KYRA

BY STEFAN SCHEUERMANN

"Kyra," by Stefan Scheuermann. ISBN 978-1-63868-111-3 (softcover); 978-1-63868-112-0 (hardcover); 978-1-63868-113-7 (eBook).

Published 2023 by Virtualbookworm.com Publishing Inc., P.O. Box 9949, College Station, TX 77842, US.

HISTORICAL CONTEXT

THE MAGYARS ARE A RACE OF PEOPLE with origins in the Ural Mountains, in modern-day Russia. In the 9th century, they took up nomadic lives, traveling west and eventually settling in Hungary. When they arrived, the grasslands of Hungary were already home to nomadic groups. But it was the Magyars who settled, formed the Hungarian Clans, built villages, towns, and cities, and established the nation of Hungary. They Christianized and joined the Christian establishment of Europe.

At the dawn of the 14th century, a new group of nomads arrived, traveling in small caravans. They were the Roma, an ethnicity from Northern India, speaking Romani, a relative of the Proto-Indo-European languages of their native lands.

The ruling Magyars had not been settled so very long as to lose a sense of kinship with the nomads. Unlike the other places they had been, the Roma Gypsies found more than tolerance from the establishment of Hungary. They found sisterhood, brotherhood. Among the Hungarians, there was still a romanticized idealism to the Gypsy life. Castle-dwelling Magyar nobles would boast of how many Gypsy musicians played at their celebrations. The fashions of the Roma people were fashionable in the cities of

Hungary. At every settlement, the Roma found eager buyers for their wares and eager eyes and ears for their performances.

In 1349, the Black Death hit Hungary, half a century after the first bands of Roma arrived. During the plague of that year, and in each subsequent outbreak, disease disrupted the kinship, for pain brings fear, and fear brings suspicion. Suspicion heralds betrayal and the worst of human behaviors. As hardship in Hungary crested and waned, so did the Hungarian love and acceptance of their nomadic Gypsy neighbors.

CONTENTS

CHAPTER ONE

IGNORED BY DEATH

A KILLER STALKED THE PEOPLE OF HUNGARY. It traveled the open roads in daylight, yet they did not see it until it was too late. They knew it was coming. Of course they knew. It had been killing in mass for two years, inching its way east, toward their towns and villages, toward Szanzar. They called it the Black Death.

Szanzar was a small village built around a tithing barn of the local diocese, where grain and cattle that were given to the Church were collected and managed. The Church's property was under the care of a man named Gellen. He was the prominent figure in the village, and the whole village seemed to take on his traits. He was an intentionally plain man, a pious man, dedicated first and foremost to his job, with no ambitions beyond his station. His second commitment was to his wife, Eneth, who suited him perfectly. She was as respectably plain as Gellen, subordinate and obedient, and living entirely for the welfare of her husband.

Gellen and Eneth had three children, a fifteen-year-old boy named Vajk, a girl three years younger named Kyra, and an infant girl whose name had changed three times in the first several weeks of her life. Gellen was not sure what God wanted him to name her. He listened superstitiously for the words of Heaven, and heard them in every sound to reach his ear.

Gellen kept Vajk always at his side, not from any sense of paternal affection, but from a desire to shape his son into a manager of God's grain. The baby was sickly and occupied Eneth to the fullest, leaving Kyra as a distant after-thought in her own home. Kyra was not a remarkable girl in any obvious way. She had a rather boyish face atop a gangly figure. She had no talents already discovered. It would not have mattered if she had. Nobody would have noticed. She was last on the minds of her parents and almost invisible to those who went about their mundane days in Szanzar.

In her twelve years, Kyra had left her tiny village only once. Four years earlier, when she was eight, she accompanied her father to the market in Bratislava. It was not Gellen's only responsibility to collect the crops and livestock of the Church. He accounted for each grain, scribbling amounts, weights, and measurements into his ledger. From time to time, he took those items to the market, sold them, and paid the Church directly from the proceeds.

The decision to take Kyra with him was logistical, not affectionate. The trip to the market was Church business, and his was a life of tedious details and particular attention to the minute. Like the tithing barn and the house they lived in, Gellen considered himself to be the property of the Church. He viewed his wife and children the same way. For this reason, he never took his family personally, never developed a husband's passion or a father's doting devotion. They were all commodities to be tallied.

He did not shed this identity once alone with Kyra. But he *was* alone with her, and the awkward silence of forced intimacy drew conversations that would never have been born in normal conditions. Once on the road together, under an early autumn sun, Gellen warmed to his daughter. In the absence of an alternative, he spoke to Kyra and showed her more attention than she had seen from either parent since she could walk. When they returned, her invisibility returned. But while they traveled and while they were together in Bratislava, Kyra felt special and could claim at least some share of her father. For the four years that followed, that trip to the market was her happiest memory.

Gellen was the only person in Szanzar who could effectively read and count, therefore, he made some effort to pass those skills to his son. But the only thing to fill the head of his daughter came from her own senses and imagination. Until her trip to the city, Kyra had little to arouse her imagination into activity, and their talk on the way to Bratislava was of the petty and mundane. The market boasted nothing exotic, nothing to be spoken of the following day by the regulars. To Kyra, it was foreign in the extreme. She saw people of varying complexion, heard multiple languages and accents, and smelled aromas far too rich for her mother's kitchen. In a glance, she saw more faces than Szanzar sheltered in a full year.

Had they explored the full market and more deeply into Bratislava, Kyra would have seen things unlike anything she could have conjured in her imagination. But this was not a trip designed for entertainment or education. They remained in that sober portion of the market where the commodities of the tithing barn could be sold at a fair price with steady temperance, negotiated calmly with placid voices. Even *that* offered Kyra so much more than she had ever experienced, and the trip home hosted conversations of far more varied topics, with questions from an awakened mind peppering the ears of a man recently softened by his well-struck bargains. It would be an exaggeration to say that Gellen and Kyra bonded and reveled in the unique brand of warmth only a loving father and daughter can know. But they spoke openly about the many things she had witnessed, and she tingled from toe to scalp.

For the next four years, the trip to the market was the only fuel that kept Kyra's mind in motion. Like most experiences at that age, the trip to Bratislava with her father distorted with the passage of time. For every detail that faded from her memory, one of a grander, romanticized nature was put in its place by her imagination. It altered with every dream and every recollection. By the time Kyra was twelve years old, it was entirely fictionalized in her head and different in every detail from her father's memories of the same event.

The faces behind each foreign accent evolved into something thrilling, and the subtle handshakes of steady tradesmen became the stunts of gypsy acrobats and flame eaters. Those memories may have grown wilder over four years, but they also grew distant. She viewed those exotic sights through straining eyes, and she longed to see them nearer, to ride with her father to the market again, or to get swept away from Szanzar entirely. Since she was comprehensively ignored by everyone who knew her, Kyra's wild musings had plenty of ground to play on. She found herself often wandering the wild grassy fields surrounding her village, with images in her head that resembled nothing in the tangible world.

That all ended one September afternoon when she returned home from her rambling. Kyra was nearly thirteen when the killer crept into their village and into their home. Kyra returned to a panicked household and a vomiting mother with a deadly fever, excruciating pains in her joints, and swelling, blackening sores on her neck and armpits.

The symptoms came suddenly and advanced with determination.

There would be no more days of wandering the fields in carefree imagination. In her mother's sickness, Kyra's father became as an infant in her care. He continued to work at his ledgers, but never leaving the house. He had no idea how to run a household or care for a baby. Kyra donned her mother's apron and each maternal responsibility that came with it. She had not been guided in the ways of a mother and wife. But the circumstances allowed no learning curve. She was in constant motion and aged several years in the days that followed.

Eneth faded quickly, and all hope of her survival withered within two days of the first symptoms. She died four days after turning ill. By the time Kyra cleaned her mother's body and laid her in a peaceful pose upon her bed, the baby's first symptoms had shown. She died one day later. Gellen buried his child behind the house and dug the deep grave for his wife. He exhausted himself in doing so. He returned indoors and collapsed, never again regaining his strength. The prolific killer stabbed him as well. The sores that formed on him blackened and distorted his features, and his face was drawn so severely that Kyra would not have known him if she had not witnessed the alterations as they occurred. He died on the floor just five days after Eneth's death and remained in the position that his final seizure set him in.

Having not stepped outside of their door since their mother went ill, Vajk and Kyra remained as the only members of their household. They were children, and they were alone. Vajk ordered his sister to prepare their father for burial, as she had done for her mother. He left the house to seek the help of their neighbors. When the door closed behind him, Kyra was left in the morbid silence of a house with more corpses than living creatures. She had had no time to cry, no time to mourn.

She knelt beside the remains of her father. He was twisted and contorted and, although he had no life in him, he looked to be the very portrait of pain. She could not bring herself to touch him. She pictured him on the cart four years earlier, riding in the autumn air, smiling and engaging her in conversation. The wrecked, discolored, and misshapen figure at her knees bore no resemblance.

She stared at him and repeated to herself, "That is not my father. That is not my father."

She almost managed to convince herself that Gellen was away and would bound through the door at any moment, still glowing with life.

Kyra was alone for three hours before Vajk returned. Her senses were awakened to what they had been ignoring. The stench of death and disease filled every space within the walls. It clawed its way through her nose and anchored itself in her head and chest. She wanted away from the smell, away from the bodies of her parents, away from the house, and away from Szanzar. She wanted to be among the many living faces in Bratislava again, and her urge to fly through the door and find that magical place was desperate.

Vajk fell through the door and sat himself in a chair. He was ghost-white and clearly shaken.

"What is it?" she demanded.

He stared past her and shook his head slowly.

"What?" she demanded again, stomping her foot near his, "Is anyone going to help us?"

Vajk continued the slow and slight, silent shake of his head.

"What is happening?" she yelled one more time.

Vajk sat erect and lifted his shirt, asking his sister, "Do you see anything? Any of the sores?"

Kyra inspected his armpits and neck. She saw nothing and she told him so. As soon as Vajk lowered his shirt, a wave of chills rushed across him. He buckled over his lap and vomited at Kyra's feet. She screamed a long and piercing note. When it no longer had the breath to maintain, it softened to a whimper, taking its turn between gasps of air. Vajk vomited again and slipped from the chair. Kyra grabbed him by the hand. His skin felt like metal that had sat in the summer sun. She ran from the house to seek the help she hoped her brother would have brought.

Kyra went house to house, building to building, barn to barn. She found nothing but distorted corpses and a stench that seemed to adhere itself to her soul. They were dead. They were all dead, or gone. She ran back to her house and found her brother lying on the floor beside the body of her father. She did not let the door close behind her. She followed her earlier urge and ran from her house, from her village. The killer had been thorough. In a week, the Black Death killed Szanzar. But like everyone she had ever known, death ignored Kyra.

CHAPTER TWO

RHYTHMIC INTRODUCTIONS

SZANZAR WAS AN ISOLATED VILLAGE. With plague in the region, the roads from Kyra's home were abandoned and seemed to stretch for eternity in all directions. Kyra's heart drew her toward her only happy memory, toward the market in Bratislava. She remembered which direction her father had taken her four years earlier, and whether consciously or not, she walked that way. She wanted away from the death and toward some unknown brightness. Once clear of the rancid stench of her dead village, she looked around her and realized she had no idea where to turn.

In a trance of rapidly flying images and memories she walked northeast for hours, until she reached the Danube River. The familiar river pulled her from her state of shock. She remembered riding along the river on the way to the market and on the way home again. With her faded and distorted memories as her only map, she thought the city was just a short walk farther. She also could not remember if the river was on her right or left as they traveled from home. She turned the wrong direction, southeast, away from Bratislava.

The sun went low and the trees grew thicker along the river. The woods were dark and the open fields to her right still clung to the fading light. So, Kyra abandoned the Danube and walked the grassy fields until the sun fell entirely and left visible only what the silvery moon could reveal. She had fled her village in fear, having witnessed everything she knew come crashing down around her. But alone in the dark field, hungry, thirsty, achy, and filthy, she came to realize her peril.

There were no houses and no people, only an endless night sky. She sat down in the tall grass and could not see above it. She cried and she wished for company, any company. Even the tangled, blackened corpse of her father would be better than the empty field and her absolute solitude. Despite her terror, her loneliness, and her morbid sense of loss, she felt relief in taking weight off of her feet. She sat with her legs held close to her chest, dropped her forehead onto her knees, and cried herself to sleep.

Her eyes did not open again until morning brought the relief of light. It was surprisingly cold. Kyra had wet and soiled herself during the night and she was chilled to the bone. The direct sun was warm and inviting, so she walked toward it. Her stomach growled with fury, and the night was not gone long enough for her legs to recover. But she walked. Waves of sorrow crashed over her, often stopping her in mid-step, turning her around, and tempting her to return to her village. She missed her mother and father, and would have given an arm to sit, ignored again, in their company.

The terrors of the previous week had occurred so quickly, with each tragedy falling in such succession, that it allowed no time for Kyra to mourn. In an open world suddenly emptied of everything familiar, with no noise around her but the subtle sounds of nature, the floodgates opened and the true measure of all that had happened and all that was lost in just over a week invaded her mind. Fear and sorrow took their turns biting and chewing at her heart. She walked a few dozen steps at a time only to stop, turn in whichever direction she thought faced her home, and sob with a heaving chest.

Her next several hours lingered on in this way. When the afternoon came, with many hours of sunlight left, Kyra began to fear another night. She had not had a bite to eat or a sip to drink in more than one full day. She was dirty, smelly, and beyond exhausted. She looked directly upward, closed her eyes, and prayed to God that her family and her life would be given back to her. She began to believe that her prayer was being answered, that she could walk back to Szanzar to find everything as it had been — her mother comprehensively occupied with the baby, her father absorbed in his ledgers, and a village of vibrant neighbors blindly looking over her. She smiled in her faith and belief that when she opened her eyes she would be ready to walk home, grateful to a merciful God.

When she opened her eyes and lowered her head, she went dizzy and fell flat on her back. She struck her head hard on the ground and the throbbing pain pushed her faith from her. There was no miracle awaiting her in Szanzar, and her splitting head fell atop an already mountainous pile of pains, fears, and sorrows. She remained on her back, looking upward, without another tear left to cry and hardly enough breath for a wheezing whine. The grass was high around her and she felt as if she was in a hole — not a hole but a grave, like the one dug by her father that sat empty awaiting her mother. Her grass-grave was not terrifying. It was comforting. It cradled her and promised to take away her pain. This twelve-year-old child closed her eyes, content to die.

Her head still pounded and she could hear her pulse. A rhythm slowly grew to accompany it, distant but piercing. As it grew louder, Kyra realized that it was not her pulse or any action of her fading body. It was the clap of hands, the slap of thighs, and the drumming of knuckles on wood, and it was working its way nearer to her. She sat up but could not see above the grass. She stood on her wobbly legs, legs that had just resigned never to stand again. Her ears pointed her eyes toward the sound. Off in the distance she saw it. A caravan of horse-drawn wagons pushed through the grass toward her.

As they drew nearer, near enough for Kyra to see the details, she saw that most of them were not standard wagons, but Gypsy wagons, *vardos* as the Gypsies called them, colorful and ornate. They appeared as little one-room houses on wheels. Some had sharp, linear angles and expanded wider at the top. Others were bulbous and rounded and covered in canvas. Most had windows and window boxes with flowers. Each had a door at the front with a little porch. Some had a door and a porch at the back. Flower designs and floral patterns were painted on them in almost gaudy excess. There were twelve of them in close succession, each pulled by a single horse. Open wagons, fully loaded, filled the spaces between them.

Lively people rode upon the vardos and on the horses that were pulling the wagons. Additional horses rode beside the wagons, some carrying people and others carrying large bundles. For every Gypsy Kyra saw riding on a horse or on a wagon, there were five walking along the sides. Sheep and goats were herded along the caravan by brightly-dressed, fleet-of-foot people with bright amber faces and bellowing voices, carrying long sticks and shouting at the animals in mysterious, exotic commands. And there were dogs. Three dogs that she could see, trotting along the herd of livestock.

The Gypsies were clapping, slapping, and drumming in flawless unison. As the front of the caravan began to pass Kyra, they began to sing. They did not sing in Hungarian and Kyra did not understand the words. There was no need to know them. It was clear. They sang of life, not death, of joy, not sorrow. Although her body was too tired to smile, her heart smiled within her. It could not help itself. An infectious spirit radiated from the Gypsies as they passed, no more than forty feet in front of her. They sang.

La na na na la na na la na
Te manges-khel! Te manges-Gilyabar!
La na na na la na na la na
Haw peeve ta Kambulin, Kumpa'nia

Most of the voices were raspy and would have been unpleasant to hear on their own. But in unison they were almost angelic. They wove intricate harmonies. Copper skinned children in bright clothing sang along as they walked, rode, or were carried beside the caravan by their parents. Kyra stood captivated as her wildest fantasies rolled rhythmically and melodically in front of her.

As if the scene before her was not exotic enough, her attention was drawn to the last vardo. A man sat upon its roof. The older man, lighter of skin than most of the others, short but lean and muscular, with a balding head and graying temples, stood up on his sharply bowed legs. The wagon rolled forward, shaking on the uneven ground, while the man stood without fear to the accompaniment of the continuing clapping and singing. He bent over, placed his hands on the roof of the vardo, and pushed himself into a handstand. A few walking nearest to him cheered him on as he held his balance on the rocking, shaking roof.

The last vardo rolled past Kyra, the old acrobat still balancing upside down upon its roof. None of the Gypsies noticed the soiled girl standing waist-deep in the grass. The front of the caravan had dwindled to minute proportions in the distance to her right. When the last vardo passed her, Kyra panicked. The caravan was passing her by and something deep inside of her was covetously reluctant to let it go. The sights and the sounds of the caravan seeped deeply inside of her and stitched itself to her innermost being. She felt those stitches being ripped with every rotation of the wheels.

Kyra tried to scream to them, but her parched throat and wispy breath could make no sound.

She mouthed, "Please. Wait. Please stop."

Even if she could have hollered with her utmost vigor, they would not have heard her over the thundering wheels and the vivacious singing and clapping. Her sorrow at watching them roll away from her was as biting as anything she had felt all day. It was as if life was being pulled from her again. She tried to run after them. After a few weak steps she fell, and could only muster the strength to stand again and watch them leave her.

Suddenly, an adolescent voice rang out from the caravan, barely piercing the other sounds. The singing and clapping smothered in waves across the shouted words. The voice came again, this time clearer, as it shouted, "Molya sprete!" The same phrase repeated in the same boy's voice, "Molya sprete!" The caravan came to a halt. The balding acrobat jumped from the roof of the vardo to the ground far below. He lifted a boy upon his shoulders and the boy pointed into the field — directly at Kyra.

The acrobat gave a loud command and a young woman broke from the caravan and ran to Kyra. She stopped nearly toe to toe with the filthy girl and stared down at her. This woman was no blackened corpse, but a voluptuous, glowing figure, with deep brown skin, billowing hair, and a flowing dress of many bright colors. She smelled of exotic perfume, which pushed through Kyra's stench like a burst of light shooting through the dark. She reached forward and invited Kyra to take her hand. Kyra placed her hand in the woman's hand. They stood there staring at each other, motionless, like they were carved out of stone.

A voice boomed from the caravan, "Milena! Milena!"

A command followed the name, and Milena shouted back, still facing Kyra. It was a shout to Milena. Kyra experienced it very differently. Milena's voice rang out with a purity of tone Kyra had never heard. It seemed to echo off of the thin air around them.

The call came out again, "Milena! Milena!"

Without another moment of pause, the woman tugged the filthy child at a healthy pace back to the caravan. She lifted Kyra onto the front porch of a vardo near the back of the caravan. An older woman came out from inside, waved her hand in front of her face to acknowledge Kyra's smelly condition, and walked back inside. She stepped out within a few seconds with a piece of bread, an apple, and a mug of water. Kyra consumed the gifts quickly as the caravan set back into motion. The rhythms that aroused Kyra from her grassy grave rose again, not at a distance this time but all around her. The singing commenced in exotic syllables that seemed to swirl around Kyra under their own power.

Between the filled stomach, the moistened throat, the singing, and the rocking of the vardo, Kyra fell asleep as she sat. She did not know what was to become of her, but she had exhausted her supply of fear and had only enough life left inside of her to relish her sudden comfort. The Gypsies gave her no reason to think they meant her harm. And wherever they were going, it was away from the death she left behind. Death may have ignored her in Szanzar, but she was seen in that grassy field, seen by a boy, seized by an angelically voiced woman, and taken by a caravan.

Kyra's dreams as she slept on the porch of that Gypsy wagon were a blend of the real and the imagined. As she rose into a shallow consciousness before fading again, she did not know which was which. She awoke briefly to find herself sprawled flat where she had sat, only to drop into sleep again. She awoke two more times while the caravan still rolled, each time noticing a lower sun whose light was more thickly filtered by the evening air.

She awoke once more before sunrise, in the middle of the night. The caravan was still and silent. She found herself as she had been, lying on the porch of the same wagon. Three thick blankets had been placed over her and tucked in snuggly beneath her with obvious care. A fourth blanket was rolled under her head. She took a few moments to savor the warmth and to appreciate the attention that had been paid to her while she slept. She fell asleep again and dreamed of Gypsy acrobats.

CHAPTER THREE

TUGGED ABOUT

THE MID-MORNING SUN BREACHED THE TOP of the wagon in front of Kyra. It stabbed its light through her eyelids and poked her harshly awake. She was still snuggled beneath the blankets. The caravan was not rolling, but the air around her buzzed with chatter and activity. Kyra rose and looked around. They were in a field with woods and hills in the distance. The closest thing to a road was the flattened grass behind them. She dismounted the wagon and walked to the side of it, where the heaviest bustle seemed to be.

There were several pockets of Gypsies, each group active with a different employment. Some were repairing the underside of a cart. Some were seated on the ground in a circle stringing beads into jewelry. One group of four was gathered around a large but shallow metal saucer. They had piled wood upon it and made a fire. That group was cooking, and from their corner of the settled caravan came the aroma of sizzling meat. Her bread and apple were long-digested, and Kyra's hunger forbade her to look beyond the cooks.

People walked all around and near her. Most nodded or tipped their hats. Each spoke some greeting or other in what seemed to be many different languages, but none in her native Hungarian. Kyra was hungry. She wanted to eat but didn't know how to ask. So, she stood still and smiled at those who passed her. After half an hour like this, a young man finally came to her with more than a nod or tipped hat. He asked her a question and waited for a response. Kyra could not understand him and she shook her head. He shrugged his shoulders and walked on. Kyra continued to watch the bustle of the Gypsy camp and waited for some indication of what to do.

A few minutes later, a tall, lean woman came by, bent eye to eye with Kyra, and asked her, "Ţi-e foame, copilule?"

The language barrier and the entirely foreign atmosphere struck Kyra's heart with cruel loneliness. Her frustration overcame her. Her face winced and her eyes welled with tears as she answered, "I don't understand you."

The woman took her firmly by the wrist and tugged her to the circle of cooks. They handed the woman a bowl filled with whatever they had been cooking in the oversized pot that hung over the fire. The woman took the bowl with one hand and, with the other, she tugged Kyra away from the fire. She released Kyra's hand and pushed down on her shoulder, forcing her to sit in the grass. She handed her the bowl, spoke something at her, and walked away.

The bowl had a broth with pieces of vegetables and grains. It was seasoned with spices that were alien to Kyra's nose as she sniffed the steam that rose from it. She blew into the bowl to cool the food, then raised it to her lips and poured it into her mouth. The flavors were shocking, and she could not decide if she loved it or hated it. When she finished, and held the empty bowl on her lap, she pondered the lingering sensation in her mouth. Her lips tingled and all of her other senses seemed to heighten. Suddenly, the breeze stroked her like fingernails being softly scraped across the skin. The multitude of sounds from the Gypsies, the livestock, and the local birds flitted spritely in her ears. Each hair on her body rose like antennas to receive what her surroundings had to offer her senses. Her previous meal had settled her to sleep on the porch of the vardo. This one provided quite the opposite effect.

Along with her enlivened senses, the spicy stew charged Kyra's entire body and mind with energy. She rose to her feet, handed the empty bowl to the cooks, thanked them with a bow of her head, and began wandering the camp, pulled by a curiosity that was much stronger than her apprehension. She went circle to circle. She had been invisible in her own home and village for so long that it startled her to be acknowledged. Each Gypsy she passed or lingered near greeted her with a smile and some unintelligible expression of concern. She understood nothing that was said, but their concern spoke in the universal languages of gestures and vocal tones. She answered each of them according to what she imagined they were saying.

While she was watching a circle of musicians sit with their stringed instruments and flutes on their laps, discussing some heated point of their craft, Kyra heard from the opposite side of the nearest vardo, "Menowin! Menowin!" A tall, thin, wiry man with baggy orange pants and no shirt answered the call of his name. On his way, he seized Kyra by the wrist. His grip was firm, and the squeeze was uncomfortable, but an indescribable gentleness in the grasp, and in the smile that passed to her from his face, dispelled the pain.

Menowin led Kyra around the vardo to the calling voice. A makeshift kiln of small stones had been constructed, awaiting the blacksmith. Menowin bent low to

Kyra and gave some sort of instruction in a language that sounded very different from those she had already heard. He pulled out two long gloves that had been tucked into the back of his pants, put them on with a dramatic flair that was clearly meant to impress his young guest, and began to receive orders from the older man who had called him over. The man giving the orders spoke as much with his hands as with his mouth. Not understanding a word, Kyra could almost picture what the man wanted made.

She had never seen a blacksmith at work, and Menowin appeared eager to have his little audience. But he had hardly stoked the fire before another tug came at her from another direction. It came not at her wrist but at her ears. The circle of musicians began tuning their instruments. Kyra had heard music before, but never like this. The best her village could offer was one stringed instrument poorly played, a pair of sticks knocked together, and voices that seemed on bad terms with the scales they sang. Among the notes coming from behind her, one sound was peculiar and exciting. She had never heard a bowed instrument. At first, it whined shrilly, but it leveled and mellowed as it came into tune with the plucked and strummed instruments.

Menowin labored away in front of her, glancing down every few seconds to make sure Kyra was entertained. He quickly saw that her attention was elsewhere, as she twisted her neck awkwardly to see under the vardo between her and the musicians. Menowin whistled loudly and hollered some name or command. In an instant, a young woman took Kyra by the hand, lifted her to her feet as if she could not have stood on her own, and pulled her back to the circle of musicians. With gestures only, Kyra was instructed where to sit, and she obeyed graciously. The haphazardness of the tuning efforts blended seamlessly into a song of extraordinary coordination.

The song began without the bow. Four musicians plucked and strummed. Two sat ready to blow into their flutes. Three kept rhythm with small drums they squeezed between their knees. Three men and one woman stood ready to sing. It was the same woman who had first fetched Kyra from the field. One deeply wrinkled man sat stone-still with a Byzantine lyra on his lap and his bow resting on his shoulder, peeking around his head to tease Kyra. The others called him Manfri. Despite the action of the circle, it was this one, still man, that captivated Kyra's curiosity. He looked both very old and very young. His hair was long, gray, and wiry. But his wrinkled face shone as if wet, and his eyes were wide as they moved in circles within their sockets. They moved with the music.

The flutes joined the strings, elevating the music. They were not spritely. They hinted at a deep melancholy that would follow. The singers began to sing. There were no harsh voices here. The three men began with staccato phrases that seemed to Kyra more like an imitation of instruments than like words. Consonants and vowels smashed together in ways she could hardly believe held meaning in any language. They paused and drew a deep inhale, ready to sing, and as voices from all sides of them shouted her name, "Milena! Milena!", the woman began to sing. Her voice quickly dominated over the harmonizing men and it had depth, like a large bowl that held the men's voices within it.

It was much more than her voice. She sang a story that transcended the language barrier. Her hips swayed like they had their own version of the story to tell. Her face winced then softened, then winced again. She clenched her fists and held her arms bent tightly at her side, only to let them drop to her hips as if severed and lifeless. Whatever the story was, it appeared very personal to her. Even her hair seemed to participate, bouncing and swaying in its own unique accompaniment.

The men singers stopped suddenly, leaving Milena's voice to hold the moment with a long-held and pure note. She held that note unnaturally long. Rather than fading as the air left her, it grew in force and penetrating purity. She snapped it to a sudden end as she closed her lips into a pucker, as if kissing that long note goodbye. The voices fully dismounted from the instruments they rode upon. The rhythmic instruments continued, waiting for the next feature to hitch a ride. Kyra knew what must be next.

She stared at the old man with the lyra. He knelt high on one knee and nestled the end of his lyra into the crook of his neck. He whipped the bow from his shoulder and waved it in the air in front of him. He lowered it slowly to the strings and began to bow. If the woman's voice was a large bowl, the man's lyra was a valley, deep and wide, carrying the echoes of every sound within it. It did not whine or cry, but wept soulfully. It did not complain of the petty. It told of every struggle it had witnessed as it traveled the countless hills and meadows between its place of origin and that Hungarian field where Kyra sat captivated.

The music took her away from everything but the sounds in front of her. She forgot the horrors she had left behind in Szanzar. She forgot about her soiled dress. Language barrier? There was no such thing as language in that circle, only vividly expressive music and the musicians who poured it forth with mournful yet spritely passion.

The song came to a calm and natural conclusion. There was no applause from outside of the circle of musicians. Kyra looked around her. Nobody had gathered around to listen. They all continued about their business. The musicians discussed and debated before striking another note. This was not a performance. These were craftsmen, like all of the other craftsmen in the caravan, working to perfect their trade.

Kyra remained near the musicians for a few more songs. Others passed by the circle and offered her water, bread, and fruit. Her need to relieve herself grew urgent. She tried to hold it in. When she no longer could, she snuck away from the musicians, away from the caravan, into the grassy field. The grass was not as high as the field where they had found her, but it was high enough. It was only then that she realized how pathetically filthy she was. Away from the aromas of the camp, the stench of urine and feces gagged her. She could not bear her own company and was mortified to return to the Gypsies. But what choice did she have? They were clean, with vibrant clothes and exotic perfumes. She smelled worse than the death she had left behind.

She walked slowly back toward the camp. With each step, her embarrassment squeezed her throat more tightly. Her whimper had a slightly longer reach than her smell, and a woman who sat on the front porch of a vardo heard her. Kyra did not single the woman out among the buzz of activity, but this lone Gypsy stared fixedly at *her* with gripping interest. She was old, much older than anyone else Kyra had seen in the caravan.

The beauty of this woman's youth hid poorly behind her deep-wrinkled mouth and eyes. Her lips were still plush and crimson. Peeking between her abundance of gray hair were strands of deep brown that sang in the sun of adventures gone by. Kyra walked along the line of vardos until she was beside the old woman.

The woman spoke firmly, grabbing Kyra's attention, "Chavaia!"

She startled Kyra, whose gasp stopped her whimper. Kyra stopped sharply and turned to face the woman. She stared directly into those old and storied eyes.

The woman scanned Kyra's condition up and down several times, then patted her lap and said, "Avas."

It was clearly an invitation, and Kyra stepped tentatively toward her. The woman called the name "Vadim" several times until a man who smelled of cooked food appeared around the side of the vardo. He bore a resemblance to the woman who beckoned him. They had the same peculiarly large eyes. His hair was a full head of those same dark strands that hid among the woman's gray.

The woman gestured to Vadim to hoist Kyra onto the porch. When he did, he winced and turned his head away from her smell. Kyra shook her head in embarrassment. The woman gave an order to Vadim, then stood, entered the vardo, and closed the door behind her. Vadim whistled and a horse trotted to his call. He hooked the horse to the vardo, sat down beside Kyra, and turned the cart away from the caravan, off into the grassy field beyond.

"They are taking me back where they found me," she said under her breath.

Vadim chuckled through a widening grin, which only made Kyra feel worse. They rode away from the caravan for about twenty minutes, during which time Kyra tried to imagine her return to the rotting corpses of her village. She was nauseous and vomited into her mouth. But she refused to add another odor to her offenses, so she swallowed it down. Eventually they came upon a large pond sitting awkward and lonely in an endless field of grass. Vadim made no attempt to bypass it. He stopped the horse with its front hooves mere inches from the edge of the water. The horse bent low and drank, but that was not the purpose of the stop.

Vadim hopped from the vardo, then grabbed Kyra by the armpits, making the same repulsive face and trying not to inhale. Once Kyra's feet were firmly on the ground, the woman emerged from the vardo. Vadim lowered some steps that were hinged and tucked beneath the wagon. The woman wasted no time walking down the steps with remarkable grace and agility, taking Kyra by the hand, and tugging her knee-deep into the water. Without a grunt, gesture, or foreign word, the woman lifted Kyra's dress off of her, then gestured for her to remove her soiled undergarments.

Kyra did not immediately obey. She covered herself as well as she could with her folded arms and looked around the vardo for Vadim. She heard his bustle inside but could not see him. The woman clapped her hands twice and repeated the gesture. Kyra obeyed and stood naked in the knee-deep water. The woman threw the dress to the shore. Kyra followed in kind with her undergarments. The woman raised her hand over her head and a cube of soap flew from the inside of the vardo. She caught it and, with her other hand, she pushed Kyra to sit in the water.

Kyra sat while the woman scrubbed away. She was so relieved by the sensation of water, the smell of the perfumed soap, and the idea of finally being clean that she was unbothered by the old hands feverishly rubbing away at her body. The woman knelt in the water, laid Kyra back over her lap, and cleaned the girl's hair. Once Kyra was fully clean, the woman yelled to Vadim, who left the vardo and walked around to the back side, out of sight. The woman stood, then helped Kyra to her feet. Hand-in-hand, she led Kyra up the steps and into the vardo.

It was not at all what Kyra expected. At the back was a bed, lush with ample folds of rich, lavish bedding. There was a polished wooden trunk with shiny copper hinges. Fine lace hung from the walls. Golden jewelry, much finer than anything she had seen being made by the Gypsies, hung from and sat upon almost every possible surface. Elaborate trinkets and knick-knacks filled what little spots remained. It was cluttered richness to a scale Kyra could not have previously imagined.

The lavish environment made Kyra forget that she stood entirely naked in front of a woman she had just met. For some reason she could not understand, she did not feel naked.

After looking at all of the things around her, Kyra faced the woman directly and said, "You are like a queen."

The woman blushed, tapped herself in the center of her chest, and said, "Iraja."

"Iraja," Kyra repeated, "That is your name? My name is Kyra."

The woman grinned slowly and slightly.

Kyra pointed to her chest as the woman had and said again, "Kyra."

"Kyra," Iraja repeated.

Iraja opened the trunk and pulled from it a full, layered skirt of flamboyant colors and a red blouse. She handed them to Kyra, who, suddenly feeling naked, rushed to put them on. Iraja took a vial from a narrow shelf and poured perfumed oil into her palm. She rubbed her hands together, then ran her hands through Kyra's hair, over her cheeks and neck, and down her arms. Kyra was cleaned with sweet foreign soap, perfumed in rich oil, and wearing a full Gypsy skirt and blouse. She had never been called beautiful, not by her mother or father, not by anyone. Despite her gangly figure and boyish face, she looked beautiful, and she felt beautiful. She smelled of exotic places far away.

Her gratitude was so abundant that she could not have expressed it adequately to someone she could converse freely with in her *own* language. She had no idea how to express it to Iraja. Her eyes filled with tears as Iraja stared at her with maternal pride. Nobody had ever looked at her so adoringly, nor had anyone, in the expanse of her memory, dedicated such attention as it took for Iraja to ride away from the caravan and clean her in that pond.

Iraja continued to stare. Kyra wanted to embrace her benefactor, but she did not want to end that moment between them. Iraja's eyes teared to match Kyra's. She nodded and held her hands to her chest. It was the first time in her life that Kyra had drawn intense emotion from anyone. She was overwhelmed by the moment. She threw her arms around Iraja and buried her head in the old woman's breasts. Iraja rubbed Kyra's head, smelled her hair, sighed deeply and whispered in her ear, "Odjus Tehara, odjus."

Iraja walked Kyra out of the vardo, where Vadim waited to see the transformation. He clapped his hands together several times and laughed heartily. He jumped onto the porch, withdrew the steps, sat down, and patted the space beside him. Kyra sat where he indicated. He turned to her, closed his eyes, drew a deep inhale, relishing her new aroma, patted her twice on the head, and drove the wagon away from the pond, toward the caravan. As relieved as Kyra was to be clean, she was all the more relieved not to be going back to Szanzar. She looked like a Gypsy princess. She smelled like a Gypsy princess, and she could not wait to walk around the pockets of the camp as just another colorful ornament in the caravan, and not a filthy, smelly stranger.

CHAPTER FOUR

THE ACROBAT

KYRA RODE ONLY BRIEFLY BESIDE VADIM. She yearned to be under the adoring gaze of Iraja. It was a drug to her, to which she was instantly addicted. After only a few minutes beside Vadim, she excused herself and went tentatively inside. She sat on the bed beside Iraja. Everything within Iraja's vardo was rich and precious, and Kyra felt like she fit well with her surroundings. She had always been plain, obscure, and unseen. It had been many years since she was hand-bathed by her mother. She had forgotten the feel of a caring hand and never recalled feeling beautiful. But there, beside Iraja and among her things, rocking within the rolling vardo, she felt reborn into something from her wandering daydreams.

The sensation was overwhelming, and Kyra's emotions rocked as roughly as the wheels beneath her. She transitioned between giggles and bursting sobs. Iraja tried to calm her by reading from a worn manuscript. But Kyra did not want to be calmed. She wanted to revel in her feelings, and she was prepared to compound them further by marching by the blacksmith, musicians, cooks, and jewelry makers in her new splendor. Nevertheless, she listened while Iraja read to her. Of course, she did not understand a word the old woman spoke, but Iraja's voice was as nurturing and cleansing as her hands had been.

Much like the singer and the lyra player, Iraja performed her reading with animated passion. The story sounded exciting and seemed to be felt personally by the reader. The outer cover of the manuscript was of deep, reddish-brown leather, with two thin leather binding straps dangling beneath it. As Iraja read, the straps swayed with the rocking of the vardo, but they appeared to be performing an interpretive dance to the story being read. Unable to understand the story, Kyra focused on the animated straps, letting them translate for her. She imagined the straps to be lovers, and an entire tragic love story played out between them by the time they arrived at the Gypsy camp and Iraja closed the book and tucked it away.

Vadim rolled the vardo to its proper place in the caravan and was already unhitching the horse before Iraja opened the door. The delay in presenting the altered child to the camp was intentional. They had all watched them roll away. It was unlike Iraja to take such a personal interest in a stranger and child. Their curiosity was piqued and the entire camp abandoned their employment and gathered in anticipation. Iraja walked first from the vardo. She stepped to the side of the porch, not acknowledging the gathered crowd, not proclaiming any introduction. She simply stepped to the side of the door to make room for Kyra's exit. It was much more of an entrance than an exit. She was exiting a luxurious vardo, but she was entering a new life and identity.

Kyra was eager to expose her radiant new self to the Gypsies, but she had no reason to think they would all gather to see her. When she stepped through the door and saw their awaiting faces, she turned as red as her blouse.

She had so long been starved of attention, and she was gluttonous for it. But as she stood on the porch, framed by the spectacular, colorful vardo, stared at by so many eyes, it was more than she could digest. She felt faint and turned an even deeper red of face. The sun shone directly on her, and she wore her reddened condition like expensive makeup.

Her face was still boyish. Iraja's feminine beauty, weathered as it was, was still well beyond Kyra's. But Iraja was not the spectacle to be adored at that moment. Kyra was. The transition was extreme and she was, in her unique and quirky way, beautiful. Her joy at being adored shone from deep within her and made her beauty all the more resplendent. Countless admiring eyes stared at her. They did not look at her with calculating eyes, as a commodity to be tallied, but as a figure to be enjoyed — and they enjoyed her. They relished her. She thought about the dancing leather straps, and thought for the very first time that she could be loved — that a passionate life could be hers.

For the first full minute, not a breath could be heard, not a mumble or comment. The silence felt like hours to Kyra. It was eventually broken by a clap. It came from the roof of the vardo in front of her, where the balding acrobat sat perched. The sun had blinded Kyra to his presence there. She shaded her eyes with her hand to see him clearly. He clapped loudly again, then more quickly again. He followed it with a cheer and a whistle. The others all joined. They were deafening. So much loud and lively, passionate approval erupted around her that she would have sworn the sound could have revived the dead. More life, more burning, extravagantly excitable and combustible life cheered around her than could have been found in every human being she had met in her previous life combined, including everyone she had seen at the market in Bratislava.

She had fallen into a whole new world unlike anything she had ever known. She half-expected to awaken from one of her fanciful daydreams, walking the fields outside of Szanzar. But this could not be one of her fantasies. They had never been this colorful, never featured such people, and she could not have previously imagined the sensations she felt when Iraja bathed her, or when the crowd's clamoring applause swelled tirelessly.

When the applause finally died down, pockets of one to five Gypsies took their turns coming to the porch and pouring their compliments on Kyra. She could not have translated their words, but she knew well what they were telling her. Once they left Iraja's vardo, they returned to their circles and continued as they had been. Having stood for so long at such an emotional extremity, Kyra's legs went weak beneath her. Vadim helped her from the porch and set a stool in the grass for her to sit upon. She took the seat and he handed her a flat piece of bread. She ate and recovered.

Once her strength and color had returned to normal, Iraja took her by the hand and pulled her from the stool. She led Kyra to the circle of jewelry makers. Iraja spoke quickly, with gestures to the jewelry and the artists who fashioned it. The jewelry makers explained and instructed. Kyra told them several times that she did not understand them. It did not deter them. They spoke louder and faster. Kyra nodded as if she understood. Once each jewelry maker had a say, Iraja took Kyra again by the hand and led her to the other side of the caravan.

The livestock were spread across the field beyond and four men and two women stood in a large circle herding them. When they saw Iraja, they abandoned their job and came to her. Much like the jewelers, the herders spoke quickly in apparent explanation of their duties. From there, Iraja led Kyra to the potters. One spun a pot upon a wheel. The wheel was turned by a foot crank beneath it. Kyra watched with amazed interest as the pot took shape and elaborate markings were added by the potter's long fingernails. Others in the circle were polishing copper urns and canisters. The copper gleamed like gold in the afternoon sun.

The livestock, the jewelry, the gleaming copper — with enough of her father still in her, Kyra tried to tally the wealth of the caravan. She had no head for such figures, but she reckoned it a substantial fortune, enough to rival any merchant in Bratislava, enough to impress the nobles in the Hungarian castles of her fantasies. She had heard of the wealth of the Gypsies, but the duality of her company was bold. Wealth was all around them, springing from their fingertips with every flick of their wrists. But a provincial simplicity filled the air of the camp, as if the wealth of the caravan had less value than the smiles on the surrounding faces. Kyra had not understood a single word since the Gypsies found her weak and soiled in the field, but she understood some things clearly. The greatest wealth of the Gypsies was not in what gleamed in the afternoon sun or what grazed in the grass. It was in the abounding passion that radiated from within their chests and shone from their extremities.

Despite the pleasures of the day, Kyra wished ardently for the ability to communicate more directly with her hosts. There were secrets in the caravan that could only be unlocked with spoken questions and answers. Iraja led Kyra through all of the circles of various craftsmen. The one Gypsy she wanted most to see in her tour was the old acrobat. He seemed to disappear from the group along with the boy who had halted the caravan when he saw her in the field.

Kyra yawned and stretched her limbs many times as she visited each group. After the tour, Iraja led her back to her vardo. She tucked her into the luxurious folds upon her bed. Kyra fell asleep with a mind filled with ample sustenance for her dreams to feast upon. She dreamed of Gypsies, and there was nothing that her dreams could conjure that was far beyond what she had experienced that day. She dreamed many strange stories, some set in the caravan, some in Szanzar, but in each, she was a beautifully clothed subject of admiration, not a plain villager in a plain dress.

Vadim woke her from a heavy sleep. It was early in the evening, and the low sun lit the sky to match the brilliant colors of the people and things in the caravan. Kyra left the vardo and immediately noticed that dozens of tents had been pitched beside the wagons. Just beyond them was one large tent. She could not imagine where so many tents had been stored while they traveled. Vadim led her to the large tent. It was wider than five vardos set end to end. A glow and a bustle came from within.

Kyra and Vadim entered the tent. There were clusters of stools and pillows along the inner perimeter, most of which held the tail end of a Gypsy. The center was clear and the grass had been trampled down. Dancing had already occurred there. Sweaty dancers panted and recovered while in conversation with the others.

"Lavinia," he instructed as he pointed to a copper-skinned, sweaty woman with thick, wavy, black hair.

Lavinia was in full, panting conversation with her other dancers and could not have heard him from her distance, but she turned nevertheless and acknowledged Kyra with a demure nod of her head before returning her focus to her dancers.

Beginning with one teenage girl, but expanding around the circle from her, chants began, demanding the presence of one particular Gypsy. "Stoyan! Stoyan! Stoyan!" they chanted. The chanting erupted into hollers and applause with the entrance of the moment's celebrity. The acrobat entered the tent with his arms held high. He pulled off his shirt and shouted a question to the others.

They answered in unison. He walked a slow circle around the inside of the tent, clapping his hands above his head. The others joined him in concerted rhythm.

Stoyan was not a particularly handsome man. He was balding. He was well shorter than the other adults. He had short, sharply bowed legs. His face was awkwardly square and his nose was unnaturally broad. But he had an exotic charisma that refused to relinquish the attention of those around him. His muscles were thick and sinuous. What remained of his hair wrapped the back of his head in wild, graying curls that he wore like a crown of untamed shrubbery.

Defying Kyra's wildest imaginings, Stoyan took three quick steps toward the center of the tent and launched himself into a front flip, landing it with a few casual steps forward. The crowd cheered more loudly than before. Stoyan began clapping again, and the musicians in the tent, who had just recovered from playing for the dancers, again struck their instruments. Milena, the voluptuous vocalist, with an infant in her arm and a small child clinging to her other hand, began to sing along. The lyra player brandished his bow and licked the strings of his instrument with the bow's coarse horse hair. Kyra sat on a vacant pillow beside Vadim and watched with a pounding heart.

Stoyan galloped around in a circle like a wild horse. He jumped into the air, spinning twice with his knees tucked to his chest. He landed from the stunt with a single step that launched him into another high flip. Forward handsprings, backward handsprings, leaps and twists and flips, all were performed in flawless unison with the music, as if Stoyan's every movement created the notes that filled the tent.

While he breathed deeply in recovery, he pointed to a few along the perimeter and barked a command. Those Gypsies he indicated took their stools from beneath them, brought them to the center, and began stacking them upon themselves. A tower of six stools high awaited the next stunt. Stoyan walked slowly to them. The crowd hushed. The acrobat raised his hands high again and held them there in front of the tower of stools. He grabbed the fourth stool from the bottom as he stepped on a rung of the bottom stool. He climbed to the top while the crowd began a unified cheer. Kyra sat spellbound by the spectacle.

Once atop the tower, Stoyan sat perched. He placed one hand on the top stool, between his legs. He set the other beside his hip. With muscles that seemed to ripple like a pond receiving a stone, he pushed himself to a handstand atop the tower. In the handstand, he bent and contorted. He slowly lifted his left hand from the platform so that he stood upon a single hand. Upside down, he spread his legs into wide splits. The music stopped entirely, as did every other sound in the tent. Stoyan pushed off with his right hand and quickly replaced it with his left, holding his handstand with his opposite hand and shaking to recover his balance.

The act went on much longer than any man of any age should be able to hold his own weight in such a way. More upside-down contortions were interrupted by shaky recovering of balance, most of which were obviously intentional, put into the act by the acrobat to add suspense. From a handstand high above the grass, Stoyan tossed himself from the tower of stools and rebounded off of the ground into a high backflip. The crowd erupted again, and the old acrobat took his bows, put his shirt on, and retreated to a stool along the edge of the tent. The tower of stools was dismantled and returned to the rear ends that had relinquished them.

Kyra felt faint. It was only that sensation that alerted her to the fact that she had not been breathing. What a magical place! What magical people that had scooped her from that grassy field!

After Stoyan settled among the others, activities and conversations waved in chaotic concert across them all, all but Kyra. She could not pull her attention from Stoyan. She could not have explained why she stared at him so fixedly, despite her terror of being caught doing so, but she could not tug her eyes away. He fascinated her as no human ever had. The fascination deepened when Stoyan beckoned his son to him. A boy, about a year older than Kyra, but shorter and just as thin, responded and bounced onto his father's lap, though he was not very much smaller. It was the boy who had stopped the caravan for her.

The boy was much darker than Stoyan, bearing the complexion of a long lost mother. Kyra's fascination was from no trait of the child's, but from the tenderness of the father's affection. Stoyan planted his nose in his son's dirty hair and inhaled deeply, closing his eyes and savoring the unique smell, while squeezing his wrapped arms tightly around the boy. He kissed his son repeatedly, rubbed his back, spoke some tender endearment into his ear, and kissed him some more. It was a display of paternal affection like Kyra had never before witnessed. It was a beautifully emotional sight for her, which pinched cruelly at her lonely, mournful heart. Never breaking her stare, she began crying, silently at first, but with increasing tremors as her chest seized and she struggled to bring air peacefully in and out of her lungs.

It was the son who first noticed the crying stranger, just as he had been the first to notice her soiled and crying in the field. He drew his father's attention to Kyra. Stoyan looked at her and, in an instant, the joyful face of a father very much in love with the child on his lap melted into an expression of richly sorrowful and authentic compassion. Stoyan whispered in his son's ear. The boy slid from his father and walked slowly to Kyra, as if approaching an animal he wanted to pet but feared being bitten.

After witnessing such parental affection, Kyra was desperately in need of human contact. Before the boy could fully extend his arm in invitation, she lunged forward and took him by the hand. With his other hand, he pointed to his chest and said, "Yubi." Kyra responded in kind, tapping her free fingertips on her collarbones, saying, "Kyra." Yubi smiled and gestured with his head toward his father. He had no need to tug on her hand. She longed desperately for the paternal love she had witnessed moments earlier. She walked hand-in-hand beside Yubi until they both stood before Stoyan.

Kyra stood several inches above her new young friend. His age was hard for her to guess. His shortness indicated little, for it stood in contradiction against the wisdom in his dark eyes. His smudged face had the soft complexion of an infant, and his features were rounded. He had none of his father's muscular build. But there was something timeless in his gaze when he locked his eyes to Kyra's.

When both children stood before Stoyan, Yubi left Kyra's side and walked behind his father. He rested his chin on Stoyan's shoulder and stared at the girl in front of them. Stoyan eyed Kyra up and down several times, not with the approving eyes that admired her from the roof of the vardo earlier that day, but with the look of strict evaluation. He stood, not much taller than Kyra, took her by the waist, and hoisted her joltingly above his head. He set her down on her feet just as quickly and sat back on his stool. He scratched his chin and evaluated her some more. He turned to his right and left and made some comment to those around him, clearly speaking of Kyra.

She would have given back the colorful skirt and blouse, and gladly put her soiled clothes back on, to understand what Stoyan was saying. Throughout her childhood, she had tried hard to gain her parent's attention, though it was never given. But her desperation for Stoyan's approval was stronger than anything she remembered feeling for her mother and father. The man carried obvious authority within the caravan. He was cheered like a king, and his vibrant character could not have been compared with any man or woman Kyra had ever met. He was a little man, not at all princely in his appearance, yet he held the captivated tent in his little hand.

As Stoyan's eyes and attention were comprehensively on Kyra, he gave her a new and strong sense of hope. She had never been praised for her beauty, yet that very afternoon she was applauded for her appearance by dozens of men, women, and children. The rules of Szanzar did not apply to the Gypsy caravan. The ways of Szanzar had no place here. Kyra still had no idea how she would fit into her new community, how long she would be allowed to stay with them, or what might be expected of her. But she knew that she tingled from skin to bone, and she felt like she had been reborn that day, in the perfumed suds of that shallow pond.

CHAPTER FIVE
SOMETHING CALLED HOME

AFTER THE SETTLING OF SPIRITED CONVERSATIONS, Stoyan and Yubi left the large tent without a farewell or invitation to Kyra. Vadim had slipped away unnoticed. For the remainder of the evening, Gypsies came in and out, eating, drinking, laughing, and telling tales. Kyra lingered, not attached to any of them, well-acknowledged by nods, smiles, and foreign pleasantries, but not *with* anyone. When the last few left the tent, Kyra was not sure what to do. She certainly did not want to remain alone. She walked out with the last group and made her way to Iraja's vardo, where the old beauty sat waiting on her porch for Kyra.

Iraja's deep eyes and welcoming outstretched arms were the warmest greeting Kyra had ever received. It told her that she had a home, at least for the night. She climbed aboard the porch and received Iraja's kiss on her cheek. Her host opened the door and Kyra went inside. Draped over the edge of the short and narrow bed was a cream-colored, silk nightgown, which Iraja handed to Kyra after rubbing it softly on her face as if to say, "Feel how soft." All shame was long lost between them. Kyra thought nothing of shedding her bright clothes in front of her new matriarch and changing into the nightgown.

The nightgown was not much too *long* for Kyra. But it had been fashioned for a woman of ample curves, and Kyra's scant figure hardly filled it. There was a tie on the back, which Iraja fastened much narrower than its tailor intended, to prevent it from dropping off of Kyra's shoulders. It was every bit as soft as Iraja's gesture suggested. Kyra's life had been one of coarse wool and linens, each stitch being the property of the Church, and nothing at all in her life existing simply for the sake of pleasure. Her skin had never touched silk. The fabric caressed her lovingly with every sway of her body. She closed her eyes, ran her palms along her body from chest to hips, and smiled with delight, stopping just short of crying.

Iraja pointed to the far end of the bed and Kyra quickly obeyed, returning herself to the lush folds of fabric. Iraja, still in her full skirt and blouse, crawled in beside her and pulled the child tightly against her. It was a strange sensation for Kyra. It was simultaneously unsettling and extremely soothing. Within seconds, she heard the heavy breaths of a half-snore. Iraja slept soundly. Kyra's mind was too occupied with her transformative day to rest easy, and her body was in the midst of celebrating the sensation of silk being pressed tightly against her by embracing arms.

She tried to keep still, but she twitched with every exciting remembrance of the day's events. After each twitch, she froze and held her breath, afraid of being thrown out as a nuisance by an old woman in need of her sleep. Iraja slept well. It would have taken much more than the little tremors of a scant-figured twelve-year old to wake her.

Kyra did not remember falling asleep. Her musings transformed slowly from vivid memories to fantastical dreams. Even fully lucid she would have struggled to draw a clear line between the two. When she awoke, Iraja was out of the vardo and voices moved quickly outside. The Gypsies were striking their camp and preparing to roll forward again. Kyra stood on the porch and watched. Each person, even the children, seemed to have a well-defined duty, and the camp was struck and packed in a scene of organized chaos. Kyra wanted to help, but it all buzzed around her so quickly that she was afraid of getting trampled or getting in the way. She went inside and changed back into the skirt and blouse. When she came out again, there were no signs that tents had sat in the field, or that meals were cooked and metals were smithed there.

Vadim appeared from beside her and hitched the horse to the vardo. Iraja ascended the steps. Vadim folded them beneath, and before Kyra's eyes could settle on one moving part of the scrambling caravan, they were all rolling forward. They were not long in motion when the sounds of the wheels, the footsteps, and the trailing herd of livestock seemed to come into an intentional rhythm. It was very shortly after that when that rhythm drew the accompaniment of clapping hands and singing voices.

It was a different song than the one Kyra heard as the caravan approached her the first time. But it carried a similar rhythm and a similar feeling. Kyra clapped and hummed along, singing along with the *Na Nu Na*s and *La Da La*s. As they rolled along singing and clapping, she thought about her filthy self, rising from the grass to watch the Gypsies roll by. That soiled little child seemed like a stranger to her, one she struggled to recollect vividly. The hours between her mother's illness and changing into a brilliant Gypsy skirt were misty in her memory, like imagining a story that was told to her by some distant relation years earlier. The sounds, the smells, the colors, and the lively faces around her were surreally contrasted to her life before, so much so that she could not think clearly of one while experiencing the other.

Kyra had no notion of geography. She was comprehensively ignorant of the country and region. Other than Bratislava, she could not name another city, town, or village but her native Szanzar. She could not have read a map. It would not have mattered if she could. The Gypsies used no map. They needed no map. The caravan rolled toward the town of Győr as if navigated by some external force, as if the Gypsies were mere passengers on a vessel captained by a higher force. The horses knew the way. The vardos knew the way. The goods and skills for sale by the Gypsies knew the way to every market and every audience in Hungary and well beyond.

The caravan paused for hours at a time, during which time the craftsmen set themselves in circles beside the vardos and wagons, just as before, preparing themselves and their items for the people of Győr. Kyra meandered between and among them without agenda. The Gypsies all fit so squarely into their groups, all but Kyra. The more time she spent drifting between them, the more she was convinced that several different languages were being spoken in the caravan. She knew none of them.

She did not long for her home, for the decaying stench of Szanzar, for a village that, in death, could not possibly ignore her more than it did in life. But she longed for some *sense* of home, for intimate inclusion in one of the several pockets of the caravan, for any place she could know for certain she was meant to be, and with each pause in travel, she adhered herself to the hip of one Gypsy or another, hoping for some magical transformation to make her one of them in language, in useful skill, and in affection.

Most of all, Kyra wanted to talk to someone, to have someone understand her and respond without queer gestures or unintelligible responses to make her feel awkward. The closest she found was a horse. It was a light-brown stallion with a white patch down the face. There was an obedient gentleness in its eyes, and as Kyra walked by it, it followed her with its head. That was all the invitation she needed. She bounded energetically to the horse, not at all with the easy and cautious approach one should use with a strange animal. The horse huffed playfully and nodded its head, seeming to be equally desirous of the encounter. Kyra rubbed its long face, introduced herself, and began peppering the creature with questions about the caravan. She called it Gellen, after her father. It was a good listener, this new friend of hers, and despite the fact that it was no more capable of understanding her than her human companions, it was far less frustrating to talk when there could be no confusion. It made Kyra a little less lonely.

Each night on the way to Győr, Kyra returned to Iraja's vardo, where the old woman shared her small bed, tucking Kyra in with a kiss on the head, a stroke of the hair, and a whispered prayer. The days were exciting and confusing, but the nights were warm and quickly became familiar. In Iraja's vardo, Kyra found something to call home. Iraja read Kyra like one of her worn books. She took every opportunity, every pause in motion, to place Kyra amid a different circle, hoping that some hidden talent or passion would stitch the child to an occupation and affix her permanently to the caravan. It was clear that she wanted Kyra to be more than a temporary stowaway.

The others followed Iraja's commands and tried to include Kyra, to instruct her in their trades. She fumbled through some half-witted attempts to follow their foreign instructions. She showed no natural talents in any of the circles, and her blunders resulted in sudden bursts of tears. Many comforting words of wisdom were given to her. Had she only been able to understand them, she could have patiently waited for her place among them to reveal itself.

For more than a week since rolling away from the soapy pond, life in the caravan went on in this way. Kyra often feared that her uselessness in a community where each seemed to have a function would grow tiresome to her hosts, and they would drop her off in a grassy field to die soiled and starving, much like they found her. Those fears arose, stung her viciously, then were melted away by the warm smiles and generosity of the Gypsies, and by the strong maternal bond Iraja demonstrated to her each night.

Kyra visited Gellen, her horse friend, many times every day. Even that small comfort began to frustrate her. One afternoon, after describing her daily walk around Szanzar to the long ears of her friend, she lamented, "I wish your kind was more talkative. Such an expanse you must have traveled, and with such people. The things you must have seen with your horse eyes..., the things you could teach me about the wide world I have entered. I would be a good student too. I promise I would. But you're not here to teach, are you? You were put here to carry the burdens of others, so God has struck you mute. It is all right, my friend. You do not need to speak. I can read about your adventures in your eyes."

She spent the next several minutes staring into the horse's eyes, trying to visualize the wonders those eyes must have beheld over the years.

In mid-morning the following day, the caravan approached Győr, a town that was growing in population and affluence. They camped in a field on the outskirts. The Gypsies gathered in one large cluster, facing Stoyan, who sat high on a large horse. He shouted instructions to eager, nodding faces, then rode at pace toward the town. Stoyan was only a few gallops away when the cluster broke into feverish activity. The wagons and vardos were formed into a semi-circle. Tents were pitched. Blankets were laid upon the grass. Goods were set and arranged meticulously upon them. It was clear to Kyra. The caravan was transforming into a bazaar.

Everyone was busy and seemed to know exactly what was expected of them. Even Iraja moved about the different groups with useful purpose. Kyra wanted so badly to help, but she could not receive instructions, nor could she ask. She planted herself on the porch of Iraja's vardo and watched the activity with an agitated heart. Once everything was set, the activity slowed, and a strange placidity came over the caravan. They waited with low, calm voices. They lounged in comfort. Kyra, feeling as out of place as ever, remained on the porch of the vardo, not eating, not drinking, hardly thinking.

In the early afternoon, her senses were aroused by the rhythmic thumping of a galloping horse. Stoyan came back, and the Gypsies returned to hyper activity. He spoke in an excited voice to a few of the others, then set immediately to constructing something Kyra could not identify. She was curious and hovered nearby, while Stoyan and Vadim secured posts into the ground, about six feet high and twenty feet apart. They tied a rope tautly between the tops of the posts. Yubi watched, inspecting the construction and giving instructions, like he was the adult, like he was in charge. The spectacle fascinated Kyra, who could not imagine what it all was for.

Everything was in place for the people of Győr. An eerie stillness held the air, an energetic calm awaiting its chance to erupt. The first few townspeople came in a wagon, followed by a few on horseback, more wagons filled with families, and hordes of pedestrians. They filled the spaces between the tents and vardos, gawking with enchanted eyes at the marvelous craftsmanship on display. The copper pots and canisters shimmered like gold in the sun. The barrels smelled of exotic wood. The jewelry was held against the skin of every lover and wife that came from her home in Győr. Foods were spiced in exotic fashion and served for a cost. The blacksmith glowed from the flames of his makeshift kiln, and hammered away, flexing his dark, glistening Gypsy arms and spinning his agile hammer in his hand.

But all of this lost its moment with the sounds of the tuning instruments. The impassioned genius of Gypsy musicians was notorious, and the first plucked note seduced the Győran crowd with fevered anticipation. The tuning stopped with the attention of all upon them. The only sounds in the entire field were the eagerly shuffling feet, trying to jockey in for a better view. The efforts were in vain. The musicians stood and carried their instruments and stools to the center of a cleared circle. The crowd moved out of their way and followed closely behind. Kyra was not one of the crowd from Győr, nor was she one of the Gypsies. The one thing she could claim to be was an intimate of Iraja, so she perched herself on the porch of Iraja's vardo, the only place she could call home. From there, she had an excellent view of the faces in the crowd, from behind the musicians.

The musicians and singers settled into a cluster. The crowd drew within an arm's reach. Stoyan walked right by Kyra. He came from behind the musicians and moved the crowd with grand gestures of his arms. The next thing he did surprised Kyra in the extreme. He spoke to the Hungarian crowd — in Hungarian. He spoke in flawless Hungarian, as if he had lived his life in the shadows of the tithing barn in Szanzar.

"Friends," he shouted, "we bring to your town items, flavors, sights, and sounds from beyond the farthest mountains."

Stoyan's charisma was in full vigor. The crowd belonged to him comprehensively. So did Kyra, once she overcame the shock of hearing her native language from Stoyan's mouth.

Stoyan drew the crowd's attention to the various corners of the bazaar, bragging in the most colorful terms about the craftsmanship of the jewelry, the gleam of the copper, and the mastery of the blacksmith. The man knew how to sell. Kyra had seen the featured items. She watched as much of it had been made, yet Stoyan made her believe that wonders beyond her imagination awaited her in the Gypsy tents and on the Gypsy blankets.

It was an unseasonably hot and dry September day. The air of the field was filled with the smells of exotic spices and perfumes for sale. It awaited only one addition — the Gypsy sounds from the musicians. The music started low, with the slow plucking of a single string. Nothing else moved, and that one string seemed like the only sound being made in all of Hungary. It tapered off and other strings were plucked by the same hand. The other instruments joined in. It was the same song Kyra heard them play on her first day with the caravan. Oh, but it sounded different that day. It chirped with wild liveliness. If freedom had its own anthem, it would sound just like that.

Kyra knew what awaited the captivated ears of the Győrans. The vocalist joined the instruments, just as she had in rehearsal. Milena's voice was even more richly seductive than before. The foreign words were beyond the understanding of the audience, giving the song an extravagant exoticism. On cue, the lyra player flashed his bow. The tempo of the song slowed dramatically, and the lyra sang from its caressed strings. It was so spritely, so aggressively dynamic, as if it had just been released from a cage whose bars it had shaken in desperate captivity for years, that it drew a steady current of tears from the townspeople.

Kyra had heard it before, but not at all like this. The Győrans loved the music, but Kyra *lived* it. She had been bound her whole life, though had not known it, and like the music, she found herself briskly afresh in a much larger, freer world. It seemed to her that the lyra was telling her story to the people of Győr. Through the music, her heart bonded with her nomadic hosts. Whether she was ready to admit it or not, Kyra was a nomad. She had no living home to return to. The exotic sounds and smells around her stopped being exotic. The music made it all intimately familiar. It felt like it belonged to her in some way she could not understand.

When the first song wound down, the dancers gathered between the musicians and the audience. Stoyan stepped between them and backed the crowd a few paces to give the dancers more room. The next song began, not slowly, and not in any way desperate. The second song sang out in joyous notes and a rhythm that put every tapping toe to the test. Milena sounded like she had swallowed everything bright in the world, everything worth loving, and spat it into the faces of the audience, again in foreign words that spurred the imagination between each pair of ears.

The people were primed to spend their money, to empty their purses for one small share of the Gypsy spirit. But it was not yet time to release them to their shopping. There were more acts of seduction to present. Another song began. It was moderately paced and the crowd clapped along. Dancers came from nowhere, appearing in the clearing. Six women crossed each other, three per side, holding their bright dresses out to their sides so they looked three times their size. All of the others from the craftsman clans began to sing with the music. Six men joined the six women, slapping their thighs and boots in perfect unison. In the middle of their dance, they split into two groups, three men and three women on each side.

Kyra scanned all within her vision for Stoyan. Just as she turned her attention back to the musicians, she was startled by the old acrobat running at full sprint between the vardos, toward the musicians' backs. Down the middle, between the two groups of dancers, the old man ran with incredible and seductive energy. He exploded into the air, throwing himself wildly into flips, while the dancers framed him. The crowd shuffled back at first, more startled than amazed. But after taking a few seconds to consider

47

what they had just witnessed, they erupted with applause, drowning out the music. Kyra stood, leaned against the porch rail, and cheered along.

The dancers maintained their positions around Stoyan, swaying their hips in rhythm like boats on an impassioned sea. Their arms rolled and waved in unison, all pointing attention to the acrobat. Stoyan took a few long and low bows before jogging around to the left side of the musicians. The crowd shuffled to give him space. He threw a high back flip, landing almost perfectly erect. The crowd shouted again. The Győrans were intoxicated by all that their senses took in. They yelled and howled like wild animals. Men shouted their love for the women dancers. Women swooned at the explosive power of the muscular acrobat, and children's eyes grew well beyond their natural size.

All cheering stopped when Stoyan raised his hands high above his head. He kept them up as he walked slowly to the vardo directly behind the musicians, the one beside Iraja's. He climbed to the roof, accompanied only by the quickly fiddled lyra. Kyra looked almost directly upward to see him, and from her perspective, the short man looked like a giant. He stood as tall as his bowed legs would lift him, placed his hands near his feet, and pressed to a handstand. He walked on his hands to the edge of the roof. He pretended to take another step, right off the edge, dangling one hand from the roof while standing on the other. The crowd gasped. He returned both hands beneath him and walked on his hands to the other side, where he performed the same trick. When he returned to his feet the crowd's scream shook the wooden porch beneath Kyra.

Stoyan flipped backward from the roof of the vardo and rolled once on the ground before springing to his feet and taking his bow. He directed the townspeople to the tightrope he and Vadim had constructed. Yubi stood centered between the posts, beneath the rope. Stoyan walked slowly to him, and the crowd rearranged themselves for a better view. They blocked Kyra's view of the tightrope from the porch of Iraja's vardo. She hopped down and walked along the opposite side of the train of wagons until she looked between two of them to get a clear view of Yubi.

All music halted, giving dramatic attention to Stoyan and Yubi. Stoyan took Yubi by the hand. The boy took one step onto his father's bent knee and jumped to stand on his shoulders. With Yubi standing on his shoulders, Stoyan inched closer to the rope until Yubi stepped onto it. Stoyan walked away, and Yubi stood balancing on the shaking rope. He gently lifted his front foot and continued to raise it until it was the height of his chin, while his standing foot shook wildly side to side on the rope. He shook his arms, pretending to fight dangerously for his balance. It was all theatrics. When it appeared that he could balance no more and would certainly fall, he went suddenly still. The gasps of concern from the crowd froze as the boy did. Yubi turned calmly to face his audience. He locked his eyes on one frightened child, gave a wink, and performed a cartwheel across the rope.

There was no eruption of applause, only wide eyes and silent, gaping mouths. Once again steady upon his feet, Yubi bent down and grabbed the rope between his feet. He lifted himself to a handstand with his feet spread widely apart above him. Stoyan, who had been near the rope, watching his son's performance, set a stool beside where he had stood and backed several steps away. He ran toward Yubi and the tightrope, but rather than running under his son, he leaped onto the stool and from that narrow platform, dove into the air, over and between Yubi's spread legs, and landed with a forward roll on the other side.

He rolled to his feet, took four large steps backward until he stood just in front of the rope. Yubi bent out of his handstand to stand on his father's shoulders. Stoyan raised his hands beside Yubi's legs. They joined hands and Stoyan lifted his son from his shoulders and set him gracefully on the ground. The two of them stood facing the dumbfounded crowd. Kyra felt like she would explode trying to hold her cheers inside of her. Her discomfort did not last long. The band struck the music as the acrobats took their bow. The dancers closed in to tightly encircle them, and the audience threw such a raucous cheer into the air and across the grassy Hungarian fields that surrounded them that it was surely heard in the streets of Győr.

It was all part of the plan — to raise such noise as to pique the curiosity of the town and send the Győrans back to their neighbors with exotic goods and fantastic stories. The performers broke and the crowd dispersed into smaller pockets, making their way from tent to tent, from blanket to blanket, buying Gypsy wares that were made all the more magical by the performance they had just witnessed. Money was spent. Tremendous wealth flowed into the caravan that day, and it was only the beginning. Family by family, cart by cart, and horse by horse, the Győrans returned to their native streets with much to boast about.

When the last one was gone, the Gypsies set immediately to recovering the grounds from the day's events. When evening fell, they were much as they had been while traveling, as if nothing extraordinary had happened that day. Kyra was the only one in the camp whose heart and mind were agitated in the extreme. With all that she witnessed that day, there was one thing that haunted her. Stoyan spoke Hungarian. Many of the Gypsies did, as they struck their bargains.

Kyra could not understand why they hid it from her and spoke to her only in languages they knew she did not understand. She felt simultaneously betrayed and relieved beyond measure. She was content to save the confrontation on that matter until the following morning. She crawled into the bed in the back of Iraja's vardo, as she had before.

But this time, she envisioned a future with these marvelous people who spoke her language. Wearing a smile that faded slowly, she went to sleep with eyes that danced with wonder behind their closed lids.

CHAPTER SIX

THE DANCER'S DAUGHTER

KYRA AWOKE THE NEXT MORNING with memories of Stoyan's voice ringing Hungarian in her ears. She rose more violently astonished by the revelation than she had been the night before. Iraja was up, seated on a trunk and latching a necklace under her long gray hair.

Kyra put her to the test and asked, "I heard Stoyan and many others speaking Hungarian yesterday. Did you know they spoke my language?"

She cringed, waiting for an answer, not sure which response would disappoint her more. Iraja patted her on the head and mumbled in another language.

Kyra was not yet convinced, and she asked, "Do you speak Hungarian? It sure would be wonderful if you do."

Iraja smiled at her and went back to picking through her box of jewelry. To give the old woman one more chance, she spoke again, "I won't be angry if you do. I would love to talk with you."

Iraja stood from the trunk, kissed the crown of Kyra's head, again called her "Tehara Odjus", and exited the vardo. Kyra was almost completely convinced that her surrogate mother did not have a word of Hungarian stored in that old cluttered closet of a head. When the door closed and Kyra was left alone, she let out a sigh of frustration, not for being unable to converse with Iraja. She had been quite content with that state of affairs. Her frustration came from the thread of doubt and that taunting, teasing voice of deception. She sat for another ten minutes in thought, then mustered the courage to confront Stoyan.

Stoyan and Yubi did not sleep in their vardo. Oh, there was a bed, somewhat larger than Iraja's, but the chamber was packed so tightly that it was difficult enough to stand inside of it, let alone sleep. It was a good thing the door opened outward, or it would never have opened at all. The acrobats slept in a small tent beside their vardo. The tent was fully enclosed, and Kyra strained her ears for signs of life within. She heard nothing, so she walked a probing lap around the vardo, rising on her toes to gain any sort of view through the windows. All seemed still inside. When she had made her way fully around and back to the tent, Stoyan stood waiting for her.

"Dobro utro," he greeted her with a bright-faced smile.

Kyra was in no mood to play games. She responded, "I don't know what that means. Why don't you try saying it in Hungarian, in my language, otherwise you are wasting your breath."

Stoyan dropped his chin and looked at her with a pouty face, then spoke in Hungarian, "Don't be angry, child. After all, you never spoke to me in *my* language."

"I don't know your language. I don't even know what your language is."

"I am Bulgarian, and Bulgarian is my native tongue, but I speak many languages. So does my son."

Kyra felt the betrayal cut more deeply, and her face demonstrated it clearly. She folded her arms in front of her and stared at Stoyan for some sign of remorse in him. It did not come.

She thought about Iraja and was afraid to ask, but her curiosity got the best of her and she blurted, "What about Iraja? I suppose she speaks Hungarian, too?"

Stoyan crossed his arms in imitation of her and answered frankly, "Of course she does. We all do... Well, most of us do. There are a few whose fingers are thankfully more agile than their tongues, or their jewelry would hardly be suitable for the dolls of young children."

Kyra's arms fell flatly at her side and her mouth gaped open. Just minutes earlier she had spoken to Iraja, who understood her fully yet answered in words she knew Kyra did not know.

Kyra raised her voice above what was necessary, and asked, "Why did she not speak to me? She must have known I was lonely. How could she be so cruel?"

Stoyan stood firmly and took one bold step toward Kyra. Her shoulders hunched in response, and her brow turned downward.

"Let me tell you about your benefactor," Stoyan spoke with a calmness in his voice that was incongruent with his rigid stance. "She is the very best of us all, the matriarch of our kumpania."

"Kumpania?" Kyra shakily probed.

"That is what we call ourselves. We who travel together are of the kumpania. Within the kumpania are clans, or at least that is the closest Hungarian translation."

Kyra nodded her head and knelt in the grass for a long lecture. She sat upon her heels and folded her hands on her lap. All anger, all betrayal, all accusatory gestures left her face and her posture.

Stoyan resumed, "Iraja is not the oldest among us, but the kumpania is hers. We are hers."

In a timid voice, Kyra asked, "Who was she?... Who *is* she? I mean who—?"

"In time, she will tell you herself. But I will tell you that she was a magnificent beauty in her day. She was a dancer, the most skilled and lovely dancer I have ever seen. I see that you wear her dresses and her jewelry. Those were gifts to her. Everything inside of her vardo was a gift."

Kyra's interest was piqued. She rose from her heels and knelt tall, and asked, "Gifts? From whom?"

"From many. Every man who saw her dance fell in love with her. Many women did, too. And they praised her with words and wealth. Iraja rejected hundreds of marriage proposals in every town between Bucharest and Vienna. Some of the trinkets you have seen of hers, I confess, came from me, when I was young."

Kyra's eyes grew wide.

"That's right," Stoyan continued, "I was in love with her for a short time, though she is much older than I."

Kyra sat back on her heels again and looked to the grass in front of her knees. Iraja's image in her head had undergone a significant transformation, and she struggled to come to grips with it.

Stoyan interrupted her tumultuous thoughts, "Iraja has been loved by many, but she gives her own devotion very sparingly. That is why it is such an honor to be taken in and cared for by her, as you have been."

There was no remorse in Stoyan, but there was plenty arising in Kyra.

He continued, "I have never seen her take so quickly and so kindly to anyone or anything. But she seems to love you, and that is enough for the rest of us. If Iraja sees something special in you, we all agree that it must be there."

With only grateful curiosity in her voice, Kyra asked, "Why did she not speak that love to me? I need it so badly."

"Listen carefully, child," he answered with new gravity in his voice, "I have seen many come into and out of the kumpania. Iraja has seen more. We don't know your past, or why we found you filthy and starving in that field.

But one thing was certain. Your previous life was dead behind you."

Kyra dropped her head quickly and fully with one fleeting thought of Szanzar and all that had been there. When the thought passed, she raised her face again to Stoyan and invited his words with her eager eyes.

"Iraja knew this best of all. Your old life is dead. We are your new life. You could never make that transition if we came to you, if we spoke in your language. You must come to us if you are to live with us, to *be* of us."

"I want to," she offered sheepishly, "I want to speak to Iraja, in her language if not in mine. But her words don't sound like yours."

"No. Iraja understands many languages, but she speaks in Romani."

"Is that the language of the kumpania?"

"It is the mother language of the Roma."

"What is 'the Roma'?"

"It is our race. We come from here and there. The kumpania picks up many things and many people, but we are Roma, either by birth or by choice. And now you have a choice to make."

"I want to learn, but I am not very smart."

"Kyra," Stoyan scolded, "I did not need an understanding of your language to know better. You are already one of the brightest stars in the kumpania. We all saw that clearly, even as you stood gaunt and filthy in that field. We have talked of little else since."

Kyra blushed and strained her swirling thoughts for a change of subject. "Iraja calls me Tehara Odjus. What does that mean?"

Clearly surprised, Stoyan tried to clarify, "Tehara? Are you sure she used that word? Not Rakli? Are you sure she did not call you Rakli Odjus?"

"I am certain of it," she answered defensively, "I have heard it from her many times."

To Kyra's surprised delight, Stoyan closed the gap between them, dropped to his knees in front of her, and embraced her tightly.

"What does it mean?" she muffled through his strong arms.

Stoyan released her and leaned back to see her face. "Odjus means beautiful. That word does not surprise me. Rakli is the Romani word for a non-Roma girl, a non-Gypsy. Tehara is the word for a Romani girl, one of our own. It seems our beloved Iraja is not just your benefactor. She has taken you as her own, as her daughter. That explains the clothes and jewelry."

"Should I give these things back to her?"

"Don't you dare. They are yours as you are hers, and she is yours. To return the gifts would be to deny your relation to her. She would see it as a rejection. Do you want to be her daughter?"

"YES!" Kyra exclaimed, as if a second of pause could cost her everything she had gained and land her filthy among the dead of Szanzar.

"Then accept all that she has as your own, and enjoy being the one person in all her years that has found a way into her heart. Many have tried."

Any lingering sense of betrayal and anger shriveled to dust. Kyra felt an urgent desire to learn Romani and speak to Iraja as a daughter speaks to a mother, not in the language of her old identity, of her old family, but in the ancient words of her new one. She insisted that Stoyan teach her immediately, at least a few phrases to express her gratitude.

"I cannot," Stoyan responded, "This is an important day, much more important than yesterday."

"How so?" she begged with genuine interest.

"Yesterday was a teaser. The real crowds come today, and with some luck, larger opportunities."

He closed all avenues of inquiry by standing sharply, turning on his heels, and stepping away from her.

After a few steps, while his shadow was still cast upon her, he turned to her and said, "Wait here. I will send Yubi to give you your first lesson, when I can free him for a moment."

With that, he winked at her and joined his rising and bustling kumpania. Kyra wanted to bounce to her feet and find a way to be helpful. Her sense of familial obligation to the kumpania was newly and immeasurably enlivened. But she also wanted to obey Stoyan and wait where she knelt for Yubi to give her the tools to speak to her adopted mother in a way that would show her commitment to her new life. So, she remained as a kneeling statue in the grass, staring at the comings and goings around her with a sense of belonging that was entirely foreign to her.

She had seen Iraja as a Gypsy queen, and she began to feel like the *daughter* of a queen. Her life suddenly seemed like a faery tale, like one of her free and wild musings as she walked aimlessly around her native village. Yet it was unlike a faery tale. The people around her were real. Her eyes and her ears had experienced the magnificent displays of the Roma musicians, dancers, and acrobats. Her scalp had felt the tender kiss of Iraja. Her nose held the lavish perfumes that Iraja had rubbed on her skin. Her reason tried many times to deny the truths before her, but her senses spoke with authority.

Kyra could not have possibly predicted her future. The experiences of her life in Szanzar had no basis to form conjecture. But she knew for certain those few things that mattered. She was treasured. She was coveted. She was cared for. And the time ahead of her promised tantalizing newness. Stoyan was correct. The daughter of Gellen and Eneth died in that field. What rose from the tall grass was an altogether different human being, comprehensively reborn into a new life. Kyra was not just washed by Iraja's fragrant hands in the shallow edge of that remote, unnamed pond. She was baptized. The naked child that emerged was the daughter of Iraja, a daughter of the kumpania. While Kyra waited for Yubi, she whispered nonsense syllables in imaginary conversations, trying to mimic the sounds of the Romani language she had heard, to steep herself in the spirit of the Roma and saturate her soul with the identity of the kumpania.

Ten thousand thoughts made their way in tight single file through Kyra's mind in the few minutes it took Yubi to come to her. Half of her hated to take him from his rehearsal. But the other half was much stronger, the half that was desperate to speak to Iraja in Romani, to find a skill and nestle into her place among her new family. That one-sided battle inside of her was put to rest when she saw the delight in Yubi's face. He was as eager to teach Kyra as Kyra was to learn.

Yubi was just a boy, but a boy with unearthly insight into the human spirit. He wasted no time with numbers or days of the week. He taught Kyra what was most urgent. He taught her how to tell Iraja those things that needed to be said. Kyra mastered two phrases in that short lesson, "Thank you" and "I love you". The syllables swelled in her chest and demanded release. They demanded entrance into Iraja's ears and heart.

The caravan was all abustle. Everyone had a duty to perform that morning, but none more important, none more urgent and overdue, than Kyra's. She practiced her new words on her teacher, wholeheartedly thanking him for the lesson. She kissed him tenderly on the cheek then put her gangly limbs in spastic motion, in search of Iraja.

Kyra found Iraja sitting on the porch of *their* vardo, dangling her swinging legs off the edge like a child. At a glance, the old woman saw a difference. There was something distinctly Romani in the swell of life radiating from Kyra's glowing form. Iraja returned her smile with

one of equal proportion. Kyra fought the urge to blurt her
new phrases unceremoniously. The moment was too grand
for such a crude outburst. She took Iraja by her soft,
wrinkled hand and led her inside.

Before Kyra could release a swelling syllable, Iraja
took a golden necklace from its perch on her collarbones
and placed it in Kyra's hand.

Kyra's first phrase burst out, "Nais tuke."

Iraja wrinkled her forehead and lifted her lips to her
nose. Her eyes reddened and began to pool with tears. The
words rang musically in her old ears. But Kyra was not
thanking her for the necklace and she did not want the
moment to be mistaken. She set the necklace aside, saying,
"Na na," and took Iraja by both hands.

She looked slightly upward to Iraja's eyes and said in
a voice much softer, much more delicate, almost
surprisingly dulcet, "Nais tuke."

Iraja's face went blank as she absorbed the meaning of
the gesture. In that brief utterance, in that short "Thank
you", Kyra put on display every ounce of her gratitude for
everything Iraja had done for her and everything Iraja had
become to her.

The tears were in full flow down the old woman's
blank face when Kyra followed with, "Me mangav tut."

It was no obligatory gesture from a position of debt. It
was as authentic an "I love you" as any daughter has
spoken to her mother. Its richness of feeling was not lost
on the Romani Queen.

Iraja repeated back, "Me mangav tut! Me mangav tut,
Tehara."

Now understanding the word "Tehara", "Romani
girl", it bounced more musically in Kyra's ear than any
sound she had heard from the bowed lyra. She understood
the sentiment it carried gleefully on its back. Kyra repeated
it back in a whisper that was broken by a sudden surge of
emotion, indicating to Iraja the child's understanding of its

meaning. Iraja pulled Kyra to her breast, held her tightly, and began to sing. With one ear smothered by Iraja's arm and the other pressed against her chest, the song sounded deep and submerged to Kyra, as if it was being sung to her by her own bones.

Never in her life had she felt so gratefully situated, so wanted and loved. The vibrations from Iraja's voice seemed to saturate Kyra's entire being. The song went on immeasurably. Kyra understood none of it. Her ignorance did not frustrate her. The sentiment behind the song was clear enough. She would come to know the words. She knew she would. But that moment was well beyond the petty, paltry, weak, and fragile grip of language. "Home" is a small word in any language, certainly smaller than its meaning. Kyra felt "home" in Iraja's arms, and no combination of words in *any* language could have encircled her feelings.

CHAPTER SEVEN
THE NOBLE'S WEDDING

WHILE KYRA AND IRAJA ENJOYED the tenderness of their intimate moments, the rest of the kumpania was in frantic motion around them, preparing for another day of visitors from Győr. Word of the previous day's delights had reached every ear in town. Győr came in force. It was on the second day, always on the second day, that the money was made and the connections were formed. There was no need to stray from the formula, no reason to alter anything from the first day, or any other day when they camped outside of any other town. Those visitors that had come the day before boasted and instructed as if they themselves were part of the caravan.

Kyra wished to remain at Iraja's side, but she also wanted to see the performers again, especially the acrobats. They were true friends of hers, and truly treasured by her. Iraja was more interested in the other trades. The jewelry makers were dear to her, which Kyra thought rather odd for a retired dancer, and they remained among them when the performers gathered on the far side of the camp. When the music began to play, and Iraja showed no signs of leaving the jewelry makers, Kyra turned antsy.

Despite her desire to please her surrogate mother, she hid her wishes poorly. Iraja read her as easily as she read the old books in her vardo. She kissed Kyra and gestured toward the music with a wave of her hand. Kyra returned the kiss and ran in the direction of the tuning instruments. She felt much more a member of the kumpania than the last time she watched them perform. She did not mix with the clustering audience, but walked casually among the musicians and between the staging dancers. They smiled at her. The alteration in her was extreme and they appreciated it. She was in no way out of place among them. She held herself and moved among them like the daughter of their queen.

The crowd was so much larger than the day before. Kyra struggled to imagine that Győr housed so many people. They were all eager for a closer look, and they shoved each other to see the show. On more than one occasion, violence erupted in the crowd. The performers continued as if there were no spectators at all. Men shouted their affection for the dancers. None were showered with gifts. They were not Iraja. But many appeals were made for greater intimacy. The seductive dancers played them like a Byzantine lyra, not giving in to them, but not rejecting them, keeping their affections on the line and their money in their hands. One spectator went too far, groping at a dancer and screaming that she belonged to him. It was a very brief ruckus. The man was pulled out of sight and sound within seconds. Kyra did not know by whom or to where. The matter seemed to evaporate with no signs of having been.

When the dancers finished and Stoyan flew onto the scene in his dramatic fashion, Kyra sat on the ground between two singers, as if her own musical talents had contributed to the success of the day. Kyra could not sing.

She played no instruments. She certainly could do nothing to compare to the wild feats of Stoyan and Yubi. But that did not matter. She was a child of the kumpania with faith that her exact place among them would soon become clear.

When the performances were over, Kyra sought the company of the acrobats. She found Stoyan in conversation with a well-dressed servant. They spoke in Hungarian and Kyra stood near enough to listen. The servant was obviously impressed with the performance. He was arranging acts for the wedding of his master's daughter. Curiosity drew Kyra closer, and Stoyan saw her inching ever nearer. Without chopping a word or breaking eye contact with his guest, he reached his hand blindly to the side with fingers extended directly to Kyra. She responded as she assumed she was meant to. She walked to him and took his hand. He did not acknowledge her, other than closing his fingers to hold her hand tightly. He continued his negotiations and settled on a price to perform at the wedding. Kyra stood silently at his side, passing her eyes between the two men.

When the servant walked away, and all the other spectators left the performance area to seek the other Gypsy wonders on display, Stoyan squared himself to Kyra, took her by both shoulders, and said, "I am sorry, I have had no chance to check on you. Yubi said that your lesson went well. Did you speak to Iraja?"

With welling eyes, Kyra relayed all that had passed between them. Stoyan was truly delighted, and he offered his son for another lesson as soon as the camp was clear of visitors. Of course, she treasured the two phrases she had shared with Iraja, but she had so many questions, and she knew there were stories to be heard. She also knew that Iraja would not meet her halfway on the linguistic road. She was glad for it. What had been a brief point of frustration was now a source of gratitude. The kumpania accepted her as Roma, but she knew that the transition would not be complete until she was more Roma than Hungarian, more of the kumpania than of Szanzar, more of the old dancer than the keeper of the Church's grain. She accepted Stoyan's offer before he finished making it.

Yubi found her mere minutes after the tents were struck. His first language lesson had been light in mood and fun. The second quickly introduced a torrent of vocabulary and grammatical rules. It was serious and often frustrating for teacher and student alike. They made no use of visuals, no writing, no conjugation charts. Speaking and listening were all they had and Kyra's progress was slower than she had expected. She wanted to converse fluently. Yubi told her to be patient and give herself time. But he, too, was young, and his irritation with her struggles was apparent. They had two very different ideas of how the lesson would go. She wanted to swallow much more than could fit in her mouth. He kept with the repetition of a few useful phrases. Had they entered the lessons with a mutual agenda and timeline, the experience would have been more pleasurable for both.

Yubi did not have many hours to commit to Kyra's lessons. His father had arranged a performance at a noble wedding. The daughter of Baron Miklos was getting married at the family estate in Pápa, in the county of Veszprém, about twenty-five miles south of Győr. It was scheduled to take place in a month and a half, in mid-November. Stoyan and Yubi were the only talent commissioned for the wedding. Cold, harsh weather was expected that time of year, and the castle interior could not hold the full extent of the kumpania's talent. The payment offered was substantial. But the acrobats would not leave the caravan, so they all packed with great efficiency and were again rolling through the grassy fields of the Hungarian countryside.

They traveled a few hours each day, but spent most of their time preparing to perform. Winter was reluctant to crawl out of bed. The Hungarian air still savored of late summer. Kyra thought it odd that Stoyan and Yubi did not prepare their act as commissioned, with only the two of them. They rehearsed as they had performed in Győr, with the full complement of dancers and musicians.

A few days before the wedding, they camped outside of the baron's estate and Stoyan and Yubi went on alone. Well, not quite alone — they brought Kyra to help them set up their equipment and serve as an assistant for their act. She tried to imagine what they would do to entertain the wedding party, with only two acrobats and a girl who felt useless.

The baron set a firm rehearsal time. He wanted everything to be perfect. The performance was set to take place in the grand hall of the baron's castle. Musicians hired from a neighboring town set themselves in the center of the performance area, leaving little space for the acrobats. Stoyan and Yubi spoke in Romani, debating how their act would be altered. With no soft ground in which to erect the tightrope, and little space for wild feats of tumbling, the act needed significant alterations. Kyra, like everyone else in attendance, waited to see how it would come together.

The baron sat on a high, ornate chair at the head of the room, the only witness to the rehearsal. The musicians struck their tunes. The music was by no means unpleasant, but it was not Gypsy, and it was poor accompaniment for the passionate performance of the acrobats. It mattered little to Stoyan. He had no intention of performing at the wedding with those musicians. He had a plan, one that was firmly in place well before their arrival at the castle.

The rehearsal went well. The baron was pleased. But it was feeble in Kyra's eyes. She compared it beside the events outside of Győr. She wanted to speak up, to tell the baron about all the talent that sat encamped outside of the estate, but she kept her frustrations and her pride in the kumpania caged within her. Stoyan, Yubi, and Kyra were invited to join the baron's family at dinner. The baron demanded that they tell tales of their travels to the other dinner guests. He was clearly intrigued. Stoyan accepted the invitation. They were shown to a single bedroom that was to be theirs until after the wedding. What happened between the rehearsal and dinner, Kyra could not have said. She laid herself on the regal bed and fell soundly to sleep.

She was awakened when a servant instructed them all to come to dinner. As they followed the servant, Kyra, who held Stoyan's hand, mentioned to him how much better the performance would be if it featured the kumpania's musicians. He squeezed her hand and shushed her with a smile and a wink. She did not know his plan, but she was proud to know that there was a secret plan, and that she would somehow be a part of it.

The dining hall was much smaller than the grand hall. It was a narrow room with a low, rounded ceiling. The long table consumed most of the floor space. It was wide and bulky and sat thirty. Most of the chairs were empty after the baron's family and a few intimate guests were seated. The baron stood to make a speech, but before a sound came from him, a servant entered with four unexpected guests. They were three musicians from the kumpania and Iraja. Kyra caught herself holding her breath. Stoyan stood and spoke to them in Romani. The baron did not mind losing his moment to preside. He was besotted by the flamboyantly dressed Roma and by the melodic language they spoke.

Stoyan turned from his friends to the baron and announced a gift in return for his hospitality. He offered a private performance, just for the intimate gathering in the dining hall. The baron clapped his hands three times and accepted the gift. The dinner was served while the musicians set themselves up at the far end of the table.

The musicians played. They played as only the Roma could play. The lyra massaged the baron's imagination with skillful fingers. Iraja, too old to dance as the dancers do, stood near the baron and swayed her hips. The baron was intoxicated. He watched as Iraja's many fine necklaces danced across her neck and chest.

When the music ended, Iraja took the jewelry from her own neck, wrists, and fingers, and presented them as gifts to the bride. They smelled of foreign oils and gleamed like the copper skin of sweaty Romani dancers. The castle boasted of many rich pleasures, but of nothing so deliciously exotic as the gifts brought into the dining hall that evening. When the food was cleared away, the baron begged for another song, which was graciously provided. When the last song finished, the secret plan was revealed.

Stoyan sat beside the baron, not like a hired hand, or even like an honored guest, but like an old friend. He told the baron tales of their travels, but included one featured story with an alternative purpose. He spoke of another wedding, of a count far away, whose daughter's wedding featured not three Romani musicians, but eight. He told of the pride and acclaim that befell the count after the wedding. The bait was in place and the baron took it. He insisted that Stoyan provide him with twelve Romani musicians for the wedding.

As that bargain was being struck, the bride boasted of her new jewelry, donning them piece by piece. Kyra saw her opportunity to join the scheme. She told the baron's daughter of all the glamorous and extravagant wares made by her kumpania. The bride begged her father to bring it all to the wedding. Before the dining hall emptied for the night, the wedding plans had altered substantially. It was no longer to be a noble Hungarian wedding, but a Gypsy one. The entire kumpania was invited, and they were to bring all that they had with them. Each part of it, each trinket, each musical note, and each stunt carried an additional price. The baron paid it gladly. He dreamed not only of his daughter's happiness, but of the grand acclaim that would follow the wedding.

Early the following morning, most of the kumpania were within the walls of the castle. The grand hall was not nearly grand enough, and Stoyan convinced the baron to move the event outside. Walls and ceilings were no friends of the Roma spirit, a spirit that was better suited to the free breeze and the birds in flight above. At the wedding, the Roma did their thing, as they always had. The guests were more enraptured than any person from any town the kumpania had ever visited. The baron swelled with pride. His payment was substantial, but was the lesser part of the wealth that came to the kumpania that day. Each guest wanted a souvenir of the imported magic, and their money seemed to hold little value to them against the exotic wonders of the Roma.

Kyra did not strike a note of music. She had not fashioned a single piece of jewelry. She did not dance or flip. But she was an intimate part of the business that day. She worked her way among them all, promoting each attraction and drawing eyes and purses to the Gypsy wonders. She spoke in Hungarian. It was all she could speak. But she forced an accent that stood her apart from the baron and his guests. It was no natural accent that could be found anywhere in the world, but one of her own invention. It did, as Stoyan, Yubi, Iraja, and the others noticed, bear the distinct flavor of the kumpania and Kyra's unique position among them. They all knew that Kyra's efforts increased their wealth. She had a way of translating the spirit of the Roma to the wedding guests in ways that nobody else in the kumpania could have. She had a foot in both worlds, and it was that position that served them all very well that day.

After the wedding, the baron's family and the guests wanted to see the vardos. Stoyan led them all in procession to the caravan. They met those who had been left behind. The herders, the blacksmith, the mothers with small children, all became attractions of the wedding festivities. The baron was given private tours of each vardo, with rich descriptions of the significance of the designs and decorations. Kyra remained nearby, learning as the baron learned, but understanding much more deeply, for each piece of information passed through the enriching filters of her understanding, an understanding that no outsider could possibly grasp.

When they got to Iraja's vardo, the old dancer gestured to Kyra. It was Kyra who escorted him inside, inside of *her* vardo. She removed one of her necklaces, opened a box, and placed it gingerly inside, indicating without doubt that it was, in fact, her vardo. What happened next was witnessed by nobody but the baron and Kyra. After closing the jewelry box, she turned to the baron and found him in a low bow to her. He had no idea that she was a Hungarian village girl, the daughter of a tithing barn manager. His eyes looked at her with the same wonder and admiration they shone upon the dancers and acrobats. Kyra's blush was in full form when the baron excused himself and left the vardo.

The wedding guests returned to the castle and left the Roma to the free Hungarian air. The kumpania was together again, and life after the wedding resumed without pause. Kyra took a keen mental note of how little the behavior of the Roma changed between entertaining the wedding guests and resuming their daily routines. They did not need to bloat themselves for an audience, or aggrandize themselves in any way. They were already exorbitantly free, with spirits unchained by any of the figurative shackles that bind human beings. The Gypsy spirit tasted by the wedding guests was authentic. They were served slices of Romani life, experiencing them as they actually lived. Kyra noticed this, and it only swelled her pride in them further.

The caravan remained outside of the baron's estate for several days, not entertaining, but simply living as they always had, breaking into their various camps, constructing their wares and perfecting their crafts. Of the many professions on display, there was only one that stirred Kyra's passions to a frenzy. No matter who she was watching or what she was doing, her thoughts rarely left the acrobat and his son. She had turned thirteen years old while they traveled to the wedding, and she had no notion of it. She had forgotten her birthday. She had forgotten the passage of time, at least as she had perceived it before. Her new life left no room for petty thoughts.

She was coveted by many. The jewelry makers, the herders, even Menowin, the blacksmith, they were all eager for a new, young apprentice. Kyra tried her hand at them all, gracing each with a few hours at a time. It is no wonder she bumbled her way through each attempt to learn a new skill. None had her full attention. She dreamed of apprenticing with Stoyan and becoming a part of his act. But Stoyan and Yubi seemed magical to her, and she could not imagine how, with her mortal limitations, she could contribute.

"I could sooner learn to blow flames from my mouth," she thought, "than to do the things they can do."

She was not frustrated. She knew that she had served the kumpania well at the wedding. Their gratitude and acceptance of her were as flamboyantly displayed as their colorful clothing.

Each day, after drifting from circle to circle, half-heartedly learning tricks of their trades, she met with Yubi and resumed her language lessons. She learned Romani phrase by phrase, and employed each new phrase to the fullest as she weaved her way through the caravan. Two weeks after the wedding, they were rolling again. Other fields, other towns, other castles were in the world around them. For the first time in Kyra's life, her vision of the world was a Romani vision. She felt as free as a bird, and she thirsted for every drop of experience her new Gypsy life had to offer her.

CHAPTER EIGHT
THE YOUNG CONFIDANT

As Kyra's knowledge of the Romani language expanded, her relationship with Iraja bounded in equal proportion. Iraja still would not speak to her in Hungarian. She held firm to that stance. Kyra wanted very badly to converse with her freely, and Iraja knew it would be great motivation to drive her studies. Kyra's lessons with Yubi were not the only place she learned. When she first joined the kumpania, foreign words bounced off of her ears and spent no time swimming around her brain. But her desperation to communicate with Iraja and others piqued her to a sharp awareness of syllables, gestures, intonations, and context.

Yubi's lessons broke the ground and exposed fertile soil beneath. It seemed that Kyra had a knack for language. After the wedding, vocabulary stuck to her. Each word she learned remained in her head and became a useful part of her increasing well of expressions. It was not only Romani. Each syllable uttered near her, in the caravan's many languages, made sense to her, and found a stable home between her ears. She began to seek words and attract them like a magnet.

Menowin, the blacksmith, was a close friend of Vadim's. His vardo usually rode in caravan directly in front of Iraja's. Aside from Iraja's, his face was often the last seen by Kyra at night and the first in the morning. He was one of the only Roma willing to speak to her in Hungarian. He did so only when the conversation went beyond Kyra's increasing Romani vocabulary. It was through those conversations, more than in her lessons with Yubi, that her Romani became more conversational. Menowin spoke three other languages, and he taught them to Kyra, not in formal lessons, but in casual conversations and friendly explanations.

Kyra usually spent the first hour of every day helping Menowin fire his forge and set his supplies. She spent her mornings with a bright face, reddened by the heat of Menowin's kiln. Their conversations were an awkward linguistic quilt, patched together haphazardly from pieces of Hungarian, Romani, and other languages. Menowin was careful not to indulge her by giving her an easy path of communication, a Hungarian path. Neither would he let their talks grind to a frustrating halt. Never too far from Iraja, he used his Hungarian as sparingly as possible. Kyra quickly grew to treasure him and relish their precious time together.

Menowin's motives were not purely altruistic or even affectionate. He grew fond of her, but he also hoped to cultivate an apprentice. Although no such arrangement was formally made, he taught her as a father would teach a daughter, and she forgot very little that was taught. For her, it had little to do with the development of a trade and much to do with the very fine company. Menowin had a hearty sense of humor. Most of Kyra's laughter came in his company. She hardly had the strength to swing his hammer, so she ran his errands, handed him his tools, and brightened his days with her eager innocence.

Kyra wanted to speak of her past, of her childhood, her family and village, and of the plague that took it all from her. There was an unwritten and little spoken of rule within the kumpania — that Kyra's past was to remain in the past and in no way taint her new life. That was a Romani concept born of Romani sensibilities. Kyra came from a firmly planted and sedentary background. Her new family could not have understood her need to speak of her past, especially of the horrors she witnessed in her final week in Szanzar.

Conversations with Menowin spanned the broadest array of topics, but could not touch the forbidden. Each time Kyra tried to bring it up, Menowin artfully steered in a different direction. Stoyan and Yubi were the only other people with whom Kyra spoke openly. It was acceptable for them to speak to her in Hungarian. They were teaching her Romani. Like Iraja, Stoyan felt that dwelling on her previous identity would stunt her growth into her new one. He would hear nothing of her life before the caravan. Yubi was altogether different. His fascination with his student grew with each hour they spent together. Her mind proved extraordinary. He saw it clearly, even if she did not.

Lessons with Yubi were usually isolated, and he sought a variety of topics to expand her well of expressions. Her past seemed to him a fertile subject to discuss. Much more than that, he wanted to know her, to know of her. She was an enticing treasure chest with a forbidding lock upon it. His time alone with her was the key to that lock. One afternoon, in a brief hour between the demands of the blacksmith and Yubi's training with his father, they found a soft patch of dry grass to sit for their lesson, barely within sight of the caravan. He had other plans. He asked her where she came from and what terrible events placed her, soiled, in that field. Not a word of Romani was learned that day. Every minute detail of her past that had been screaming mutely inside of her flew at the chance to escape.

Kyra told him everything. He listened. He did not say a word, nod his head, or shift his position. He barely blinked, but gazed wide-eyed at her in absolute fascination. Having that secret chest opened for him and gazing upon its contents did nothing to reduce his enchantment. Her life in Szanzar was as foreign to him as Gypsy life had been to her. The story of her final week with her family gave her image a heroic luster in his eyes. When she had said all that she could think to say, he erupted with questions. The weight that was released from her that afternoon was immeasurable, and her gratitude to Yubi embroidered him most fixedly to her heart.

Iraja was a mother to her. Stoyan was some lofty Gypsy ideal, sprung directly from her childhood fantasies. Menowin was a teacher. None of them were peers, none but Yubi. A bond formed on that soft patch of dry grass. She found a peer, a friend, her only true friend. His gazing eyes made it clear to her that she was more to him than an assignment given to him by his father. She had as much to offer him. After that afternoon, they sought each other as often as they could both be spared, not for vocabulary, but for company, for treasured company.

Yubi was the only person in the caravan who knew where Kyra came from and exactly what she had suffered. This gave him a distinct sense of ownership, like she was his more than any other's. He gave her a secret release valve through which any thought that demanded release found its way to a welcoming ear. The necessities of the nomadic life spared them little time, but what time they found together was stretched beyond its measured length. More Hungarian than Romani passed between them, but he also taught her Bulgarian. What *was* learned stuck thoroughly, for it came to her under pleasurable circumstances and on the wings of fascinating topics.

The bazaar at Győr and the extravagant wedding had been successful in the extreme. A great deal of wealth came into the caravan. They sold almost everything they had to sell and were in full acquisition mode. They caravanned from market to market along the Danube, purchasing food and drink, and the raw materials needed for their various crafts. They always camped at a distance, never parading as a whole near the urban areas. Never more than two or three rode out to the markets. It was only in the open fields that they felt a sense of home. Kyra took note of the obvious changes in their demeanor when the caravan found itself within the comings and goings of society.

One evening in late February, they camped outside of the town of Paks. Stoyan and Menowin rode alone to the market. Kyra took the opportunity to speak with Yubi. They sat together in the grass, as they often did, and she asked him why the Roma seemed to fear society.

He answered, "A thousand memories from a hundred years stick to them like damp dust."

Kyra simply stared at him, not because of what he said, but how he said it. Yubi had a serious nature. Himself only a young teenager, this boy had the look of a man in his expression — of a man who had seen more than most men.

He put a hand on her shoulder and explained, "You have been with us for many months. In that time, have you seen a weapon, a sword or a shield?"

She did not need to scour her memory for an answer. The thought of one of her fellow tribesmen swinging a sword and hollering the cries of battle was absurd to her. She could more easily imagine them growing a tail and wings, and flying into the air to gather the clouds. She shook her head quickly in response.

He continued, "Terrible violence has been inflicted on our people, yet we never arm ourselves against it. We are peaceful, wanting only to be free and to bring delight to others. Our people shed their sorrows and discard them like worn shoes. I do not. I cannot. I ought not. I think you understand me."

She nodded vigorously in agreement.

He continued, "There is one curse to our nomadic life. We are constant and perpetual strangers to the world. We are the easiest target for blame when anyone near us suffers. A crop fails... it must be the Gypsies. A mother dies in childbirth... the witchcraft of the Gypsies. A turn of bad weather... blame the Gypsies. We love the crowds, and we fear them. We have watched each other hang, and we have watched each other burn."

Each word he spoke to her seemed to place additional weight on his young shoulders. He felt every one of the kumpania's pains, accumulated over hundreds of years. Kyra had shared her sorrows with Yubi. Now Yubi shared the sorrows of the Roma, which he alone held tightly. Kyra could not help herself. She threw her arms around him and embraced him like she was embracing all of them at once. She gave him a long and firm kiss on his forehead. He understood what she felt and what she meant. She was kissing the Roma, her people. She was kissing them all, attempting to nurture them all with her lips. Yubi's forehead was simply their representative.

When she pulled from him, the weight was gone from his shoulders. The anguish was gone from his face. A joyous light shone from him. He had a different face entirely, as if flipped like a coin. His resilience astonished her. He had shown a very non-Roma embrace of sorrow. But in his sudden radiance, she was reminded of who he was. She had been with them long enough to recognize, in his buoyancy of spirit, something quintessentially Roma. There was no fearful child in front of her, nor was there a seasoned sage or a wild and thoughtless animal, only Yubi, the boy, and her only confidant.

CHAPTER NINE

FROZEN PLAINS

STOYAN AND MENOWIN RODE BACK to the camp having struck many bargains in the Paks market. The rears of their horses were thoroughly laden with samples of materials for each profession in the caravan. They unloaded the horses, distributed the materials, and spoke with great exuberance of the opportunities Paks had to offer. Stoyan was eager for another performance. He and Yubi had been expanding their act, and he was excited to display the new stunts. Stoyan gathered the people around him and began to lay the plans for the Paks bazaar. Many threw their ideas into the bustling clamor.

They were all brought to stillness when Iraja walked among them, waving her hands in the air, yelling "Manush! Kumpania!"

Kyra had the Romani of a three year old Roma child, but it was enough to get the gist of the following announcement. Once all eyes and ears were on Iraja, she looked directly upward and watched the movement of the birds. She closed her eyes and drew a slow and deep inhale. Although the March air was warm and the sun shone directly on her, Iraja ordered them to prepare for the cold and snow. Nobody questioned. Nobody doubted. They set immediately to obey her. They drew the caravan into a tight circle, two to three vardos deep. The smaller tents were pitched within the circle, leaving a large space in the very center.

As the sun set, it was still quite warm. Still, nobody questioned that cold and snow were coming. They built a large wood pile in the center of the camp and hunkered into their tents as if it was already cold. Kyra nestled into Iraja's vardo and was soon joined by the great matriarch. They crawled into the bed together. Iraja pulled two extra blankets over them and held more tightly to Kyra than normal. The excessive warmth drew Kyra quickly to sleep.

She was awakened in the night by a howling wind and a shaking vardo. It would have terrified her if not for the woman sleeping beside her. Iraja foresaw the storm, and that fact comforted Kyra. She was convinced that the tents would have been swept away by the angry wind and deposited in France, if stationed as they usually were. But they were not usually stationed. Because of Iraja's observance of the birds, and her deeply pulled inhale, the tents and the people within them were safe within the circle of heavy, bulky Gypsy wagons. The livestock were all hitched tightly between them.

Kyra felt safeguarded by Iraja's wisdom, and by the obedient hands that had prepared the caravan for the night. Yubi had spoken much of the Kumpania's history. Kyra knew that this storm was one of a multitude that had been well-weathered by the caravan, and the first of many such storms to be weathered by her. The storm was a mild hardship, no real hardship at all, and Kyra went through it with her nomadic family. That thought comforted her. The howling wind was like a lullaby, and the shaking vardo was like the gentle swaying of a nursing mother. Kyra dozed off again, much more comfortably than she had hours earlier.

She awoke to a gray, dingy sunlight pushing with all its might to get through the thick clouds and falling snow. Iraja still slept soundly. Kyra had to break a seal of ice to open the vardo door. It opened to a strange scene. The air was bitterly cold. The snow came in tiny crystals that seemed to shake with their own protective shiver. The strangeness of the scene was not in the cold, the layer of thick frost that sealed everything, or even in the shivering snow. It was in the behavior of the kumpania. Such weather would have sent the people of Szanzar into the deepest corners of their homes. The Roma behaved like they felt no difference between that morning and the one before.

Kyra put on an extra blouse and wrapped herself in two blankets before she dared step from the protection of the vardo. The others wore no additional layers. They worked and laughed within the same light shirts they wore in the warmer weather. The men's sleeves were rolled up and their open shirts showed their bare chests, as they tried to light the pile of wood that had been set the night before. Milena sat barefoot and bare-breasted on a stool, nursing a baby that was swaddled only by a diaper. Neither mother nor baby seemed to notice that the sun hid its light and warmth from the Hungarian plains. The winter was very late to come. But when it came, it came with a vengeance. Its icy teeth could not sink into the Roma, not into their bodies and not into their spirits.

Kyra's additional layers, thick as they were, felt like nothing at all to her. She stood near the woodpile and silently cheered the men who were lighting it. Eventually, a spark grew and the fire shot up as if it was trying to shake God's hand. Kyra had to step back and turn her ruddy face from the heat. She turned it in time to see Stoyan, Yubi, Vadim, and Menowin a few short strides from her, gawking at her. Kyra took three steps away from the fire and looked all around her, believing that she had done something wrong, or violated some ancient kumpania tradition. She had done no such thing. That was not the reason for the faces that stared at her.

Menowin interpreted her reaction and spoke to her in Hungarian, "It is alright, my friend. Please…" He gestured to where she was standing when she saw them.

She stepped slowly back to the fire, looking sheepishly at them with each slow step. The men did not move. They only stood and stared as she had first found them.

"What things are?" she ventured in Romani.

Vadim cocked an eyebrow and tilted his head in confusion. Menowin and Stoyan smiled softly. Yubi stepped forward and corrected her verbiage.

"What is it?" he instructed her.

"What is it?" she repeated.

Menowin giggled and assured her, again in her native Hungarian, "It is nothing that you did. It is only how you look."

Kyra looked around her at all the thinly dressed Roma, and she felt self-conscious. She pulled the blankets from her shoulders.

Stoyan stepped to her and replaced the blankets, as Yubi told her, "It is not how you are dressed. It is how your face holds the light of the fire."

Kyra did not understand, and she signified that fact with a subtle shake of her head.

Yubi tried to clarify, "Your cheeks are reddened, and the glow makes you look… it makes you look…"

"Beautiful!" Stoyan finished, "It makes you look beautiful."

Kyra's red face reddened deeper.

Yubi nodded vigorously, but finding himself also blushing, turned the moment into a lesson, instructing her, "Odjus. That is the Romani word for—"

"Odjus," she interrupted, "Yes, I know that word. Beautiful."

She turned from the fire to face them, and she thanked them in Romani, "Nais tuke."

Vadim, who was not updated on her linguistic progress, told her that he understood her, "Me razumiv!"

She replied to him with a wide smile across her glowing face, "Me razumiv tut."

Yubi's infatuated stare, which was as scantily veiled as the nursing baby, turned to one of pride, and he congratulated her, "Baxtalipe!"

"Nais tuke," she returned with a roll of her head.

He pressed himself against her shoulder, then sat facing the fire. She took the invitation and sat beside him.

He fell easily into his role as teacher, pointing to the fire, saying, "Yog."

"Yog," she repeated.

The men stood behind them and admired the scene playing out in front of them. Kyra forgot all about them. Her thoughts were on Yubi and his lesson. A few minutes later, she turned back and the men were gone, bustling about their chores like everyone else.

Kyra and Yubi spent another hour in that way, learning and laughing in front of the fire. There was little else for them to do. The snow grew deep around the camp. The caravan would not have moved easily. It was obvious that they intended to entrench as they were until the weather improved.

The weather did not improve. For three weeks it raged on. The stores of food were abundant, yet Kyra sensed some nervous concern. Finally, Vadim rode to Paks. He returned to the camp and reported that the markets and shops were not open. The town was shuttered up tightly. There was no place to buy provisions and even Iraja could not tell how long the snow and cold would continue.

The following weeks were a delightful time for Kyra. The camp was not a bustling place. Kyra used the time to foster relationships with the entire kumpania and to understand these people who were still in many ways strange to her. Still in search of her place, still seeking her employment, her future, she spent time getting to know each of the professions, hoping that one of them might place some fertilizer for a dormant seed of talent that would sprout from her on the frozen Hungarian plain.

Word by word, expression by expression, her Romani expanded. It happened so gradually that she hardly noticed her impressive strides. The others noticed. Yubi noticed. Most importantly to Kyra, Iraja noticed. Their small sphere of endearments expanded to stories of Iraja's many years.

While Yubi and others gave Kyra thorough histories of their people, they were told from an impersonal distance. Iraja carried the history not only in her head, but in her heart and in her memory. She told stories, personal stories of her many decades with the kumpania. She had seen it grow and dwindle. Some left. Some died. Newcomers joined to take their places. Iraja was born in the grass beside the caravan. The kumpania had been her only family and her only country ever since. She knew them all, all who had traveled with them and every town and village they visited.

There was an endless horde of stories bottled up inside of her like a genie in a lamp, just waiting for Kyra's Romani to grow up, give it a rub, and make its wishes come forth. In their weeks snowed in place outside of Paks, Kyra grew in many ways. With decreasing impediments and decreasing frustration, Iraja's nightly stories became longer and much more in-depth. Their tightening embraces each night reflected the deepening of their relationship.

There was little for Kyra to be but a daughter and student, little for her to do but assist Menowin at his forge and take a shift attending the huddled livestock. The days were long, but they were filled to their limits with thoughts. Even her time alone among the sheep and horses was an incessant and tireless stream of ponderings and reviews of the previous day's lessons. Had any one of the kumpania slept through their frozen weeks, they would hardly have recognized the Kyra they awoke to. As the Romani language came from her more naturally, her understanding of the people who spoke it expanded in kind. It would be an exaggeration to say that Kyra had become Roma. But she had a much greater understanding of them than any non-Roma, and with that understanding came an indescribable degree of admiration, respect, and love.

CHAPTER TEN
MORE ROMANI THAN THE ROMA

AFTER NEARLY A MONTH of almost constant snow and oppressive cold, the sun reacquainted itself with the Hungarian air. A heavy layer of snow and mud held the young spring grass tyrannically beneath it. But the April sun was direct and penetrating, and the snow melted quickly. As the snow thinned, the mud thickened. The wagons could not be pulled through it. The camp outside of Paks was home until the ground dried and hardened. The sun and warmth brought the performers out of the tents and vardos and into the open air, where their skills flourished. Stoyan and Yubi finally resumed their rehearsals. They ended the days as exhausted as they were muddy, but they were again flipping through the air and vaulting off of each other.

The need for supplies bordered on desperation. Menowin and Vadim rode their horses to Paks. It was a slow, slogging march. The ride, which would have taken less than an hour in ideal conditions, took three hours. Although the days were getting longer, six hours round trip left little time to peruse the market. Nobody expected them to return the same day. But they did return. They rode back much harder and faster than they rode out, arriving in the afternoon with nothing more upon the horses than the men who rode them.

The camp was out of doors, so all witnessed their hurried return. It was news, not supplies, that they brought back from Paks.

Before Menowin's boots hit the ground, he announced, "The plague has come to Paks."

Stoyan shouted from the cluster, "How bad is it?"

Vadim answered, "It is not yet very bad, only two cases that we heard of."

Menowin added, "But the people there are not clean. I expect it will spread quickly."

Kyra thought this to be a strange assessment. She could not imagine how the cleanliness of Paks could affect the spread of the disease.

"Quickly," Iraja shouted to Menowin and Vadim, "to the bath!"

Kyra watched with confusion as several hands stripped the two men and meticulously cleaned them. Four others took the two horses and washed them thoroughly. Stoyan grabbed the saddle and saddle blanket from one, and instructed Yubi and Kyra to take the other. Yubi knew what to do. He set the large cooking basin on the fire, and with Kyra's help, dragged the saddle and saddle blanket to the fire. Both blankets, as well as all of the clothes the two men had worn to Paks, were thrown into the boiling water, along with soaps and perfumes. Yubi took two rags, handed one to Kyra, and instructed her to help him clean the saddle.

As the buzz of panic subsided, Kyra finally asked him to explain the kumpania's reaction.

He answered in Romani, "The disease is not the punishment of a vengeful god, or the connivance of an evil person."

She understood the words. The topic had deep, personal relevance to her. She had not given much thought to what had brought the plague to Szanzar, or why it swallowed her home village so quickly and comprehensively. But Yubi spoke with confidence. He seemed to understand what nobody in Szanzar had.

"Go on," she pleaded.

"It is a matter of sanitation."

She had not learned that word, so Yubi switched to Hungarian.

She stopped scrubbing the saddle and slipped into a deep trance of reflection. The weight of thought was heavy on her, and Yubi continued to clean the saddle, throwing occasional glances at her, but not saying a word.

Finally, she looked up to him and asked, "Are you saying that my family died because they were dirty?"

"Nobody has ever died from dirt," he assured her, "but there is a difference between being dirty and being unclean."

Kyra snapped defensively, "How can you know this?"

Yubi stopped scrubbing the saddle and scooted closer to her. He put a hand on her shoulder and said, "The people of Paks, like the poor people of Szanzar, have only seen the plague in their own little village. They do not have the luxury of comparison, as we do. Plagues have come and gone many times through the cities and villages we see. It has long been understood by us and by all of our kind that the places with good sanitation fare well. Where the streets are dirty and the people unclean, plague has always been worse. The pious and prayerful still die alongside the debauched, while the clean live on."

Kyra took a moment to compare in her memory the cleanliness of her mother and father with that of her Gypsy hosts. The odor of her daily household in Szanzar had been overpowered by the stench of death, but she thought back before the plague struck her village. She remembered, and she compared. She saw the truth as Yubi explained it. The fresh open air, the smell of exotic soaps and perfumes that saturated the caravan, even her own laundered clothes, they all seemed like saviors to her. Her memory held the images of her native villagers, while her eyes and nose held her Roma company. The contrast was severe.

Kyra thought about the people of Paks. Who would be their Kyra and who would be their Gellen?

With pity in her heart, she blurted, "Shouldn't we tell them? Shouldn't we return to Paks and tell them how to save themselves?"

Yubi's lips grinned slightly, while his eyes showed tremendous sorrow. He answered, "How do you imagine that will go? Gypsies ride into their dying village and tell them to bathe. They believe in superstitious causes and they turn to superstitious remedies. They would not believe us. They would burn us, as they have before. They would offer our lives as sacrifices. When one dead Gypsy does not end the plague, they offer another, and another."

Kyra's blood left her extremities. She turned pale as she shivered.

"There is more," he continued, "When they see that they are dying and we are not, they will say that we have poisoned them. They will accuse us of witchcraft and devilry."

Kyra again compared the people of Paks with her own family and neighbors. She could not imagine her father or brother setting her on fire because she traveled with Gypsies. She asked, "How do you know they would do such things?"

"I do not know that they would. I only know that they have."

Kyra was not satisfied. Her mind was increasingly Romani, but her heart was still of Szanzar, and she took his prediction personally.

"I don't imagine Paks is so very different from my home village," she argued, "My neighbors would never have done such terrible things. Paks may soon die. We know how to save them."

Images of her dead village flooded her inner-eye, and the memory of the smells filled her nose and clogged her throat. A weak cough pushed through her pathetic whimper. Her cruel, lively, and oppressive sorrow was on bold display, and Yubi felt the pinch of compassion. But he was never part of a settled community. He never knew pride in a place. He felt for the people of Paks, but Paks itself meant nothing to him. He cared for people but not for places, and very little for things.

Kyra, on the other hand, had seen her home die. Her villagers died, but that was not all that she had lost. Her house had also died. The Church's barn died. The same buildings she saw every day, the routines of her life, the daily barking of the village dogs, all of those minute things that go mostly unheralded died along with all of the people she had ever known. The Roma had a very different notion of possessions. They sold everything they made. Nothing was permanent. Nothing was routine. If every possession in the caravan was to suddenly disappear, the kumpania would rebuild their vardos and replace their tools and instruments with no sensation of loss. There was nothing in Yubi's life that could relate to Kyra's feelings. Her compassion for the fate of Paks was beyond the understanding of a nomad.

Yubi's fear was not rooted in recent and fresh experiences. They were rooted in centuries of Romani culture and stories. The Roma had long borne the blame for every sort of human mishap, from plagues and famine to bad weather and accidents. They had borne the blame *and* the punishment. This deeply rooted apprehension was as far beyond Kyra's comprehension as village life was from Yubi's. They both felt fear and sorrow, yet their pains were of such different backgrounds that they could not see eye-to-eye.

After an awkward moment of silence, Yubi spoke softly and tentatively, "We don't have a home beyond our people. They are all that we have and all that we are. If we lose each other, we lose everything. You come from a village. I don't think you can understand that."

Kyra slapped him on the shoulder, not a playful slap, but one intended to sting. She stared directly into him and refuted, "Can't I? Do I not know what it is like to lose everything? What do you think was happening when you saw me alone in that field? What did I have? I had no place. I had no things. I had no people. I laid down to die before I heard the caravan. I wanted to die. Yubi, don't you tell me what I can't understand!"

He thought vividly of that sad little creature in the soiled dress. He remembered what he felt when he shouted the caravan to a halt. He may have been rooted in hardship, but she had been thoroughly encased in it. Yet she broke from that casing and began spreading her new, colorful wings. It was that very resilience that endeared her to the kumpania. It was a brand of human recoil that was distinctly Roma, as much so as any in the kumpania. That is what Iraja saw and recognized in her. She and the other elders who had lived to witness all that they had witnessed in their many years identified that strength in Kyra the moment they saw her poking from the Hungarian grass like a lone tree in the desert that refused to shrivel, die, and turn to sand.

Yubi did not have Iraja's vision, but he was drawn mystically to her deeply buried sorrow, which he alone shared. Her scolding lecture pierced into him like a nail. There was power in her words, and even more in the way she delivered them. He had been the teacher, and she the student. But she reprimanded him for his thoughtlessness and short-sightedness, and he cowered and diminished in response. He wanted to apologize but could think of no words.

She scooted away from him to sit on the opposite side of the saddle. She doubled the speed and fierceness of her scrubbing and refused to look at him. They went on in that way until the saddle itself was tired of being cleaned. Neither wanted to leave the other, to leave things as they stood between them, but neither knew how to progress from there. What she did not know was how deeply she had moved him. In his silent scrubbing, he thought very differently of Paks and its people. He began to see them as a suffering cluster of Kyras, and he had already grown to love her very much.

Finally, Kyra stood. She stared at Yubi, inviting him with her eyes to say or do something that would resolve the tension between them.

He stood quickly in response and told her in Romani, "Bi kashtesko merel i yag."

She understood the words but not the meaning, and she translated it questioningly into Hungarian, "Without wood, the fire would die?"

He lowered his head in a reverent bow to her, as he whispered his gratitude, "Nais tuke."

She may not have understood the idiom, but she felt his sentiment. He straightened from his bow, cupped the back of her head with one hand, and gave her a long kiss on her forehead. That kiss expressed his understanding — of her, of her past, of her compassion for the people of Paks, and of her need to act on their behalf. She wanted to throw her arms around him and squeeze with all of her might. Her arms refused to express themselves. Her feelings found their escape through the half-giggle, half-cry that her shaking chest pushed through her nose.

He took her by the hand and led her to his father and the other leaders. As they worked their way through the kumpania, they heard the fears being expressed around them. None of them feared the plague. They feared persecution *because* of the plague. They feared for their livelihoods and for their lives. They all spoke in Romani. Yubi did not translate. He did not want to speak more of Gypsy fears. He was with Kyra in every way. He wanted to speak only of compassion. Kyra did not need a translator. Her Romani had developed far beyond the vocabulary and conjugations taught to her by Yubi. Her Romani lessons were constant and from every mouth in the kumpania.

Kyra observed them all closely. These were not the faces of prejudice and judgment. They were the faces of authentic fear based on real experiences. They had both been right. They had no direct knowledge to assume the worst from the people of Paks, but they would have been foolish to disregard the deadly lessons of the past.

They found Stoyan, Menowin, and Vadim outside of Iraja's vardo. They were in the heat of furious debate. Yubi interrupted them in Hungarian and told them that they should ride into Paks to see how they may be helpful. All three men stared at him like he had suggested that they walk to the moon and back. Menowin and Vadim continued their debate as if Yubi and Kyra had never come to them. Stoyan saw his son holding Kyra's hand and, in their unity, he saw strength that could not be brushed aside. Their suggestion had to be addressed, if only to be shot down.

He silenced the other two men by asking Yubi loudly, "Why do you think we should go into Paks? What is to be gained that could outweigh the risks?"

Stoyan looked at Yubi, waiting for an answer that was slow in coming. Kyra squeezed Yubi's hand more tightly and answered, "Their lives! You ask what is to be gained and that is the simple answer."

None of them had seen such boldness in her, nor could they have imagined her challenging one of them so brazenly. But Yubi stood firmly by her side and supported her words with a puffed chest and raised chin.

Vadim addressed Kyra scoldingly in Romani, "Te na khuchos perdal cho ushalin!"

"What does that mean," she demanded, "To try to jump over my own shadow?"

Vadim was not expecting her to understand the words. She demanded again, "What does that mean?"

Iraja stepped up from behind Kyra, ran her fingers maternally through Kyra's hair, and explained, "Vadim is suggesting that you are an ignorant child, attempting the impossible."

She followed the explanation with a strong gaze of disapproval at Vadim, who sheepishly focused upon a single blade of grass between his feet. Kyra's gaze was much harsher, and it slapped him when he raised his eyes to her. But Vadim was not alone in his opinions, not alone in his fears. After he apologized to her for the insult, he explained his apprehension in terrible detail. Others around him added their own experiences and their own trepidations.

The wave crashing upon Kyra was large and powerful, but she did not collapse beneath it or let it wash her away. She stood boldly and insisted that if nobody would go to Paks, she would go alone, and assist them in any way she could. Menowin and Stoyan, who both tried to claim paternal authority over her, adamantly denied her. Only one person in the kumpania had a true parental claim. In watching Kyra stand her ground, Iraja saw in her a very Roma-like strength and independence. She had no interest in dissuading Kyra, or stifling her in any way. She silenced them all by giving her blessing. She made her proclamation and walked away, leaving Kyra as astonished as the others.

It was spoken by the matriarch and it was final — Kyra would go to Paks. Nobody would refute her. How and with whom were not details for Iraja's consideration. It was decided that Stoyan would take her to the outskirts of Paks and wait for her there. They could not prevent her from going, nor would they allow her to go dressed flamboyantly like a Gypsy. Vadim pulled Kyra's old dress from a sack. It was clean and respectable. He demanded that she wear it. Kyra wanted to appear in Paks as the daughter of Iraja, as a Romani princess, not the daughter of a Hungarian villager. She prevailed over Stoyan and Menowin's fears when Iraja gave her blessing, but yielded to them on the manner of her dress.

She had grown during her many months with the kumpania. The dress was tight and it was short, but it was the dress of a Hungarian village girl, not of a nomad. Kyra's evolution had been gradual. Her old dress was a tangible metaphor for virtually every changed facet of her being. She did not realize how much she had changed until camouflaged beneath her old dress. In putting it on, she felt dishonest. She felt like an imposter, dressed to deceive. It seemed a rather fraudulent way to present the truth to the people of Paks. Nevertheless, it was under that disguise that she mounted behind Stoyan on his horse.

As they trotted along the caravan, receiving wishes of good fortune, Kyra noticed that the blocks that were normally placed beneath the wheels of the wagons to keep them from rolling while they were camped were not there. The caravan was ready to roll. It was a subtle reminder of a tremendously heavy truth — the kumpania was frightened. They had placed a great deal of faith in Kyra's opinion. She held tightly to Stoyan as they turned away from their friends, and the two of them raced from the caravan toward the uncertainty of the dying village.

CHAPTER ELEVEN

THE RESCUE

STOYAN STOPPED WITH THE VILLAGE of Paks barely in view. He dismounted the horse. When he helped Kyra down, before releasing her to her own feet, he held her tightly and kissed her head several times. There was clear anxiety in his rapid breaths, a sickening fear that radiated from him and crawled through the embrace to burrow beneath Kyra's skin. She began to doubt her plan. Her moral convictions and her pride coupled to outweigh her fear. She pulled herself from him, turned toward Paks, and took a few timid steps away from Stoyan.

Stoyan halted her, saying, "Kyra! I will be right here. Do what you feel you must do, but come back to me quickly. You look like a village girl. You sound like one, but you are a child of the kumpania. If I don't bring Iraja's daughter safely back to her..."

She stood with hunched shoulders, watery eyes, and a quivering lip, and simply nodded in response.

He wished her luck in Romani, "But baxt!"

She may have looked like a Hungarian village girl in her Szanzar dress, but she sounded Romani in tone and accent, as she responded, "Nais tuke."

She turned from him and walked away, her heart pounding more ferociously with each step toward Paks.

She walked through the heart of the village. It was eerily quiet. She waded slowly between the buildings until she reached the river. She was simultaneously relieved and terrified to see that the market was open and boats were at the docks. A distinctly somber sobriety hung over the market. Deals were struck without laughter, without smiles, without a single unnecessary word. Kyra was not the only girl walking the market, and no eyes were drawn from their business to her.

She heard a few mentions of ill family members, of prayerful well-wishes and of mournful regrets. It all seemed like a dampened version of a normal day at a normal riverside market, but with a heaviness in the air that weighed down every syllable from every pair of lips. There were no tears on cheeks, but they were in the eyes, too brave or too scared to leave the shelter of the eyelids.

She was in the market for nearly two hours before hearing of the Gypsy camp outside of town.

Two tradesmen spoke of the caravan, when a third, a man named Balázs interrupted, "May the Devil take them all back to Hell."

Kyra's gasp was noticed but quickly forgotten, as the debate continued, "Balázs, you do not believe that the Gypsies have brought the pestilence."

"Yes, I do. They have flaunted their witchcraft. They have sold us their strange spices and their unholy relics, brought from ungodly lands far away. And now the disease comes just as they camp outside of Paks."

"The first signs appeared before they did."

"I warn you not to misunderstand the limits of their magic."

"What are you proposing?"

"We should ride out to them and run them away from here. We should burn and bury anything purchased from their caravans. Maybe then we will find ourselves again in favor with God."

The man spoke with a silver tongue and an impassioned voice. The people of the market gathered, listened, and were convinced. Many wicked conspiracies came from the growing mob, and many violent proposals.

Responding instinctively, without forethought, Kyra blurted, "The Gypsies did not bring the death!" She shouted it several more times until the market gave her its attention.

Balázs' eyes went piercingly to her. He was a man of influence in Paks and was not accustomed to being contradicted. He scolded her, "Child, what authority can you claim on such things? Go home to your father and mother!"

All eyes turned to her as she stood her ground and answered firmly, "My father and mother are dead." There were many sympathetic sounds pouring toward her from the crowd around her, which encouraged her to continue, "I watched them turn hot. I watched the sores grow on them. And in a few days, I watched them die."

A man with a kindly voice asked with deep concern, "For the sake of God, child, who were your parents?"

"You would not have known them," she answered, "They were Gellen and Eneth of Szanzar."

The man dropped to a knee in front of her. He took her hands and told her, "I knew your father, the manager of the tithing barn. I did not know that Gellen had a daughter, and I did not know that anyone from Szanzar lived."

Kyra dropped her head. She cried and shook, in part from mournful thoughts of her parents that had been too quickly buried by the adventures that had swept her away, but also from the terrifying thought that her kumpania would be blamed for the death of Szanzar.

The kind man put his hands on Kyra's shoulders and asked her urgently, "How did you get to Paks? Where have you been? Who is taking care of you?"

She thought in silence about the answers to his question, about Iraja, Menowin, Stoyan and Yubi, and all of the familial kindness and care she had received since wandering from her dead village. She feared for them all and began to weep more intensely.

"My name is Gergely," the man spoke calmly, while rubbing her shoulders with his thumbs, "Your father was a good man, and I am truly sorry to hear of your misfortunes."

In a piercing tone, Balázs shouted, "Do you call it misfortune? It is far more sinister than that. Tell me child, did the Gypsies come to Szanzar? Did they sell anything to your father?"

Kyra stood stiffly and resolutely, and she answered loudly, "I had never seen a Gypsy until I was saved by them!"

Gergely stood, and looking down to her, he asked, "What do you mean, 'saved by them'?"

All eyes volleyed back to Kyra, who replied, "Szanzar died because it was unclean. There were no Gypsies nearby. I walked far from my home, alone, the only survivor. I was nearly dead from hunger and thirst when the Roma took me in. They cleaned me and fed me. They gave me a warm, safe place to sleep. You asked me how I got to Paks, where I have been, and who has taken care of me. That is your answer."

Gergely took her in his arms and assured her, "You no longer have to live like that, to live with them. You will be part of my family now."

Balázs warned Gergely, "Be careful, friend, taking this Gypsy child into your house."

"Look at her! Listen to her!" Gergely shouted, "This is the daughter of Gellen, the keeper of the Church's grain. She has escaped the Gypsies, and we shall care for her."

"I did not escape from them," she corrected, "They let me come here, to tell you what I know about the Black Death."

"That is a relief," Gergely sighed. Kyra smiled at him. Her smile disappeared when he finished, "They wished to be rid of you and will not come looking for you."

Balázs warned that Kyra was an unwitting weapon, sent by the Gypsies for some devilish ends. Gergely argued that God would not let a pure child, like Kyra, be used for evil. The people in the market took sides and the arguing drowned out all of Kyra's protests. Gergely prevailed, and Kyra was pulled into his home.

Once in Gergely's home, Kyra took tally of her good fortune. She was under the care of a man of influence, a man who knew and respected her father. It would be through Gergely that she would attempt to help the people of Paks, and to acquit the kumpania of all blame. As the day went on, she learned how poorly Paks fared. The disease had struck many homes. Sin was blamed, and prayer was the only attempted remedy.

Gergely left his home shortly after placing Kyra in the care of his wife and children. Kyra tried to explain all that she had come to understand about the disease, and how the Roma successfully kept it away. But with each mention of the Gypsies, Gergely's superstitious wife shushed her and changed the subject.

Kyra was committed to her efforts, so much so that she had forgotten that Stoyan waited for her outside of the village. The day grew old and the sun went low. Kyra believed that she could get through to Gergely, that she could convince him to seek the help of her kumpania and follow their guidance to stave off the plague. But he did not come home. He was still away when twilight came. Through that dim, cool air came Stoyan's voice.

He rode into the heart of the village, yelling for Kyra. Gergely burst through his door and warned Kyra that the Gypsies had come to steal her away. She shouted at him that Stoyan is no kidnapper, that he is a friend. She begged Gergely to invite him in and learn from him. Gergely heard nothing of it. He rushed into the street to face the invasion and protect his new charge. He was not alone. Leading an armed mob was Balázs. Hateful torches lit the surrounding homes.

Stoyan shouted from his horse at the mob, demanding Kyra. He dismounted his horse and marched forward bravely. Not only was Stoyan dressed distinctly like a Gypsy, he had unique features and was recognized quickly as the phenomenal Gypsy acrobat who had performed for the village a few years earlier. But there were no cheers for him this time. They threatened and taunted him.

Although he was facing an armed mob, Stoyan did not back away. He continued to march toward them, shouting for Kyra. They surrounded him, with shouts of "burn the devil" and "purge the evil". Someone knocked him from behind, and he fell to his knees. They encircled him with their weapons raised. But he did not fear their weapons. He feared only for Kyra and would have suffered any wound to bring her back safely. They closed in and were within a lunge and thrust of him when his horse pushed through the circle. Sitting heroically atop the horse was Kyra.

She reached her hand to Stoyan and ordered him to arise, shouting in Romani, "Opre!"

Kyra appeared very differently to the mob, as she sat on the horse, lit only by the torches in front of her, yelling commands in the Gypsy language. This was no captive victim. They were stunned and frozen in place. Stoyan obeyed her. He sprang to his feet and vaulted onto the horse like only a Gypsy acrobat could have. He landed behind

Kyra. She shook the reins violently and shouted commands at the horse that none in the mob could understand. They stared, not at the timid daughter of the Church's employee, but at a fiercely bold Gypsy girl, whose hair seemed to fly about her head under its own power, and whose voice echoed with strength off of the surrounding houses. The horse heeded her commands and raced them both from Paks.

In the panic of the moment, Kyra kept her head. She did not steer the horse directly toward the kumpania. She left Paks in another direction and circled around when they were well-lost to all eyes, enshrouded by the comfortable arms of the dark Hungarian grassland. Riding toward Paks, Kyra had held tightly to Stoyan. Riding back, Stoyan held to Kyra. She was still a thin and gangly girl, but to Stoyan's arms, she felt twice her size. They rode in the dark, but not blindly. Kyra set them in the general direction. The horse took it from there.

If only Kyra and Stoyan could have seen into each other's hearts. He was filled with gratitude and admiration for the brave child who charged through the mob to save his life. She was filled with remorse. Against the warnings of the very man she saved, she had marched naively into the unknown dangers of Paks. Stoyan could have been killed. They both could have. She placed the blame on herself, and she rode toward the kumpania expecting all of the others to do the same. More haunting still, while she was within the settled walls of Gergely's home, being tended by his wife and children, she gave a few passing thoughts to remaining with them, to leaving Iraja and Menowin, Stoyan and Yubi, foregoing the sounds, flavors, and smells of the wider world for a return to village life. Her recollection of those fleeting thoughts haunted her like shrieking ghosts as she hollered at the horse. Her heart arrived back in Iraja's vardo well before the horse got them there, and she scorned herself cruelly for her moments of mental betrayal. Each squeeze of Stoyan's grateful arms from behind her drove the nails of guilt more deeply into her.

CHAPTER TWELVE

FROM ASHES

IT WAS NOT VERY LATE INTO THE EVENING when Kyra and Stoyan returned. Still, the tents should have been pitched. They were not. The caravan was ready to roll. The horses were hitched to the wagons. The livestock was herded into travel formation. All tools of trade were packed. They awaited only Stoyan's word. He gave the order to move. The horse that had driven them so fiercely from Paks was hitched to Stoyan's vardo without a breath of recovery. Stoyan escorted Kyra to Iraja's vardo, lifted her onto the porch, and disappeared into the dark. Within two minutes, they were rolling.

Kyra did not look Iraja in the face. She could not. Her shame was resplendent, and Iraja could not have mistaken it. Two things weighed on her. Her momentary thoughts of abandoning her adopted mother were silent and secretive inside of her. It was *no* secret that Iraja's trust in her had nearly proved deadly. The events of Paks were still known only to Kyra, Stoyan, and the horse that carried them away. But the details would spread through the kumpania faster than the plague through Szanzar, the moment they could camp and mingle. How boldly she had insisted upon going into Paks, how defiantly she demanded. She feared that none of them would look at her the same way again.

Iraja did not dress for bed. Few did. There would be little sleep in the kumpania that night. Most of them walked or rode alongside the vardos. Those within shook and rocked from every pit or stone in their hurried path. Iraja sat on the bed and offered her lap to Kyra's head. Kyra *did* dress for bed, and she pressed her ear against Iraja's lap like it was the only safe place in the world. Somehow, Iraja knew. She always knew more than it seemed she could. Perhaps the minute details still hid from her, but she read the truth in Kyra's every gesture, and she knew what to do.

Iraja took Kyra's head onto her lap, stroked her hair, and began to speak softly and maternally. Her words swelled beyond Kyra's vocabulary, and seemed to slide in and out of various languages. But Kyra got the gist. Iraja spoke of the Romani spirit that radiated from her, of her courage, her strength, and her compassion. When Kyra began to cry, Iraja spoke of her tears, of the Romani tears that sought freedom on her cheeks, just as the Roma sought freedom in the open fields. The words turned to song, then to a lullaby she composed on the spot, which Kyra understood perfectly.

Miri cino
shej
(My little
daughter)

Kaski san?
(Whose are
you?)

Stefan Scheuermann

Devlesa
avilan
(It is God
who brought
you)

Devlesa
araklam
tume
(It is with
God alone
that we
found you)

Amaro baro
them
(In our big
land)

Feri ando
payi
sitsholpe te
nauyas
(It was in
that water
that you
learned to
swim)

Akana
mukav tut le
Devlesa
(I now leave
you to God)

Ashen
Devlesa,
Romale
(May you
remain with
God)

Dza devlesa
(God go with
you now)

Aldin
Devlesa
mura sa
(God Bless
my child)

When the song was finished, Kyra sat up from Iraja's lap and whispered in a strong Romani accent that she was tired, "Me sim khini."

The simple phrase rang musically in Iraja's ears. She closed her eyes and let Kyra's voice and the Romani language play gleefully together in the echoes of her memory. She pressed her lips against her daughter's forehead and held them there long enough for Kyra to drift in and out of consciousness several times before the lips pulled away with the subtle smack of a soft kiss.

With every rotation of the wheels away from Paks, Kyra felt lighter and more confident. Iraja did not. She had been around long enough to see this before, to know that Paks was not an isolated incident, that the plague swept

Hungary, and blame for the deaths would point at them from many different directions. They did not ride toward a destination, but away from danger, not in search of people, but in an escape from them. Hard times were ahead. Trade would be difficult and dangerous. The dancers, musicians, and acrobats would have to bottle their skills for safekeeping until the violent, hateful, suspicious cycle ran its course.

In the morning, it did not take Kyra long to notice the difference. The caravan was still, but not in camp. They were strung in travel formation, ready to roll at a single shout. The herd did not roam to feed. Like the Roma themselves, the livestock sought the protection of the caravan, not from cold or wind, but from a danger that could be seen by none but was felt by all. That is how the following several weeks proceeded — rolling by night and resting by day, working their way at the greatest possible distance from any human settlement, into the open pockets of Hungarian land.

Food began to run scarce. Their treasured livestock had a better chance of meeting the flame than the grass. How quickly it had all turned on them. Kyra felt guilt for every morsel to touch her tongue, so she refused meal after meal, sometimes passing the entire day without a bite. She was already thin but turned so much thinner, but she never complained. It was a silent sacrifice that announced itself loudly in her appearance.

The townspeople of Europe held strong to their Gypsy stereotypes, and the Roma held to theirs. They viewed the settled citizens of Europe as decadent, self-pleasuring, and over-indulgent. Kyra was anything but. Her sacrifice and its effect on her already thin figure was impossible to ignore. Very few of the kumpania still viewed her as a villager, as a guest from a different culture. Her heroic refusal to eat stood in such contrast to their stereotype, and the humble quiet with which she bore it was distinctly

Roma. But one thing was clear to all of them — she could not go on long in that way. None of them could.

Yubi begged Kyra to eat. When she refused, he offered her a deal, "If you must skip meals, skip them one day, and I will skip mine the next, while you eat. The same amount of food will be spared."

His care for her was obvious in his gesture and in the way it was presented.

She refused him with a statement that seemed logical enough to her, "I will be fine. Death ignored me in Szanzar, and I am sure it will ignore me now."

"Death did not ignore you in Szanzar!" he rebutted.

She fixed her eyes on his with a sternly questioning grimace, waiting for him to explain his contradiction.

"It just doesn't like wasting its time," he finished.

"What do you mean?"

"You are strong, Kyra, so much more than you know. You were going to survive. Death didn't take you in Szanzar because it knew it couldn't. It has better things to do than waste its time on the strong."

He did it again as he had before. With a few passing words, he fundamentally altered the way she viewed herself. She blushed heavily before refusing his offer again.

Despite the painful circumstances, the weeks went by quietly and peacefully. Kyra was just beginning to doubt the danger when the scars of hate presented themselves. As the May dawn began to brush the sky, the brightening pink was cut in half by a line of smoke rising from an isolated patch of countryside. The caravan halted, and Vadim rode out to explore. Almost an hour later, he came back with passengers. A young woman, clinging to her infant with one arm and buckling herself tightly to Vadim with the other, rode behind him on the horse.

They were Roma. That was undeniable in the woman's dress and complexion. Vadim escorted her and her child to Iraja's vardo and asked Kyra to tend to them.

Without explanation, he ordered the caravan toward the rising line of smoke. Nobody doubted. Nobody questioned. They obeyed his command and rolled the kumpania forward.

Iraja left the vardo, leaving Kyra alone with their guests. The woman was dirty, bruised, and scraped. She cried steadily but said nothing. Kyra tried to relieve her of the burden of the baby, but the woman would not let go. Kyra wept with her, but did not realize it until she instinctively wiped the salty water from her own cheek with the back of her hand. With a luxurious scarf, she rubbed perfumed oils on the woman's forehead and cheeks, and on the infant's head. Whether from the cool oils, the fine scent, or the compassion with which it was applied, the woman and infant were both soothed.

The mother finally spoke. She thanked Kyra in a dialect of Romani that was undoubtedly different, but not foreign. Kyra understood and she comforted them with a recitation of Iraja's lullaby. She giggled as she sang. She giggled with a realization that delighted her to the core. This woman, this Roma woman, did not know Kyra as a Hungarian villager rescued by a caravan of Gypsies. She knew Kyra as Roma, as a member of a Romani kumpania that had come to her aid. They were the same — this woman and Kyra. They were the same in many ways, not only in their dress and language, but in a way far more fundamental. They had both been rescued from the grassy fields by the kumpania, though what this woman and child were rescued from, Kyra could not guess. She could not guess and she would not ask.

Within half an hour, they found the source of the smoke. They rolled upon what remained of another caravan, of another kumpania. It had been attacked. The smoke rose from a vardo that was clearly glorious a day before but was still aflame. There is little more tragic to the Roma than the destruction of something exquisitely

111

beautiful. The vardo was aflame, but maintained enough of its former self for them to easily imagine its previous artistry. They wept for it, for each hour spent on its construction and decoration, and for each hand that calloused and blistered building it.

They all broke from their travel formation and worked to extinguish the fire. Once that effort had succeeded, they gauged the full damage. There were only seven people left of the dozens attacked, one older man, three women, two little girls, and an infant, including the mother and child who had returned with Vadim. Many were missing and others lay dead where they had been slain.

Lying in a tight row and covered in blankets were the bodies of nine people. Some were taller and some shorter. Kyra could not tell which were men, which were women, and which were children. Her attempt to conjecture what had happened strangled her and seized her breath. There was no time for long explanations or storytelling. The seven survivors blended in with Kyra's kumpania to bury the dead and salvage what could be saved. Of the fourteen vardos attacked, only three could be repaired to full function.

Menowin moved like the wind. He constructed his forge, fired his kiln, and set to making parts for the damaged wagons. None of the horses remained. They had all been taken by the attackers. Perhaps more of the vardos and wagons could have been fixed, but there were not enough horses in Kyra's kumpania to pull them. What did remain of the other caravan was of greater value than horses. Their full stores of flour and grains were unspoiled. The large sacks had been knocked from a toppled wagon, but ignored during the mindless and uncalculated violence of the attack.

One of the salvageable vardos belonged to the old man. His name was Patrin and he was a tailor. Kyra's kumpania had no tailor. They stitched and mended their own clothing, usually quite poorly. Patrin's kumpania was poor, and their tailor had very little in the way of cloths and textiles. It embarrassed him as his rescuers repaired his vardo. Vadim, being Vadim, took Patrin by the hand and guided him to one of the supply wagons. He gave Patrin a sack filled with rolls and folds of exotic fabrics, much of which had been given as gifts by the baron and the wedding guests. It sat useless without a tailor and served only as something to trade. Vadim needed no poetic words of welcome, no diplomatic speech. The fabric spoke well enough. It said to Patrin, "You have a home with us, and your skills are needed."

Kyra's kumpania had traveled all night. Few rested. Yet they worked all day to get what remained of the slaughtered caravan back in motion. Kyra joined in the effort of tending wounds and comforting terrorized hearts. But what would become of the victims? Kyra was afraid to ask. By the end of the day, her question was answered. The attacked kumpania was absorbed into her own. The sudden and seamless integration inspired Kyra, and she began to see her own group as they really were, a body built of many parts, which made her own inclusion seem more natural.

As the sun set, they all set back into motion. The mother and baby stayed with Iraja in her vardo. Kyra rode behind Stoyan on the horse that pulled his vardo. She burned with questions and comments about the day's events, and about the history of her own kumpania. In the middle of the night, as if reading her mind during the hours of silence, he spoke to her.

He explained that his father came into the kumpania under similar circumstances. He was of a Bulgarian caravan that had been attacked and slaughtered near the Hungarian border. He had been taken in just as the seven they had rescued that day. It was that very day that his father met his mother, and in his mother's compassionate nursing, that love formed. His father was not born in the

Bulgarian kumpania. He was from a Bulgarian village, taken in as a young man by the Roma.

Although he lived most of his life as a Hungarian Roma, and he married a Hungarian Roma, Stoyan's father remained very much a Bulgarian villager. Stoyan was raised as a Bulgarian villager in a Hungarian Romani caravan. He did not truly become Roma in spirit until he fell in love with Yubi's mother, a Roma of a pure Indian line, with a rich bronze complexion and deep, dark eyes. She was a dancer, the sort who could tell a thousand tales with her hips. By that time, Stoyan was already an acrobat. He and his wife put together an act like none who watched them had ever seen. A dancer and an acrobat blending their arts in the most elegant, expressive, and breath-taking feats. He lifted her. He threw her and caught her. She danced upon his shoulders and spun inside of his hands.

When she died, their unique art form died with her. Stoyan was again just an acrobat. Remarkable as he was, he was just an acrobat. But he dreamed nightly of his old act with his wife, of the extraordinary passion that flowed from them both as their bodies united to do what had never been done. Stoyan confessed all of this, his whole history, including Yubi's birth, his wife's death, and all that he could remember until he saw Kyra for the very first time.

Oh, he was a magnificent storyteller. Kyra relived the storied moments as if watching them occur before her eyes. She laughed when the moments were comical and cried when they were tragic. Her bond with Stoyan and with his son was strengthened and glued fixedly to her that night, as she held to his back and listened to his history.

When the caravan stopped at sunrise, Kyra returned to Iraja's vardo. Iraja alone awaited her inside. The old matriarch had been nursing and nurturing all night. It was her turn to rest, to rest with her daughter. They held tightly to each other in bed and slept through the day. When Kyra awoke in the late afternoon, she sought the rescued Roma.

She found them, and she distinguished them well from those she had known, but she remarked within her own head how quickly they had become one with the whole, how comfortably they joined the practitioners of their own crafts, and most remarkably, how they spoke and laughed.

Kyra found such resilience to be both admirable and repulsive. Of course, they still carried the sorrow of their very recent tragedies, and of the violent loss of loved ones. But the sorrow seemed to be something beneath them, not upon them, something that they stood upon to see the light of a brighter future. It was beyond Kyra's comprehension and it troubled her mind all afternoon and evening.

She tended the two girls they had taken in. They were half her age and twice her strength. They told her about the fathers they had lost, about the dolls and toys that had been taken, torn, or burned. They told of those things not in terms of bitterness, not with tones of revenge, not in the whimpering voices of victims, but as one might speak of honored things from long-bygone days. They were a peculiar blend of mature perspective and youthful innocence. Once in their company, Kyra could not leave them, and she traveled the following night with them in one of the repaired vardos.

Kyra was good with the children, or perhaps they were good with her. In either case, a mutual bond formed. They were similar and very dissimilar. Like Kyra, they had suddenly lost parents and friends. But while the tragedy of Szanzar lined the inner side of Kyra's skin, perpetually smelling of decay, the children held their tragedy in the palms of their hands, something they chose not to put down yet. It had not grown into them. They possessed it by choice and seemed capable of tossing it aside when it suited them.

Over the course of the following days, the full details of the attack were pieced together from the memories of those who survived it. They had been set upon by a hastily assembled party of men from the town of Kecskemét, which had hunted them for hundreds of miles. Weary from travel, the attackers had forgotten the reasons for the pursuit. The attack was violence for the sake of violence, and theft for the sake of theft. They burned, struck, stabbed, and killed. They plundered, turned on their heels, and rode directly toward Kecskemét. It all happened less than an hour before Vadim rode out to investigate the line of smoke.

Their resilience from such trauma confounded Kyra, but it also attached them to her affections. They were fully integrated, fully of her kumpania, fully of her family. How quickly and comprehensively they dusted themselves of the ashes from which they were pulled. After only a day of being tended to as victims, they took to contributing in equal measure with the rest. Kyra had briefly believed that she had found her calling among them — as nurse and nurturer to the afflicted. But her patients were not long afflicted. They were soon Roma among Roma, much more so than Kyra.

Comparing herself in recovery beside the victims of the attack set Kyra back many months in her efforts to integrate. The seven victims may have been newer to the kumpania, but they were more of the same ingredients added to the stew. Especially when tending to the children, Kyra felt savory among the sweet, like a flavor that stood out, and although not repulsively contrasted, did not quite compliment the meal. Again, a clearer view into the hearts around her would have done her good. She, and she alone, saw herself that way.

CHAPTER THIRTEEN
THE FALL OF THE HAMMER

THE FOLLOWING WEEKS OFFERED KYRA many challenges and opportunities in her effort to sculpt herself into a shape that fit snugly into the kumpania. She was inspired by the rescued. Each kumpania of Roma has its own distinct flavor, its own traditions and culture, but it also shared traits with all others. These newcomers to Kyra's kumpania adapted and adjusted with remarkable ease. They motivated her to do the same. She began this new effort as she began the first, with lessons from Yubi.

The caravan was often in motion, forbidding Yubi and Stoyan from rehearsing their craft. This liberated Yubi's attention. Kyra captured it. She sought to improve her language. Of course she did. But she was less intent on the Romani language than on the Romani spirit. She did not wish to stand out, but to blend as the rescued had blended. There was something she did not see. In her attempts to blend, to be more Roma, she distinguished herself, not as an imposter but as a higher level of Roma, as an ideal that some of the others found themselves striving to match.

One evening, the kumpania gathered and celebrated the survival of those who had joined them. It was a much quieter, subtler celebration than what Kyra had seen from them before. She snuck away into Iraja's vardo. She helped herself to the piles of letters, papers, and books, hoping that her increasing vocabulary might unlock some hidden understanding and finally shine a light on the elusive Romani spirit. Her answers were plainly in front of her, yet she could not press her finger upon them, like straining to remember the words to a forgotten song. Like everything else since she first slept on a vardo porch, it crept into her rather than falling on her.

With an uneasy blend of satisfaction and frustration, she left the vardo and sought Yubi. When she returned to the gathering, he was not among them. She found him flat on his back, a hefty stone-throw away from the caravan, staring at the stars as their light intensified with the sinking of the sun. He heard her walking and began to sit up. But when she plopped flat beside him, he returned to his thoughtful sprawl. As confused as ever, she asked him about the rescued Roma, and how they could so easily put aside what they had been and press themselves into the shape of their new kumpania.

"Is that what it means to be Roma... to be so fluid? Is there nothing constant within them ..." she asked, "to disregard all that they were?"

"They disregard nothing," he answered in a dreamy, thoughtful tone, "The core inside of them is as constant as the stars above us, as bright and as reliable. Everything else is like clothing. It can be changed and altered to fit the circumstances. When you changed your dress to go into Paks, you were not altered. You did not suddenly become the same girl who wandered from Szanzar. Did you? My father told me what happened. He speaks to me of little else. Oh no, what changed is only what covered you. You proved that with your heroics that night."

Kyra felt her face turn hot and was grateful that their position and the darkness prevented him from seeing her blush.

Yubi continued, "Compare them to others you have known, whose exterior is unchangeable while their cores are moved with ease."

Kyra rolled her eyes to the side in retrospection. She set Yubi's words against all the people she had known, and the truth was plain. She ventured to continue his point, "Oh yes, I know the sort of people you are talking about. But the cores of the Roma are the same and need no adjustment to fit in with us."

She turned her face from the stars to look at him for a response. She saw his wide smile before he answered simply, "Mm hmm."

They reclined in silence for several minutes, each staring upward, until Yubi sat up sharply. Kyra responded in kind, asking, "What? What is it?"

"It takes a solid core," he blurted, "to come through strongly from what they have suffered."

Kyra dropped her chin to her chest and said thoughtfully, "It must have been terrible."

"It was unspeakable, yet they forced themselves to speak it for our sake."

"What do you mean?"

"While you were away in your vardo, they recalled every detail of their flight from Kecskemét. They finally thought they had escaped pursuit, and they rested for the first time. They were set upon in that dark hour before dawn."

He proceeded to tell her all that he had overheard, every gruesome, vengeful, barbaric detail. When she was fully horrified, he finished, "That is why the celebration is subdued. Noise, light, movement, these things have proven treacherous to them."

Still deeply mortified by the details of the attack, she shook her head and spoke more to herself than to him, "I don't understand how they can celebrate at all, how they celebrate tragedy."

Yubi stood and stepped to face her. She folded her legs in front of her, and he sat down mirroring her, knees against knees. He took her hands and answered her, "They do not celebrate tragedy. But their miseries rest always on a scale, opposite their blessings. Can't you see how the scale tips? It seems that their blessings carry more weight."

Kyra's mind was in such turmoil, fighting, wrestling, and struggling with the contradictions before her.

Still holding tightly to her hands, he asked, "Do we not have our hardships?" She parted her lips to answer, but he shook his head and continued, "Yet we celebrate. We celebrate because our lives are beautiful, and love outweighs our misery."

He released her hands, took her gently by the sides of her face, and pulled her in for a brief but tender kiss. The strange energy that shot from her lips through her entire body was like nothing she had ever imagined — simultaneously nurturing and fundamentally unsettling. She had little time to ponder it. Yubi stood abruptly and walked away from her without another word or glance. Kyra's mouth hung open, begging words to come forth from inside of her. Hardly a breath responded.

He was well gone from her sight before she closed her mouth. She returned to her back and gazed at the stars above, hoping that their steadfastness would instill some order into her chaotic mind. They did no such thing. After some unguessable amount of time, she stood, shaking from scalp to toe, and returned to her mother's bed, where she slept through dreams of the most varied themes, from the very horrid to the exquisitely sublime.

The warnings of the rescued changed the air of the following morning. Much more quickly was the caravan packed and rolling, farther from the scene of the attack and farther from any settlement of human beings. Before Paks, and before the attack, the caravan moved toward destinations, or simply to be in motion, never away from something. It was a very different air, indeed, as each roll of the wheels had such a new and terrible motivation.

There was a spastic quiet, a muted expediency to their movements. There was no singing or clapping, no handstands on the top of a vardo. Kyra began to wonder what they had planned. Surely, they could not survive in constant motion, keeping the greatest possible distance from every gathering of people. At midday, they rested.

Kyra took the settled moment to ask Menowin, "How will we go on this way, not playing and dancing, or making jewelry, or crafting metals?"

Menowin seemed perturbed by the question, or perhaps more perplexed than perturbed. He answered impatiently, "We will not go on like this. Things will be different for a while, and not so very different. How much of our time do we spend in the towns? We will caravan and camp where it is safe to go, and be as happy as we can be."

Menowin looked around them, and gestured with his eyes for Kyra to do the same. She scanned a full circle and saw what she needed to see. In subtle, huddled form, the groups did what they had always done. The jewelers clustered tightly and threaded their necklaces, but they were pressed against the caravan and spoke in whispers. The musicians polished and repaired their instruments in silence. The dancers stretched and exercised. They had not abandoned their crafts. They continued them in a very different manner.

"What about you?" Kyra asked Menowin, "You cannot fire your kiln or bang loudly on metals."

"I am more than just a blacksmith," he told her.

Kyra smiled widely, embraced him, and told him, "You are *much* more than a blacksmith to me!"

He giggled authentically, returned her embrace and said, "I am also a friend and brother, a confidant and advisor, a teacher and a student. My hammer needed a rest and I shall now give it one. Let the other parts of me perform for a while."

Menowin's words and observations brought some softness to a sharp atmosphere. Although it had his intended effect on his young friend, it did not entirely wipe the truth from Kyra's senses. There was fear in the kumpania, a just fear, brought on by real dangers, and it did not appear that any amount of cautious travel would bring them to normalcy soon.

They permitted themselves only half an hour before returning the wheels to motion. Kyra needed more information and more soothing. Rather than riding in her vardo, she asked Menowin to carry her on his horse. He gladly agreed, and Kyra shared a saddle with the blacksmith. She asked her questions and he gave his answers.

He told her that there were settlements and trading posts where they could safely conduct business. They would work their way as obscurely as possible between them. Kyra was greatly relieved to know that trade would happen, that new food and new items would come into the caravan, and the labors of the craftsmen would still be profitable. She had enough of her father left in her to measure the success of a lucrative transaction. Still, in her dreamy moments of quiet, still holding to Menowin's back, she thought of the noble wedding. She reminisced about how useful she felt as the barker, as the Roma-whisperer to the mesmerized Hungarians. She wondered if they would ever see such times again.

The hypnotic trot of the horse had lulled her into a sound sleep, drooling on Menowin's back with a gaped mouth. She was jolted awake by yelling. Her neck was not yet ready to be snapped side to side. She felt a hard pinch as she tried to turn her head like an owl. Her breaths were panicked and she shook the saddle beneath her.

"Calm yourself, my friend," Menowin assured her, "There is nobody here but the kumpania."

As they caravanned, riders had gone out as scouts in all directions. It was the shout of a scout that awoke her so violently. One of the scouts had returned with news that appeared urgent but not panicked. There was a brief gathering of leaders. When the gathering broke, the caravan took a sharp turn to the left and continued onward at a quicker pace. Kyra must have asked Menowin one hundred times if they were safe. Each time, he insisted they were, but that they needed to make adjustments to their plans.

They did not camp at dusk, but rode a full two hours past the setting of the sun. Although the moon was nearly full and silvery-bright above them, to Kyra, to many of them, the dark had never been so dark. As they finally broke the caravan to camp, there was a strange, foreboding energy in the air. Kyra immediately sought the refuge of Iraja and her luxurious vardo. By the time she went inside, Iraja was already in bed, soundly asleep. Kyra dressed for bed and curled beside Iraja. She was tense-bodied, and not calmed at all by the soft and rhythmic breathing of the sleeping matriarch beside her.

She caught herself holding her own breath, and still, once becoming aware of it, continued to hold it longer. She held it to take note of the activity around her. There was none. The kumpania was fully settled and fully silent. Kyra's face clinched and her breath was in her throat, like the very moment before a cry breaks free. But she was locked in that moment. Her tears and her sobs were stuck, waiting at the gate. They were waiting for something, for something horrible that seemed to cruelly tease her from just out of sight.

The stillness of her lungs was interrupted by her own gasp when a shadow suddenly blocked the moonlight from the window that her wide eyes stared through. The gasp made way for calm and comforted breaths. It was Menowin's shadow she had seen. Kyra was certain of that. The moon shadow across the window was soft and kind, and appeared more as a projection of light than an obstruction of it. Such a shadow could have belonged to nobody else. The blacksmith was up and about, keeping his keen eyes and strong arms alert for the safety of the others. The thought soothed Kyra dramatically and she fell asleep within a dozen deep breaths.

There was no way of telling how deeply into the night she had slept. The moonlight no longer came through the window when a loud, low knock shook her vardo. Still wrapped in her comfortable thoughts of Menowin, she did not spring upright, but opened her eyes slowly and remained pressed against Iraja. She heard another knock, and a clang, this time farther away. The sound warned of violence, and Kyra sat up quickly. Her chest seized when she heard the holler of a strange voice, followed by a familiar scream of distress. It was Menowin's voice, no doubt at all.

There was quite the scuffle. A struggle, a violent struggle, took place in the camp, and Kyra's imagination tried to place imagery to every sound. She stood tentatively and looked from her window. She could see nothing. The night had gone very dark. She heard Menowin's screaming voice go fainter and from a farther distance, like he was running from the camp. The bustle of many people seemed to follow him. When the sounds had fully died, she stepped from the vardo. Others had risen and began to gather in hushed but frantic conversations.

Kyra interrupted them all, asking, "Where is Menowin? Is he with us? Where is he? Where is Menowin?"

The faintest brush of deep, sunrise-red was dully coloring the eastern horizon. The caution of the previous weeks was thrown to the wind. Lamps were lit and voices rang out, calling for the blacksmith. He was gone. The search around the edge of the camp revealed trampled grass, but no tracks could be seen. Vadim conducted a survey of the kumpania. All were accounted for but Menowin. He was gone, and no tracks could be found in the dark that would indicate which direction he had gone, and how many of what sort of people were with him.

Kyra ran several strides away from the camp, turned, and made several strides in another direction, looking out into the obscurity of the dark plains. She returned to her vardo to arouse Iraja, but the matriarch was already up, fully dressed, and in rapid conversation with the others.

"Which way did he go?" Kyra shouted at her in Hungarian, her mind too panicked to translate.

Stoyan broke from the group, took her by the hand, and led her into the tight huddle like an equal.

"There is no way to track them," he told her, "not until light."

"Them?" she questioned, returning to Romani, "Who was with him? Who was with him?"

"We don't know," Iraja answered.

"But he was not alone," Vadim continued, "We know that."

Kyra pulled from Stoyan's hand, took one strong step backward, and commanded, "We have to get him!"

As they stood still and stared at her, she took three more steps backward, holding both hands to her belly and buckling slightly forward, as she commanded more fiercely, "Go! Go get him! Go get Menowin!"

Vadim dropped his chin and shook his head slightly.

"What is wrong with you?" Kyra screamed.

She turned and ran east, toward the slowly brightening horizon. She ran at full speed, but Stoyan caught her and held her as she kicked and punched at him.

"Go get him. Go get him," she repeated in slowing and weakening repetitions, as Stoyan hoisted her tightly into his arms like a baby. He carried her back to Iraja, while Kyra continued in a quiet whimper, "Go get him."

Stoyan carried her into her vardo and set her in bed. He left and closed the door behind him. Kyra stared out of the window, wishing the sky to brighten. With each noticeable degree, she looked to the door, but it did not open. When the orange gave way to hints of blue, she stood and opened the door. Stoyan stood outside with his arms extended to her. She jumped from the porch to him.

"Let's go get Menowin," he said to her with determination.

He threw her upon his horse and mounted quickly in front of her. As they rode to the west, away from the camp, Kyra saw other riders heading off at great speed in other directions. She sighed in relief, but the sigh did not push her fear from her. A clutching dread gripped her heart relentlessly. She battled it in the only way she could — by straining her eyes into the distance for any sign of her friend.

They rode in outward spiraling patterns for about an hour. Kyra had no idea how far from the caravan they had traveled, nor in which direction it waited. Stoyan rode hard with his eyes ahead. Kyra held tightly, pressing the side of her face against his back, watching the blur of grass beside them. She saw the orange pants off to their right, and she knew it could be nothing else. With no thought of her own peril, she thrust herself away from Stoyan and fell from the back of the horse. She landed hard and awkwardly on the back of her neck, but she sprang to her feet as if getting out of bed after a restful sleep.

Stoyan shouted her name and halted the horse. He turned to see her running to the orange fabric. He leaped from the horse and ran after her. He caught her as she stood beside Menowin. Stoyan could see that he was dead. So could Kyra, but her heart refused to believe. She fell upon the body and shook him, wildly screaming his name. Stoyan grabbed her by the collar of her blouse and pulled her to her feet. She stood with her sleeves soaked with blood.

Kyra buried her face in Stoyan's neck. They held each other tightly and cried. After several minutes of crying together in uninhibited sobs, Stoyan stopped abruptly and returned to a calm rate of breath. He pulled himself from Kyra's embrace and looked down at the body of their friend.

Kyra's sobs continued until Stoyan announced, "This is better than I feared. Tonight, we celebrate!"

She was stung by the announcement. She was confused, and she questioned indignantly, "Better? Celebrate?"

She stared at him defiantly, waiting for his explanation. He took her by the hair above her ears, pulled her within a breath of his face, and said, "Menowin's hands are not bound. His feet are not bound. He died as we all hope to die… free. It is far better that he lies dead as we see him than alive in a cage."

Her expression of bitter indignation changed to one of inner conflict. Her heart felt nothing but anger and sorrow while her mind pondered Stoyan's words. Those opposing organs had no chance of immediate reconciliation. She could not celebrate, but she knew enough about the Romani spirit to understand. She thought about her last conversation with Yubi. Her heart overcame her thoughts and her face returned to one of fury. Her eyes reddened, her cheeks shook, and she began to hyperventilate.

Stoyan tightened his grip on her hair and shook her head, as he said, "There is no animal in the wild world that fears being caged more than a Roma. There are many things we suffer bravely, but not that. Menowin was not bound and caged, tried and executed. He was not strung by the neck or bound to a pile of firewood. I do not know what happened where we now stand. But I know this. His feet ran free in this field. His fists swung free. And he died under the control of nobody and nothing but the sky above him. He died free, and tonight, we celebrate his freedom."

He released her hair, ran his thumbs across her eyebrows, kissed her head, and said, "Help me, my dear. Let us bring him back to the kumpania."

Kyra wanted as much as Stoyan to bring Menowin back to the others. Yet she obeyed reluctantly. Stoyan's love for Menowin was plain to see, and his grief pronounced itself, but it did so in strange terms that Kyra could not understand. Her mind understood, but her heart could not get on board. She cooperated with a heart that viewed Stoyan adversarially. But cooperate she did. Stoyan continued to shed tears, but they were spaced between sudden, wide smiles. Kyra did not smile. She alternated between stone-faced anger and bursts of sobbing.

They set Menowin across the shoulders of the horse. Kyra sat atop the saddle with both hands on the lifeless body of her kind friend. Stoyan led them back to the caravan, which was in full readiness, awaiting the return of its riders.

CHAPTER FOURTEEN

SOLITARY SORROW

As STOYAN AND KYRA APPROACHED the caravan with Menowin's body, Kyra's stomach knotted fitfully. She knew what the blacksmith meant to the kumpania. He was kind and adored by all. In her intense compassion, she dreaded their sorrow. As the first few gathered to greet them, her nerves shook her and disrupted her breath. Stoyan could not help but notice. He looked back to her and smiled.

Stoyan halted the horse and walked ahead to meet the others. By the time they all gathered around the horse, they already knew that Menowin was dead. Kyra didn't have to tell them. She didn't have to see their faces up close as they found out. For that, she was relieved. Many hands contributed to pull Menowin from the horse and carry him away. One pair remained to help Kyra from the horse. Stoyan took her into his arms and did not put her down again until he set her on Iraja's porch.

Kyra was covered in blood, standing on the porch when Iraja climbed the steps of the vardo from behind her. Kyra still shook. Her breaths were still rapid and uneven, until Iraja wrapped her fingers behind Kyra's neck. The soft stroke of her thumb settled Kyra enough for her to draw a slow inhale, hold it with a wincing face, and release it with a whimper.

Iraja stripped Kyra of her bloody skirt. Kyra hardly noticed. But when her shirt followed, Kyra grabbed at it defensively and held it tightly to her chest. It was not from any sense of nakedness, but from a desperate reluctance to release Menowin's blood. Iraja tugged the shirt from her, and with that, Kyra felt Menowin being taken from her again. Iraja climbed from the porch with the bloody clothes while Kyra walked into the vardo and dressed herself without drawing another breath. Once dressed, she stood in front of all the fine things hanging and lying about. How cheap they all appeared to her, of what little value. Such a paltry thing is a gold necklace. Gems that Kyra had believed to be worth the world itself appeared as lumps of rock.

Stoyan and Kyra were not the last riders to return. The others arrived at once. Kyra did not realize that she had not breathed until she heard a horse gallop in beside her window. It was Vadim. She knew it by his howl. It portrayed a depth of anguish that matched Kyra's. She ran from the vardo to be with him, to mourn with him, and to be a comfort to him. When she got to him, Stoyan was describing the scene where they found Menowin's body. Vadim expressed his gratitude for Menowin's freedom from shackles and a cell, much as Stoyan had, but he followed with a growling demand to see the body.

Stoyan led him to where they had laid the body. Vadim stood before his slain friend, giggled and smiled, but then fell to his knees and screamed. Kyra, who had followed silently behind him, lunged at him and grabbed his shoulder. Vadim screamed again, and Kyra felt every bit of his sorrow through her hand. The scene was too much for her. Her vision faded and she fell unconscious to the ground.

She awoke, under the familiar folds of her own bedding, to a timid knock at her door. The door creaked open slowly and Lavinia slid inside as only a dancer can. She seemed afraid of disturbing the air and sending Kyra into another fit. It was already late in the afternoon. Kyra sat slowly, trying to gain her bearings. Once she did, she stood sharply worried about what she might have missed. Her mind was in no condition to accurately translate. She stumbled through a few attempted questions.

"Calm yourself, child," Lavinia offered in Hungarian.

Kyra shook her head as if the syllables of her native language caused her pain, and she blurted, "Romani!"

Lavinia gave the same gentle demand in Romani. Kyra sighed deeply and obeyed.

Lavinia took her by both hands and explained that they were taking the caravan to the place where Menowin died. They intended to bury him there. Kyra wanted to protest, but did not know how to speak her objections in Romani, not at the speed her mind was moving. She would not speak Hungarian.

They were to bury Menowin that evening, but Kyra buried herself that afternoon, not into the ground but into the kumpania. She ensconced herself inside of her adopted family, shunning the world around her, shunning Hungary. She feared and hated them all — those who killed Menowin, those who attacked the other Roma caravan, those who knocked Stoyan to the ground in Paks, and the ones who raised her from birth in Szanzar. She hid from all but the Roma, all but her kumpania. In shunning Hungary, she rejected all things Hungarian, especially her native language. She never again spoke Hungarian in the kumpania.

It is hard to say if it was good or bad for Kyra to return to where she had spotted Menowin lifeless in the grass. It turned her sorrow to anger, and as she imagined the violence that took place where she stood, her anger turned to fear. The transition happened slowly and silently inside of her as the grave was dug and her friend was placed beside it.

They dressed Menowin in the finest outfit in the caravan and laid him on a blanket beside the grave. The moment reminded Kyra of kneeling beside her dead father.

"That is not my father," she vividly remembered repeating.

That long dead horror was given new life inside of her as she looked at Menowin lying on the blanket. If she had been ignorant to all that had happened that day, she would not have believed that the cold, brightly dressed, but sunken-eyed, lifeless figure before her was the spirited blacksmith she had grown to adore.

"That is not my dear friend," she thought in a horrible echo of her past, "That is not my dear Menowin."

But when the blanket and body were lowered into the hole and covered forever in earth, it was obvious to them all who was resting in that grave. Menowin's spirit was agonizingly absent from the company. His hearty laugh and his bellowing cry were muted forever in the ground. The gentle, encouraging touch of his mighty hand was locked beneath the dirt.

These were the thoughts that twisted and wrenched Kyra's insides as the songs of tribute began. She heard none of them, but she heard every sound around them. Each nightly noise of the wild Hungarian plains sent her eyes darting in defense. She felt that Menowin's murderers were closing in on them, stalking them from every direction.

In a sudden swell of panic, she broke from her place beside the grave, her place of honor between Vadim and Stoyan. She sought her greatest source of comfort. Near the back of the gathered company, near her vardo, she found Iraja. She buried her face in Iraja's neck and cried. It was not a cry of mourning. It was one of fear and Iraja knew it. She led Kyra inside where they both prepared for sleep, with the sounds of Menowin's tribute muffled by the walls that separated them from the celebratory songs of the kumpania.

Iraja held Kyra tightly. The cradling embrace put the frightened girl quickly to sleep. The songs ended and the caravan set back in motion, quickly putting many turns of the wheels between them and the resting place of their blacksmith. Kyra awoke briefly to the rattle of the wheels beneath her, but Iraja's embrace remained tight. Kyra's consciousness was brief.

The next time her eyes opened, the caravan was still and silent. The night was not silent. The wind howled dreadfully. It was less of a howl than a tortured wailing. The night wind blowing across the grassy field and through the spokes of the wagons, which served Kyra as a lullaby on so many thoughtful nights, screamed dismally, mournfully, and ominously. It shook the door and windows of the vardo, as if it too sought refuge from the spiteful world.

In her compassion, Kyra had half a mind to open the door and let it in to be comforted under Iraja's ample folds of luxurious bedding. She was too frightfully disturbed to do any such thing, so the wind remained out of doors, loudly lamenting its exclusion. For a moment, as the sounds outside fluctuated in pitch, Kyra thought she heard the voice of Menowin, calling her to his kiln on one errand or another. Chills shot outward from her very depths, ejecting in their wake a torrent of tears from her eyes.

The morning sun did nothing to brighten Kyra's heart. Iraja was up and out when she awoke. In the absence of Iraja's arms, though she was quite warm, a haunting chill wrapped her. She had no way of knowing how far they had traveled. She knew, by the position of the sun, that they had caravanned southwest, but to what destination, to what real or imagined safety, she could not guess.

When she stepped onto the porch of the resting vardo, she was surprised to see that the kumpania had camped. They were not in the huddled, ready-to-roll formation of people in flight for their lives. Tents were pitched. A fire was in the basin. Foods were cooking. And the musicians were gathered in their circle, preparing to rehearse. More surprising still, there was a lightness of mood that contrasted severely with the darkness inside of Kyra. Not since her earliest days with the Roma did she feel like she stood so unlike her kumpania. She felt like a lone dark stain on a pristinely white sheet.

She made her way to the rear of the camp, all along encountering conversations of disturbing normalcy. They spoke of Menowin. He was first on the tongues of them all. But they spoke as if he still lived, or if he had died long ago and the pain had been softened by time.

There, at the end of the caravan, was Stoyan's vardo. She sought him in a subconscious reaction to what she felt was the too-rapid, even jaded recovery of the others. He had cried with her when they discovered the body together. It was he who had shared her adventure in Paks. She believed that only he would speak to her of Menowin with the proper amount of weight still hooked to his heart. She was angry when she found him setting up the equipment for his father-son act.

She was not jealous of him. She was insulted, insulted for Menowin. She wanted Stoyan to be suffering as she was and to show it demonstratively.

She caught his eye, and he turned to her and shouted, "Kyra! Perfect. I'm glad you're up. Please, help me."

Stoyan was struggling with the rig, but she did not respond. She stood and stared at him with a twisted grimace.

"Kyra, please," he begged.

She sat where she had stood, crossed her legs and stared at the grass between her knees. Her face was pressed into the mold of a worldly adult, or of a child who had felt the compounding stings of a trying life well before her time. Stoyan noticed the stone expression from his distance, just in time to witness it soften and rise to a subtle smile.

He dropped what he was doing and ran to her, knelt beside her, and asked, "What is it, Kyra?"

"Now I know for certain," she responded.

"What? What do you know?"

She raised her eyes from the ground to look at him, and her slight smile was pulled beneath the surface by a sober and thoughtful gaze.

She answered him, "I used to walk and dream of a life like the one I have had with the kumpania. Since joining you all, I have often wondered if I am not still in Szanzar, fading in a fever on the floor of my house, dreaming all that has happened since my father and mother died. But now I know this is real."

He inched closer to her, intrigued by her dreamy tone, and he asked, "What is it about this moment that convinces you?"

Tears streamed down her cheeks in a sudden squall, and she answered in a faltering voice, "It is Menowin. I would never have dreamed such sorrow because I have never known it, until now."

She leaned toward him and began to raise her hands from her sides. He stood and hoisted her from where she sat in one quick motion, holding her with his powerful arms and setting her softly to her feet. He kept the embrace until she pulled from it. He looked at her with pity for her deep sorrow. She did not want his pity for *her*. She wanted him to hurt as she did, and she could not understand how he and the others could go about a normal morning.

He tried to help her, encouraging her, "Come and help me set up. I have some new ideas."

She took a strong step backward, away from him, and she shouted, "No! I cannot. I should not, and neither should you. Neither should any of you."

He closed the gap between them with a strong step to her. He held firmly to the outsides of her shoulders and said, "The death of one is not the death of all. We live, and we insult the dead by not living each moment when we still can and they cannot."

Kyra understood well what he meant, and she would have agreed wholeheartedly a month earlier, but she was too low sunken for such thoughts.

She leaned into the embrace and said, "His loss is an affliction that cannot be repaired, not with new ideas, not with repeating old ones."

Stoyan's insight into her was keen and he told her, while squeezing her tightly and rubbing the back of her head, "You must feel out of place. You are not. *This* is your place. *We* are your place. Hearts that are in unison move each other as they are moved. When only one is lifted, it lifts the others. Our unity, our oneness is the reason for our buoyancy. When your heart moves with the kumpania, as if sewn to it, you will be *of* the kumpania. You, too, will be buoyant. How many times was Menowin the one who lifted the others? How many times have *you* lifted us? Today it is not you. Today it is others. Let the kumpania lift you."

Whether from the words or the embrace, Kyra no longer felt like an emotional adversary, not with Stoyan, not with any of them. Her heart still trudged through a rancid mire. It did so for that day and many that followed. But she took Stoyan's hand as he led her to the collapsed rig. She helped him erect it as she had many times before. When it was up and secure, Yubi, as if waiting for that moment, walked from behind their vardo. With a hand behind her head, he kissed Kyra firmly on the temple, turned to his father, clapped his hands together loudly, and inquired about the new ideas for their act.

Kyra spent the rest of that day quietly observing the acrobats' rehearsal, in deep thought, on a great many subjects. That night, she slept more soundly than the night before, but she awoke a dozen times with a new, heavy, intense, crippling understanding of her mortality and that of the people she loved. She thought of Menowin and developed, in that mournful state, her first concept of eternity — the Forever that Menowin would be gone from the world.

CHAPTER FIFTEEN
BLESSINGS AND WARNINGS

THE CARAVAN ROLLED IN THE WEE HOURS before sunrise and remained in motion through the noon hour. They set camp in the afternoon and set themselves to doing what they always had done. Kyra remained in bed while they traveled. They were well settled and active in their various pockets when she made her first appearance of the day. She did not cry. She did not demand tears from others. In a lethargic trance, steeped in thoughts of death and eternity, she meandered a haphazard circle around the camp, not acknowledging anyone or any sound around her. She didn't even notice the aroma of the cooking foods.

It was obvious to all that Kyra needed to be forcefully yanked from her somber stupor and into her future with the kumpania. Each hand in the caravan gave a pull in that effort. Kyra was destined to do more than assist Stoyan and Yubi with their equipment, nor could she hide her life away among the sparkling trinkets inside of Iraja's vardo. It was a well-debated topic long before Menowin's murder, and it was clear to everyone but Kyra. Many small gatherings featured the subject.

The elders and leaders of most groups pinpointed minute facets of Kyra's character and behavior in efforts to convince the others that Kyra should join their profession. The sole exception was Milena, the singer. Milena had two children, one being an infant with an infant's constant need for care.

While Kyra walked mindlessly and heedlessly by her and the band of musicians, Milena commented, "I, too, am glad she is with us, but I see no need to force her into one of our trades. She is not one of us and never will be. She cannot play an instrument or dance. She is no acrobat. The dear thing has never cooked a meal. God knows she cannot sing. We rescued her, and we were right to do so, but she is not one of us."

Many moans of disagreement came at Milena from the people around her, but she continued, "That is not to say she is unuseful. There are many tasks that take us from our duties, tasks that Kyra could do."

"Like what?" Manfri, the lyra player, growled in a rare projection of his voice.

Milena stood tall with both hands on her hips. She raised her chin and answered, "I am sure she is capable of tending to our small children. She seems bright enough. I would trust her with that and many other tasks."

The words were praiseful, but the tone was derogatory. Milena hid her bias poorly. She authentically wanted Kyra's help, but not for the same reasons the others wanted her. Milena believed her incapable of rising to the Roma ideals of the professions represented in the kumpania, but quite capable of the menial tasks of the talentless. It took little time for her opinions to become well-known, even to Kyra. Stoyan and Yubi began to regret having her help assemble their tightrope rig. They believed Kyra was well on her way to finding her place among them, a place where she could do remarkable things. They certainly did not want to contribute to Milena's vocal opinions by assigning her to the peripheral details of their act.

That was the contentious atmosphere as they briefly camped that day and the many days that followed. Kyra mourned Menowin while those that he had lived with for decades seemed not to, and she began to hear and understand the factious mumblings about her place in the caravan. Her spirit was assaulted on two fronts, weighed down on one side by sorrow and pricked abrasively on the other by her sense of inadequacy.

The caravan continued southwest in this manner, at a snail's pace, traveling from pre-dawn into the early afternoon. They made their way toward the Drava River. The survivors of the attacked kumpania had acquaintances in many of the communities along the Drava, and it was well away from the treachery of the Danube. They had no way of knowing the condition of those communities until they arrived.

Their path to the Drava took them near the city of Pécs. It was an area of substantial influence and wealth. The caravan paused as it brushed the eastern outskirts. Many believed them to have come dangerously close to the city. They were right, but it had to be done. Supplies were low and bargains needed to be struck, no matter the risk. Vadim volunteered to ride to the market and attempt trade. The others remained in caravan, ready to roll in an instant. Stoyan and Yubi rehearsed their acrobatics. The dancers danced. The musicians played in pairs and trios within the vardos. No tents were pitched. No tightrope was erected. Noise was kept to a minimum. And Kyra hid in her vardo from the various forces at work against her poor heart.

Vadim rode to Pécs at a casual trot, with equal portions of hope and trepidation. As he slowly disappeared into the distance, every eye in the caravan witnessed his back side dwindling beyond sight. There was no expectation of his return that day, no realistic expectation on the following day. The fields around them remained abandoned by all life but the kumpania. Still, they scrupulously maintained their quiet and were outspoken by the gentle breeze. At any given moment through the first three days, there were ten to twelve pairs of eyes straining to focus on the distance to the west.

The fifth and sixth days went by with decreased speed and increased anxiety. At the end of a full week in Vadim's absence fear turned to despair and despair turned to a stout resolution to get the towns far behind them as quickly as possible. It was already a cool November and the winter was poised to snow them in and lock them from escape. It was decided that they would resume their path toward the Drava River at sundown on the eighth day. Kyra was among the first shift to drive the caravan. She was ordered to sleep that day, but she could not. She tried. With Iraja up and about, Kyra sprawled her limbs across the full expanse of the bed, but she could not close her eyes.

The common assumption was that Vadim was either imprisoned or already executed. Kyra made no such assumptions. Her heart would not allow it. She remembered her valiant heroics in Paks and was determined to ride into Pécs and perform the same service for Vadim that she had performed for Stoyan. This time, she asked no permission. She rose from bed, strode with steady determination to Stoyan's horse, unhitched it from the acrobats' vardo, and began to walk it west.

Yubi found her mere steps from his vardo and asked what she was doing. She bore an expression of guilt, of a person caught doing what she knew she should not. The look was enough for Yubi to read the entire plan in her face. He scolded his disapproval but managed only the first syllable before shouts of warning came from the center of the caravan. Yubi and Kyra both ran to the noise, and there, standing tall on the porch of her vardo, was Lavinia. She pointed west to an approaching cart.

There was a horse walking beside and two men on the cart, riding hip-to-hip. Not a breath was expelled by the kumpania, as they watched the approach for any sign of identity or intention. They released their held breaths with a concerted sigh when one of the passengers stood and waved his hand high and wide in the air. He shouted his greeting in a familiar voice. It was Vadim.

Some stood where they were, while others ran out to meet Vadim and his mystery companion. When the cart arrived among the others, Vadim introduced the kumpania to Matthais, a Dominican friar from the monastery in Pécs. The cart was filled with sacks of grains, canisters of dried meats, a barrel of beer, and a chest full of crosses and other Christian icons. These life-saving items were not the result of some masterful bargaining by Vadim. They were gifts from the monastery. They came from Matthais' kind heart, and they came with his stern warning.

"Our abbot has offered you lodging within our walls," he admitted, "but I warn against it. Plague still lingers in the streets of Pécs. There is great fear and despair, and where those things exist, violence is sure to follow."

Matthais helped the others unload the gifts and pack them for immediate travel. From each vardo and wagon of the caravan came Roma wares and treasures. Matthais refused them all.

"I cannot ride through Pécs with such things in my possession," he warned, "Even if I could, I would not diminish your stores, not now."

Stealthily, Iraja and Kyra gathered what little local currency the kumpania had. Iraja offered it to Matthais, not as a payment for supplies and not in gratitude for his kindness. Matthais would not have accepted it. She offered it as a donation to his order, and the friar accepted.

An intimate gathering of elders huddled near the front of the caravan. Stoyan was there, so Yubi was near him. Kyra clung to Yubi's arm and found herself a member of the select group. Matthais gave them many warnings of the dangers of the region. He provided names and locations of safe places for the Roma to trade along the Drava. By the time the sun began to fall from the high point of the sky, plans for the caravan's travel in the next several months were in place.

Matthais mounted his cart, stood high upon the bench, and chanted a blessing in Latin. Some few understood parts of it. None of them understood it all. But there was no need to. Matthais' voice was deep and reverberating. His chant sounded like a line of four men. It sounded like kindness. It sounded like compassion. It sounded just like the blessing it was. When it was over, Matthais stood, scanning the faces in front of him. His eyes rested on Kyra and remained there for an awkward pause.

"You are different," he spoke directly to her.

Kyra's face turned red. She was ashamed. She didn't want to stick out. She didn't want to be different. The others turned to her, trying to see the difference he spoke of.

He drew their eyes back to him as he noted the awkwardness and apologized to her, "I am sorry. I do not mean that you are different from the people traveling with you, and I do not mean to stare, but I find you strikingly beautiful in a way that my eyes do not understand. I have seen many kinds of beauty. You are different. In an increasingly ugly world, my eyes are reluctant to break from you."

The awkwardness only thickened, and looks passed back and forth from the friar to Kyra. Some understood that Matthais was not speaking strictly of physical beauty, that his spiritual eyes saw more deeply, yet even they strained to define what he saw.

With his gaze still on her, he said, "God Bless you, child, and keep you from evil."

He followed the blessing with one mumbled in another language. He signed the cross to them and sat. Vadim untied his horse from the friar's wagon and escorted it to its place in the caravan. Matthais turned the cart around and rolled west to his monastery.

The warnings they received were frightening. There was much danger in the region for the Roma. But the decision to caravan to the Drava proved fortuitous. They knew where they could go, who they could safely encounter, and they knew which towns and villages to avoid. Matthais had given Vadim a well-marked map, explicit instruction on where they could trade, where they could camp, and most importantly to some, where they could perform.

The evening turned cold and the clouds threatened snow, but the outlook for the immediate future was not nearly as bleak as it had been earlier that same day. Following Matthais' advice, they rolled immediately from Pécs, continuing southwest toward the Drava, but they did so with surging excitement.

Traveling away from Pécs, they altered their travel schedule. Matthais' warnings, and the attack that took Menowin from them, made one resounding point that was clear in their minds. The night was more treacherous than the day. The dark was deadlier than the light. So, half of the kumpania at a time turned nocturnal. They traveled by night and made camp by the glow of the sunrise. The late fall nights were long and they traveled with new energy, covering much more ground between camping. The performers began planning their next performance with fervor, and the artisans began tallying what they had to sell and what they needed to buy.

CHAPTER SIXTEEN

EVOLUTIONARY ART

THEY EACH TOOK THEIR SHIFTS driving the caravan by moonlight, even Kyra. She didn't mind at all. She slept better, safer, during the day, with the clamor of a bustling camp as her lullaby. When she was awake during the latter part of the day, there was a strong, coordinated, community effort to find her employment. She was given intense lessons in every craft and profession. She gained a deeper appreciation of them all and enough proficiency to be considered useful, all except herding. The animals did not listen to her. They paid her no mind at all. They neither followed her nor turned from her, no matter how she barked at them. It reminded her of being a small, ignored child in Szanzar. The feeling was distasteful to her in the extreme.

Milena and a few others saddled her with their personal tasks. She tended to Milena's baby and hustled up and down the caravan, fetching this and delivering that. She knew Milena's motivations. Echoes of those debates still stung her inner ear. But she was glad to be useful in any way she could, so she obeyed. She fetched things. She swaddled and rocked the baby. She cleaned every mess, and she did it with a gracious smile. She was so focused on her tasks that she did not recognize the other efforts on her behalf.

She received a surprise commission one morning from Stoyan. One of his new ideas was to construct a narrow metal bar, about his own length, and mount it horizontally on tall posts. He imagined himself, and later his son, performing large, swooping, swinging circles on it, and releasing it in grand, dangerous, flipping dismounts. Oh, the giddy, child-like fervor with which he described it to Kyra.

Unaware of his intentions for her, she gladly offered, "I will be happy to assist you in raising it."

"Oh no," he replied, "I don't need your help raising it, not yet. I need you to construct it."

"What? Me? How?"

"I need you to forge the bar. It needs to be perfect, and I trust no other."

She stared at him, jaw-dropped and stone-faced.

"Menowin is gone," he continued, "You apprenticed with him. You helped him construct his forge and strike it again for travel. You know the tools of the trade. I have seen you hammering away with his guidance in your ears. Who else, if not you?"

Kyra closed her gaping jaw to stutter in response, "I... but he..."

"Listen," he calmly commanded, "my dear friend, my spirited little Roma. If Menowin had one minute of life granted back to him to choose any Roma in the wide world to wield his hammer, he would need only one second of it. He would think immediately of you and no other. I knew the man his whole life, and I never saw him take to anyone the way he took to you. He wants his hammer in your hand, his apron tied around that narrow waist of yours."

Kyra pondered in silent stillness for a moment, while Stoyan gazed at her with paternal pride and confidence.

She recalled every word, every example Menowin passed to her of his trade. She had spent most of that time half-heartedly listening, with thoughts on the musicians, the dancers, and the acrobats. She was more than slightly mortified by her childish inability to focus on the lessons at hand. She always assumed she would have more time, as we all often do. She bit the inside of her lips in a painfully self-administered penance. But her regret on that account did not gnaw on her long, not as it would have.

Kyra never felt more Roma than in company with Stoyan — her Gypsy ideal. Their shared adventure stitched their affections tightly to one another. His encouraging stare shoved the village girl aside and made a wide path for the young Roma woman growing inside of her to march confidently to the occasion. There was no regret for the lost knowledge, or the lost intimacy with Menowin, which she had so blindly discarded in favor of more romantic notions. There was only determination to put on her friend's gloves, construct his forge and fire it as he taught her to do, to swing his hammer, and make Stoyan's high bar.

Stoyan provided the scraps of metal, and Kyra submerged herself in the commission. During the brief hour of dusk, while they still camped, she constructed and fired the forge. She could almost see and hear Menowin instructing her as a phantom-like shadow constantly looking over her shoulder. She found herself in conversation with him, speaking aloud, laughing at their imagined conversations, and leaning in against his imagined figure. She was finally the student he always wanted her to be, and she never felt closer to him.

Each one of her phantom conversations was witnessed by at least half a dozen curious, stealthy spectators. The truth is, they wanted her to be successful. They had no blacksmith after Menowin's death, and the skills of the trade were in constant demand. They also missed

Menowin, and they hoped to see him reborn in her. They looked for his traits in her every mannerism.

She worked and worked, firing and hammering and firing again. She single-handedly extinguished and struck the forge for travel, and reconstructed it the following afternoon. For more than a week she worked on Stoyan's bar, much later than he had hoped to have it. Eight days after being given the commission, it was still not what Stoyan had asked for. She took her time, being reluctant to relinquish her new position. It was in the last days of November and the afternoons were cold. It snowed during that week, but Kyra was blind to it. The heat of the forge created a timeless summer while she worked.

There was another reason for her delay. The metal did not obey her. The bar bowed slightly. It was not particularly round. It was lumpy and could never be used for Stoyan's purpose. Kyra knew the futility of further efforts. She did not have Menowin's skills. How could she? It was a gradual realization that she tried to deny until she finally dropped the hammer in disgust.

Matthais had directed them to a community, one that would buy their wares and delight in their entertainment. They were nearing that friendly destination, and the bar was not ready. After eight days at the forge, Kyra brought the bar to Stoyan. She had toiled industriously and came up short. She had no excuses, but she did rehearse an apology. When she stood before him with the warped bar in hand, her words left her. Stoyan stared at the bar, and Kyra stared at Stoyan.

"Hmm," he grunted, while cocking his head to one side, "I don't think I can do what I had planned with this. Still, I have no doubt I could put it to some use."

He took it from her, still inspecting it with a puzzled look upon him. He hardly had it in his own possession for two full breaths before Kyra snatched it from him with the strength of a blacksmith. She ran with it away from him, not in anger, not in embarrassment, not really *away* from him, but toward her forge in excitement.

For the next three days, in every minute the caravan was still, she fired at the bar. She hammered it feverishly and constructed from it a sign to hang upon Stoyan and Yubi's vardo. It was a thin, metal silhouette of the acrobats at work, Yubi upon the tightrope and Stoyan balancing on one hand. Beneath the figures were the words, "Made in Fire."

The artistry was exquisite, and although she could not make a functioning gear, the cap of a wagon wheel or an acrobat's high bar, what she forged in those three days was both invaluable and uniquely hers. She was so excited as she marched it to Stoyan and Yubi that she did not notice the growing trail of admiring Roma in her triumphant wake.

With a half-circle of intrigued faces engulfing her from behind, she presented her gift to Stoyan and Yubi. It was Yubi who stepped forward to accept it from her. It was large and heavy, and they lifted it together until Stoyan relieved Kyra of her share of it.

While tracing the metal figures lovingly with her fingertips, Kyra whispered to them, "I am sorry I could not make your bar, as Menowin would have, but I have made this for you. Now people will know. You are the wonderful acrobats. Little girls will know that it is you they have been dreaming of as they wandered around their villages."

As she whispered her dreamy praise, she continued to lightly caress the silhouetted figures with her fingertips. She ran her fingers up and down the image of Yubi while her face blushed brightly.

The crowd behind her could not hear what she was saying, but they heard Stoyan's response, "My dear friend, you are no starry-eyed village girl. You are a star from the heavens, if one has ever brightened a kumpania. You have my gratitude, my admiration and affection, and my obedience."

Similar sentiments came from the rising murmurs behind her. Even Milena was impressed by the sign and began to imagine the one she would ask Kyra to make for her and the singers. The compliments abounded, but she could not appreciate them as they were intended, because she did not hear them. Her thoughts were comprehensively in front of her, where Stoyan's words filled her from bone to skin, and the hand of Yubi, her closest friend, rested upon hers while she caressed his metal likeness.

The Roma remained and watched while Stoyan and Yubi mounted the sign above the front porch of their vardo. When the acrobats stepped back to admire it, the kumpania, young and old, cheered, raising more clamor than they had dared to raise since their flight from Paks.

It was not only the sign that lifted their voices. They were in different country, away from the darkness of previous months, carrying with them a map to guide them away from danger and toward success. The future looked brighter than it had, and each circle of professions envisioned their efforts being profitable again.

They were a day's hard ride from the first community on Matthais' list. They were not a day from being prepared, so they camped early and broke late. The Romani wares were crafted feverishly. The musicians played hard. The singers bellowed with full-throated vigor. The dancers rolled their hips, while beads of sweat flung from their brows.

Kyra was an equal part of the hysteria. After making the acrobats' sign, she received commissions for five more, each from a different circle of craftsmen. Unlike the others, she could not complete them before setting their next performance and bazaar. Rather than completing one, she toiled a little on each. Perhaps she could have made one for sale, one to be sold to the people who would flock to see them, had she not been so eager to please them all.

They finally reached their destination, setting up between the towns of Siklós and Harkány, about four miles from the Drava River. Like Matthais, the inhabitants of the region were not Hungarian. They were Swabians who had migrated across the Alps and along the Mur River, to settle in pockets along the Drava.

It was the first time since Paks that the wooden blocks were placed beneath the wheels of the vardos. The sun was direct and cut through the cold. They unpacked, entrenching themselves where they rested, not ready to fly in haste from danger. They camped for two full days before sending a rider to herald the bazaar. During that time, Kyra was not sure of her place among the frenzied activity. Iraja, the old dancing queen, knowing more than could be perceived by the senses, took Kyra aside to teach her. Alone on the far side of their vardo, Iraja rolled her hips for Kyra. So very full of life and vigor they were, swaying and rocking in a nautical rhythm. The swings and flicks mimicked the waves that lap against the sides of ships.

She grabbed Kyra's hips tightly in her hands and tried to rock them as she had demonstrated. Kyra's body simply did not move that way. Iraja let go and resumed her demonstration, adding an opposing and counter-rhythmic sway of her shoulders and chest. Kyra took a step back and admired her mother. Iraja looked like the ocean itself having its way with Kyra's helpless eyes. Old as she was, Iraja was still a superior dancer. None in the kumpania, not even Lavinia, could compare.

Iraja stopped and invited Kyra to imitate her. Kyra tried but could not copy or even vaguely resemble Iraja's movements. She knew that she was not succeeding, but she would not stop trying.

When she finally paused, Iraja took her by the hand, saying, "Not every great artist is a great teacher. I must put you in better hands."

She led Kyra to the circle of rehearsing dancers and placed her hand directly into Lavinia's.

"Teach her to dance," is all she said before returning to her vardo for a nap.

All of the dancers stopped rehearsing and committed to the effort. It is hard to say through what traveling vine Yubi heard that Kyra was dancing, but he left his father on the spot to watch. What he saw when he found her was so pathetically endearing. In her awkward failure, she appeared more adorable than ever. Yet, he saw more in her than the choppy movements. She had fashioned the sign out of love — love for Menowin, for Stoyan, and love for Yubi. If she were to move like a dancer, she would have to move out of love not obligation.

"Stop! Stop!" he yelled, as he rushed among the dancers.

He stopped in front of her, took her by both hands, quickly released her hands and took her by the cheeks, and said, "You are *trying* to dance. If you watch Lavinia, she does not dance. She speaks with her shoulders and neck, sings with her hips. You have as much to say as any of us. Your heart is bigger than words. It must express itself in bigger ways."

In all earnestness, eager to learn, she asked him, "If I am to speak with my body, like Lavinia and Iraja, what should I speak about?"

He gave it only the briefest thought before returning, "Say what your heart wishes to say but has not yet found a way."

He backed away and signaled the musicians. He indicated the desired rhythm with a steady, repetitive nod of his head. The music started low and moaning, lamentful and regretful, unlike how it had sounded before, as if

Kyra's deepest thoughts somehow directed it. Kyra accompanied it with a simple, stiff-necked sway of her head. But as the music began to build, and rhythms bounced more celebratorily from instrument to instrument, Kyra's movements began to match them. She did not sway her hips like Lavinia, or rock her shoulders like the ocean, but her body moved freely and without thought.

She closed her eyes and pictured Iraja, not as the old woman teaching her mere minutes before, but as a young Romani wonder, with suitors along every waterway between the Black Sea and the Austrian Alps. She moved as she never had before. She mimicked her tutors admirably, matching sway for sway, but she did not burst with the passion that a Romani dancer must display. Yubi watched her studiously from a distance. After a few minutes, he ran into the circle of dancers, stopping the musicians in mid-note. The dancers stood still, staring at him as he closed the distance between him and Kyra. He stood directly before her, staring with a puzzled look.

His face dropped as she said, "I thought I was dancing well."

"Your body danced well," he responded, "while your heart whispered."

She knew what he was telling her, that she did not dance with the passion of a Roma, and she did not believe that she ever could.

"You must dance to something," he instructed in a slightly vocalized whisper, "You must dance *for* something. I know you well. You know that I do. I see how badly your heart wants to scream. Scream, Kyra. Let your body be your heart's voice."

They stood gazing at each other, each with thoughts that swam and grasped.

Finally, his eyes widened, and he took her by the shoulders, saying, "Dance for Menowin. Let your body tell him all that you wish to say to him, all that you want the world to know about him, all that you feel when you think of him."

Her eyes widened to match his. She turned her head sharply to the musicians, who took their cue and struck a tune. Yubi backed away from her, as did all of the dancers. What she did next poorly resembled the Roma dancers. Kyra threw one arm in the air in a fluid wave, as if it contained no bones. She contorted the same shoulder and slid into a deep lunge. She held that pose for the length of the note, then rolled across her hips, fanning her feet above her. The fabric of her dress spread like a giant fan. She stood and jumped into the air, swinging her arms in a circle. She contorted her back and her neck in ways that would have seriously injured any of the other dancers, had they ever the imagination to attempt it.

Yubi was fascinated with the sight before him. Kyra did not look like a gangly girl, nor like a woman. She looked like a spirit without a body, without any of the restraints of a physical form. Everyone around her stood dumbfounded. Her dancing did not resemble her tutors or appear as the movements of any creature they had heard of. She rolled her spine and snapped around, dropped to her knees, jumped into the air, bent and twisted as nothing they had ever seen.

The music stopped. Kyra stopped. She stood breathing heavily and smiling through her abundant tears. This was not a dance to seduce the gold from the pockets of men. This was Kyra's soul speaking to the world about Menowin, and using as its medium the only body that could have expressed it so vividly.

Kyra's face went blank when she realized that everyone around her was motionless. She became self-conscious and regretted such an unchecked release of her feelings. That sensation lasted only a few seconds before the other dancers rushed to her with enthusiastic praise, comments, and questions. They asked her to repeat the more peculiar movements. She did so as well as she could remember, and the dancers tried to imitate her. Yubi walked backward, smiling, as Kyra transitioned in a moment from student to teacher.

Her dance would have mesmerized strangers. Yubi was no stranger. He knew her. He knew her mind and he knew her spirit. It was raw. It was real, and Yubi recognized her innermost self in what she displayed with her body. Her dance grasped him deeply, restricting his breaths. As the others occupied her attention, Yubi wasn't sure if he wanted to hug her, raise her on a pedestal for the world to see, or run from her at a full sprint. He did none of them, but continued to walk backward until his sight of her was obstructed and replaced in his mind by a glowing figure in his imagination. His mind's eye projecting nothing else upon his inner eyelids that night.

Kyra slid into bed with keen contemplations of her evolution. She had often thought, while lying wide-eyed against Iraja, how unlike her days were from what she had known as a young child. That night, she thought of how different *she* was. She had already traveled farther, done more, and seen more than four full lifetimes in Szanzar could have given her. In many ways, she was already a much older woman than her mother Eneth, older, in ways, than anyone she had known in her previous life.

She had always thought of her father as wise and worldly. He traveled regularly to Bratislava. Bratislava — the name had once rung in her ears with foreign exoticism. So very plain it seemed to her now. Very plain seemed the common tradesmen whose brief appearance in her life had spawned so many wild imaginings. Her image of her father, and of their heavily romanticized excursion to the city, had been slowly gaining the clarity of worldly retrospection. By the time she pondered him that night, she saw him for who he was, the faithful, good-natured, but simple and provincial employee of a rustic tithing barn. Kyra's life was so much bigger, and expanding by the day.

CHAPTER SEVENTEEN
THE RELUCTANT CELEBRITY

KYRA ROSE EARLY THE NEXT morning determined to make progress on the signs she had been commissioned to make.

She had not yet fired the kiln before Lavinia confronted her, "What are you doing?"

Kyra, suspecting greater depth behind the question than was intended, stood motionless, except for her eyes, which darted back and forth between Lavinia and the blacksmith tools beside her.

This went on awkwardly until she finally answered, "I have many signs to make, but yours is first. I am making the dancers' next."

Lavinia did not reply with the relief and gratitude Kyra was hoping for. She lifted her hands to her waist and shifted her hips to one side. She turned her head slightly and looked at Kyra sideways through a squinted eye.

"I am working as quickly as I can," Kyra spoke defensively, "I was the first one out of bed today. I was up before the herders."

Lavinia stood straight, dropped her arms to her sides, shook her head, and replied, "To the devil with those signs.

You are a dancer now. We perform soon, and we have much to teach each other."

Kyra raised her eyebrows suddenly, wrinkling her forehead, and she answered, "I am not a dancer. I cannot move like you move. Look at me." She gestured with her hands down her body from shoulders to knees, and continued, "I will never seduce money from pockets with this."

Lavinia took a scolding stance and tone, as she responded, "You underestimate yourself and me."

"I cannot dance like you!" Kyra insisted.

"No, you cannot. And *I* cannot dance like *you*, which is why we must begin now if we are to perform together today."

"No, no, no, no, no," Kyra stuttered in a panic, while waving her hands in front of her, "I am not dancing in front of people today. I will stay here today and work on the signs."

Lavinia stepped to her and took her by a hand, saying, "My friend, you are not a blacksmith. Surely you must know that. Stoyan's sign is beautiful, but you must know after yesterday, that you are a dancer."

"But I don't dan—," she began again, before being interrupted.

"This is not only my wish. All of the dancers have agreed. What is more, Iraja insists upon it."

Well, there it was. There was no higher authority and no turning back. Kyra was going to have to work with the dancers that morning. She had a few hours to either prove to them that she was not fit to dance among them or connive some other excuse to hang in the rear of the Roma attractions, as she had done before. Come what may, she struck the kiln, put away the tools of Menowin's trade, and followed Lavinia.

With only a single musician accompanying their rehearsal, Kyra stood amid the dancers.

"First," Lavinia commanded, facing the dancers, "we must teach Kyra to dance with the corp."

Kyra parted her lips as an infant protest tried to crawl through. It was frightened back into the egg by the sudden striking of musical notes. The dancers did what they do. The music infiltrated them through every pore. It commandeered their hips and thighs. It possessed their thick, wavy hair like a lively and expressive demon. Kyra simply stood among them, motionless at first from profound admiration, then from frustration and embarrassment.

Lavinia locked her eyes on Kyra and snapped her fingers loudly. Kyra drew a deep inhale, followed by a sharp sigh and a half-hearted attempt to imitate the dancers around her. She was not listening to the music, not inviting it to possess her. Her eyes had command of her thoughts, as she anatomized every sway and flick on display around her. Her hips were relentlessly bound to her legs and torso. They would not move independently. Kyra looked less like a dancer than a stick, broken in the middle and being waved above a child's head.

She froze altogether and stared at Lavinia as if to say, "See, I told you!"

Lavinia held her palms up toward Kyra, took a deep breath, and closed her eyes. Kyra took it as a command to do the same. She drew a deep breath, closed her eyes, and exhaled slowly. As the breath exited her, the music entered. It did not go directly for her hips, but opted instead to start with her fingertips. With her eyes still closed, her fingers curled in, then straightened again. Kyra thought she was still completely motionless. The movement was subtle, but grew steadily. Her wrists began to roll. A shoulder lifted, followed in rhythmic response by the other. Her ribs made small circles, not disturbing the stillness of her hips.

The breeze blew and swirled around the camp, and seemed to have its way with Kyra, as though her body, from the waist up, was lighter than a hair. Iraja, who had been watching stealthily from behind a vardo, made her way to stand at Lavinia's left side. The other dancers continued on all sides of Kyra, surrounding her. They moved very differently than her, like two different substances.

The music rose in power and emotion. Kyra matched it note for note. Her hips joined in, not in fluid sways like the Roma dancers, but in twitches and rolls. It looked like her pelvis was trying to break free from the rest of her body. There was an edginess to the spectacle, a sharp desperation that might have been irritating and awkward were it not so intriguing, were it not so intensely expressive. Kyra's dancing was concentrated spice, not meant to be eaten by the mouthful. But amid the other dancers, like pepper in a stew, it seasoned them to perfection.

It was such a personal expression of Kyra's heart that the others stopped, not because they did not want to dance with her, but because they were captivated by her rawness and freshness. With her eyes still closed and tears rolling from her eyes and crashing against her cheeks like waves on a beach, Kyra danced on. With no idea she could do such a thing, she lifted a leg high in the air in front of her, arched back, grabbed the ground behind her, and kicked through a handstand to land back on her feet and continue dancing.

There were gasps and applause, but she could not hear them. Yubi heard them. Stoyan heard them. They both ran to the sound of the music to see what was wowing the dancers. Yubi stood to the right of Lavinia, opposite Iraja, and Stoyan took his place beside Yubi. Iraja, wanting to see how the act might come together, gestured to the dancers to continue. They resumed, framing Kyra's unique style with their traditional Romani dancing.

Kyra's exaggerated movements revealed changes in her figure that none had noticed before. The previous months had taken her several steps nearer the form of a woman. She did not have Lavinia's figure. She was still a gangly adolescent, but not awkwardly so. In fact, it suited her quite strikingly, almost magically, especially while she danced. Her face had thinned in the lower cheeks and broadened at the cheekbones. Her chin had grown more pronounced, and her lips had filled. These changes happened so gradually that nobody but Iraja had noticed. But when she danced, with tears flowing to brush her cheeks with an almost mystical glisten, and she winced, grimaced, gasped, and puckered, those maturing features pronounced themselves. She seemed to blossom into adulthood right before their eyes.

What's more, her body was not expressing the light and shallow moods of a teenage villager. They spoke of the horror, recovery, love, loss, admiration, and regret of a woman who had lived a full and traveled life.

Lavinia leaned toward Yubi, pointed at Kyra, and whispered, "This is not a Roma interpretation of the music."

Yubi was offended for Kyra, and he almost spoke up in her defense, until Lavinia completed her thought, "It is the Roma music itself, pronouncing its identity through her in ways I never imagined."

Yubi smiled and took Lavinia by the waist, pulling her in. He took his father's waist with his other hand and sandwiched himself snugly between them, and he said in a dreamy tone, "I would say that the spirit of the music passes through her and comes out the other side covered in what is uniquely Kyra. She has old, dark sorrow in her, and yet she remains as fresh as dew."

Stoyan and Lavinia were surprised by Yubi's words. They turned to him. Besotted adoration was plainly visible on his glowing face as he watched Kyra dance. Unaware of the other, both Stoyan and Lavinia gave the boy a tighter squeeze. They recognized the affection swelling within him, and they were grateful to him for finding the words to express their own opinions of Kyra's dancing.

As the music calmed and slowed, fading to its conclusion, the dancers dropped to a knee and gestured their inside arm to Kyra. Kyra rolled to the ground, folded her legs beneath, collapsing onto her bent knees and resting the right side of her face on the grass. She looked like a newborn, laid to a peaceful sleep by a nurturing mother.

Yubi's heart grew in that moment. It grew to love as a man's heart loves. He had a strong urge to hoist her from the ground into his arms and run with her until no living creature was near. But she was not his to take. She was the moment's celebrity and the eyes of many were on her. Many would have things to say to her, many compliments and many words of admiration. Yubi wanted her to hear only his. He did not get his wish or even an opportunity to speak to her at all.

Iraja rushed to Kyra, helped her to her feet, hugged her, kissed her, hugged her again, and repeated this cycle for a full two minutes before saying to her, "My love, my dear child, you are a better dancer than I ever was."

Lavinia stood behind her and interjected her own compliments, placing between them her plans for the performance. Stoyan and many others shouted their enthusiastic opinions from their distance. Yubi stood silently. His frantic mind could not muster a word. There was nothing he could have said that would have captured his feelings. Had he been given an hour to compose a single sentence, he would not have succeeded. He did not understand his feelings. His throat closed and his lungs restricted. His stomach seized and he felt sick.

He ran from the crowd to where he and his father had been practicing. He pressed himself into a handstand, as Stoyan had taught him, but he had no strength. He shook and faltered. He cursed himself, tried again, and failed again. Not truly understanding his feelings and frustrations, and being entirely unable to account for his physical reaction, he wedged himself amid the things in his father's cluttered vardo, and alternated between growling and moaning until he fell asleep.

When the admirers broke from the scene, leaving only the dancers, Lavinia's mind erupted with artistry. With the youthful energy of a girl half her age, she effused with ideas for the afternoon's performance. Kyra was overwhelmed by the response to her dancing, by the applause and praise, by Iraja's words, but mostly by the urgency with which Lavinia tried to embroider her onto the dancers' performance.

Lavinia beckoned the rest of the musicians. They gathered and tuned while she placed the dancers around Kyra. She directed them in every detail, all to accentuate Kyra's unique expressiveness. It was all happening so fast, in double-time, so it seemed to Kyra. Her head was cloudy. Her performance that morning, her dredging of the deepest emotions within her, exhausted her fully. She was weak in the knees and foggy in the head. Lavinia buzzed at a rate Kyra could not keep up with.

While the other dancers followed their director's instructions, Kyra went faint. She collapsed to the ground. The world spun around her for countless hyperventilated breaths before Lavinia noticed her and tended to her.

"Go and rest," she instructed, "You must be tired. I can work with the others first. I will send for you when we are ready for you."

Kyra rose with her own strength and staggered away from the dancers. It was not only her dancing that dropped her to the ground. It was the rush to place her before an audience of strangers, the expectation that she would capture the Roma spirit and make enticing all that the kumpania had to offer. She did not feel up to it, not nearly so. She wandered the camp, but not aimlessly. She sought the comfort and advice of her one confidant. She sought

Yubi. She knew that if she was not ready to perform with the others, Yubi would tell her so. She also knew that if she was ready, he would convince her that she was.

Kyra found Stoyan near his vardo, gathering and arranging the equipment for his performance. She asked for Yubi. Stoyan said that he had no idea where his son was. On nothing more than a draw in her gut, she knocked on the side of the acrobats' vardo. She knocked again, and a third time before she heard the door open to her right. Yubi bent his head around to the side of the vardo. When he saw Kyra looking back at him, he blushed. He stumbled through a greeting. A massive collision of thoughts and feelings occurred in his throat. Nothing made it cleanly to his tongue.

Kyra raised an eyebrow at his linguistic clumsiness, then relieved him of the pain of his efforts by asking, "I need your opinion and your advice. Will you give it to me?"

Being of use to her sobered him from his stupor, and he answered quickly and sharply, "Of course, yes. I am yours. I mean, of course."

He hopped down from the vardo and the two of them strolled side by side, hand in hand, cutting a gradual arc away from the caravan.

Like the others, Yubi was mesmerized by Kyra's dancing. Unlike the others, he knew her very well. He knew her past, and he had shared, through conversations with her, almost everything she felt and thought. For this reason, he understood her dancing as no others did, and it affected him so much more profoundly. She was most especially his in that way, a fact that she was aware of but he was not.

In the light of her new bloom, he was not content with his fair portion of her. Her dancing belonged to Lavinia. It belonged to Iraja. It belonged to the whole kumpania, and that frustrated him. After all, it was he who saw her in the field and stopped the caravan. It was he who had spoken to her in Hungarian and listened to the horrors of her past when nobody else would. It was he who suggested that she think of Menowin when she danced, he who had awakened the talent within her and, therefore, he who should enjoy the largest portion of her now.

To most of the kumpania, this was a new Kyra, one that replaced the awkward girl they had taken in. Yubi did not see her as a new Kyra. He saw the revelation of her talent as the steady maturing of his same old friend. He was beguiled by her dancing, but not astonished. To him, there was a natural continuity from the soiled girl in the field, through the hero in Paks, to the strangely enchanting dancer he strolled with in that moment.

In Yubi's attempt to gain greater ownership in her dancing, rather than simply praising her as the others did, he tried to dig more deeply, to pull even more poignant expression from the depths of her soul to the extremities of her body, using something he alone shared with her.

"I think," he suggested, "you should think of Szanzar when you dance for the crowd today."

Kyra stopped sharply, still holding his hand, and asked, "Of Szanzar? What do you mean?"

"Perhaps you could think of what you went through before I found you, of losing your parents, your village, and walking alone into the fields."

Kyra, entirely misunderstanding his intentions, pulled her hand from his and asked, "Why should I do that?"

She interpreted his suggestion as a criticism of her dancing and a complaint that she was not expressive enough, that she somehow needed to be more. It violently burst the bubble of her recent attention. How very differently the following pages would have been written had they been able to see into each other's hearts.

She was hurt and offended. That was easy to see. He thought she was rejecting his involvement in her art, like she was above his paltry suggestions. She thought he saw deficiencies in her performance and in her character.

They stared at each other in awkward silence until his words bubbled accidentally and clumsily, "I... I don't know. I just thought... I thought I could help you. Not help you, but... I don't know."

Were his heart less agitated, much more proper words would have compiled in his mouth before bursting through his nervous lips. All his stuttering did was harden the film of inadequacy that coated her. She did not know it at the time, but in great part, she danced for him. She may have thought of Menowin, but she danced for Yubi. The disapproval she thought she perceived from him was deeply cutting.

He reached for her hand again, but she recoiled. Who knows how the scene would have played out had Lavinia not called for her at that moment? Lavinia, the performance — whatever building confidence may have been leading her to perform that day in front of a crowd of strangers was shattered to oblivion by the sad, pathetically awkward, and grossly misleading talk with Yubi.

Kyra answered Lavinia, she went to her, and with quivering cheeks, a reddening face, and watering eyes, she said, "I can't dance today. I can't dance."

Kyra ran away from the dancers and buried herself beneath the folds of bedding in Iraja's vardo. Lavinia had a performance to rehearse, one to rethink without Kyra. She stifled her urge to chase after her talented protégé, and she went immediately back to work.

CHAPTER EIGHTEEN
UNINTENDED INFLUENCE

THE WINTER SUN WAS AS HIGH and direct as it would get. It cut well through the chill in the air. The ground was dry and the camp was set to host the townsfolk before Kyra composed herself enough to venture from hiding. The bazaar of Romani goods was polished and placed to seduce its way into the hands of their guests. The dancers were flamboyantly dressed, with flushed cheeks and glistening sweat. The instruments were tuned and the acrobats were warm and limber, while the intended feature of the festivities snuck behind them all not wanting to be seen.

She did not want to be seen, but she wanted to see. Never was her blood more charged with mystic energy than when watching the Roma perform and barter. A strange pall rested over her excitement. She knew her reluctance to dance was a disappointment to Iraja and Lavinia, and she thought her dancing was a disappointment to Yubi. Well, she was certainly half-right. The people of Siklós and Harkány were sure to be enthralled, but much less so than they would have been with Kyra's signature addition. That is what was on Lavinia's mind all morning and into the afternoon, and Iraja was saddened by the reluctance of Kyra to embrace her destiny and seize the world around her.

Kyra observed the day much as she did outside of Győr, when she first joined the caravan. She peeked from between wagons, constantly maneuvering for a better view. She watched the dancers. As she did, the stories of her past surged into her chest. Her heart thundered, and her urge to dance took all of her self-control to temper. There was something in the music and in the coordinated sway of dancer hips that reached inside of her and found Yubi's words. She saw clearly that he was right, that her horrid past provided a blend of deep, dark, but vibrant colors, which her dancing could put to dynamic use.

She had tried so hard to find a profession within the kumpania. In that moment, she realized she had one. A true calling took her in its grasp. That was the one Roma trait she had so long envied. All in the kumpania seemed to have a career they were born to do, as well-fitted to them as their own skin. Menowin did not *decide* to be a blacksmith, nor Stoyan an acrobat, or Lavinia a dancer. The herders seemed to speak the language of the animals. Beads, stones, and gems seemed to spawn from the fingertips of the jewelry makers. Most of them inherited their professions from a line of ancestors beyond memory.

While Kyra peered between vardos, fighting the deep, arcane urge to rise and dance, she was grateful that her father had ignored her, that she was not pressed and molded into the career of Gellen or the maternal responsibilities of Eneth. Kyra was a dancer, of that she was suddenly certain, and her muse was her own experiences. It was a monster she had caged. Again, it was Yubi who saw her more clearly than she saw herself. She was mortified at how she had reacted to his suggestion.

"Think of Szanzar," she recalled him saying.

How very insightful he was. Kyra stood at the threshold of her destiny, and again it was Yubi who escorted her there. Not unlike how he shouted from the rolling caravan and stopped it for Kyra to join, he spoke again, stopping Kyra in her tracks so she could finally join the kumpania with a Romani profession.

Yubi!

Kyra's heart left the dancers completely. She had no thoughts of Szanzar or her more distant past. She thought only of that morning, of Yubi, and of all she owed to him. She ran at full sprint behind the train of wagons, to the far corner of the camp, where the acrobats rehearse. Their equipment was already struck. All that remained of Stoyan and Yubi was the matted grass where they had jumped and flipped and rolled.

Kyra cared not for hiding. She was single-minded in her attempt to find Yubi, apologize for her behavior and thank him for all he had done and been for her. She ran through the crowd of enthusiastic voyeurs, back toward the dancers, where she knew the acrobats would perform next. Stoyan was securing the second post that held the tightrope. She could not see Yubi. She worked her way aggressively to the front of the crowd. By the time she caught a glimpse of Yubi, he was already walking up beside his father to mount the rope.

There was no acrobatic introduction by Stoyan. He did not flip among the dancers as he had before. The dancers finished to the lustful calls of young men, then silence fell as all eyes turned to the acrobats. Stoyan simply walked regally beside the rope and offered himself as human scaffolding for his son's mount. Kyra knew they had been reforming their act, and she waited with the same ignorant anticipation as the strangers around her.

The local communities were inhabited largely by Swabians. They spoke German. The language was as foreign to Kyra as Romani was to them, placing the same exotic flavor on Kyra's palate.

Yubi began as he had before. He faked a wobble and a gasp, only to recover to perfect balance. The crowd "oohed" and "ahhed" and whispered to each other in words Kyra did not know. Stoyan barked at the crowd in their language. Kyra's admiration of him spiked. She could not imagine there could be a place in the world where Stoyan could not speak the language and translate the essence of the Roma to the people.

Whatever Stoyan yelled, it froze the audience into silence. The subtle shuffling of feet, as they nervously fidgeted for a better view, was all that could be heard. Yubi cartwheeled off of the rope into a one-handed handstand on Stoyan's head. The wobbles of the stunt were not faked, and there were no "oohs" or "ahhs", but one collectively held breath. Stoyan raised one hand beside his ear. Yubi placed his other hand into it, then shifted his weight onto it, took his hand from his father's head, and set it slowly and gracefully into Stoyan's other hand. Stoyan straightened his arms and lifted Yubi into the air.

There they stood, hand-in-hand, reverse images of each other, one atop the other. Still balancing his son upside down above him, Stoyan lowered himself to one knee, rotated while switching to his other knee, and stood tall again. He shuffled his feet, setting himself perfectly beside the tightrope, and Yubi bent at the waist, setting a foot back on the rope. Stoyan bowed low, and Yubi stood alone, high above him, on one foot. He placed his other foot on the rope, ran three quick steps along it, and sprang from the rope to land on the ground in a bow that mirrored his father's.

The passionate frenzy of the erupting crowd needed no translation. The feats before them were beyond anything they had dreamed before that day, and would spice each of their dreams from that day on.

The applause settled down when they realized the act was not finished. Yubi stood to face his father. Stoyan remained low in his bow. Yubi ran at Stoyan, leaped onto his back, and stepped onto his head. Stoyan extended his hands to the ground beneath him and pressed himself into a sharply angled handstand, almost horizontal, with Yubi standing one-footed on the back of his head. From there, Yubi bent down and replaced his one foot with two hands. He lifted his handstand on the back of his father's head, while Stoyan continued his angled counter-balance. It was a fantastic display of human architecture, high and sprawled upon each other, only connected to the solid ground only by Stoyan's two hands.

The audience relished the demonstration of strength and balance. So did Kyra, but her vision of the spectacle quickly focused, until she saw only Yubi. He appeared quite mystical to her, not just in his strength, not just in his skill, but in a more comprehensive beauty that was well beyond the vision of those who stood mesmerized around her. Like the dancers, he glistened with sweat. It was not only a result of his exertion. It was a designed part of the day's festivities. Yubi had grown muscular. His copper skin shone seductively in the afternoon sun. His physical beauty was yet another exotic display to make the Romani trinkets for sale all the more irresistible.

Kyra's gratitude for Yubi, her appreciation of all he had done for her, blended with the very intentional showcase of his physical attraction to create a fuel in her that burned intensely hot. It turned her flush. She could feel the redness of her face. She knew she should not interrupt the performance, but she could not help herself. She was driven by a force that her timid mind could not barricade against.

She broke from the crowd, ran onto the matted grass where the dancers had been, and yelled in Romani, "Yubi, I'm sorry!"

Yubi did not raise his face to her. He was so embedded in concentration that he heard nothing of the world around him. Everybody else heard, and they saw. When Kyra realized that every face surrounding her stared directly at her, she ran behind the wagons that separated the performance from the empty fields beyond. She sat with her back against a wagon wheel, tightly squeezing an occasional bursting cough between her violently heaving breaths.

The Swabian spectators could not understand her. To them, she was part of the act, a young Roma woman, busting from among them to shout some profession of adoration in their mysterious language, all to add to the scene. Stoyan could not imagine why Kyra did what she did, or what she could be apologizing for, but he played upon it. He shouted in German that Kyra must wait her turn for Yubi's attention, like all the other bewildered young ladies. The crowd laughed and the incident blended into the rest of the act. Kyra did not hear Stoyan's attempt to recover his act from her interruption. She heard nothing but her heaving breaths and the pulse that felt as if it was beating in her ears instead of her chest.

Lavinia and the dancers were not fooled by Stoyan's words. They did not see in Kyra's outburst a part of the act designed to make it more alluring, a Roma actress performing a well-rehearsed scene. They saw the truth. They saw a girl they knew well, and they saw a love in her that they had seen growing since Kyra's earliest days in the kumpania.

The stunts of the acrobats continued, and they were magnificent. Kyra knew that by the almost deafening appreciation of the audience. She wished so badly to be part of the attractions. She cursed herself for not having the Roma talents to impress Yubi, and for not having the wisdom to graciously accept his feedback. As enticed as she was by the sounds behind her, she would not turn around.

When the performances were complete and the purses of their guests were liberally loosened, Kyra stood. She observed the bustle of the bazaar from behind horses and between vardos. She thought she was invisible, but she was not. Many sought her, and many saw her. Lavinia in particular watched her with pity and frustration. She was aware of Yubi's influence over her, and she approached him on the matter.

Yubi, still breathing heavily from his performance, was watching the cooks prepare treats for the visitors, when Lavinia grabbed him by the hip of his trousers and yanked him a few stumbling steps away from the cooking fire.

"You must speak to Kyra!" she demanded.

Yubi, still frustrated from their earlier encounter, answered defensively, "She doesn't want to hear from me. Nothing I say matters to her."

Lavinia slapped him on the side of his head and scolded, "Blind boy! Her heart is sewn to you. It moves when you move. It moves where and how you move. You must be careful where you go with it."

Yubi respected Lavinia. They all did. As an expressive artist, she kept, always, a tender awareness of the human heart. Her words on matters of the heart carried tremendous authority. Yubi did not respond. He only lowered his head and softened his posture in contemplation. It was enough for Lavinia to know she had gotten through to him. She walked away triumphantly, while Yubi's mind subconsciously composed, revised, and frantically rewrote what he would say to Kyra. No opportunity seemed quite right. He followed her from a distance as she snuck around the bazaar, concealing herself as well as she could while sampling a scene that still enticed her as seductively as it had the very first time.

The days were short, and the festivities were much briefer than in the summer months. It ended without a good opportunity for the awkward adolescents to speak. The townsfolk returned to their homes, and the kumpania began to clean and strike for the night. The visitors had been reluctant to leave. The sun was low when cleanup began. All hands in the kumpania contributed. Even Lavinia's young son toddled from tent to wagon with what his tiny arms could hold. The rain started. It was a heavy and cold rain. It smelled of snow but was wet and saturating and soaked everyone, young and old, to the bone. The frigid rain did not slow them. Roma of all ages worked through it as if it was the warmest and clearest of evenings.

By the time Kyra pressed herself against Iraja in bed, she was chilled to the marrow. The old woman, who had herself only just gone to bed, was already warm. Kyra held especially tight to her that night, never fully regaining warmth. She awoke many times during the night, with cold feet and shivering shoulders.

The first time she felt warm was when she awoke in the morning. Her comfort freed her mind to consider how she would handle the day. Would she rehearse with the dancers? Would she try to apologize to Yubi, or would she hide behind wagon wheels and horses until the second day of visitors was done? She knew only one thing for sure. She was warm in bed with a mother who would always love her. There would always be comfort there, no matter what the day before had done to her or what the next day threatened.

Kyra's surge of affection for Iraja pushed her into a tight embrace. Kyra was warm, but Iraja still felt much warmer. There was a hot clamminess to her skin. Prompted by slight concern, Kyra shook her shoulder and softly called her name. She repeated the effort with increasing force and concern until Iraja turned onto her back and whispered "Good morning."

There was something in that affectionate smile and maternal glow that surged Kyra with confidence in her day. She returned the greeting and stood quickly to dress for the challenges that awaited her. Before she stepped out, Iraja called to her. In a voice that seemed not quite herself, Iraja encouraged her to join the rehearsal and perform that afternoon.

"You are the brightest star in the kumpania," she told Kyra, "Shine, my dear daughter, shine like…"

Iraja did not complete the thought in any form Kyra could understand. Her Romani drifted lethargically into other languages, more mumbled than spoken. A moment of worry lunged into Kyra's mind. Her heart jumped into her throat in a single beat. But the blissful smile on Iraja's face as she continued to dreamily mumble allayed Kyra's concerns and gilded her confidence to join Lavinia and the others as they prepared for another afternoon's performance.

CHAPTER NINETEEN
THE VACATED THRONE

KYRA WAS STILL RELUCTANT TO PERFORM, but her desire to do so rode on the wings of Iraja's request, and the obedient daughter followed the mandate of the matriarch. She walked confidently to the area where the dancers had rehearsed the previous morning. The grass was still trampled flat. Kyra squatted down in the center of the clearing and thought about Szanzar. She mustered all of her memories, with all of their associated feelings, from the moment Eneth went ill until she heard Yubi's voice stop the caravan.

Her body may have remained still, waiting for Lavinia and the others to join her, but her spirit did not sit still. It swirled within her, banging against the inside of her skin, infiltrating her bones, and demanding that she stand, sway, leap, roll, and fling herself as only Kyra's spirit did. With eyes pressed tightly shut and grinding teeth within her mouth, she remained as motionless as stone, until Lavinia touched her on the shoulder from behind.

"You are ready to rehearse, I see. Yubi must have spoken to you."

Kyra did not know which assumed conversation Lavinia was referring to, and she answered, "No! He... ah... He..."

Lavinia relieved her of the effort of answering, saying, "Well, I am glad you are here. Our visitors will expect more today than yesterday. Their dreams alter their memories and they always expect more. Their tales of what happened here yesterday exaggerate with every retelling. Oh, they will expect more, but they will not expect you. Perhaps it is better this way, better that you held out yesterday. Their dreams of us last night will fall short of what you will give them today."

Lavinia's attention was drawn past Kyra, over her shoulder to Yubi, who stood, shyly, observing from a distance.

"Come here, boy!" she demanded.

All shyness left Yubi, and he ran to them. Lavinia greeted him by taking his hand and placing it in Kyra's.

"Go, walk, while I gather the others," she instructed.

Lavinia disappeared as quickly as she could, removing herself from their senses and leaving them alone. It took an awkward minute for them to look at each other, but once they did, they were the same old friends. Their steps began in concert, as if signaled when to begin by some third party.

They were only a few steps from the trampled dancer area before Yubi broke the silence, "I spoke clumsily yesterday. It was not until last night that I realized how I must have come across to you, how arrogant I must have sounded to you."

"You didn't sound..." she began.

"No, please, don't excuse me. I don't deserve it."

He drew a few deep breaths, preparing himself to continue, before he added, "I am very attract— I am very drawn to your dancing. There is something very magical, almost unearthly... Lavinia put it well."

He scratched his head with the hand that was not in hers, trying to recall the quotation, "Something about the Roma music pronouncing itself through you."

Kyra did not want to hear Yubi struggle to reproduce Lavinia's words. She wanted his own words, in description of his own feelings.

They came forcefully, quickly, and bluntly, "I think you are the richest treasure of the kumpania. There is nothing and nobody among us more Roma than you, especially while you are dancing."

He paused his words to put them in proper order, which she graciously but impatiently allowed, while they walked in silence for dozens of synchronized steps.

Finally, he continued, "If you notice one thing that we all have in common, one universal trait we all share, it is that we are discontent. We strive to capture the essence of life and love, emblazon it onto our art, and share it with the world. It is an ideal we have all reached for. Yet it remains always just beyond our grasp. What we have always tried to capture has come to you of its own free will."

"Believe me," she said with a reddening face, "none of you should be jealous of *me*."

"None of us *are* jealous. How could we be? You have brought to our caravan what we have always sought, what has been a hair away from our outstretched fingers as we pushed forward across the world. Whether we are stringing beads or balancing on our fathers' heads, we now sit in the company of an ideal, and we all are better for it. I assure you, my dear friend, we are nothing but grateful. Even my father, who may seem always engrossed in his own actions, studies you."

Preceded by a brief, forced giggle, she refuted, "Not Milena. I am no ideal to her."

"You read her as she wishes you to, not as she really is. Like the rest of us, she hopes that your light will shine on us all, and that the Roma ideal will finally be realized in our kumpania."

She let out a quiet sigh with a subtle shake of her head that he neither saw nor heard. He gave her a squeeze of the hand, which he held for several exaggerated deep breaths. Lavinia was right. Yubi had every bit of influence she foresaw. Although Kyra's humility forbade her to take him at his word, to believe she was truly all that he described, his sincerely expressed sentiments inspired her to rise as close to his description of her as her talents would lift her.

Their conversations softened into mundane topics. By the time they circled around to the dancers, there was no talk of Gypsy ideals, nothing of Szanzar and feverish fathers, nothing of her horrid flight from her childhood home. Her mind was a blank canvas, awaiting the brushstrokes of the artist that sat comfortably and confidently inside of her. Lavinia could see it in her. Kyra was going to dance and that dance would take the performance of the others to new heights.

Lavinia called Vadim and instructed him to get Iraja. She would know how to set the dancers to accentuate Kyra's contribution. Vadim laughed. It was not a laugh of ridicule. He was not humored by the request. The laugh was his body's chosen reaction to the swell of pride and excitement inside of him. He revered Iraja above all others, and he saw Kyra as her second. Once the hearty laugh had settled to a lingering chuckle, he turned on his heels and walked at pace to Iraja's vardo.

Several minutes passed without a sign of Vadim or Iraja. Kyra excused herself from the group to fetch them. When she stepped inside, Vadim was kneeling beside the bed. Iraja was ghostly white, and Vadim was trying to rouse her. Iraja did not respond.

Kyra's breath was stolen the moment she saw her mother's lack of color, and with only the air that remained in her mouth, she weakly pushed out, "Vadim?"

Vadim turned to her, looking nearly as ill as Iraja. He stood and walked past Kyra, who followed him, nearly tucked into his back pocket. Vadim yelled for the attention of the kumpania. The camp was in full bustle, and only a few responded. He announced that all activities of the kumpania were canceled. Stoyan heard him. The gravity of Vadim's voice and the shaking girl who stood tightly behind were all the explanation he required. Without question, he quickly saddled two horses. He rode towards the towns with one of the herders, to tell them there would be no Gypsy attractions that day.

Vadim went back into the vardo, refusing to let Kyra follow him. She waited on the porch while he checked Iraja for the sores that might indicate plague. There were no sores, nothing that would declare that the pestilence that had swept through the country with indiscriminate violence had infiltrated the kumpania. There was only a deadly fever. The danger to the rest of the kumpania was minimal, but the danger to Iraja was extreme.

Vadim loved Iraja dearly. Before Kyra came to them, he was her closest relation. But Kyra had nestled in between them. She had become Iraja's only child and dearest possession. Vadim was not jealous. Not only did he also come to adore Kyra, but he saw clearly the peace and happiness she brought to Iraja, and he was grateful to her. Vadim knew Iraja was fading and unlikely to improve. He spoke to her, asked her questions, and begged her with a faltering voice to respond, to place her voice in his ears one more time. Submerged just beneath lucidness, she whispered an incoherent response, winced her face, and went silent again.

Kyra waited on the porch for what seemed, to her, a static eternity. She stood stiff-legged. She was weak. Her knees ached and shook beneath her, but she was too afraid to move, or even adjust her stance. She was hesitant to breathe. She did not draw enough breath to noticeably move her ribs, and she held that paltry taste of air much longer than it cared to be inside of her. Other members hung nearby, pretending to be busy with minute details of their trade, but accomplishing nothing. Their thoughts, if not their eyes, were on Iraja's vardo, most of them biting the insides of their cheeks, or chewing too deeply into their fingernails, or performing some other form of nervous self-mutilation.

Finally, the door began to open slowly. Kyra looked up to where she knew Vadim's face would reveal itself. She saw nothing, so she took a timid step forward. Vadim appeared suddenly. Kyra gasped and shifted back, almost falling backward from the edge of the porch. Manfri, the old Lyra player, who stood nearest the porch, lunged forward with arms extended to catch her. She recovered herself before falling, and the old man dropped to his knees from the sudden exertion and the emotional strain of the moment.

Kyra's stumble was partly from the suddenness of Vadim's appearance and partly from the look upon his face.

She blurted, "Is she asking for me?"

He did not answer, but simply took her hand and led her inside.

Kyra was relieved and let out a long sigh when he said, "There are no signs of the plague."

She sucked that same air back in through clenched teeth and puckered, slightly parted lips when he told her to remain with Iraja until the end. He instantly regretted his phrasing and explained sympathetically that Iraja would not live to see the next sunrise. The wet chill from the night before had done her in. She had danced in the snow in her youth, slept bare-backed on the frozen ground and rose all the more invigorated from it in the morning. But cold had reached her bones one too many times. It had burrowed itself into her marrow, and there it would remain, impervious to her desperate fever, until it took her into the ground.

Kyra shook hysterically. Illness had taken everything from her in Szanzar, beginning with her mother. Despite Vadim's assurances, she saw Iraja's illness as the first crashing wave of a similar storm, which was sure to wipe from her life everything and everyone she had grown to love since. Vadim pulled her into him and squeezed her tightly against his chest. The embrace was not nearly long enough for Kyra.

He took her by the arms and pushed enough distance between them to look into her eyes and tell her, "You are her most beloved. You must lie beside her. Hold her tightly and talk to her. Do this and she will not be in pain. She will not be in fear. She will die as we all hope to die, and she will rest in peace."

Chills ran through Kyra's body, but they were quickly overcome by love for Iraja and a strong sense of duty and obedience. She turned to Iraja and bit hard on her lower lip. She had known enough death to recognize it when she saw it coming. She turned back to Vadim with a full flow of tears and raised her hands to him. Although she could have crawled into that bed under her own power to lie beside Iraja, as she had countless times before, she kept her hands extended to Vadim until he hoisted her into his arms, kissed her head, and laid her on the bed against Iraja. She turned her back to Vadim and pressed herself as tightly as she could against the dying matriarch.

Kyra heard the door close behind Vadim when he left. She was with Iraja, and yet alone. She obeyed the demand placed upon her. She began with a slight hum, feeling the vibrations of her chest travel into Iraja. There was no need to compose a speech, no search for the proper words. When her long hum ended and her lungs pulled in the next draw of air that would carry to Iraja's ears the last words she would ever hear, words spoken by the voice of a loving daughter, Kyra spoke. Her heart commandeered her tongue and her brain simply listened.

She told Iraja stories that her childhood mind had conjured during her walks around Szanzar. She spoke of her parents and siblings. She recalled her every thought and feeling as the people of Szanzar died around her. With great animation, she told of the first rhythms to reach her ears as the caravan approached her. Exuberantly, she spoke of her first days in the kumpania, and the vicious duel that took place between her sorrow and her excitement.

Her story eventually came to the pond where Iraja had washed her of all that was stinky and ugly, and replaced it with brightness, richness, and more loving beauty than she had ever imagined. Kyra's mind was forbidden to interrupt. Her heart wielded her tongue as only a heart can, as only a *Roma* heart can. The words that her heart poured onto Iraja like warm honey, had they only been written and survived to this day, would be among the most treasured, admired, and revered language to ever inspire the human spirit. But they were not meant for the species. They were an ephemeral and intimate gift, given in one moment then gone for all eternity. I will not dare try to reproduce them for you here. The frail and paltry scribblings of this author could never do them justice.

Kyra's storytelling did much more than Vadim had wished. It ensconced a mother and daughter in a shared blanket of mutual love for the ages. There is no way to tell how much of it seeped down to Iraja's deeply buried consciousness. Some things were certain. Iraja's shallow breaths were steady, unlabored, and peaceful, and found synchronization with Kyra's. Her body was not tense, but settled into an affectionate press against Kyra. Her face held no grimace. It neither lifted a smile nor pushed a frown. There was a calm sense of rightness about the dying woman that filled Kyra with so much gratitude that there was no room in her for sorrow.

Somewhere between recalling the wedding of the baron's daughter and the flight from Paks, Kyra's heart lost its grip on her tongue. It continued on, weaving its tale directly into Kyra's dreams. She slept against her mother one last time. The love of each one of those nights they spent together collected and poured itself over them both.

Kyra awoke at dusk. Iraja was no longer feverish. In fact, she had gone cold. Kyra was familiar enough with death to know when it lay pressed against her. Iraja was gone from her life, gone from them all, and the world was a much uglier place for it. Kyra cried, beginning with a silent whimper and a shaking chest. As disturbed as she was by the cold corpse against her, she refused to relinquish her embrace. The memories of life were warm enough to overpower the coldness of death.

Her whimper grew to a vocalized cry. There was one moment — one moment when she consciously opened the doors of her grieving heart, and her cry erupted into screaming sobs. The walls of the vardo were no barrier against the sounds of such a lost love. The entire kumpania heard her and knew that their matriarch was dead. Stoyan had returned to the camp and stood a defiant sentry post at the head of Iraja's vardo. All were pulled by compassion to comfort Kyra, despite their own sense of loss, but Stoyan forbade it. Iraja was Kyra's, and Stoyan knew that the crying would tell when she was ready for the affection of others. He would not dare barge into the vardo she had shared with Iraja, nor would he allow others to do so, not until Kyra emerged and looked out into the wider world again.

Many anxious ears heard the crying from within the vardo subside in the same order it rose. There were about ten minutes of silence before the door opened and Kyra looked out at dozens of faces that awaited her. I struggle now to describe the look on her face. Anguish and peace blended in her expression in a way that did not contradict.

Her sobs had drawn intense color into her cheeks, made all the more resplendent by the orange sunset reflecting off of her tears. There was nothing immature or boyish in her face. She glowed in their eyes as a true beauty, a Roma beauty, as the one and only daughter of Iraja. It was that rare sort of beauty that seems to command the world around it. It certainly commanded the hearts of her fellow travelers.

Kyra was expecting one of them to say something, or to do something. She had no idea what to do next. None of them said a word. They just stared at her as if God had placed her before them at that the very moment to sum up the splendor of Creation. It was more than the duality of her shimmering face, more than the seemingly sudden eruption of magnificent physical beauty. The intensity of her love and loss shot forth from her spirit and bludgeoned them all in the chest. It was a sensation they did not know, a brand of mourning entirely foreign to them. It was what they were all slowly becoming, strange creatures never before known by the earth — a blend of what is Roma and what is Kyra.

None of them reacted with a sound, except Yubi. He was so astonished by her glowing loveliness and radiating spirit that he drew a forceful gasp. The air surrounding them all was a pungent stew of deep, dark, piercing sorrow and an almost unsettling display of human beauty and brightness. It appeared to them all as if Iraja had emerged from the vardo with her, filling her from the inside until she shined through Kyra's pores.

The scene was broken, the pungent stew spilled out, when Kyra began to shake and cry. It was not a cry of sorrow, but a cry for help, an invitation to her only remaining loved ones to reach inside of her and remove her pain. There was no holding them back. They rushed to the porch, none knowing quite what to say, none but Stoyan. Stoyan knew what to say, and he knew what to do. He reached her before the others could. Kyra fell from the porch into his arms, surrendering herself utterly to his wisdom and affection.

He carried her through the crowd, as they yielded and parted into a human passageway. Yubi followed behind his father with a hand on Kyra's head. As badly as they all wanted to comfort her, she was Stoyan and Yubi's concern. The body of the matriarch was theirs. Kyra had yielded Iraja and now Iraja belonged to Vadim.

Kyra felt too soothingly comforted by Stoyan's arms and Yubi's hand on her head to spare a thought for the others or for the disposition of Iraja's body. Stoyan carried her to his vardo. He held her while Yubi pitched their tent. When the tent was ready and filled with comfortable pillows and blankets, Stoyan set Kyra on her feet.

"Please understand," he insisted, "that you are not alone. You are never alone. Stay with us tonight, while Vadim and the others prepare your vardo for you."

Your vardo! The phrase was a poignant reminder that Iraja was gone and Kyra began to cry again.

"No, no, no," Stoyan instructed, "Think of nothing now. Settle in with us and sleep."

Kyra stopped crying as if his words corked her emotions on the spot. She turned to Yubi. His eyes were wide with welcoming compassion, and he nodded his head slightly. The evening was early and much needed to be done, considered, decided, and prepared for. But those were not the concerns of the three of them, not that night.

Kyra was not yet aware, but with Iraja's death, she inherited the matriarchy of the kumpania, not through any rule or constitutional byline, nothing discussed and agreed upon by the leaders of the kumpania, but by an unspoken and universally shared respect for Iraja's love for her, coupled with the sudden birth of her very Roma talents of artistic expression. Had there been any wavering of this opinion, it was cemented into place as they all stared up at her that evening, with the light of the fading sun seeming to set the spirit of Iraja ablaze inside of her.

As she was pressed between the acrobats, before she fell asleep, she was unspeakably grateful for them. She wanted to thank them, but could not find words that could carry the weight of her thoughts. She could not imagine another place in the world that could have soothed her to sleep that night. She dreamed, or as she described it years later, she was visited. She dreamed of Iraja, of a young and radiant Iraja, dancing beside her. Iraja danced as Iraja did, and Kyra danced as Kyra did. The breeze, the birds, the growth of new flowers, the breaths of all living creatures paused to watch and admire them.

Iraja stopped dancing and held a hand out to Kyra. There, on her palm, was a tiny vardo. Kyra leaned in to admire the detail. As she sharpened her focus on the miniature figure, she realized that it was not one vardo but a train of them. Around and between them walked the tiny figures of Stoyan, Yubi, Vadim and Lavinia, and all other members of the kumpania. They were not merely figures. They were real, and they went about the workings of their day right there, on Iraja's palm.

Young Iraja gestured her head toward the figures. Kyra leaned in closer. Iraja took Kyra's hand and turned it palm up, with fingers curled slightly upward. She placed the kumpania in Kyra's hand, took her tightly by the same wrist, and raised their hands to the sky. Iraja released her grip, bowed to Kyra, and walked backward away from her, fading more than reducing from Kyra's vision. When she was gone, Kyra lowered her hand and inspected the figures on her palm. They all stood staring at her, waiting for her to say something. She knew what she needed to say, and she began to speak it.

She awoke from the dream early in the morning, not remembering what she was going to say, but resolved to fulfill Iraja's wishes for her, and determined to fill Iraja's shoes in every way she could.

CHAPTER TWENTY
THE POETIC TRIBUTE

FEW WERE UP WHEN KYRA SNUCK from Stoyan's tent. She had a devotional draw to be among Iraja's things, yet a morbid reluctance. She did not know what had been done with the body. She could not bear to see the sunken, lifeless face. But she needed to be embraced by Iraja in some way, and being among her possessions, among her smells, and among the many little things they had shared was the only way to feel Iraja's touch. She walked from the tent, near the rear of the camped caravan, toward Iraja's vardo.

She passed near an open wagon, where she saw an enshrouded figure lying flat, a corpse bound tightly in lavish linen. After the briefest glance she turned away and continued walking. The image stayed in her inner eye, as clearly as if she had stared and studied it. She curled her lips inward, between her teeth, and bit down on them, continuing several steps forward, away from the body, but with slowing steps, like she was walking through water that slowly rose from her knees to her waist.

She lost the power to push forward. The image of Iraja's wrapped body remained in her eyes, covering them like thick cataracts and blinding her to the world in front of her, though her eyes were opened wide. She stood in place, afraid, as though another step forward could somehow hurt Iraja or be perceived by the dead as a rejection of her maternal love.

She heard the shuffling of feet at a distance. The sound cleared her eyes, bringing into focus what was right in front of her — Iraja's vardo. The body was not in the vardo. It was in the wagon behind her. The pull of the vardo was intense. Kyra ran to it and leaped onto the high porch with a single stride. To any observer, it would have appeared as if some large, invisible figure hoisted her by the waist and tossed her onto the porch. There was no large, invisible figure, only the love of a blossoming, passionate young Roma dancer with a powerful desire to be with the things she had shared with her beloved.

In the vardo, Kyra began slowly and dreamily sifting through Iraja's possessions. She took in the exotic smells of every breath and held them in her lungs until they seeped into her heart. She rubbed Iraja's clothes against her face, kissed her jewelry, and caressed the books and papers. She had seen, touched, and smelled it all countless times before, but never had the sensations been so dynamic, and never had her heart been so tender in their reception.

She opened the chest and found sheets of Indian paper. She had never seen them before. They must have been a recent acquisition, perhaps from their Swabian visitors two days earlier. In Kyra's mind, Iraja had purchased them for her, for that moment, to write Iraja a letter, a farewell, a final effusion of all her love for the woman who took her in when she had nothing in the world but an empty stomach and a soiled dress.

Kyra's Romani had grown conversational, but still lacked the vocabulary to express all she wanted to write in the letter. What came from her hand was not a letter but a poem, and an epic poem it was. It began in a drawn and dragging meter. It was a lamentation of the loss of Iraja to the wider world, in poetic measures that seemed reluctant to let the eye pass through them without wounds. The rhythm began to shorten and lighten, as the poem pranced through stories Iraja had told Kyra of her many decades of travel. It ended with a confession of immense gratitude, not through Kyra's narrative voice, but in the words of the world and its people, thanking Iraja for the goodness she shared and the beauty she bequeathed upon her death.

Kyra did not finish the poem with a heavy heart and drenched cheeks. She felt light and lifted, almost celebratory. For that brief moment, she mourned like the Roma. It lasted for only a few grateful sighs before disappearing like a puff of warm breath on glass. What it left behind was Kyra, as she had always been, and as she had always mourned. Her sense of loss clenched her heart fiercely and pulled it sharply and violently into her bowels. She fell from her seat on the edge of the bed, onto her knees, and vomited down her blouse and skirt.

She gagged and choked, cried and gagged again. She was part Roma princess and part Hungarian village girl. The Roma part of her wrote the poem and savored it like a Gypsy. That very same poem was a bludgeon to the gut of the village girl. One half of her was cruel to the other half, causing great pain before fading away, leaving a kneeling, gagging, sobbing Kyra. Her convulsing body was the war-ravaged battlefield in the continuing conflict between what she had been and what she wanted to be.

Kyra would have been thankful for an interruption, but as the camp awakened with Kyra on their minds, nobody dared violate the sanctity of Iraja's vardo, so she was left in that miserable and lonely condition for the full hour that followed the writing of the poem. At the end of the hour, she removed her dirty skirt and blouse and changed into a set of Iraja's. Kyra's physical growth had snuck up on her.

She was surprised at how well the clothes fit. It was a special outfit, one that Iraja did not wear often.

The shirt had narrow sleeves that accentuated Kyra's long and slender arms. It was of the brightest white. That sort of gleaming whiteness was rare and exotic among clothing of the time. Colorful beads bejeweled the swooping lace hung across the breast. The skirt was of the most richly flamboyant red. It would have caught a sharp eye from a quarter mile away, but it was not fully layered. It was thin and hung snugly on the hips and narrow down the legs. It, too, accentuated Kyra's changing figure. The outfit lengthened and narrowed her waist, while widening her hips above her long legs.

Kyra bundled her dirty clothes and set them aside. She picked up the poem and reached for the door, hesitant to be seen in Iraja's clothes. Her fingertips were an inch from the door when it pushed open from a hand on the other side. It was Yubi. Lavinia had prompted him to check on her. Kyra grabbed him by that same hand and pulled him inside. She felt a strong need to share the poem with someone, and who else would do but her only true confidant? Yubi had long received those tender thoughts that were not strong enough for a large audience. When the door closed behind Yubi, Kyra handed him the paper.

He did not immediately take it. He gawked at her. The scene before him was a confusing swirl of sensations. He could smell the vomit. In contrast to the foul odor was the richly dressed girl in front of him, clad gloriously in the skirt and blouse of their honored dead. Her face was red and radiant from the turmoil of the morning. She bore a fragile expression of tender vulnerability that begged for his help. The beauty that filled his eyes struck him dumb, while her morbid reverence for the walls and items around her gave the air of the vardo the feel of a tomb, dark, dusty, and spiteful. With that step into the vardo, Yubi felt as if he had fallen into a dream — spellbindingly beautiful, yet dreary and dismal.

Although he understood her far better than anyone else, her sensibilities were still as foreign to him as his were to her. He continued to stare at her in his dreamlike state, feeling simultaneously brightened and poisoned. She awakened him to the moment when she shook the papers in front of her. He looked at the waving scribblings in her hand, then back to her face, where she stabbed at him with eyebrows pushed together, a puckered frown, and eyes that seemed to scratch at the inside of his skull. He turned his eyes defensively downward and took the papers from her with a shaking hand.

A layer of awkward silence thickened between them, pushing him back against the door and her to a seat on the bed behind her. His eyes strained to rise from the papers to her face, which he wanted desperately to adore. They were forbidden to do so by a strange terror he did not understand. A foreign and mysterious darkness swelled before him. It pierced deeply into his soul and kept his eyes cowering downward. So, they remained on the paper and began to consume the words in tiny nibbles.

The atmosphere in the vardo may have been strange to him, but the poem was not. It was as Roma as Yubi, as freely Gypsy as the rhythms of the clapping kumpania as they caravan across the open fields on a sunny day. With Kyra's scribbled words, she managed to hold the spirit of Iraja in a light that showed all sides of her at once. It was a very Roma tribute to the most Roma of them all. It captured Yubi, body and soul, and held him in a benevolent cage. The words she had chosen, the dramatic and fluctuating rhythm of the measures, and the feeling they cooperated to express were exhilarating to his mind and succulent to his heart.

He finished reading, shook the paper in front of him, much as she had done to him, and stuttered the demand,

"You... you... you must... you must read this to them all. Th...they... they need to hear it."

There was a hint of hesitation in Kyra's heart, but it did not show its face. She sent it away. Yubi's fervor convinced her of the poem's merit. The tension between them dissipated. In the vacuum it left behind, they were pulled to each other. She stood and they stepped together as if coordinated with a count of "three". With hardly enough room between them for the paper he still held in his hand, they discussed, like comfortable old friends, how the poem should be included in the evening's tribute to the fallen matriarch of the kumpania.

They left the vardo together and stepped into an atmosphere that shocked Kyra. When Menowin died, danger dictated their response. It was no accurate depiction of a Roma funeral. Kyra was expecting more of the same, a similar dismay in the air, something more like a funeral in Szanzar. She had seen many village funerals in her earliest years. A heavy pall of silence always fell over the village, no matter how important or how insignificant the dead. A neighbor's dog died when Kyra was seven years old. She walked around somber for a week, speaking to nobody.

With the death of the kumpania's most significant member, Kyra expected the air of the camp to be oppressively heavy. It was not. In fact, there was seldom a lighter mood than the one that gleefully greeted Kyra when she escorted Yubi from her vardo. It irritated her. She expected — her heart demanded — the sounds of pitiful wailing to match the sounds her heart made within the muted cage of her ribs. The people did not go about their usual business. They all prepared for Iraja's celebration, but they did so with laughs and stories, jovial slaps on the back, and with song. It crept its way into Kyra and tried to infiltrate her with grateful peace. She was repulsed by it. To her, laughing and singing in the hours after Iraja's death would be the same as laughing in the hours preceding it. She stood in horror and watched her friends, her only family carrying on that way.

She turned to her vardo and begged with weak knees, "I am sorry, mother. I am so sorry."

There is no way of knowing if it would have been better or worse had Yubi heard her lamentation. He had walked away and her dreadful apology had no witnesses. She went back to the porch of her vardo, but she could not mount it. She could not enter. Her heart had a frenzied need to do something and do it quickly, but every movement at her disposal seemed wrong — wrong to enter the vardo, wrong to join the lighthearted preparations, wrong to run alone, screaming through the high, dry grass that surrounded the camp.

She had half a notion to take Vadim's horse and ride to the familiar confines of the neighboring villages. But they spoke German and she did not, and she could not leave the vardo she had shared with Iraja. She was chained to it and shoved from it at the same time. Her poor soul felt every bit of that violent struggle, tearing, bleeding, and swelling inside of her. Relief came in the sudden sensation of Indian paper on her fingertips. She held the poem, with no memory of taking it back from Yubi.

With her poem in hand, she walked a direct line away from her vardo, away from the camp, in the opposite direction of the villages, where the grass stood unmolested by human feet. Where the grass was highest, she trampled a small plot for her to sit, and submerged herself chin-deep. She spent the next hour rehearsing her poem, hoping to revive in her the peace and gratitude she felt as she wrote it. It was slow-going. She paused many times for recovery, but she was satisfied with the words. They spoke everything in her heart that fit within her Romani vocabulary.

When she could speak the poem easily without referencing the paper on her lap, she stood. Her quiet rehearsal had not turned her heart fully Roma, as she had hoped, but it brought her comfortably half way. Once standing high above the grass, she could see that the large tent was being pitched. She walked to it and found half of the kumpania cooperating to raise it. She found Yubi. His hands were full of rope and canvas, but when Kyra held the paper to his chest, he dropped everything and took it reverently. Kyra walked away from him and secluded herself in the womb of Iraja's vardo.

Yubi was done working for the day. It was clear to all that the paper in his hands was a commission of great importance. They did not ask, but excused him from any further responsibility. If the paper in his hand was some sacred commission, Yubi didn't know what it could be. He stood with it, exchanging glances between the words he held and the shut-up vardo that encased his dearest friend. Finally, with no other notions in his head, he carried the paper with two hands, like a precious artifact, back to his vardo, where he tore through the clutter to find some way to press and preserve it. He found a leather apron, which he folded and pressed the paper within. He did not let it from his hands for the rest of the day.

In the late afternoon, the kumpania gathered around the wagon that held Iraja's body. The ground was cold and hard and difficult to break. But a grave with meticulous, pristine edges had been dug. So much more care went into it than had ever been put into the digging of a grave in the long history of the kumpania. Vadim was sent to fetch Kyra. He opened the door and found her asleep.

Her face was red and her shut eyes were swollen. Her hair was a tousled mess, yet there was something spectacular in the image before Vadim's eyes. A helpless child, an expressive artist, a powerful warrior, and a wise sage seemed to combine in cooperation to possess her. Her breaths were as calm and shallow as an infant's, yet her face bore the anguish of her heart and the wounds of fitful crying. She was not like the rest of them, but diverse in many ways. That beaten contradiction asleep before him was splendid, and he stood in captivity, his spirit shackled by her strange and intense form of beauty.

A gust of wind rushed through the door Vadim had left open behind him. It roused Kyra, who was startled to see her frozen friend looking down at her. She gasped and sat up sharply. He raised a hand to calm her, and he told her that it was time to bury Iraja. She sucked her cheeks inside of her mouth, puckering her lips. Her eyebrows pushed hard together furling her forehead, as she painfully nodded her consent. Vadim turned away from her and walked onto the porch. He looked back to see that Kyra was standing, and he returned to the gathered kumpania.

Kyra was not far behind. She walked onto the porch. From that vantage point, she saw the dancers lifting Iraja's wrapped body and carrying it to the grave. She drew the attention of all with the slamming of the door. She had gone back inside. Nobody knew what to do. It was wrong to bury Iraja without the presence of her dearest one. But it had to be done. All of the preparations for the celebration were in order, and the kumpania could not return to their newly improved lives until it was done.

They buried Iraja without Kyra. Kyra was not the only thing conspicuously absent from the event. Nothing that was prepared to say was said, nothing sung. In somber silence, they placed Iraja into the ground and covered her with earth. It was not a very Roma funeral. Their moods were not sobered by the loss of Iraja. They were deeply darkened by the absence of sorrowful Kyra.

Kyra would have been comforted to witness it. Finally, they acted like she wanted them to act. It looked and sounded like a Szanzar burial. She was too entrenched in her own mourning to notice what she could not hear. The kumpania finished the burial without a word passed between them, and they all shuffled into the large tent with no idea how to proceed with the painstakingly planned celebration.

They sat still and quiet for what seemed to many of them like hours. Boisterous conversations never rose, but sighs turned to whispers and whispers to mumbling. It was into this muted scene that Kyra finally entered. No sooner did eyes perceive her than their associated lips were pinched shut. It took less than ten seconds for every wide-eyed stone face to be on her. Yubi sat with the poem pressed in leather on his lap. Several times he thought he had stood and began walking to her with the poem extended in front of him, only to realize that he had not yet moved.

He did not need to move. With the attention of all, Kyra walked to the center of the tent. She cleared her throat, took two deep, loud breaths, and recited her poem. Entranced, her eyes locked on a pair of feet in front of her as she paid her poetic tribute to Iraja. When she raised her face to meet those around her, she saw that every one of them had glistening cheeks. The silent flow of their tears was only broken by an occasional sniff and the wiping of salty water from their faces.

Kyra had not cried, not while she recited, but when she saw the wet faces surrounding her, her prolific eyes produced a new squall of tears. But she did not understand her audience. They did not cry because they lost Iraja. That was not their way. They cried because Iraja lived on in Kyra. Her poem captured the Roma spirit like nothing they had sung, played, danced, or fashioned in all of their years traveling together. Nothing of the filthy, gangly girl they found in the grass remained with them. Her transformation was complete — not into a Roma. What stood before them was something more than a Roma, more than a villager from Szanzar. Some heightened, enriched, pure, and radiant blend of them all put off its own atmosphere in the tent that evening, and they sucked it in like it was their first breath in an hour.

Yubi was as moved by the recitation as the rest, but he had read the poem. It didn't surprise him. And he knew Kyra. Although he still struggled to understand her, he knew her inside and out, having long been the only one to share her many terrible secrets. He sucked that atmosphere like the rest, but had the wherewithal to stand and walk to her. He handed her the leather-encased poem. Others were swept in his wake and trailed behind him under some unknown power.

The poem was passed from hand to hand, admired by eyes and hearts. It made its way to Milena. She snatched it covetously and rushed to gather the musicians. The celebration went on as planned, while Milena and the musicians huddled and debated how the poem should be set to music.

The scene became jovial as stories of Iraja circulated. Kyra understood that the Roma mourn differently. She was not angry at them, but she could not bear the scene. She walked quietly and secretly from the tent, noticed only by Stoyan. The old acrobat drew his son's attention and gestured toward the tent entrance. Yubi's quick glance caught a brief flash of Kyra's back before she cut out of sight. Stoyan gestured with his head and Yubi obeyed, following Kyra from the tent.

The noise from the tent hid his approach, and he took her by the hand before she knew he was behind her. They were mere steps from Kyra's vardo.

"You are welcome, you know," he tentatively offered, "to stay again with us, in our tent, as long as you like."

He was holding her hand, but she flipped her palm upward so that she was holding his. She turned a placid face to him, but lifted a smile from one side of her lips when their eyes met.

She squeezed his hand and spoke through that same half grin, "That would be a great comfort to me. But I don't desire comfort tonight. I want to be irritated. I want to be lacerated. I want to bleed inwardly. Tonight I must be in Iraja's bed. It is the only place I can mourn her properly."

Just as Kyra was more than a villager, Yubi was more than a Gypsy. His time with Kyra evolved him. He understood what none other in the kumpania would have. He felt an insatiable need to comfort her, but he appreciated her need to suffer that night. He offered to tuck her into bed, which she gratefully accepted.

With Kyra tucked in tightly, Yubi sat on the edge of the bed and hummed a tune. He thought intensely of her, of her kindness, her courage, and the fiercely hot flame that burned inside of her. His heart took control of his throat, and it hummed its admiration.

It did not sound like a Roma tune, nothing like the melodies that billowed from the caravan for countless decades. There was a pinching sadness to it that spoke well to what was happening in Kyra's chest. She closed her eyes and let the song infiltrate the melancholic smells around her to lull her to a mournful sleep.

She awoke minutes later with Yubi's melody in her head. He sat silently staring at her, still perched on the edge of the bed as he had been.

"That is exactly it," she whispered.

"What is it?" he asked.

"Your song. Your melody. That is the song that should carry my poem."

He ran his fingers under his nose and grasped his jaw, trying to imagine his melody married to her words. His eyes slowly widened as he realized how right she was. They were a perfect fit. Kyra fell asleep again, and Yubi left her. He walked back to the tent with a hungering soul that increased his speed with each step. He found the musicians still debating the poem.

He ran among them, raised his hands over his head, and yelled, "Stop. Stop."

When he had their attention, he began to hum the melody. The folded leather sat on a stool beside Milena. A flute began to accompany Yubi's voice. It stayed with him until it got it right. Yubi sat and watched as the other instruments joined in, and his melody took full orchestration. Milena unfolded the leather and removed the poem. She sang, not as Milena or any Roma. She sang in a new way. Her voice adhered itself to the spirit of the poem, to Kyra's spirit.

She had always been wrong about Kyra. She was blind to the subtle evolution that was recognized only by Iraja, Stoyan, Yubi, and Menowin. To her, Kyra's recitation of her poem was not the completion of a gradual climb, but a sudden ascension, as if Kyra had been grabbed by the gods and lifted above them all. She could not account for it, and it moved her deeply.

She was astonished at her own singing as her voice produced the words on the paper. The words and the melody seasoned her voice with almost too much radiant soul to handle. She smiled through her tears as she continued singing in a new, richer, more dynamic voice than had ever come from her throat, celebrating Iraja, celebrating her new heights as an artist, and celebrating the young woman upon whose towering spirit she stood.

Everyone in the tent heard the song. How could they not? They were dumbstruck by it. Not only was it a new song, it was a new form of music entirely — more Roma than the Roma, as if the richest, purest, freest portions of them all had been extracted, melted down, simmered and thickened, and poured directly onto Milena's tongue and onto the fingers of the musicians.

Iraja would have loved what happened in her honor that night. It was more of a celebration of Kyra than of Iraja. They all knew the source of the rich beauty that flowed from them. What would come to be known for centuries across Europe as "Gypsy Music" sprang to life and took its first breaths under the large tent of Kyra's kumpania that night, while she danced with Iraja in her dreams, and her still body slept like an infant in the embrace of Iraja's maternal bedding.

The moment Kyra opened her eyes the next morning, she felt different. She could not have described the nature of the difference or the reason for it. She felt transformed, renewed, like she had just released a great burden that had weighed her down for years. Her new lightness was not energetic. It was too new and did not yet have its feet beneath it. Her skin tingled, like it was made aware of a secret from which her mind was excluded.

She could not have known how fully she had stepped through a door. She was ignorant of what had happened in the large tent through the night. While she slept, the musicians and dancers rehearsed and the whole kumpania watched. They retired moments before dawn. It was Yubi who insisted they practice the new song until it was ready to accompany Kyra's dancing. He hoped it would bring her deepest passions to the surface. The others required no coaxing. Milena was not the only artist to bloom into a newly radiant version of herself that night. The atmosphere Kyra left behind her when she walked from the tent was richly exotic and intensely inspiring, not only to the performers. Every profession in the caravan was revolutionized.

The kumpania was in need of a leader, and they were all in agreement. Kyra made them feel bigger than life. That Roma ideal they had pursued across fields, through forests, into castles, and around cities, which had remained near enough to touch with their fingertips but not near enough to grasp in their hands, was served to them in healthy portions by the most unlikely leader among them. Iraja had brought them near it. Kyra plunged them into it.

With every note played or sung through that long night, with every swing of hips, and with every teary face that sat breathless in observation, they were collectively transcended. By the time Kyra awoke in the morning, she was their queen, and she had no idea.

CHAPTER TWENTY-ONE
THE THRONE REFILLED

PREPARATIONS FOR THE DAY'S BAZAAR went on as usual, but with a saturating flavor that sat strangely in the mouth. Kyra had weighed down Iraja's funeral. The camp hardly felt Romani. Yet she also brought an electric energy to all around her. She unwittingly transcended them into something more Romani than the Roma, at least more of what would later be known as Romani. They each carried within their ribs Kyra's somber heart and her radiantly outstretching, hypersensitive spirituality. In her own bumbling, unwitting, accidental way, Kyra was sculpting the very character of the kumpania.

As they prepared for their performances and set up their wares for sale, it was written plainly upon them. They were less jovial, more focused, but carrying an energy about them that tried to burst through every utterance and gesture. They were doing what was always done, in preparation for what had never been done. Nowhere was this strange duality more focused than at its root. Kyra's heart was agitated in the extreme. She was useless to any practical endeavor. She dared not assist the acrobats in erecting their equipment, as she had done before. She knew she would be performing. That alone would have shaken her nerves. But that consideration was only a grain of salt in a stew of variously swirling thoughts and emotions.

Nobody called on Kyra to assist them. Over the years, even Iraja had calloused her hands, contributing her sweat to the manual efforts of setting up the bazaars. But as much as they revered her, Iraja simply held the Roma ideal. Kyra expanded it and redefined it, and they set her as a polished idol in their midst. So, when active employment would have served her best, her hands were idle, and her thoughts were not bound to any duty. By the time the first visitors arrived, she was abuzz with frantic, fretful nerves.

Stoyan rode out early to spread word of the day's events. When enough townsfolk had gathered for them to begin, the musicians, dancers, and acrobats all took their places. Kyra sat among the cooks, offering neither hand nor mouth to their efforts. The crowd came to be delighted by an encore of the last performance. They had no idea what was coming their way. The Roma performers were themselves unsure of what would cascade from their throats, fingers, and limbs once the first notes were struck. All they knew was that Kyra was their talisman, and they felt powerless without her.

Milena's throat was bound while Kyra sat obscurely among the cooks. Lavinia's legs trembled and her fingertips drummed nervously on her hips. This sensation of nerves was entirely foreign to them. It washed away with the beginning of a new sound. Vadim, never a musician, had stretched a hide over a large canister to make a bass drum. The day's performance began with his slow and steady rhythm.

Boom... Boom... Boom... Boom...

The crowd quieted with each reverberation until nothing could be heard but Vadim's palms on the stretched hide.

Boom… Boom… Boom… Boom…

Milena's mouth opened before she knew it. Her voice poured forth without permission from her brain. Her low note rode steadily on the shoulders of the drum, then rolled up a colorful scale until it looked down upon the scene. Her voice was Kyra's sorrow wearing the clothes of Gypsy freedom. The strummed strings took up a counter-rhythm to the drum and provided a stronger stage for Milena's voice to stand upon. Manfri put his bow to his strings with none of his usual flare. He wove a harmony through the other instruments, stitching them together. They had rehearsed all night, but the sounds that filled the field that afternoon were unlike anything that had filled the large tent the night before.

Kyra closed her eyes. Her chest pulsed increasingly forward and back, waving outward until her arms waved at her sides and her head rolled in circles. The spirit of Iraja rode the music directly into Kyra's core, and it shouted, "GET UP!"

Kyra opened her eyes, and there stood Yubi with his hand extended to her. She put her hand in his and walked with him to the cluster of waiting dancers. Lavinia led a corps of five dancers toward the crowd, on the left side of Milena and the musicians. The visitors made way for them and a clearing was established. Lavinia stood at the center of the clearing. She gripped her dress and waved it side to side to the rhythm of the drum, while rolling her hips in opposition. Her shoulders jutted forward to the counter-rhythms of the strings. Her head swayed to the voice of Milena. The other dancers withdrew from the perimeter of the clearing and joined her in a tight center.

The dancers pulsed out from the middle in waving lunges that imitated Kyra's dancing, while Lavinia remained centered among them, letting the music speak through her, as Kyra had taught her to do. The music rose to a clamoring height, then withdrew like the outgoing tide, slowly quieting until all that remained was Vadim's drum and Milena's soulful voice. Lavinia joined in line with her dancers, framing an open space of trampled grass that awaited the polished idol.

Yubi released Kyra's hand. That was all he needed to do. He did not push her forward, but simply opened his palm, and she flew gently from him like pollen in the breeze. Her nerves were still there, but they were stood upon by everything else inside her, clamped, immobile, and without a voice. She floated into the space framed by the dancers. Her walk transitioned without seam into her unique brand of movement. She contorted her shoulders in ways that drew gasps from the audience. She kicked a leg to the side and held her foot above the height of her head, held it there, then collapsed suddenly and surprisingly to her hip. She rolled across the ground and sprang back to her feet.

Milena stopped singing. Vadim drummed on. The dancers swayed side to side while Kyra shifted in deep synchronized lunges from right leg to left. Milena's voice re-entered the scene, this time in Yubi's melody. The melody was born during Yubi's adoring gaze at Kyra while she slept. That was its purpose, and it served its purpose well. Everybody in attendance, Roma and Swabian alike, stared at Kyra with the same adoration. The other instruments joined exactly as Milena began to sing Kyra's poem.

Her voice sounded like two different voices in passionate communication with each other, two voices that had been distant and out of contact and could now finally share with each other their triumphs and tragedies. Each note, each word, elevated her above any place she had been as an artist, shocked those who knew her, and bewildered the guests who did not. She delighted in her new supremacy, and she knew who to thank for it. Her voice flowed around Kyra like a warm and lazy river, gentle but powerful, washing her toward a stormy ocean.

Any grip Kyra's mind may have had on her body was severed. Her spirit snatched it covetously and set it on the river that ran its course all the way to the ocean. If Kyra's poem and Yubi's melody were a stormy ocean, Kyra's body was sea foam, rising, sinking, waving, and tossing about. It did not move her by the skin, nor by the bone. It took every portion of her body to its whim. Every wave of Kyra's love, sorrow, fear, and regret crashed out onto the crowd like breakers on a beach soaking the sand, again and again. The Swabian visitors were in raptures, knocked silent at first by the spectacle. But soon they found their voices again. The scene before them was a rich concentration of their every Gypsy fantasy, and Kyra was its face.

They called her Wild Woman, and began chanting in unison in their native German, "Wilde Jungfrauwe! Wilde Jungfrauwe!"

Everyone in the camp was held in the hand of a single spirit, one that was reluctant to abdicate. The song continued. Milena continued Kyra's poem in recycled verses, and Yubi's doting melody rolled on and on. All of it pointed at Kyra. While she danced, there were no Gypsy wares, no jewelry, no food waiting to be consumed. There were no primed acrobats. There was only Kyra. Even the voice and instruments that accompanied her seemed to be extensions of Kyra — Kyra, the embodiment of all that they were becoming as a kumpania.

As if meticulously rehearsed together, Kyra rolled to the ground as the instruments faded. Milena's voice died out on the same note that had begun her performance. Vadim's final deep, thumping boom ended its reverberating echo as Kyra squeezed into a tight ball, lying on her side on the cold, December ground. The chanting of the crowd fell silent. The camp fell silent. The field and countryside took a soft sigh of recovery from what it had just witnessed. Many an unconsciously held breath waited while every eye remained locked on Kyra, who was still curled in a tight ball on the ground.

She lifted her face to the people surrounding her, to the wide eyes and gaping mouths that awaited permission to proceed with their lives. She revealed a face reddened by exertion and glistening with sweat and tears. Her eyes glowed. Her eyes — those seductive orbs — seemed to the audience to simultaneously push at them with brightness and pull at them with a deep and hollow darkness. None of them, not one man, woman, or child among them, had ever felt as they did in that moment. They did not know which of the mandates of her eyes to obey, to shield themselves from the brightness or to allow themselves to fall into the depths that beckoned them.

Kyra remained in her tight ball, scanning her dewy eyes back and forth, from imprisoned face to imprisoned face, without a blink. The moment was broken by Lavinia, who stepped forward, took Kyra's hand, and escorted her to her feet. She put her arm around Kyra's back and forced her into a shared bow. The depth of the bow detonated an explosion of cheers. Lavinia backed away, leaving Kyra alone in the clearing, alone in her reception of hollered compliments and shouted professions of esteem, none of which were understood by Kyra. Yubi understood. He knew their German, and their admiration flustered him in strange new ways.

The shouts continued at an unwavering level until Kyra turned her back to them and walked from the clearing. She walked by Yubi, squeezed his hand, leaned into a hard brush of his shoulder, and disappeared behind the Roma and their tents and wagons. The crowd began chanting again in unison, "Wilde Jungfrauwe! Wilde Jungfrauwe!" It gradually became clear that Kyra would not resume her place amid the clearing. Proportionally with that spreading realization, the Swabian visitors broke from the clearing and made their way to the other exotic delights that awaited them.

Stoyan and Yubi were primed to perform immediately after the dancers, but that was out of the question. Even their exciting feats would lose all flavor after the free effusions of Kyra's spirit. They determined to wait until the end of the day, to give their patrons one last thrill before sending them home to their wild Gypsy dreams. The visitors flitted from display to display, barking and bartering. But not a trinket was purchased, not a morsel eaten. They were stuck in their hazy trance.

It was Stoyan who knew what to do next, what the kumpania needed, and what Kyra needed. He sought Kyra. He found her lying in his tent. She wasn't asleep, quite the contrary. Her eyes were wide, her face still red, and her breaths were heaving. She was so harbored in her own emotions that she did not hear him enter.

"Kyra," was all he said, softly and reverently.

She turned her face to him and saw something for the very first time — the doting gaze of a proud father. She saw in that look that she was *not* orphaned again by Iraja's death. She sprang to her feet and had her arms wrapped around him before he realized what was happening. She had grown slightly taller than him. She held him with one of her arms over his shoulder and the other under his opposite arm, forcing his face into her neck and burying his proud smile within her hair. She released several breaths in a half-giggle, half-cry, as he slowly wrapped his arms around her.

There were a thousand things he wanted to say to her, but none of them could congeal into words, in any of the many languages he knew.

In the midst of the embrace, he whispered simply, "Your family needs you."

The horde of galloping emotions inside of her disbanded, leaving only devotion. She pulled from him and begged him with a look to direct her, to guide her as a father guides a daughter.

"Our visitors are still in your hands," he informed her, "They will buy nothing. They will do nothing, without your permission."

Kyra took Stoyan by the hand and yanked him from the tent. She dragged him to the jewelers, pulling him behind every human being they passed. Three jewelry makers sat behind a blanket that held their handiwork on display. Kyra bent down and kissed the nearest one on the cheek. The Swabians surrounding her stared at her, their arms still flatly at their sides.

Stoyan's boyish grin rode on the bubble of a surfacing idea. He took a necklace from the display and draped it over Kyra's head. She looked down to her chest, stroked it twice, and looked up to Stoyan. He nodded in approval, then extended his hand to receive it back. Kyra removed the necklace and handed it back to the jewelry maker. That necklace never again touched the blanket. The visitors shouted for it, barking offers and shaking purses of coins. The jeweler settled on a ridiculous price — three sheep in their prime for a single, simple, understated necklace worn very briefly by Kyra.

Kyra stared in amazed confusion at the spectacle, until Stoyan leaned into her and asked, "Now do you see your power?"

She saw it, and she understood the truth. To those entrammeled in her depth of soul, she left a magical residue on everything she touched. The necklace had become a relic for its brief contact with a living fairy tale. From that point on, the rest of Kyra's day was scripted. She went from display to display. Each thing she touched was purchased. Each thing she tasted was coveted.

She received hundreds of compliments, invitations, and proposals. She understood none of the language, but the sentiments were clear enough. Yubi feared for her. It was not a fear he comprehended. He had never felt it before. But he pushed and squirmed to be nearer to her than those who drank her intoxicating company like wine. Stoyan saw his son's interference. He saw how it hindered their access to her. He took Yubi firmly by the wrist and pulled him away.

Once clear of the swarm, he reminded him, "The day ends with us, my son. Kyra is doing her duty. Let us prepare for ours."

Yubi reluctantly obeyed, but while he prepared his body for its athletic feats, his thoughts were cleaved violently in half.

No longer shackled to Yubi's jealousy, Kyra maneuvered with ease. Everything that was for sale was sold. Many things that were not for sale found their way into Swabian hands at an exorbitant price. One gentleman offered a large plot of his land for Kyra's vardo. The deal was almost struck until Kyra's permission was asked. More than one man offered all he had for her hand in marriage. They were graciously and gracefully rejected by those who spoke their language.

The visitors were filled with exotic flavors, with Romani wares dangling and clanging from them. One thing remained to close the most successful day in the kumpania's memory. The musicians gathered near the tightrope. They strummed, drummed, fluted, and fiddled, while Stoyan barked for attention. The crowd gathered around, but their attention was not seized. Their eyes drifted.

Realizing that he and Yubi needed the same magical touch as everything else sold that day, he took one step toward Kyra, who sat against a wagon behind them. He stopped himself and gestured to Yubi. Yubi jogged to Kyra and offered his hand. When she took it, he lifted her to her feet with an arm that had longed for her all day. He escorted her to his performance space. The crowd went silent.

Kyra did with Yubi what she had done with the necklace. She tried him on. She took the side of his face with her hand, stepped tightly to him, and gave him a long, soft kiss on his lips. But he was no trinket handed to her by his father. If destiny had found Kyra, Yubi was the road it took to get there. The kiss was no performance meant to add enticement to the recipient. It was a kiss of gratitude, but also one of admiration. It was a kiss of love.

To say it affected him would be to say the moon affects the tides. It would be more accurate to say that it caused him to be everything that he was during that moment. It also served the purpose Stoyan hoped it would. Yubi had always been a beautiful boy, but Kyra's kiss elevated his beauty. Kyra's kiss ensured that every stunt he threw during his performance would exude the same magical aroma that had saturated the entire afternoon.

Kyra released Yubi and took a seat near the tightrope pole. The eyes of the audience did not follow her. They stayed on Yubi, and the performance of the acrobats began. Stoyan flipped and Yubi balanced. One stood high upon the other, and the besotted onlookers fell more deeply into their dreamlike rapture. In their past performances, the acrobats surprised their audiences. This audience was not surprised. Kyra's kiss had them expecting magic. In their eyes, it had endowed Yubi with unearthly powers, so that his amazing feats of athletics seemed as natural as flight to a bird.

At the end of the performance, Lavinia led her dancers to the acrobats' clearing. They stood in a semi-circle around Stoyan and Yubi. Milena and the musicians filled in the tight spaces between them. The herders, cooks, and jewelry makers joined. The entire kumpania wrapped the acrobats in a rough and bulky frame. Milena broke from them and found Kyra. She pulled her between Stoyan and Yubi, whispered a heart-felt apology in her ear, followed by a suggestion, then she stepped back in line with the others.

Kyra followed the suggestion. She began to sing. She sang the lullaby that Iraja used to sing to her. Her voice was hardly dulcet. It was a rough voice, broken further by the lump of emotion swelling in her throat. Rough as it was, it was not unpleasant. How could it be? It cracked and cried with the love of a daughter still in the throes of mourning.

The song ended and nothing but breaths could be heard in its wake. The quiet was broken by a single voice, asking in its native tongue if they could return for more the following day. Without a word of response, the Roma broke from their formation and made their way to their tents and vardos. The visitors broke a few at a time and headed back toward the river, toward their homes.

Much of what was purchased that day was given back as gifts to Kyra as they departed. Some of the smaller, more elegant gifts went with her into her vardo that night and joined the stash of trinkets that had been gifted to Iraja over the years. It was as if a rejuvenated, glorified version of Iraja still occupied that same bed. The kumpania poured Kyra into the void left by their queen, not until it was refilled, but until it overflowed.

CHAPTER TWENTY-TWO
SNOWY SUITORS

KYRA WOKE TO FRIGID SILENCE. There was no wind pushing against her windows, no song birds above, and no rustling of busy feet about. She tried to investigate the silence. When she looked to her window, the answer was before her, not in what she saw through it, but what she saw on it. It was frosted corner to corner with thick, translucent ice. She opened her door to a scene of natural beauty. Large flakes of snow, as big as her widening eyes, floated calmly and majestically from the gray sky above. They fell onto a glistening and thickening rug of white.

Lovely as it was, it was poorly timed. There would be no Romani jewelry laid seductively on a rug that day, no stunts from a rope, and certainly no dancing. This was not the sort of snow that is easily pushed aside by a determined sun. It had claimed the country for its own and had no intention of dislodging until the spring. No sooner had Kyra's new self been uncorked and poured out than it had to be re-shelved for safekeeping through the winter.

The snow signified the end of the season and the beginning of nature's long hibernation. It coincided poetically with the end of the kumpania's long held identity. But there was no hibernation for them. They packed and pushed through the thickening snow with a strange and unsettling newness in their hearts, away from the river and away from the towns they had teased. They abandoned the payments that had been promised but not yet provided.

Kyra's mind strongly associated her new identity with the plot of ground where it blossomed. As she sat in her vardo alone, while they slowly marched away, she felt herself being torn from an exciting future and returned to a confused past. But as slowly as they moved, the past could not catch them, and Kyra's sensation of being torn did not last.

The cold never bothered them. They sat upon horses, and on the porches of their vardos. They marched along the sides of wagons and walked beside the huddled livestock, when, like the heartbeats within their breasts, their feet found synchronization. With a few joining at a time, their clapping hands gave accompaniment.

To the much slower rhythm of their snowy travel, they began to sing. There were no words, only a tightly concerted "lanalana" and "dadudana". If their singing had a smell, it would be of the Hungarian wilderness in early spring, when adolescent leaves and infant flowers put off a smell of freshness and newness. It started weak and shaky, like a newborn horse struggling to its feet, but soon gained strength. Within a few minutes, it was galloping.

That is when Kyra realized that her new self was not being left behind, buried beneath the snow where she had performed, for the song was very different from the rhythmic melodies that had long fueled their travels. It savored strongly of the new artistry to which they had just collectively awoken, the one pulled from them all by Kyra. It traveled through the walls of Kyra's vardo, through her skin, between her ribs, and into her heart like a benevolent specter. It warmed her from the inside out, flushed her skin, and raised every hair growing on her body.

The following day, a new song rose from them as they traveled. It doubled in time and thundered in volume. It was interrupted by fiercely galloping hooves behind them. Two horses carried riders, one middle-aged man and one younger man. They were from the town of Siklós and had been among those men chanting for the "Wilde Jungfrauwe".

They rode beside the caravan and called again for Kyra, "Wilde Jungfrauwe! Wilde Jungfrauwe."

Their chants were not in unison and certainly not in cooperation. They shouted, each in competition over the other, each jockeying his horse in front of the other, to make a bolder claim for Kyra's heart. The caravan stopped. The kumpania broke from their travel formation and emerged from their vardos. They formed a shield of humans and horses between the two desperate Swabians and their desired prize, all but Yubi. He had been resting in the clutter of his vardo, wearing no shirt and no shoes. Exactly as he was, he mounted Kyra's porch and braced a foot against her door.

The two men shouted from their horses, effusing their passion for Kyra, boasting of their wealth and prestige, and proposing marriage. The younger of them dismounted and rushed on foot toward the wall of defensive Roma. In a furious voice, he demanded Kyra, referring to her as his destiny and his rightful property. He promised her a home in Siklós, or rather a house, but he chose a word that translated to Romani more closely to the word "cell" or "cage".

Yubi lost all control of his reason. He sprang from the porch like only a Roma acrobat could have. He pushed through the defensive line and charged at the young man. He was a foot shorter, carrying significantly less weight on his frame than his target, and rushing forward barefoot and shirtless. But Yubi's strength greatly exceeded his age, height, and weight. He was a full twelve feet from the man when he launched himself through the air. His swinging fist connected to the man's head while his half-naked body still soared horizontal to the ground.

The strike knocked the man to the ground, and Yubi careened and crashed over him. The commotion spooked the older man's horse, which neighed and reared in response. Its rider almost fell, sobering him quickly from his deranged infatuation. His eyes stopped seeking Kyra and suddenly saw the protective faces staring at him and the fierce young acrobat who had leveled his competition. His fear defused his scheme and he rode at haste toward Siklós.

The remaining young man was not sobered. He stood from the assault even more determined to fight his way to Kyra and take her as his own. He was blind to the other Roma. He saw only Yubi, who growled at him with skin reddening from the cold. The two were primed to charge at each other in a beastly battle. It never came to that. The young man was pelted in the face with a snowball, followed by another and another.

The projectiles came at him fast and furiously. He ran for his horse and the snowballs kept coming. One hit the horse and sent it riderless in the direction from which it had come. Kyra's mad suitor ran after his horse screaming its name and ordering its return. Kyra watched from her window as the man and his retreating horse dwindled from view. When he was entirely gone from sight, the kumpania rushed to their previous formation and pushed the caravan forward with new zeal. Yubi wanted to run to Kyra and hold her in his frozen arms, but he was swept by the rush to move, and he dutifully took his place in the effort, still barefoot and shirtless, until they were all as they had been, but with hearts that pounded with vigilant, defensive service to their queen and inspiration.

The incident with the two riders added urgency to their travels away from Siklós and Harkány. For more than a week they did more traveling than resting. When they stopped, cooked, ate, and conversed in huddled clusters, they addressed Kyra with reverence — none more than Milena. The singer brought her children to Kyra, not demanding services, but seeking exposure. She placed them in Kyra's arms hoping something of their new queen might rub off on them. Kyra did not handle the cold and snow like a Gypsy. She remained almost constantly in her vardo, and in almost constant company with Milena and her children, Lavinia and the dancers, Manfri and the musicians, and all of the other artists who wanted to elevate themselves by her influence.

The potters and jewelry makers, even the cooks and herders, took their turns breaching the sacred confines of Kyra's vardo. They all wanted to extract from her, to be endowed with that mysterious something that seemed to glow inside of them when they were in her company. The only ones who sought to serve Kyra, to provide her with what she needed, were Vadim, Stoyan, and Yubi. But they had few chances.

Vadim and Stoyan were content to delight from afar in the evolution of their kumpania and the luminous girl who had become the bright center of them all. Yubi's experience during those days was very different, different from all of them, and infinitely more agonizing. He was in a state of constant agitation. The feelings during his attack on the young suitor lingered just under his skin and itched and irritated him from the inside. He mourned deeply the loss of the long and intimate walks he had shared with Kyra. She had belonged to him when no other hands clutched at her attention. As mystified as he was by her evolution and the changes she inspired in others, he cursed it.

His portion of her dwindled to a share no larger than anyone else's, just when his craving for her was at its strongest. While they traveled, he never had a full minute of her attention to himself. It was not that she did not want to give it. She too missed their former intimacy. The constant distractions drew an opaque curtain over the fiery love for him that smoldered in her bones. But his longing was deeper than hers. There was no curtain over his feelings. His maturing body, mind, and spirit demanded her in equal measure, resulting in peculiar behavior that did not go unnoticed. He was short of patience and sharp of tongue, isolating him while she drew human hearts to her like eyes to a sunset.

The snow fell with few interruptions for nine days, and finally gave the sun permission to see the whitened world beneath it, just as the caravan settled on a plot of field to claim as its own and wait out the winter. It would be a long wait. The snow that had fallen that week held fast to the ground for the many months that followed. It would have paralyzed Szanzar, locking its timid hermits within their walls until flirtatious birds again swam together in the warm air of a new season.

The Roma had much to do before that happened and, as usual, the cold slowed them little. They trampled the snow around them and made for themselves a whiter version of the same creative rehearsal spaces. The spaces may have been similar, but the rehearsals themselves stung the soul with freshness, like the raw skin under a newly removed callus. There were no thoughts of plague and fearful prejudice, no thoughts of violently desperate suitors. There was only youthful giddiness and the plotting, planning, and scheming creativity it fueled.

There were two sad exceptions to the general spirit of the kumpania — Kyra and Yubi. Kyra's celebrity status did not afford her the time she needed to process her new identity or mourn Iraja with the degree of intensity that would satisfy her sensibilities. Yubi's legs always burned in their desire to run to her, and his tongue curled in its desire to speak to her all that it wanted to speak. Rather than setting those parts free, he bound them and isolated himself, waiting for a perfect moment that did not come.

He thought of his father's early passion for Iraja, as it was told to him many times. Although he knew Stoyan overcame that passion, falling in love with Yubi's mother, marrying, and finding the heights of pride and happiness as a father, Yubi did not want to get over Kyra. He feared it, so he fueled the fire in him by constantly shoveling the fuel of adoring thoughts upon it. He feared seeking her and professing himself, afraid he would appear like the two riders from Siklós.

He wanted to show the difference of his affection, different from the two suitors and from the affections of everyone else in the kumpania. He grinded his teeth in regret for not securing her heart earlier, in the calm language lessons and the confidential conversations they shared during the previous year, when nobody else sought her attention. He did not realize that he had already done just that, and the slightest gesture from him would have had the power to brush everyone else from her and secure her as entirely his own. But she did not need him in the same ways she needed him before. She needed him in ways that did not pronounce themselves demonstratively enough to pierce through the swarm of distractions. In ways that would catch his attention and pull him from his regret, jealousy, and self-pity.

Although the artists of the kumpania were inspired by the searing darkness inside of her, simultaneously rancid and delicious, they did not yet fully understand it. In this disconnection, Kyra was in constant company yet never in communion. Yubi understood her but barricaded himself behind ramparts of reclusive emotions. That is how they passed the frozen weeks, two brooding teenagers, suffering from voids only the other could fill, sinking beneath the clamorous excitement of loved ones whose eyes were too focused forward to see the turmoil boiling inside both of them.

CHAPTER TWENTY-THREE

POSSESSIONS OF THE DEAD

THE PERFORMANCES OUTSIDE OF SIKLÓS and Harkány had been fruitful, and they came in the nick of time. Few would have admitted how desperate their situation had been since their flight from Paks. But as it stood, they had money. They had supplies. They had Matthais' map and list of trusted connections. Plague had subsided from the nearby communities, and the world seemed itself again.

The kumpania's artistry had new fervor and new purpose. The winter months, which had loomed ominously, were suddenly treasured by most of them as a perfectly timed opportunity to experiment with their new identity. The only thing missing was Iraja. It was not in their nature to mourn for long, and they were not darkened by the loss, but Iraja had led them for so long, and her absence was conspicuous. Mindless and aimless activity buzzed around the camp. Their excited newness had no navigation without Iraja to focus them. Fruitless energy without direction resulted in bodies scurrying from point to point on no particular errand. Like the body of a snake, the kumpania wiggled and writhed without a head, in spastic motion yet moving nowhere.

It is not as if Iraja had been taking them by the hand and pulling them through their days. They were quite capable of doing what they had always done. But in their hearts, there was a staleness to their old ways. It was not the Roma way to shuffle habitually through life. They were intentional in every movement and in every breath. They had no map to guide them on this exciting new path. They did not need Iraja. They needed their queen. They needed Kyra — the inspiration for their changes. They turned to her for constant guidance and, in her adolescent timidity, she turned away. The kumpania was stuck in futile hyperactivity.

The camp was thoroughly entrenched. The tents remained pitched, the horses unhitched, and the forge assembled. Kyra prepped it for work every morning, but rarely set the fire. There was nothing they needed that was within her blacksmithing skills. The empty forge and the still hammers reminded Kyra daily of her lost friend. Still, every morning, with whispered conversations to a ghost, she pensively set Menowin's tools for another day of inactivity.

Once a week, Vadim took a wagon into Harkány to purchase supplies and maintain business connections. One afternoon in early March, he returned with a passenger. A young man sat beside him. His name was Ernko. He was an ambitious apprentice to the Harkány blacksmith. Ernko had apprenticed since he was seven years old. He was ready to make his own way, and Harkány had no room for another independent blacksmith. He was there that day, when Kyra danced, when she sang her lullaby to the people of Siklós and Harkány. He craved adventure and idolized the Roma lifestyle. It was not difficult for Vadim to recruit him into the kumpania.

Ernko was pure Swabian, without any of the physical features that walked and worked around the camp. He had a large barrel of a rib cage. His hair was fine and sandy in color. He had a wide jaw and a pronounced brow ridge. He was not what anyone would call at first glance a striking beauty, even among his own kin. Yet a confident sparkle shone from his eyes that matched the sun reflected from his light hair and skin. His smile was friendly and contagious, and his company was pleasant.

He owned no tools of his own and was eager to see what the kumpania had to offer. Vadim took him directly to the forge, without introductions. The forge in Harkány was a grand one. The blacksmith there was well-known and supplied the metalwork for several towns. Menowin's little forge was humble, just a small kiln and an apron full of tools. Ernko stood staring at his new forge, while the curious kumpania gathered thickly around him.

The forge was just outside of Kyra's vardo. She stepped onto her porch and had the best view of Ernko and Vadim. Ernko folded his arms in front of him, drew a deep inhale, and grunted as he compared the forge to the one on which he had been raised. He looked around him at the Roma wagons and the Roma faces. He closed his eyes and drew a deep inhale, breathing in the excited freedom that flavored the camp. He unfolded his arms with a wide smile and embraced his new life.

Vadim had shown him his new life, but he had not yet offered it. He had no authority to do so. In the eyes of the kumpania, only one person could make such an offer, and she stared dumbfounded from her porch. Vadim took Ernko by the shoulders and turned him to face Kyra. There she stood, elevated above all, looking down on the scene with deep uncertainty.

Vadim began to introduce Kyra to him, but Ernko interrupted, addressing Kyra by the only name he knew for her, "Wilde Jungfrauwe."

"Her name is Kyra," Vadim instructed in High German, "and she is the very best of us. Your place among us is hers to grant or deny."

Yubi climbed atop his vardo to observe the exchange from an elevated distance. The truth is, he needed a new blacksmith as much as any of them. Stoyan's innovations awaited the construction of metalwork. But Yubi ground his teeth as he sat on his vardo. He did not see a desperately needed professional in Ernko. He saw another pair of eyes on Kyra, another voice in her ear, another consumer of her attention.

Ernko's opinions of himself matched his age more than his actual merits. He had no doubt about his ability to impress the fourteen-year-old grimacing down at him. He pulled Menowin's hammer from the apron and spun it on his palm with impressive skill. He stopped it with a sudden grip of the handle, swung it down beside his hip and flung it behind and over his shoulder, catching it blindly while still staring fixedly at Kyra.

Perhaps the trick would have impressed her, had she not been so wretchedly offended by the lack of reverence with which he grabbed and tossed Menowin's hammer. It was not a tool to her but a relic, one she hardly felt deserving to take in her *own* hands. To Ernko, the trick with the hammer was an audition meant to impress a girl. Vadim knew Kyra was above such flirtations. He saw the scowl on her face and whispered into Ernko's ear. The young blacksmith returned the hammer to the apron, bowed to Kyra, returned his eyes to her with a much more serious gaze, and spoke to her.

Kyra did not understand his language, so Vadim interpreted, "He humbly asks you for a place among us, to join our kumpania and fill our need for a blacksmith."

For the life of her, Kyra could not understand why the request was made to her. But as she turned her eyes from Ernko to the people gathered around, *her* people, she understood clearly. It was in that moment that her authority as their queen came clear to her.

A strange new weight tugged downward on her rib cage. She felt utterly unqualified for the decision placed upon her. Still, a decision had to be made.

She turned back to Ernko and spoke quietly, so that all had to keep still and hold their breaths to hear her, "That is Menowin's apron, and those are Menowin's tools. He may use them, but he may not have them."

Ernko did not know a word of Romani. He looked to the people around him for some hint of what she was saying. The kumpania had not forgotten Menowin, but the Roma move on. That is what they do. The notion of the blacksmith tools somehow being the property of the dead was foreign to them. But they had grown susceptible to Kyra's sensibilities, and they quickly understood her. Ernko looked to Vadim for translation. Vadim smiled at the young man, patted him twice on the shoulder, and handed him the apron.

Ernko was eager to show his skills, and the kumpania had a long queue of needs. First among them was Stoyan, with the long-awaited plan for his high bar. Instructions and debate ensued in Ernko's language, followed by shouts and translations from many others in the kumpania. Ernko's arrival seemed providential, a newness, just as they were born anew. Innovation swelled in them as they overwhelmed Ernko with all they wished him to make for them.

Kyra stood on her porch and observed with mixed emotions. She understood little of what was spoken in front of her. Her thoughts were not on Ernko but on the tools in his hands, on the apron he had already wrapped around himself. She could not help but compare the young man to the friend she had lost. There was no comparison. How could there be? Her eyes volleyed between the stranger, who had suddenly usurped Menowin's forge, and the excited faces of her kumpania. Yubi remained atop his vardo, misinterpreting Kyra's expression, gripping, pulling, and squeezing the hair above his ears.

Ernko was certainly the celebrity of the moment, not from the affection of the kumpania, but from their needs. Kyra could bear no more of the chaotic scene. She went inside and prayed to God for Menowin. Her prayers for Menowin turned to conversation with Menowin. Yubi was given no time to brood. His father called him down and swept him into the excitement of new ideas for their act, ideas that would finally include the high bar.

The following morning was much warmer. Springtime, with all of its renovation, grabbed the air and pulled it to its breast like a mother reunited with her child. As usual, Kyra was the first to rise. She began the day as she usually did, setting Menowin's forge, painstakingly setting his tools as he taught her to do. But this time, she did not set it for a phantom, but for a blacksmith, one who was eager to set the fire and strike the hammer.

When the forge was set, Kyra stood and evaluated it, speaking to the dead with fond reverence. She did not notice Ernko, who stood behind her. He spoke, and she started and turned quickly to face him. He asked her some questions and made some comments, none of which she understood. He stepped around her and began setting the forge as he preferred it. The moment he released the hammer, she snatched it and returned it to where she had set it.

"Don't you forget," she demanded, "This is Menowin's forge. You may use it, but it is his and it always will be."

He stared at her in ignorance, shook his head, then began to fire the kiln.

"No, not like that," she instructed.

She elbowed him aside and continued his efforts, but in Menowin's way, in the way he had taught her. Ernko raised his voice, clearly agitated. He put on the apron, patted it a few times in a gesture that clearly meant that he is a blacksmith and knows what he is doing, and he reached around her.

She stepped back and shouted, "STOP!"

He did not know the word, but the sentiment was clear enough. He stopped, as ordered, and stood, staring at her with a frustrated expression on his face. She stared back with a similar look. They both looked around for someone, for anyone who could translate their words. Nobody was nearby.

Finally, Kyra yelled for the one person who had served her most in such matters, "Yubi! Yubi! Yubi!"

She yelled his name nine times before he ran up beside her. Ernko was relieved to have someone to translate. No translations occurred. Kyra seized Yubi by the sleeve and yanked him from Ernko, away from the forge, around to the other side of her vardo. She pushed him against it, knocking his head on the wall. He did not notice. Neither did she.

She demanded with the authority of a queen, "You have to teach me his language. I need to know what he is telling people, and what they are saying to him."

They remained face to face, mere inches apart. She held him against the vardo by tightly clenched fistfuls of his sleeves. She blushed with frustration. He felt a strange need to obey her, but an equally strong reluctance to bring her and the stranger together in the intimacy of a shared language. As she stared at him, waiting for a response, her face changed from a look of stern demanding to one of pitiful pleading. It was a face he had seen on her many times, one of needing, of needing *him*.

He had known hunger. He had known thirst. He had known many deep physical urges, but none as deep as his desire to kiss her at that moment. Her look reminded him of when she was his and nobody else's, when she was awkwardly out of place in the kumpania, with no useful employment and no discernable talents. He not only wanted to kiss her. He wanted to pick her up, lock his lips to hers, and run with her away from every living creature who might want a share of her.

Still in her tight grasp, he pushed his chin forward slowly, raising his shoulders and imagining his arms wrapping around her while they remained flatly at his sides. He observed her closely for changes, for any sign that she would accept such a gesture of affection from him.

She showed no signs, but shook his arms and begged, "Will you teach me the language?"

He withdrew his chin, dropped his shoulders, let out a sigh that seemed to expel from him much more than just breath, and he answered, "Of course I will teach you, if you wish to be with me... I mean, if you can spare the time to learn."

She let go of one sleeve, but squeezed all the more tightly to the other. She pulled him a good fifty paces from the camp, to a small piece of ground where there was more grass than snow. She released him and began to sit.

"Wait!" he demanded.

She stood tall again and watched him run to his tent. He came back with a blanket wadded in his arms. He folded it thickly upon itself and made a seat large enough for one. He placed it on the ground in front of her. She sat on the blanket and he knelt on the cold wet ground in front of her. He took just a single breath before he began instructing her, teaching her the first fundamental phrases of Old High German.

She interrupted him to ask, "How many languages do you know?"

"I know as many as my father knows. When we are alone, he rarely speaks to me in Romani, but insists I learn all that he knows."

"How many languages does he speak?"

"My father is the barker. He must speak wherever we go."

She was not satisfied with the answer, and her face showed it, so he told her, "He can speak to the people in any town between Delhi and Rome."

Kyra knew of Rome. She had never heard of Delhi but imagined it must be very far away. She was satisfied, and she sat back to continue the lesson. The German words stuck to her mind like pine sap on the fingers. Her progress in the first few hours astonished and delighted him. Most of all, he was delighted to be teaching her again.

Swaddled in the warm familiarity of the situation, he forgot the cold, and he forgot the purpose of his lesson. He was alone with Kyra, with her full attention upon him, teaching her a language, much as they had spent their earliest days together. In that lesson, she was his and his alone, and he was comprehensively hers.

CHAPTER TWENTY-FOUR
SOAPY MEMORIES

DURING THE PREVIOUS YEAR AND A HALF, Kyra and Yubi were like two stars sharing an elliptical orbit, passing very near each other then very far away in a pulsing and repeating pattern, each caught perpetually in the gravity of the other, yet never quite connecting. Like the celestial metaphor, they often appeared as one bright star to those at a distance, only to peel away into two very distinct and separate points of light in the kumpania. As the snow gave way to the pale green of infant grass, their orbits brought them near each other again.

Ernko made himself instantly useful, creating and repairing the many things that sat neglected since Menowin's hammer lost its master. He worked feverishly. Stoyan had his high bar exactly as he envisioned it. The wagons had new axles. The cooks had new knives. Few in the kumpania spoke German, but a translator was never far off. Well, one translator was always far off. Yubi was slow to embrace Ernko. He savored his long hours teaching the blacksmith's language to Kyra, but despised the ultimate goal — to share Kyra with yet another person. Kyra ignored Ernko. It disturbed her deeply to see him wearing Menowin's apron and swinging his hammer.

It would all be disrupted soon. Life in a Roma camp was very different than life in a rolling Roma caravan, and it was time to travel. They had plenty to eat and plenty of supplies for the construction of their wares. They were short on the more exotic items. The foreign spices and alien trinkets that gave their bazaars such glamorous romanticism could not be found in the open fields, nor in the villages speckled across the countryside. They were to be found in the ports of the sea and in the larger markets along the Danube.

Great and often heated debates pushed them into April, debates between east and west. Stoyan and the dancers wanted to go west, through Croatia, to the fantastic markets of the Venetians. The musicians, jewelry makers, and herders saw more benefit in traveling east and returning to the riches of the Danube. Everyone had a voice and many voices were heard, but only one had the authority to command the caravan, the one who knew the least about such matters.

They arranged the caravan for travel, but left the large tent pitched. Everyone above the age of twelve gathered there in the morning, and there they would remain until the decision was made. Through Croatia and along the sea to Venice or the Dalmatian Coast, or to Mohács and south along the Danube into Bulgaria, it was a big decision. Before them were two completely different paths that would lead them into very different futures.

Had Kyra the chance to witness such a gathering while Iraja was still there to preside over it, she would have been prepared for what came next. Had she truly understood her authority, she may have had some inkling of the chaotic scene that awaited her. A chair was set for her against the inner edge of the tent. Pillows and blankets were strewn around it so that none sat above Kyra. Entirely ignorant of the expectations on her, she was led into the tent and to her chair by Lavinia. Once she was seated, the rest of the kumpania filed into the tent and took their seats on the pillows and blankets, all facing their fourteen-year-old queen.

One at a time, people rose to their feet to express their opinions and explain the benefits. Ernko, not understanding the rituals of the Roma, stood near the entrance to the tent. His head rose above Kyra's. When Vadim looked back and saw him, he gestured vigorously for him to sit. Ernko plopped suddenly and harshly to a seated position on the spot.

The setup of the tent made it quickly clear to Kyra what was expected of her. She knew nothing of geography. She did not know Naples from Bombay. She listened closely to each argument, hoping that her heart would be swayed strongly one way or the other. There was no talk of fear. Apprehension of any sort was entirely absent from the deliberations, but not absent from Kyra's heart. As the options were described to her in detail, she began to lean, not toward one, but away from the other.

The path of the sea would take them through dense urban areas, which offered both treasure and terror. To Kyra, who held long and hard to each tragedy of her life, the terror outweighed the treasure. Kyra hardly felt adventurous. As Stoyan described the Venetian ports, with their tents full of commodities from Africa, Asia, and Western Europe, Kyra stood suddenly erect, with shoulders lifted almost to her ears. She silenced Stoyan in mid-sentence.

"East!" she shouted, "to the Danube, then south into Bulgaria!"

Stoyan cocked his head to one side, raised his eyebrows, and lifted his lips to his nose. It was not in disappointment that she chose against his plan, but in astonishment at the desperation with which she declared her decision. His surprise and the associated physical response lasted only a few brief seconds. As much as any of them, he respected her authority over them all. He was the first to defer to her with a nod of obedient approval before returning to his seat on the ground.

Milena rose from her place against the wall of the tent, walked to Kyra, turned to face the others, and said, "We go to Mohács, then south along the Danube."

She offered her hand to Kyra, who rose to take it. She escorted her through the kumpania, from the tent, and to Kyra's vardo. Not another word was spoken on the matter, and no time was wasted putting Kyra's decision into action. Within half an hour, they were rolling east, toward the town of Mohács.

Leadership exhausted Kyra, but more than wanting rest, she wanted to again be the child who was cared for by others. Vadim rode on the back of the horse that pulled Kyra's vardo, and although there were more comfortable places to ride across the miles ahead of them, Kyra sat behind him, with both arms tightly around his waist and a cheek pressed firmly against his back, drifting in and out of innocent, childish dreams.

She awoke in the afternoon from a deep sleep, still pressed against Vadim's back. She felt as if she had transitioned from one dream to another. They were away from the caravan, alone, just Vadim, his horse, Kyra, and her vardo. The porch behind them was loaded with empty jugs and canisters. Vadim settled her uneasiness when he explained that the caravan was resting behind them. They had broken from the others to fill the jugs and canisters with water from a nearby lake.

She ached from the awkward sleep, seated on the back of a horse, and asked Vadim to stop and let her off to walk beside him. He lowered her to her feet. She gripped the cuff of his boot and kept that embrace while she marched beside the horse.

They came to the lake. Vadim unhitched the horse to let it run freely while he filled the containers with water. The porch of the vardo faced the lake, and Kyra climbed upon it and sat staring at the glistening afternoon sun on the surface. She turned thoughtful and pensive as she pictured her twelve-year-old self naked in the water in front of her, with Iraja's fragrant, soapy hands rubbing away at her filth. She was not entirely in the memory. She also imagined where she would be and what could have happened to her had she not toddled into the path of the caravan. She thought of her immense debt to the people who revered her as their leader, and she dismally regretted her inability to repay what she owed to Iraja.

She hummed a long note that broke whiny, crackly, and pathetic as it ran out of air. It drew Vadim's attention. His concern evaporated as he looked out at where she stared and recognized, as she did, the similarities between the bank of this lake and that of the pond where Iraja had bathed her. He was the only other one there that day, and the only one who could have understood the nature of her wistful stare and whimpering hum.

He knew that her mind was not where her body was, there, at that lake, on that day. He had come to know her enough to understand how tightly she held to the past and how deeply she mourned the dead. As strong as his instinct to embrace her was, he would not snap her back to the moment at hand. Her mind was where it needed to be. He gathered the horse and rode it in large laps, at enough of a distance not to interrupt Kyra's daydream.

For more than an hour he left her alone to her remembrance. But the sun sank in the sky and the ride back to the caravan could not be delayed any longer. When he returned to her and began hitching the horse to the vardo, he found her in a trance, unbroken by his noisy activity. She sat on the porch with her chin on her knees and her arms wrapped defensively around her legs, as if someone was trying to steal them from her hips. Her eyes were wide open, staring at the edge of the porch.

"Kyra," he prodded tentatively. "Kyra," he repeated with greater urgency and concern. "KYRA!" he finally shouted.

She drew a sharp inhale as she shook violently from her trance. She turned to him as her mouth tried to speak without consulting her brain, "I... I... I..."

"Shhh, shhh, shhh," he calmed her, reaching onto the porch and cupping her knee with his palm, "We have to go back to the kumpania, or they will come out looking for us. We have already been much longer than..."

He cut his thought there, not wanting to concern her with the worries of others. He patted her knee a few times before she stood slowly, entered the vardo, and swaddled herself in the bedding. As Vadim turned them around and drove them back, Kyra pulled out, in turn, every cloth item in her possession, drawing deep inhales, trying to extract from them the strongest scent of Iraja. She did not cry. She was too wrapped in comfortable memories.

The experience at the lake and the smells of Iraja's things made her almost forget that her mother was gone. Such a vivid string of delightful memories passed through her mind that there was no chance for reality to speak up and remind her that she was alone in the vardo and the body of Iraja was left miles behind her. She spent the ride back in a giggling, whispered reliving of moments of the past. Vadim drove the horse, feeling Kyra's wrapped arms around him in his imagination, slowly coming to a richer understanding of the deep darkness inside of her that had long been an enigma to her adopted family.

When they came within sight of the caravan, Yubi ran out to meet them. Several others followed at half the speed. Yubi ran beside the horse and skipped backward to keep pace with its return, peppering Vadim with questions and demanding, "Where is she? Where is Kyra?"

"Settle down, Yubi," Vadim instructed, "She is inside and she needs some space. I think we should let her be. Let us camp where we are and let her lie in peace until morning."

Yubi tried to imagine what could have happened to delay them, and why Kyra would suddenly need rest and isolation. Had Vadim explained all that he knew, Yubi would have understood and his heart would have settled. That is not what happened. Vadim led Kyra's vardo to its proper place in the caravan. He dismounted, informed the others that Kyra wished to camp for the night, and he joined the cooks in preparing the evening meal.

When Kyra awoke, she was no longer swaddled in soft memories. She was alone, and she *felt* alone. She was still dressed from the day before and wasted no time on her appearance. The morning was cool. She took a moment to pull Iraja's shawl from under the bed. That small delay was all that slowed her. She left the vardo looking for Vadim. It was not Vadim that she sought, but the lake. She had an inexplicable fear of rolling away from it, like it would somehow sever her connection to Iraja. The months behind her had put many layers between her and the freshest feeling of grief for Iraja, but the lake cut right through those layers.

She found Vadim as he so often was, gathered with the cooks, bathing nose-deep in the aromas of a boiling soup and simmering beans. He made a comment to her about moving forward toward Mohács. She hardly let him finish before asking if they could remain camped where they were. The request struck him as strange, in light of their needs and of her recent bloom as an artist.

"I really do believe we should move on to Mohács, to the markets there and to the crowds who will see you dance."

"Not yet!" she shouted in a panic.

Her outburst hushed every conversation around them. The cooks held their spoons and ladles like statues of themselves, all staring at Kyra.

Kyra calmed herself and continued, "Not yet, please. I would like you to take me back to the lake."

One of the cooks spoke up, "We have enough water to get us to Mohács."

Vadim, understanding her well, held his hand up, shushing the cook, while keeping his eyes locked on Kyra's eyes.

"We could fill one or two more," he suggested in a soft and nurturing tone that displayed to her his understanding.

She lifted a smile so slowly that it looked like time was distorted. He matched her at an equal pace.

Debate on the matter would have been fierce, had the matter been open for debate. Kyra wished to stay, and regardless of urgent needs, they would obey her. Kyra turned on her heels, mounted the porch of her vardo, and sat ready to roll. Vadim stared at her, as did the cooks until they turned their eyes to Vadim for an explanation.

"Oh, now? Yes, of course, now," he stumbled.

To maintain the pretense, he put a canister beside Kyra, hitched his horse, mounted, and pulled away from the camp, toward the lake.

The bustle drew others from their tents. It drew Stoyan and Yubi, and they watched in wonder, with no idea why Vadim would be taking Kyra's vardo away from the camp just as they were expecting to assemble the caravan for travel.

Vadim, aware of how it must appear, yelled from a distance, "There are things we must do. We might take some hours."

Yubi took one determined step toward them, but his father caught him by the cuff, as he shouted to Vadim, "Do you need help?"

"No, no," was all he heard in response.

Yubi tugged against his father's grip. Stoyan pulled him into an embrace and said, "Whatever he is doing, he seems to have it under control."

"Is Kyra with him?" Yubi asked fretfully.

"I imagine she is."

"Why? Where are they going? What could they be doing?"

"I am sure we will hear about it when they return."

Stoyan's voice was calm, but the terrors of the previous year had not entirely evaporated from his contemplations. Worry was not pulsing violently from his bones to his skin, like it was inside of Yubi, but the small hairs on the back of his neck stood erect, and his jaw clenched with his puckered lips.

He took a deep inhale, followed by a curt sigh, then he spoke more to himself than to his son, "Vadim must know what he is doing. They will be well."

Many curious thoughts followed Vadim and Kyra as they rolled away, but no bodies. The kumpania remained in camp and went about the day as usefully as they could.

Back at the lake, at the very same spot as the day before, Vadim unhitched the horse and left Kyra to her memories. He did not ride again in free circles. Like most of the others, Kyra had already altered him fundamentally. After about twenty minutes of keeping his distance, he returned to Kyra, but not to hitch the horse and take her back. For the first time in his life, the past anchored him. He thought about Iraja. He thought about many things and many people from days gone by. He thought about Kyra, and about how, inch by inch, she had rooted herself into his heart. When he dismounted the horse and walked up to the porch, gazing at her with a depth of love, admiration, and confused wonder that was new to him, he realized how altered he was, how altered they all were, and he wondered how the little girl they had found in the field could have the power to change what had remained unchanged for centuries.

He crawled onto the porch and sat beside her. She seemed unaware of him until, with eyes still glossed over with memories, she lethargically drifted her hand toward him, until his hand was firmly in her grasp. Something in her touch, in the raw and open flow from her innermost self, through her palm, and into him, completed his transition. He looked out over the glistening surface and saw vividly what Kyra saw. He saw Iraja kneeling in the shallows, a newly cleaned girl in front of her. A wave of emotion surged from inside of him, finding, as its only port of escape, his eyes, which poured forth tears as they never had before.

He did not think only of the day at the soapy pond. Images of Iraja from their decades together, everything she did for him and was to him swam freely in his mind. With each intense memory, a pop of air shot through his nostrils. And with each pop from his nostrils came a tender squeeze from Kyra's hand. They both knew what the other was doing, and they cherished each other's company and their shared sorrow for their mutual loss.

Vadim could not have guessed how long they stayed like that, but when he came out of it, he came out fully. He transitioned radically into a very Roma state of mind, but energized beyond measure by what he had just experienced. He was ready to embrace the world around him with an agitated vigor that would not let him sit for another moment.

He expected Kyra to transition with him, but he had become much more like her than she had become like him. When he stood abruptly, he looked down at a girl weighed down by oppressive sorrow. He wanted so badly to inject her with a little of what he was feeling. It was because of her that he radiated with such excitement. She had anchored him to the past, but he was able to pull the past easily with him into the future. She was not yet able to do so.

He hopped from the porch and paced beside the vardo until he simply could not wait longer. He hitched the horse and pulled away from the lake, while Kyra remained as she sat, rocked and jostled by the hard wheels beneath her. She ran into the vardo and looked out the back window. As the lake shrunk behind them, she felt Iraja tear from her again. When it was gone from sight, she fell onto the bed and cried.

Vadim had never felt so beholden to another, yet the only gift of gratitude he wanted to give her was the one she was unable to accept — liberty from her oppressive sorrow. As he returned Kyra's vardo to its place in the camp, with confounded eyes pretending to go about their business, he knew that Mohács would have to wait. Kyra would not leave the lake, not yet, not until her spirit found a way to take it with her.

Kyra recovered enough that day to have conversations on mundane topics. What burned in the minds of the others was of a loftier nature. They wanted to speak to her of Mohács, and of the performances that would happen there, of her dancing and theirs, of their acrobatics and singing, and of all the things she had transformed in them before the winter froze it all in place.

Kyra did not have a single thought to commit to such things. Her mind was too weighed down by helpless indebtedness that had no viable avenue of resolution. She had not eaten since before Vadim broke from the camp and took her to fill the canisters two days earlier. Her regret was a potent and poisonous drug that numbed her to all other sensations. She felt no hunger. She felt no thirst. She felt no adolescent love for Yubi, and no excitement to experience and expand her new career.

CHAPTER TWENTY-FIVE
A STROKE OF THE THUMB

ON THE THIRD DAY, Vadim did not wait to be instructed. He hitched his horse to Kyra's vardo and pulled it out of formation while Kyra was still asleep inside. Jostled to alertness, she stumbled to the porch in her nightgown. It was the same nightgown Iraja had given her, the same one that her twelve-year-old figure could not fill when she wore it for the first time. She had since filled it admirably, and admired she was. But when she emerged from her vardo that morning, the nightgown seemed to hang again from her younger self.

Her weight loss was disturbingly apparent. When the door closed behind her, and Vadim looked back in response, he gasped at her skeletal form. He flung himself from his horse and fetched a piece of flatbread from his own tent. When he rushed it back to her, she was off the porch, leaning her back against the side of her vardo. He began to lift the bread in an offering to her, but she halted him with an order that surprised him.

"Manfri," she spoke in a rusty voice that frighteningly befitted her emaciated figure. She cleared her throat and a much more familiar voice repeated, "Manfri, I want to see Manfri."

Vadim's emergent need to feed her relaxed, and the hand with the flatbread lowered to his side. He was increasingly persuaded that the trips to the lake did her more harm than good. Kyra's request to see the old musician set him at ease. He allowed it to convince him that they would move forward to a healthier future and stop sitting on the sticky ashes of a decomposing past. He woke Manfri and relayed the request, then made his way with steady-breathed ease to his horse.

He had begun to unfasten the hitches when Manfri made it to Kyra. Vadim held his breath to hear the hushed words behind him. He did not hear what he had hoped, no order to push the caravan forward, toward the Danube.

She told Manfri, "I need you. I need you at the lake."

She confessed to the old musician that her mental images of Iraja were fading, that she could hardly pull a clear picture of Iraja's face from the receding pool of her memories.

"I need you to come with me and play the lullaby she used to sing."

"I don't know th—," he began.

"I need you!" she creaked more desperately.

Her position of leadership in the kumpania would have been enough for him to obey her. The wincing grimace on her face and the wretched creaking of her voice excited his compassion. He nodded to her and backed away, returning in less than a minute with his lyra and bow. Vadim heard the entire exchange. In the brief time Manfri was away, he refastened his horse to the hitches. He did not steer the horse from the porch of the vardo, but sadly mounted the creature's back, hoping that Manfri's contribution to the day might set Kyra at ease and return her and the caravan to course.

They were all concerned for her, and for themselves, but none more than Yubi. Poor Yubi! Each time the boy grew near to Kyra, something pulled her away from him. He never felt so "away" than when he watched her roll from the rising sun with Manfri and Vadim. Such a pathetically apt metaphor shone on the back of Kyra's vardo. She rolled away from brightness, away from the new day, away from their decided destination, to dwell on long gone moments of her past.

Only Vadim understood the reason for the daily excursions. But even if they had all been at the pond that day with her, Iraja, and Vadim, even if they had all contributed a hand to washing Kyra of the stench of Szanzar, they still would not have understood. To them, there was no debt owed by Kyra, not to Iraja or any of them. They saw in her a shining Roma. They were blind to the shackles that chained her to that lake, chained them all where they sat, and forbade them to explore the horizons beyond.

Yubi was the only exception. Only he saw the darkness inside of her. He was drawn to it. He loved it, and he would have been the perfect passenger to sit beside her, not Manfri, and not Vadim. As it was, he had no idea why she rode away from him each morning, why she did not eat, or why she demanded the company of Vadim and Manfri when *he* had always been her confidant.

As Kyra rolled away again, concerned curiosity filled the space between the tents and wagons. But curiosity was not *Yubi's* master. He was in the Herculean grasp of a much deeper emotion, one he did not fully understand, but one that had its fingers on each of his organs. As he watched her vardo diminish on the horizon, his stomach cramped. His lungs seized. His guts pinched. His brain went foggy, and his senses could not clearly detect the things around him. The following hour moved slowly, begrudgingly releasing each second into the past. In those cruel minutes, the grasp on Yubi tightened malevolently.

As they rumbled to the lake, Manfri sat in silence on Kyra's bed. He stared at her, waiting for some sign of what he should say. She stood and ran her fingertips over everything that was Iraja's, hoping to release her spirit into the air like a freshly agitated scent. Arriving at the lake, Vadim again performed his ritual. He pulled the front of the vardo to the shore, took the horse, and rode large laps, barely within sight. Kyra sat on the porch facing the water. Manfri sat beside her with his lyra and bow in hand, but with no idea what to play.

He locked his gaze on the side of Kyra's head as she stared forward. After several awkward minutes in this way, she turned to him. He was an old man and had seen many things, beautiful and horrid, in his many years caravanning across the region. Very little startled him, but her face, as she slowly and hauntingly turned her starved lips and sunken cheeks toward him, unsettled him deeply, and a shiver pulsed from his very bones to shake the bow in his hand.

They held each other's eyes for what seemed a moment to her and an eternity to him. She dropped her chin to her shoulder, drifted it forward again, raised her eyes to the water in front of them, and began to hum Iraja's lullaby. The tune was familiar to him. Before she finished the first phrase, he began to scratch his bow on the strings. Her hum faded seamlessly and was replaced elegantly by Manfri's lyra. The old Gypsy was keen of heart. As he played for Kyra and watched her gaze onto the water, the reason for his company became clear to him. He had not been there at the pond that day, yet an amazingly accurate image formed in his mind's eye as he followed Kyra's eyes to the water and he pictured his old friend bathing a young girl.

Although her adhesion to the past was still foreign to him, his new vision allowed him to serve her well. He angled his bow differently, trying to change the tone to best imitate Iraja's voice. She did not notice his efforts. Starvation, exhaustion, and extreme sorrowful guilt buried her thoughts and muffled her ears to the world around her.

Manfri watched her closely as he played, seeking some sign of improvement, some indication that his music revived her. He found no such thing in her stone-still and hollow, entranced gaze. His knowledge of his art was deep and filled with decades of experience. He employed every bit of it in his effort to recreate the voice of the dead with the instrument in his hands. He failed, and it frustrated him.

"Different strings... a different kind of bow," he thought to himself, "I could make the sound she needs, but not with what I have."

He played on, as well as he could, to motionless ears on a motionless head that seemed deaf to every flick of his bow.

Back at the camp, Yubi's blood churned excruciatingly through his veins. Regardless of where his eyes were and what was before them, he saw one thing only. He saw Kyra's gaunt figure and starving face. His father was in mid-sentence, talking to him about some topic he could not have recited later, when he bolted to the cooks, hoarded scraps of this-and-that into a sack, vaulted at full sprint onto his father's horse, and rode off at full gallop along the tracks left behind by Kyra's vardo.

Finding them easily, he rode right by Vadim, paying him no gesture, for Kyra's vardo was in sight and he saw nothing else. Vadim rode behind him, yelling at him not to interrupt. Yubi dismounted beside the vardo and marched to the porch, where he could make no sense of the scene before him. Manfri played on, while Kyra's dark, sunken eyes remained as they had been for an hour — pasted forward as if dead. Vadim remained mounted and took his horse into the shallows in front of the vardo.

He barely opened his mouth in protest to Yubi, when Yubi turned in a rage to him and yelled, "Go! Both of you, go back to the others!"

Yubi's word did not usually carry much weight in the kumpania, certainly not as much as Vadim's. But he screamed with an irrefutable authority that clearly indicated he was not going to yield. Vadim drew a deep inhale and, before releasing it, he considered Kyra's deteriorating condition. What he had been doing during the previous days was doing her no good. He yielded to the violence of Yubi's demand.

He gestured to Manfri with a nod. Manfri responded, creaking his old joints to his feet and crawling from the porch with his instrument in hand. Vadim took the lyra and bow from him, then pulled his passenger up to sit behind him on the horse. They both took one more glance to Yubi, as if to say, "I hope you know what you are doing, boy." As they rode toward the camp at a steady trot, Manfri stretched his neck to look behind him. Vadim did not. He focused forward with an unfamiliar feeling of helplessness. To the heart of the Roma, the sensation can only be compared to being captured and caged.

Yubi did not wait for them to be out of sight or sound. He tossed his sack of food onto the porch, then flung himself aboard with equal force. He stood where Manfri had sat, looking down at her while the sack of food sat as neglected by Kyra as she had once been by her family and neighbors. He did not stare at her long before his rage melted away. Yubi was Roma, and he had a Roma notion of beauty, a comprehensive notion of beauty. As he watched her gaze into God-knows-what, he did not see dark, drawn eyes or sunken cheeks. He did not see an emaciated figure. He saw the beauty of Kyra, her comprehensive beauty. He saw her heart and he saw her mind. He saw her hair and her skin, the way she pulled her feet beneath her skirt, and the way she wrapped her arms around her folded legs.

Contentious words that had demanded freedom from his clenched jaw evaporated away. He curled into a bookend pose on the opposite side of the porch. They both stared out over the water, but with very different minds on very different things. His thoughts were on her, but his eyes were not, so he did not see her turn her head to him. To her, it was as if he magically appeared there, or like a sudden and intense thought of him played tricks on her eyes. She peered at him, not sure if he was real. In a transition she did not notice, her thoughts left Iraja and turned to Yubi.

She had a strong urge to hold him, or to be held by him, but she could not move, like she was buried neck-deep in the hard ground. She struggled to break free of whatever invisible force locked her as she sat nauseated. It would not relent. It would not release her. She remained as his opposite bookend. She surely would have emptied her stomach, had there been anything within her to empty. She turned from him and returned her gaze to the lake.

The very instant after she turned from him, his eyes drifted to her. His urge to embrace her was as strong as hers was to be embraced, but no invisible force held him in place. He rolled, turning onto his knees then continuing to turn, until he ended sitting near her. Once settled to stillness beside her, he placed his hand on her elbow and ran it down her arm until he reached her hand. Her arms tensely gripped her legs. But when he took her hand and pried it from the other and interlaced his fingers with hers, her arms went limp, allowing him to unwrap her legs and pull her hand onto his lap.

She didn't unglue her eyes or shift her head in the slightest toward him. But she had yielded her hand to his care. Her next sign of being a living human came in the form of a slow and deep inhale, which she released with an even slower hummed whimper. To that sound, he pulled her hand to his lips and kissed her thumb knuckle. He held it to his lips for a few deep breaths, then returned their held hands to his lap.

Yubi's eyes made repeated journeys between her hand on his lap, the side of her face, and the sack of food that her wasting figure so desperately needed. He could make no demands of her and give her no orders. He only hoped that she would snap from her trance, thank him for his company, and devour the food he brought. That did not happen. Change came in a much subtler fashion. After nearly half an hour, sitting as they sat, she pulled her eyes from the water, sinking her gaze downward to her legs in front of her, then resting her chin on her knees.

Yubi scooted closer to her, pressed firmly hip to hip, as he placed her hand in his far hand and draped his near arm over her shoulders. He leaned his shoulder into her and tilted his head toward her head. Had she responded in kind, they would have rested their heads against each other. She did not. But she slowly tightened her grip on their interlaced fingers, so slowly that he did not notice until they were in an equally tight embrace of hands.

Looking over the water, as she had done for days, she was surprised to realize that her thoughts were not of Iraja, but of Yubi, not of being bathed in a pond, but of being taught Romani in the grass. She owed a debt. She was right about that, but Iraja was not the only creditor. The boy beside her had saved her life, and was later instrumental in transforming it. Her subconscious grip on his hand began a very intentional caress of her thumb against his.

That slight stroke of his thumb was enough of an invitation for him. Freeing his hand from her grip, he took the sack of food and placed it on his lap. She stretched out her legs, lowering her knees from beneath her chin. In the most casual manner, like two old friends sharing the most mundane moment, they divided the food between them into small piles on their laps and they ate together. Kyra could not eat much. When she stopped, he stopped. When their mouths were no longer occupied with essentials, they spoke. They talked casually of the minutest topics, as if continuing with an ordinary conversation from any ordinary day.

He stood slowly, looked down at her, and asked, "Are you ready?"

It was a complicated question with a multitude of meanings. She answered each of those meanings with a simple, "Yes."

Yubi offered his hand to her. As soon as she gripped it tightly, he hoisted her to her feet. He hopped from the porch and hitched his father's horse to the vardo. When he returned to the porch, she was inside. He had hoped to be seated at her hip as they rolled together back to the kumpania, but he was pleased with the victory he had already accomplished and felt in no position to demand more.

He turned them around and set them on the same tracks those same wheels had repeatedly trampled for days. After perhaps a dozen rotations of those wheels, the door to the vardo opened and Kyra appeared behind him. She ran her fingers through his hair then sat beside him. They swung their dangling feet in perfect synchronization, saying nothing and never looking toward each other. They both looked forward. They did so literally, and they did so figuratively. Yubi smiled widely in his triumph. Lavinia was right. His influence over her was profound, as were her obligations to him — to him and to them all.

Their approach was spotted from some distance, which was no accident. At any given point during the day, twenty eyes were posted in that direction. Quite the huddle of Roma greeted them and enveloped them like a stone plunged into deep and welcoming mud. There were two conspicuously absent members. Vadim and Manfri were not among them. Kyra inquired of them, and Stoyan informed her that they had ridden east together to the markets of the Danube.

Yubi shushed and shooed them all away. He brought her vardo to its place in the camp, opened the door for her, closed it behind her, and went about his day with a great deal of relief and self-congratulations. He passed near Lavinia, who smiled at him devilishly. He stopped and studied her face, trying to interpret the smirk. He raised his eyebrows and shook his head, as if to ask, "What is that look for?"

She closed the small gap between them with slow, intentional steps, patted him twice on the shoulder, and said, "Do you believe me now?"

He looked blankly at her. She let out a sigh, shook her head, and said, "Her heart is in your hand. Until you realize that, you cannot hold it as it ought to be held."

Yubi turned his palm upward and looked into his hand, half-expecting to see Kyra's bright and beating heart, or to see her in her entirety, tiny and fragile, curled up with her arms around her knees, just like she had sat on the porch near the lake. When he looked up from his empty palm, Lavinia was gone.

He heard Lavinia's voice shout from behind him, "Don't you forget it, boy."

A proud grin spread over his face. He held that same palm to his chest, and made his way dreamily to his tent.

Kyra spent the evening poring over Iraja's things, rubbing with her hands, seeing, smelling, and feeling those precious items they had shared. Already, the minute details of Iraja's face began to fade from distinction in her memory. She feared that eventually the vardo and all its contents, which she had turned into a shrine, would just be her own things. They would lose Iraja's smell. As they gained association with other things, people, and events, they would carry less pungently the spirit of Iraja. She feared that day, as she focused to stitch each item to a particular memory that would last.

CHAPTER TWENTY-SIX
THE DEBT TRANSFERRED

WITH KYRA BACK AMONG THEM, everybody was eager to progress, but they could not, not until Vadim and Manfri returned. For three more weeks they lingered in stagnation. There is a moment in the life of a Roma when, camped too long in one place, an unsettling intimacy develops with a particular plot of ground, with its view of the neighboring hills, with the nearby trees, when even the grass beneath them taunts them, whispering into their antsy ears, "You know me too well, and I know you."

Only the performers used this time wisely. Lavinia had her star dancer back and wasted no time working and reworking the performance. Stoyan had his high bar. He and Yubi pushed themselves to their physical limits experimenting and choreographing. It was an exciting time. What most of them did not know is that Stoyan and Lavinia had been collaborating during the days when Kyra was at the lake.

Stoyan had dreams of reviving the act he had with his wife — a glorious hybrid of dancing and acrobatics. If ever there was a dancer to do it, he was sure Kyra was it. Lavinia was not in agreement. She was loath to lose her extraordinary protégé to Stoyan's acrobatics act.

"Kyra is a dancer!" she reminded him, "Everybody can see that."

"And yet you must admit," he retorted, "she is much more than a *dancer.*"

Lavinia was insulted by the belittling tone he used with the word "dancer", and she contorted her lips to one side, tilted her head, and chastised him with her eyes.

"You know what I mean," he excused himself, accurately reading her gaze, "She is more than you. She is more than me. Let us see what she is capable of doing. You must admit, some of what she does is as much acrobatics as dancing."

She relaxed her stance, unable to refute him, and conceded, "You can have her once a week, but don't you injure her. I tell you, Stoyan, if she hobbles back to me in pain, I will pay it back on you tenfold."

Stoyan smiled, and his eyes rolled to the side in deep, imaginative thought.

"I don't know what you are thinking of doing," she interrupted, "but it looks dangerous."

They giggled together and parted as the dear friends they were.

But Kyra had no strength to experiment with acrobatics. Her days of fasting had taken their toll and she was too weak. Nevertheless, Stoyan took her for the few hours Lavinia would give her to him. These were delightful hours for Kyra. Stoyan and Yubi kept closed rehearsals. Nobody knew just what they would do in performance. As Kyra sat with the acrobats, discussing and theorizing plans, she was part of an exclusive circle, a circle of only three. Her sense of belonging was elevating. She had felt adored. She had felt revered. Not since Iraja died had she felt like family, like immediate family. In the intimate and secret company of the acrobats, she felt a sense of belonging similar to what she felt in Iraja's embrace. She also felt as if she had fallen into a past dream. It had always been the acrobats that fascinated her.

A few hours, one day a week, was all that Lavinia gave the acrobats. Kyra's strength returned in steady increments. As it did, Lavinia used every drop of it in rehearsal with the other dancers. Kyra's inclusion in the planned acrobatics remained theoretical. That is not to say it was undefined. By the end of the three weeks camped, the full act was plotted in detail. Kyra was excited but hardly credulous. The feats proposed by Stoyan and Yubi seemed impossible, not for them, nothing seemed impossible for them, but for her. She went along, throwing her doubts to the wind, as long as it remained theoretical.

It was nearly dusk, at the end of the three weeks, when the distant sounds of galloping hooves heralded the return of Vadim and Manfri. They were greeted with fervor by all. Stoyan lifted Kyra upon his shoulders and stood first among the reception party. Still at some distance, Vadim saw her, and she saw him. She saw the glow of a face shining with relief and delight. He dismounted the horse and ran to her, leaving Manfri on horseback. He grabbed her by the waist and took her from Stoyan's shoulders. Her color, her figure, her smile, all told him she was well.

Manfri laughed and clapped, reminding Vadim of his fellow traveler, still high upon a tall horse and unable to dismount on his own. Vadim directed others to help the old musician, then returned both arms to the effort of embracing Kyra.

The ride had been hard and strenuous for the old man, yet he maintained enough power in his frail body to yell, "Pitch the large tent!"

Hands of every age and size contributed to the effort. Even Milena's children assisted. But not Kyra. She was not permitted. She had her strength back and she wanted more than ever to be part of the kumpania in all that entails, however, she was shooed away each time her hand grabbed at rope or canvas. Yubi took notice, and knowing her as he did, he asked for her help. She responded, grabbing, tugging, and hoisting alongside him.

The large tent was up before the sun was fully down. It was lit from within more brightly than it had ever been. Whether the radiant light was from extra torches or from the hearts that gathered, I will leave for my readers to determine. In either case, it appeared as midday within. Once the entire kumpania was situated, Vadim took the floor and explained all that he and Manfri had done and seen during their travels. In the ports along the Danube, plague was withering, but life was not returning to normal. The massive loss of the labor class left fields unattended, crops unharvested, and markets scant of wares. In the wake of the plague, uncertainty dominated.

"These communities," Vadim informed them, "have little to offer us right now, and they have little need of what we offer. We should return to the southwest, to the sea and its ports."

The kumpania was Roma, if not by blood, then certainly by pride of identity. But they were also Hungarian, like birds who may fly over human borders at will but always return to the same nests in the same trees. They had been to the Croatian coast decades earlier, when Vadim was a boy. He spoke of a boy's experiences, romanticized by a man's faded memory. Oh, but he did so with charismatic flair, enough to convince even those whose memories were clearer. By the time he finished, the plan awaited only the nod of their queen. All eyes turned to Kyra. Kyra turned to Yubi who froze, without a gesture, so as not to sway her judgment. Kyra turned back to Vadim, and seeing in his eyes and hair glimpses of Iraja, she nodded her consent.

Discussions on the matter immediately erupted in several small pockets around the tent, until Vadim hushed them all, announcing, "We came back from the Danube with more than news!"

All eyes returned to him. He gestured to Manfri, who sat alone tuning his lyra.

Vadim continued, "Manfri sought one thing on the river's markets, one rare thing, and he found it."

Vadim set a stool at the center of the tent and bowed to Manfri. The old man waddled to the stool. He sat and waved the kumpania to gather more tightly. They huddled close, sitting on the ground like children. Manfri directed them to make space in front of him for Kyra. Once she was seated at his feet, he explained his reason for accompanying Vadim on the expedition. He was in search of a special kind of string for his lyra and a unique hair for his bow. He would not have left the river without them. He went on to explain the particular qualities of both and why they were important to him. He spoke in the technical terms of his trade and few understood. But they could see the obvious, that it brought a youthful glow to the old man.

Just as he began to bore them with the details, he raised his lyra to his lap and rested his bow on the strings. It was very different from how he usually held his instrument. When he began to scratch at the strings, every ear in the tent understood the necessity of the venture. Manfri played Iraja's lullaby. With the new strings and bow hair, and his new method of holding the lyra, he mimicked the tone of Iraja's voice to a haunting similarity. He played the lullaby with his eyes fixed on Kyra's face.

He still looked old. His hair was still white, his face deeply wrinkled, his nose still red and bloated, but there was a distinct and remarkable youthfulness about him as he played. As he thought of a young Iraja, he remembered a young Manfri. His heart beat like a crazed adolescent. If his heart was all that people could see of him, they would have thought him younger than Kyra.

Kyra closed her eyes and listened, wrapping her arms in front of her and caressing her own shoulders the way Iraja used to. She listened to Manfri play for her, and her thoughts, as he had hoped, were on Iraja. It was more than the new strings and bow hair, more than the way he held the instrument. The man's artistry was on brilliant display. Not only did he imitate Iraja's voice, he closely mimicked her spirit. In other words, he did what Kyra could not in her starving hours at the lake. He captured her. He captured Iraja and placed her on Kyra's lap.

Under the music, Kyra was again able to vividly picture every wrinkled contour of Iraja's face. Manfri returned Iraja to her. As Kyra's consciousness let go of her mind, it drifted in many different directions. By the time she seized her thoughts again, they were not on Iraja. They were on Manfri. She listened and watched him intently. She admired his skill, but what was more, she felt his love. Although it sounded like Iraja's voice that filled the tent, it was not Iraja's voice she heard. It was not Iraja's love she felt. It was Manfri's lyra. It was Manfri's love.

Her tears flowed, but not mournfully. They were the sort of tears one sheds when reunited with a lost loved one. Now, it was not at all the way of the Roma to cry for the dead, or to wrap their hearts so tightly in things of the past as to cause a flow of tears, but when Kyra opened her eyes and looked around her, each cheek glistened. It was in that moment she realized that she had also transformed them. She was not alone as she faced a future without Iraja, and the kumpania was not leaving their departed queen in some unmapped plot of Hungarian soil. They kept her as Kyra kept her.

Manfri concluded with a long note that faded so gently that Kyra could still imagine hearing it after the bow was lifted from the strings.

He set his lyra beside the stool and spoke softly to Kyra, so softly that only the few nearest could hear, "You see, my child, Iraja is still here. We take her with us to the sea."

"She is in your lyra," she smiled as she answered.

He added, "I see her nowhere more distinctly than in you. I keep my old friend in this vessel," as he gestured to her from head to toe, "and this is where I will find her when I need her company."

Kyra's heart was still bound by sorrow, still shackled to the weight of past pain, still burdened with debt. That is who she was, and no expanse of years with the Roma would change that. Despite that weight, her heart flew. It had the strength of wing, with Manfri's words, to carry any burden, to the sea, over mountains, anywhere. As she stood from her seated position, it rose higher, and with more wild freedom, than any Roma caravanning across the free fields of the world. As to her debt — she looked around her and saw many opportunities for repayment. She determined to repay her debt to Iraja by being for the kumpania what Iraja had been, or as close to it as she could. She had been placed on the vacant throne, but, under the large tent that evening, she sat upon it willingly and determined.

She quietly walked to Vadim and whispered to him, "We need to sleep. Tomorrow, we travel."

He repeated her words loudly, for all to hear. With purpose of step, they struck the large tent in the dark of night and made their way to their vardos and tents, obeying Kyra, sleeping and dreaming of Adriatic ports.

CHAPTER TWENTY-SEVEN
PERILOUS CELEBRITY

THE DRAVA RIVER HAD LONG BEEN THE BORDER between the kingdoms of Hungary and Croatia. Culturally, it very much still was. But in 1102, a succession crisis in the Kingdom of Croatia placed Hungarian King Coloman on the Croatian throne. The kingdoms were not united, not culturally and not politically. Hungary and Croatia were two separate kingdoms ruled by the same king. Such was still the case in the 1350s, when Kyra and her caravan of unique Gypsies returned to the settlements along the Drava.

The king was Louis I, a strong and ambitious Hungarian with a tender affinity for the Dalmatian coast and the Croatians who called it home. He spent more time sailing the Adriatic Sea than feasting in his Hungarian Castle. The Croatians felt his affection, and they recovered from the plague with a vengeance. They were inspired by their king, who himself fell ill with plague. Like Croatia herself, Louis survived and, in the wake of illness, surged to his greatest achievements. While Greater Europe reeled in the throes of a labor shortage, Croatia thrived. It enjoyed what historians now call its golden age.

Kyra and her kumpania lived a similar rebirth as they rolled, walked, and trotted toward Siklós and Harkány. It was not so much a return to those towns, for they were different people entirely from the ones that had visited the previous year. The difference became more distinct with every mile traveled. A strong aroma of innovation filled the camp each afternoon, a literal aroma as well as a figurative one, for two things had been purchased by Vadim and Manfri, the new strings and a box of eastern spices. The cooks wasted little time playing with the flavors the way a child plays with a new toy.

The jewelry makers experimented to astonishing effect. Manfri and the musicians rethought the creation of each and every note. The melodies were new. The chords were revolutionary. Even the strings themselves seemed determined to sound differently than before. Stoyan's mind was abuzz with feats even he was not sure were physically possible. Milena hid herself in a vardo and belted notes, opening her throat, restricting it, singing from the chest, then from the head, switching between them all in cascading scales, trying to find that new sound that would keep her at pace with the rest of them.

And the dancers — Lavinia yielded much control to Kyra. They were a creative duo at the dawn of an exciting partnership. Each time the wheels stopped rolling and were locked in place with wooden blocks, pungent newness wafted from every finger, mouth, foot, and eye. Although each was fully cocooned in a specific craft, they were all inspired by the untrodden spirit of the others.

It was their plan to revisit those Swabian communities that had been so profitable, then cross the river into Croatia and work their way to the sea. But travel was not their vocation, and it took a subservient position behind the things that happened while they camped. They went days at a time without moving at all. For this reason, movement was slow. In the thirteen weeks it took them to finally camp outside of Siklós, they developed a trove of new and exciting jewelry, foods, songs, stunts, and dances.

As promised by Lavinia, Stoyan took Kyra for a few hours each of those weeks. He planned, plotted, and described to her many tricks, most of which were new even to him and beyond anything he had performed with his wife. Oh, how thoroughly his mind disobeyed the mandate of Lavinia. These stunts were dangerous, hardly seeming possible to Kyra's ears. She listened, imagined, and nodded, silently feeling like she could more easily learn to turn herself inside out as perfect the skills he described like a giddy child.

He had already gained remarkable proficiency with his high bar. He swung giant loops around it, gripping the bar with both hands, then with one hand, releasing it on the upward swing and flying above it, then regrabbing it as he dropped. He had a notion of performing his giant loops with Kyra hanging from his waist. As he described how Kyra would release him in mid-swing, fly through the air, and roll across the ground as only Kyra could roll, even Yubi, whose imagination knew few limitations, winced incredulously.

At the end of their hours, it was all speculation and no practicality. Kyra was committed to being all the kumpania needed her to be, so she mustered enthusiasm for the impossible stunts and watched the acrobat glow with glorious ambition. Then she returned to Lavinia and the dancers to refine the very practical innovations occurring among them.

Although each group had their own craft. They were not uncooperative. In fact, they were interdependent. The new act of the dancers simply would not fit the old music, nor could the new music be dragged into the past by the old dancing. Patrin, the tailor, imagined new fashions for the performers and for them all. They shared in the innovations of the cooks and held exotic breath on their tongues as they debated within their own little circles. Every ingenious invention flavored every other. When they camped outside of Siklós, they were, in most ways, a group who had never been there before, and they could hardly wait to place it all in front of the same townsfolk they had bewildered and besotted the previous year.

In new, bright striped pants and a shirt that battled it for attention, Stoyan, the great barker, set out as he had before, to announce their arrival and muster excitement. Even this was hardly recognized by its recipients. The voice of a much younger man came from his weathered lips, one with an authentic ring of youthful delight. His siren call was seductive in the extreme. Many tried to follow him from the towns, back to the Roma camp, rather than gather at the determined date. He was as fleet as his horse, and he made it back to the camp alone. Such a stir of anticipation was left in his wake, one that ripened further in the three days before the planned bazaar.

It was early on a warm Friday afternoon when the first of them arrived at the camp. Everything was set differently than it had been. The wagons, open tents, and blankets were set in a tight crescent formation, crowned on both ends by a vardo, the two most colorful in the caravan, creating a sort of passageway through which the visitors must pass to see the attractions. This was Vadim's idea.

"In coming to see us," he had explained to them days earlier, "they must exit their lives and enter ours. They will not be walking around an open field with Roma wares upon it. They will be walking into a Roma kingdom, where nothing is familiar. Even the untouched sky above," he added with a wide-eyed whisper, "will appear foreign to them."

As the visitors approached, even the aromatic tang of the eastern spices seemed to stop at the border of their makeshift kingdom, waiting inside to pounce on the unsuspecting immigrants. Once that border was breached, each bewildered eye, ear, and nose felt swept into a dream — and not their own dream, for their imaginations could never have constructed such a scene. As the jewelry makers sat on their blankets, their sprawling dresses haloed them with new flamboyance. Colorful new patterns were stitched in bouncing textures.

Among Vadim's ideas was to present each visitor with a small sample of food. One step across the threshold of the colorful vardos, each one was gifted a piece of flatbread. It had been fried in exotic new spices that stung the palate, far more exciting than pleasant, the extraordinary flavor permeating through the mouth, into the sinuses, commandeering the blood, and storming into the brain like a powerful but benevolent army. It was an army of liberation, for it freed their confined consciousness to experience the bazaar unfettered by the petty details of their mundane lives. It worked just as Vadim imagined. Eyes were widened, both literally and metaphorically.

The next part of the experience was Kyra's idea. Rather than bombarding their guests with an immediate performance, the kumpania went about what appeared much like an ordinary day for them.

"Let them soak in it," she recommended, "... in us, in what we are and do. Let them feel fully relocated before we strike a note or dance a step."

They did precisely as their queen wanted. The visitors walked among them as they strung bracelets, tuned instruments, cooked and laughed, stretched and debated, as they fed their children and performed the necessities of a normal day. Each Roma paused to greet the guests and share a pleasantry before returning to what they were doing. It worked masterfully. The townspeople felt Roma, like they lived among them and traveled beside them from God-knows-what imagined location across the world.

Ernko, the kumpania's new Swabian blacksmith, was as fully transformed as the rest of them. He had not returned to his home when they encamped outside of Siklós. He was no longer a Swabian blacksmith. He still spoke German. He was much better with a hammer than with a noun or verb. He picked up enough Romani to greet his fellow Roma in the morning, congratulate them, and wish them peaceful sleep at the end of the day. That was all. Still, he dressed in Roma clothing and blended in every other way (except language) with those who had returned, like a mystical story, to the Drava River.

The tidal wave of newness unanchored his skills from what he had been taught by his master. He had long been able to repair or reproduce anything he saw. In the thirteen weeks of travel to the Drava, his hammer created things he had *not* seen, things that were conceived in *his* imagination before being born in his forge. The hubs of the wagons were capped with the brass heads of strange beasts whose likeness had never roamed any field or forest in the real world. Many additions to the craft of the jewelry makers were born of his head and worked in minute detail by the tiny, sharply pointed tools he invented for that purpose. Ernko presented himself like the rest of them, allowing his former neighbors to wander around him, watching him invent. He had a new Roma apron wrapped around him, and the strangely Roma fire in his forge was reflected in the distinctly Roma fire in his eyes.

Two hours after the first family entered the camp, it was filled with more people than it had a right to hold, each of them fully inside the Roma crescent. It was difficult to create a performance space, but this too was part of Kyra's plan. Rather than settling the audience to one side of the performance, they were allowed to experience it as the Roma do, to walk among it and around it.

It was a far more intimate presentation of their skills than any villager or townsperson had ever seen in the long history of the kumpania — or any kumpania for that matter. What they were doing had never been done. What they presented had never been seen. What they cooked had never been tasted. What they sold had never been fashioned. And what they were about to play, sing, and perform was entering the wider world for the very first time.

The music began as it did every afternoon for the past months, not with a well-placed note or boom of the drum, not meticulously timed to have the greatest effect. It began in conversation and debate among the musicians, while the dancers milled about them stretching and directing each other. Those nearest when it began must have felt themselves to be another Roma, with a flute in their hands, ready to contribute. Those farther away were drawn away from their current interest and toward the rising music the same way members of the kumpania are drawn to a rehearsal.

Not all could see. The crescent camp was too packed. But all heard. In squirming, shuffling waves, they all worked their way to view a portion of the performance up close. The happenings within the crescent were not only new and exciting to the people of Siklós and Harkány, it was all new to the kumpania. It was less of a performance given from one group of people to another than it was a shared experience by all within the womb of the colorful vardos.

With the spiced bread already convulsing their lips in fitful ecstasy, the colorful patterns on the skirts and vardos and the exotic brass faces on the wagon wheels in their eyes, and a melody that was both heavy with sorrow and yet savagely free whirling from Manfri's lyra, Milena sang. "Sang" is such an inept verb. It falls so short, but there is no word in this language or any other to describe the sounds that galloped fiercely from her throat. Dozens of widely varied vocal tones, some sounding less human than others, played in concert with each other, uniting in her mouth and springing as one from her tongue. If those who shared the experience would have closed their eyes and listened to her with a blank mind, it would have been easy to imagine not one vocalist but several, of differing form, some familiar, some strange.

Milena sang a new song, one she composed in silence and debuted in that moment, even to herself. The song was of a star that fell on a caravan of Roma, bringing a new darkness and a new light into their lives. It was sung in Romani, so the visitors understood none of it. They took it for an ancient Roma song passed through the generations. Most in the kumpania understood its meaning, knew it was a tribute to Kyra, and thought keenly of Kyra's influence on their lives as Milena sang. Others, including Kyra, were too enraptured by the sound to coherently piece together the words.

The scene was perfectly set for the dancers. If there was a tallest possible peak from which one could jump higher and farther than humanly possible, Kyra stood atop it, ready to leap to a place that no dancer had ever been, no artist had ever been. Lavinia led a single-file train of dancers through the thick crowd, like a worm burrowing its way through earth. Kyra was the last of them. They slithered their way as one to the center of the crescent, near Milena and the musicians. From there, they split and opened to a diamond shape, with Kyra in the middle, kneeling with her skirt billowing out from her waist. She looked downward and her hair fell over her face obscuring her identity. She looked like a praying angel, emerging from the peak of a colorfully patterned mountain to bestow a blessing upon the planet below her.

The dancers swayed and waved, kicked and rolled. The audience recognized their movements, not as theirs but as Kyra's. Their eyes leaped from one dancer's face to the next, looking for the "Wilde Jungfrauwe". The winter had not withered Kyra's celebrity in the region. It fertilized it. Whispers of "Wilde Jungfrauwe" waved out from the dancers and crashed against the wheeled walls of the crescent. As it did, the outside pushed inward, stirring the contents of the camp vigorously. But they did not disturb the dancers' sanctuary. The anticipation of Kyra's appearance made it sacred to them.

Kyra's position in the middle, her angelic pose and her obscured face, drew eyes to her as it was intended to do. One mouth at the end of a long, pointed arm shouted, "Wilde Jungfrauwe." Eyes followed the pointed arm, and when enough eyes were upon Kyra, Lavinia broke from the diamond and danced in circles around her. She spun and twirled, brushing Kyra with her skirt, as if trying to polish her for display. At last, she stood still beside the kneeling wonder and held her own skirt over Kyra, like paper and a bow over a gift.

Slowly, over what seemed like minutes, Lavinia pulled her skirt back to her legs, revealing Kyra, whose head was not down, whose hair no longer obscured her face. Kyra looked up boldly, but she did not stand. Lavinia resumed her place in the diamond that framed the featured attraction. Lavinia and the others expected an enthusiastic roar of "Wilde Jungfrauwe" but it did not come. There was no sound at all, but a silence. A silence that waved outward from Kyra's position. Silence and utter stillness. The shouting stopped. The talking stopped. The music stopped.

Kyra lifted her arms sharply and stiffly above her head and held them perfectly still, then waved them in boneless, pulsing ripples upward from her shoulders. What she did next came as a shock to all but Lavinia. Kyra's hands swam in complicated patterns from their perch high above her head to rest side by side on one of her hips. Her fingers worked to unfasten her skirt. She stood, leaving her skirt on the ground at her feet. She was wearing men's trousers, but of a bright rose color. The trousers went down midway from her knees to her bare feet.

She stepped away from her skirt, that skirt that had limited the language of her expressive body. She danced around the skirt, not as Lavinia did. In trousers, she could fling her legs suddenly. She could bend as never before. She lifted one knee to her armpit, then straightened her leg until her foot was above her head, as her hands had been. Like her arms, her leg waved bonelessly from the hip. The well-fitted trousers showed every curve, as her foot danced freely above her, while she balanced steadily on the other.

Her dancing foot came back to the ground like a leaf falling from high on a tree, drifting in a thoughtless breeze, and only the sound of the breeze accompanied it. Once it joined its partner on the grass, Kyra remembered her dream, when Iraja placed the tiny kumpania in her hand. That debt, that beautiful debt that she was so happy to owe, and so happy to repay to *her* people, balled up in the center of her heart then erupted outward to her extremities. The musicians struck a concerted note at the very moment, and the performance began.

Kyra danced. Perhaps it would be better to say Kyra did Kyra. It was so unlike anything that had ever worn the name "dance". Her legs took full advantage of their new freedom. The audience took no offense by her unconventional clothing. They did not see a woman dressed like a man. They saw a mystic creature too unearthly to be judged by human expectations, too free and too far above them all. Even the most prudent chambers of their hearts refused to cast judgment. Every portion of them, body and soul, stood in admiration and in hope of receiving some magical gift from the fascinating creature before them.

There were no chants, no other movement around her. The only movement was from those outside of view of her, shouldering their way to a better position. Most in the kumpania climbed atop wagons, vardos, and horses to witness the spectacle, in equal expectation of internal transformation.

When the music and dancing ended, a long silence covered the camp. It was silent but not placid. A corked agitation was bubbling. Without cue, the corked popped and the crowd erupted. They did not chant in unison, but shouted as covetous, self-interested individuals. They reached for Kyra and shouted the name they had given her. But they would not breach the diamond of dancers. They wanted her, yet feared her power over them. Kyra stood as she had stopped, with a heaving chest and a glistening face and neck. Her eyes looked around her for one target. She sought Yubi and his approval, of her dancing and of her stunt with the skirt.

Like Vadim, Ernko, Stoyan, and many others, Yubi watched from atop his vardo. The others foresaw the profits that would come. They saw the circle of moths drawn to the flame by some arcane instinct. As Yubi saw the crowd reach more desperately for her with every gasp of her recovering lungs, and he heard the things they shouted, his eyes saw a different metaphor, not helpless, fragile moths to a powerful flame that would consume them, but a band of wild dogs ravenously encircling his dearest friend, drawn to the succulence of her passion, wanting to sink their teeth into her heart, which was delicious to them.

A new and tyrannical brand of jealousy came upon him. As eager as he had been to see her dance before the world and shine her unique light, he was suddenly all the more desirous to hide her from humanity and hoard her for himself. The sensation surprised him. It struck him from behind and knocked the breath out of him. But he was no less captured by her performance than the rest. In fact, he experienced much more, and the duality of his emotions was straining.

He was inexpressibly proud of the glory on display in front of him, and more drawn to her than anyone within the crescent of the camp, for he saw deeper than the strange leaps, spins, and contortions. He saw the woman beneath it, and he knew what each movement was saying, as if it were a language they had made up together and shared with nobody. Everything and everyone seemed to stare at Kyra — the visitors, of course the visitors, but also the Roma, their horses and wagons, each brass face forged by Ernko, even the jewelry on display seemed sad to go to anyone else. The staring sun in the sky lit the way for the grass and trees to stare at Kyra, or so it seemed to Yubi.

Stoyan also saw the potential peril of the moment. To Yubi's delight and gratitude, he muscled his way to the diamond of dancers and whisked Kyra into the crowd, throwing a blanket around her shoulders and moving so quickly through the chaos that she was soon obscured, just another shifting figure in the Gypsy kingdom. He shoved her into his own crowded vardo and told her to rest there until after the acrobats' performance. As he closed the door behind him, it did little to mute the sounds from outside. Kyra did not hear everything that was shouted, but she heard enough, and the walls of Stoyan's vardo seemed like a paper castle. It concealed her, but it would hardly protect her.

CHAPTER TWENTY-EIGHT
A TRIO TO BE RECKONED WITH

KYRA'S DISAPPEARANCE ADDED MORE MYSTIQUE to her already mystical persona. The crowd was no longer interested in spiced foods or jewelry. They wanted Kyra and seemed violently committed to having her. Amid the tight, shoving bustle, Stoyan and the dancers erected the high bar in front of Milena's vardo, at the center of the crescent. Milena's husband and the other herders, with their deeply tanned faces, pushed the crowd back using their rough hands and herdsmen barking. Milena climbed atop her vardo and struck a piercing note with her voice. It was something between a commanding scream and an angelic blessing — not so much *between* the two as a combination of both.

There was one thing the whole kumpania knew. It would take something extraordinary to calm the frenzied passion of the crowd and return the bazaar to something both safe and profitable. Fortunately, they had just what they needed. They had Stoyan, Yubi, and the high bar. The acrobats joined Milena on her roof. Milena's long held note mellowed. It calmed, but there was still a commanding

273

quality to it that was not to be ignored. Her height above the crowd and her piercing voice drew the attention of everyone within the crescent.

When all eyes were on them, Stoyan removed his shirt. Short, balding, bow-legged, but sinuous and carrying a fire in his eyes that could be recognized from the farthest edges of the crowd, he silenced them. Milena drew a breath and resumed her pure note. Kyra noticed the sudden hush from inside the vardo. When Milena sang again, no wood or glass could get in the way. It sounded to Kyra like she was inside with her. She looked out of the window. The crescent formation gave her a view of the three of them standing together, but not nearly a satisfying view. She ignored Stoyan's advice and stepped onto the porch. She draped over the rail and gained the view she desired.

While Milena still pushed her second breath of piercing song, Stoyan looked to Yubi. Yubi nodded with a smile. Not only was the boy ready to present his new stunts, he was eager to divert the crowd from their desire for Kyra. When Milena exhausted her breath, she backed away satisfied, knowing she had cut through the chaos and steered the day back on track. She climbed down and joined her husband in holding a perimeter around the high bar.

The bar stood about ten feet from the vardo and was as high as the roof. Stoyan jumped belly-down from the roof. He caught the bar with both hands and swung with speed and force into four giant swings around the bar. It was clear the crowd had never seen anything like it. The fascinated "oohs" and "ahhs" spoke well enough to their success. Their guests were again guests, not intruders, and not hunters. For the moment, they thought of nothing but the amazing acrobatics happening in front of them.

After the four giant swings, Stoyan released the bar and flipped backward to land beside his son, on the roof of Milena's vardo. The sounds that followed from the audience were loud but controlled. They were again respectable townsfolk enjoying an exotic performance.

Kyra had seen some of the acrobats' new stunts, but not that. In light of the amazing feats of Stoyan and Yubi, she could not, for the life of her, understand any attraction to her. Her fear left her. In fact, she almost forgot about the tightly packed people standing between her and her dear friends. When Stoyan urged the crowd into a concerted, rhythmic clap by clapping his own hands above his head, Kyra joined like the rest of them.

Once the onlookers were able to keep their own anticipatory percussion, Stoyan stopped clapping and mounted the bar as he did before, but this time, he performed his giant swings splitting his legs apart at the top of the swing and closing them together at the bottom. After two such swings, Yubi leaped from the vardo and landed on his feet, balancing on the bar. Stoyan swung up quickly from the bottom and the crowd gasped. Just before his father would have smashed into him, knocking them both violently to the ground, Yubi jumped. Stoyan spread his legs again and Yubi cleared him, landing again on the bar.

The crowd gasped again as Stoyan came swinging to the top. Again Yubi jumped between his father's split legs. This went on for several more swings and jumps. Yubi added mid-air poses before landing. He jumped and spun, each time landing just in time to spring again and barely miss his father's next swing. After a dozen or so swings like this, Yubi jumped to the side, landing on the edge of the bar. Stoyan slowed his swing to a handstand at the top, bent at the waist, placing his feet on the bar, and rose to stand beside his son. The swell of appreciation from the guests was almost as uproarious as their shouts for Kyra had been.

Kyra had an idea, a risky one, but one she believed to be right. She snuck around the back of the vardo and stealthily followed the outside of the crescent. When she got to Milena's vardo, she climbed to the roof.

As she stood, she heard someone yell, "Wilde Jungfrauwe!"

She immediately gestured to the acrobats and began to clap. The crowd joined her in another ovation for the stunts they had just witnessed. Stoyan jumped backward off the bar, grabbed it and swung into a flip back onto the vardo, leaving Yubi as the solo feature on the bar.

Kyra and the others thought the high bar stunts were Stoyan's alone. She was as surprised and delighted as any to see what came next. Yubi bent down and laid himself flat on his belly along the bar. He tucked his hands under his chest and grabbed the bar with both hands tightly pressed together, one on each side of the bar, and pressed himself to a handstand. It was an amazing display of strength and balance.

But that was not all. He walked on his hands along the bar. At the end, he turned himself around and walked back to the other end. He turned again and walked to the center, where he allowed himself to fall away from the vardo, toward the crowd. He kept his grip and performed giant, sideways, circular swings, picking up speed and power with each full swing. After six swings, he released the bar near the top and flew to the vardo roof, spinning several times in the air before landing next to Kyra, on the opposite side of his father.

There they stood together, high on the roof of a colorful Gypsy vardo — the day's features, the Wilde Jungfrauwe, framed on either side by the most amazing acrobats any of their guests had ever imagined. Kyra's plan worked. Her appearance at the end of the acrobatic act set her again as she should be, not as an object of thoughtless desire, but as a subject of fascination and the recipient of admiration. She and the acrobats were a team, a family, and the audience could no longer separate them. They bowed together from the roof, and applause was the heart-felt appreciation of enthusiastic, but thoughtfully calm, visitors to their Gypsy Kingdom.

The three of them dismounted the vardo and made their way through the crowd together, leading people and money to the various wares for sale. Hands still reached to stroke Kyra's arms, shoulders, or any part of her they could reach, but they also reached for Stoyan and Yubi, not to grope and not to seize, but in curiosity, not sure if their hand would feel a human or some magical dust in the form of a human. Kyra was quite human, so were the acrobats. Nevertheless, their visitors withdrew their hands, staring at their own palms, wondering what might have passed from the magical Roma to them.

The unified clapping started by Stoyan had grown so loud that it drew more people from Siklós, almost emptying the town. Harkány was farther away, but it was heard by everyone on the road between the two towns, and they all came. By the time the sun went low, twice as many people had come to the camp as those who had witnessed the performances. The kumpania sold everything that was for sale and many things that were not. Incredible wealth came into the caravan that day, and although a hundred people begged them to stay longer, there was nothing left to sell, nothing left to gain from Siklós and Harkány.

They could not camp as they were. They broke from their crescent formations and assembled the caravan for travel. When they were ready to roll, the leaders gathered. Kyra was asleep in her vardo. Yubi woke her with a knock. When he opened the door, he said nothing. He simply stood and stared at her as she rose to her feet. She stood and stared back. His slowly lifted grin spoke of their many shared experiences. Her lifted grin in response added that day's exciting affairs atop the pile.

He reached a hand for her and said, "We need your permission…, your guidance."

She took his hand and he led her to her porch, where the leaders had gathered to see her.

Lavinia spoke up, "In light of today's... mmm... occurrences, we think it might be best to camp away from Siklós tonight. What do you say?"

During their travels, Kyra had seen fields and hills, mountains and forests. She had never been to the sea, and the Adriatic Sea sounded very alluring to her, an expanse of water so vast that its opposite shore is unimaginably distant. Yubi had explained to her that the Italian peninsula sat on its opposite side, that they could stand in water and look out toward Rome.

Kyra had had enough of provincial Swabians along the Drava, enough of Hungarian villages, enough of petty, ignorant tradesmen along the Danube. She was ready for the sea, and she told them, "I agree. Let us go around Siklós, to the south at top speed, until we reach the Drava."

Vadim informed her, "We cannot reach the Drava tonight."

"What is south of here?" she asked.

Vadim answered, "A thick forest lies between us and the river, but there are roads through it."

"No," she answered suddenly, "no roads. We can camp in the fields outside of the forest and get to the river tomorrow."

It would not have mattered much if they disagreed. They would have counseled her but obeyed her. As it was, they did not disagree. The plan was sound and it was safe. They packed the wealth tightly and caravanned south in the dark. About a mile of forest banded the banks of the Drava. They settled at the forest edge and set camp for the night. Most slept, some stayed up in conversation about the strange events of the day. Kyra sat on her bed, her heart too stirred to sleep.

She went to Stoyan and Yubi's tent and heard a loud snore from within. She put her lips to the canvas and whispered, "Good night."

Yubi's voice lifted above Stoyan's snore, answering her with the hint of an adolescent giggle in his voice, "Good night, Kyra."

She smiled widely, turned on her heels, skipped back to her vardo, and fell into a sound sleep, a sleep filled with dreams of swinging acrobats, chanting crowds, bustling port markets, and mighty ships on endless bodies of water.

CHAPTER TWENTY-NINE
RISING BLOSSOM

THE DAWN CAME IN A BLINK. Few slept for more than two hours. You would never know. The camp broke with energy and excitement. Croatia promised adventure, and the Dalmatian coast was notorious for exotic goods from across the continents. There was no reason to think the Croatians south of the Drava would be less enthusiastic than the Swabian settlements on the northern banks. But first, the river itself must be conquered.

The sun had barely shown its full form above the eastern horizon before the caravan was rolling again. They traveled west along the outer edge of the thick band of forest that girdled the river. When they were directly south of Harkány, they encountered a promising road through the forest. It was wide and welcoming, with sparse forestation on both sides, so that the path before them was well-lit by the rising sun. And where there is a road to a river, there is a bridge or a ferry.

It took less than an hour to reach the banks, and there on the other side was a ferry. The ferryman saw them but did not come for them. He stared and tried to make out what sort of people sought his service. Colorful vardos, flamboyant dresses, it was clear from that distance. He crossed halfway for a better look, but stopped and waited.

Vadim pulled Kyra to the edge of the water and suggested, "Yell to him in Hungarian. That might set him at ease."

Kyra hollered, but not in Hungarian or any language. Hungarian words clustered heavily in her belly but would not move toward her throat. She still could not bring herself to speak her native tongue. Few understood her reluctance. Stoyan understood, and his Hungarian sounded native enough.

He jogged to Kyra's side, wrapped an arm tightly around her shoulder, settled her anxiety, and shouted to the ferryman in Hungarian, "Hello brother!"

The ferryman eased closer to the northern bank, near enough to see the kind faces waiting. Stoyan added, "We have righteous business with the people of Croatia. Will you escort us on our way?"

Stoyan was hard for anyone to resist. His affection for the girl at his hip was spoken in the universal language of a fatherly embrace. Such charisma, such lightness of spirit and enthusiasm for life easily overcame the suspicions of the cautious ferryman. Those standing nearest the bank could see the smile that preceded the wave of his hand. He made his way in haste to the kumpania.

The ferry was long enough to easily take the vardos one at a time, but barely wide enough for two people shoulder-to-shoulder on either side. It was dangerous to cross the river inside of the vardos, so Vadim and Ernko crossed first with the children and two horses. The vardos and wagons followed with only one passenger standing beside each vehicle. After an hour, less than half of the caravan was across. The ferryman needed rest. He restored himself on the Hungarian side, where he was treated to food and song that expedited his recovery.

Kyra oversaw the provided services. It was quickly evident that she carried great authority, and the ferryman was as honored by her attention as if waited on by a queen in a palace. The riches of the caravan were on brilliant display around him, and he anticipated a generous fee. What the ferryman could not see was the inner turmoil churning within them. He could not see it and they could hardly understand it.

The kumpania was cut in two, divided by a river, but not for the first time. Yet, it was the first time any of them felt such panic by it. It was a foreign sensation to them, but not to Kyra. Each time she looked across the river to see the tiny figures of her friends waving back at her, she became suddenly and violently nauseous. They all felt it, and again they realized how deeply affected, how fundamentally altered they were by the hands of the young stowaway they had picked up two years earlier.

Such separations had never affected them so. The Roma never felt possessed by anyone, nor in possession of anyone, but the wide river dividing them seemed to separate their hearts from their minds and their bodies from their spirits. Each passing minute increased the sensation cruelly. It was a very Kyra-like emotion, and they all recognized Kyra in their shared feelings. But they were compassionate to the labors of the ferryman, and they served him until he was fully revived.

Once again on his feet and handling his ferry, he worked twice as quickly as before. In well under an hour, the kumpania were reunited in Croatia with what felt like a much wider world in front of them than behind them. The ferryman suggested a fee well above his usual price. Kyra told Vadim to double it. They paid the man more than he would have made in three months of manning his ferry. They kissed him and embraced him like old friends, then turned their backs to the ferry and the river and cut from the road, to the familiar arms of open country.

The first stop on their way to the coast was the town of Požega. It was almost forty miles from where they crossed the Drava. They had supplies for living well and traveling leisurely, so they caravanned for a few hours every afternoon. They took three days to get there, giving them three mornings to perfect their crafts, three afternoons to relish each other's company, and three nights to dream of the wonders ahead of them.

Lavinia had already been dreaming. Since they had left the crazed audience of their last performance, she began imagining more dramatic and breathtaking ways to present her star dancer. Just as Stoyan had incorporated Kyra into his act, Lavinia envisioned a way to put Stoyan into the dancing. She had discussed it with the other dancers while they were separated from the kumpania by the slow ferry. At dawn on the first morning in Croatia, Lavinia and the corps of dancers gathered around Kyra's vardo. They did not knock or call her name, but their excited murmur was alarm enough. Kyra awoke to the giggles and rising whispers of her dancing sisters and brothers.

She knew them all well and could accurately visualize each one of them and where they stood. It would be no slow, leisurely beginning to her day. By the time she opened her door, she was dressed to rehearse, with her rose-colored trousers beneath her dress. Lavinia told her nothing of her plans, but only extended her hand for Kyra to take. She escorted Kyra to Stoyan's tent, with the other dancers trailing behind like the tail of a comet.

Stoyan needed no rising murmurs to wake him. He was, as was consistent with him, already up and preparing for his day with the energetic excitement of a man half his age. With much on his mind, Yubi's nights were restless and it was not until the wee hours that he had finally found deep sleep. Stoyan met the dancers outside of the tent, and seeing in their faces that elaborate plans were in the works, he rushed them away from his sleeping son to hear their plans.

They made one more stop before trampling the ground for rehearsal. They went to Patrin, the tailor, a quiet old man, a hidden and internal man, who was so understated that Kyra could only recount three or four conversations with him in all of the time since they rescued his kumpania. His was a plain vardo. It was brown throughout. But within were colors enough for any foreign exotic palace. Fabric — trunks and rolls and folds of colorful fabric left him little room to move about. At each market and each bazaar since Vadim gifted him the sack of fabrics, Patrin had been collecting.

Lavinia went alone into his vardo, but before she did, she demanded Kyra's dress. With her pants underneath, she unfastened her dress and gave it obediently. Lavinia took it into Patrin's vardo and emerged seconds later without it. Curiosity about the dress was washed away by the general excitement, and they all paraded to their rehearsal space and trampled the grass together.

When the ground was ready, Lavinia gave her orders, "Stoyan, kneel down there, in the center."

The acrobat obeyed, and Lavinia walked to him, took his right hand, brought it to his ear, and turned his palm up. Still holding Stoyan's hand she gestured to Kyra with her head. Kyra walked curiously to stand in front of Stoyan.

"Now sit," Lavinia ordered her.

Stoyan understood what she wanted, and he smiled. Kyra sat on the ground where she stood.

"No, no, no," Lavinia impatiently corrected, "Here, on Stoyan's hand."

Kyra stood, turned her back to Stoyan, and perched herself on his hand.

Lavinia backed away from them, raised her hands upward, and directed, "Up, up, take her up."

Kyra had grown taller than Stoyan. Her figure had filled, and her muscles were dense. She knew Stoyan was strong, but doubted his ability to lift her above his head with one hand. She squealed as the old man stood quickly and thrusted her into the air. There she sat on his hand, atop his extended arm. She shook and squirmed and wrapped her ankles around his arm at the elbow.

"Hold still, child," Lavinia barked, "or you will break his arm."

Kyra clenched every muscle in her body. She locked. She froze. And there she sat, like a nervous goddess atop a ray of light.

"Now, relax," Lavinia calmly suggested, "Unwrap your legs from his arm. Cross one leg over the other and pose like a queen. Roll your shoulders back. Raise your chin. Smile."

One direction at a time, Kyra obeyed, until she sat regally looking down on the other dancers from above. She smiled, but not in obedience. Her smile was authentic.

Lavinia clapped her hands twice together and said to Stoyan, "Wonderful! That is how I want her. Now try again, taking her up slowly, very slowly."

"Slowly?" Stoyan questioned.

"Very slowly."

He lowered Kyra to the ground and returned to one knee. He shook his shoulders, made three wide circles with his right arm, returned his right hand palm up by his ear, repeated Lavinia's command, "Slowly," and nodded his head to Kyra. Kyra sat on his hand again and he repeated his earlier performance at one quarter the speed. He stood from his knee while raising his arm. There was no nervous squeal this time. Kyra's eyes were forward and upward. Her smile was wide and radiant. By the time Stoyan's arm was fully extended over his head, she sat again like a goddess, not a nervous one, but one in full command of all that she could see from her lofty perch.

Stoyan lowered her again to the ground and demanded, "If I am to do this many more times, I must eat first."

"Yes," Lavinia consented, "Get some food. Come back when you are ready."

The fire had just been lit, and Stoyan followed the smell of the wood to where he found the cooks beginning their day.

In his absence, Lavinia explained the new beginning of their act. She directed the dancers to circle around Kyra in deep lunges, with skirts and baggy trousers spread wide to obscure the acrobat who would be kneeling behind her. She told them to reach their arms in toward Kyra's narrow waist. The dancers, with their weight forward over a deeply bent leg and the other extended behind them, reached in toward Kyra with their heads down and their arms and fingertips extended, never quite touching her. Lavinia ordered them to peel away from her, beginning with their extended fingertips and opening outward like the blossoming petals of a flower.

Kyra suddenly remembered the mystery of her dress and the tailor who was ordered to alter it. With penetrating vision, she saw into Lavinia's mind and shouted out, "The dress! You mean to extend it to cover Stoyan when I am high in the air."

Lavinia's pride in her protégé erupted with her words, "Yes, my love. Yes."

She explained to the dancers what was to happen with the dress. By the time she finished, Stoyan had returned from his breakfast with the tailor beside him. Patrin held a cumbersome mound of bright red fabric. It looked like four dresses laid upon each other.

Lavinia began explaining how they would incorporate the extended dress into the one-handed lift, but Kyra, in her excitement, interrupted. She rambled, incoherently at points, often injecting words in Bulgarian and German where her Romani fell short. She would have appeared as a strange, unintelligible creature to any villager from any country, but Stoyan got the gist of the explanation. He nodded his head and assumed his position.

The dancers unraveled the dress and wrapped it over Stoyan and around Kyra's waist. Kyra fastened it tightly with a buckle. The dancers lunged and reached. Kyra sat on Stoyan's hand, and there they stayed, awaiting Lavinia's word.

"Now! Slowly," the director ordered.

The dancers peeled away as they had rehearsed, while Stoyan slowly stood and lifted the seated queen above his head. The dress had been extended perfectly and hung down to one inch off the ground, entirely obscuring the acrobat beneath it. Kyra looked like a long-legged giant, descended from some smoky, arcane mountain for the first time in centuries. She unbuckled the dress, and the dancers each grabbed a portion of it. They opened it from behind Kyra and walked it forward in front of her, holding it in a taut, straight line above their heads, like a curtain, obscuring Kyra from the waist down and entirely hiding the acrobat beneath her. The dancer to the far left of the line yanked on the dress as the others released it. It flew out of sight like smoke that instantly dissipates, revealing Kyra in her trousers, perched on her acrobat.

It went exactly as Lavinia had envisioned it. But she had no time to revel in her success. Her mind was cluttered with ideas that needed organizing.

"Alright, alright," she said to Stoyan, "Let her down. Go. Take her and come up with some of your stunts."

"Stunts? What sort of stunts?" he questioned.

"With her over your head, like your old act. You remember."

He did remember, and he took Kyra tenderly by the hand and led her to his rehearsal space. When they got there, Yubi was still asleep.

"Troubled boy," Stoyan spoke out loud, "he needs to rise and help us. It will be good for him."

Stoyan went into his tent. Kyra stood awkwardly outside, wanting to hear what might be said inside, but trying not to actively listen. She heard stirring but no words. A few minutes later, Yubi came out of the tent. He stood and stared at her. She stared back. She thought she had said "Good morning," several times but she had not, and neither had he. The moment was finally broken when Stoyan came out of the tent.

"Son," he asked, "would you get Vadim? We will need more hands for this."

Yubi kept his eyes locked on Kyra while he whispered, "Vadim."

Kyra, staring back with equal intensity, whispered back, "Vadim." She shivered herself free and said more forcefully, "Your father thinks we need Vadim."

Yubi shook free of his trance and spoke, "Vadim? Yes, we need Vadim. I will get him."

Kyra giggled and Stoyan shook his head. Yubi ran to find Vadim, and Stoyan began to explain his ideas to Kyra.

"Like your old act?" Kyra questioned him, "What did Lavinia mean?"

"She was speaking of the act I had with my wife. It was dancing and acrobatics. She danced. She danced on my hands and on my shoulders. I spun her and threw her, flipped over her and flipped her over me."

"I cannot do that!" Kyra protested.

"No," he answered, "not in one day. Let us begin with some different poses as you sit on my hand."

Together, they worked out a few poses and transitions, simple ones from her seated position that could be done without danger. Vadim and Yubi joined them as Kyra sat on a stool and practiced.

With Yubi on one side and Vadim on the other, Stoyan lifted Kyra above his head. As he turned slowly, she went through her choreographed poses, falling once into Vadim's arms and once into Yubi's, learning and adjusting, until it was ready to show to Lavinia.

Before taking it to the captain of the dancers, the four of them huddled and recovered, while Stoyan told stories of his years performing with his wife. He was so clearly still in love, in love with a memory, with a phantom he could not touch, could not spin or lift or flip over his head. But he spoke with giggles not tears. As he regaled them with such tender tales of his love, Yubi thought of his mother, and he thought of Kyra. The feelings Stoyan described were not unknown to him. Kyra was no phantom. She was flesh and blood, and seated beside him. But to Yubi, she was as phantom-like as any living creature could be, like smoke he wanted to grasp in his hand but knew he could not.

Kyra could not visualize Yubi's mother. She could not picture a young Stoyan. The faces she placed on the stories being told were ones she knew well — hers and Yubi's.

CHAPTER THIRTY
INTO HIS FATHER'S SHOES

LIVELY AND RESOLUTE ACTIVITY swarmed around the morning camp. There were miles to cover and a seductive future pulling them. They were so industrious in the hours between waking and traveling that the rolling caravan featured none of the clapping and singing that had drawn Kyra to them years earlier. The summer had not yet fully yielded to the fall, and the days were long. They camped after a few hours of travel with a long, bright afternoon still ahead of them.

The less strenuous professions returned to work. The dancers and acrobats did not. They ate and slept. When the sun went too low to work, the herders and jewelry makers raised the large tent and set the inside for a grand gathering. They gathered in the evening, but it was not grand. It was a calm recovery, with light conversation and sober planning.

When the morning came, they were reenergized. Stoyan joined the dancers, and Yubi, not having his father to rehearse with, sat and watched. Lavinia completed construction of the act, beginning with the long dress and the blossoming stunt with Stoyan. Once Kyra was on her own feet and with the other dancers, Stoyan was no longer needed. He tried to bring his son back to the high bar and their own rehearsal, but Yubi would not budge. He watched Kyra dance. He watched her rest and receive instructions. He watched her laugh with her fellow dancers, and he laughed with them. He was very much in love and he lingered near Kyra all morning. Stoyan worked on his high bar, but he worked alone.

In the afternoon, they traveled. In the evening they gathered. In the night, they slept. On the third morning in Croatia, they started again. Lavinia wanted Kyra to end the act the way she began it, high on Stoyan's hand, wrapped in her long red dress. She kept Stoyan from his high bar and rehearsed all morning. In the hour before travel, Stoyan was determined to work on some new stunts.

His idea was this. Yubi would stand on the bar, as he had in the last performance, and jump over his swinging father. But on Yubi's last jump, he would grab his father and ride him around the bar in one giant swing. Stoyan could have performed the stunt easily. He had the strength, but not after a full morning of lifting Kyra. Nevertheless, he attempted it, but when Yubi grabbed him and they swung under the bar, Stoyan's right shoulder gave out. It dislocated, and both acrobats flew from the bar and careened across the ground.

Yubi was fine. He thought his father had simply lost his grip, and he began to laugh. He was silenced by the scream that followed. It was one, short, loud scream. Stoyan stood quickly and Yubi could see the deformity of the shoulder. The herders were the first to respond to the scream. Milena's husband forced the shoulder back into place. Patrin fashioned a sling, and the cooks mixed herbs and spices to reduce the pain. Once all of this was done, the kumpania took a breath and considered the situation.

Stoyan was badly injured. There could be no acrobatics act, and Kyra had no high perch to begin her dance.

Travel that afternoon was painful for Stoyan. Kyra placed him in her own bed and wrapped him tightly. She rode with him and read to him until he slept. That evening, they arrived outside of Požega. They camped with no idea how to proceed. Stoyan slept in Kyra's bed, while Kyra dozed in and out of sleep seated on her trunk. In the morning, Lavinia wasted no time replacing Stoyan. Only one in the kumpania had the strength to do what Stoyan could do. She pulled Yubi from his tent and dragged him to Kyra's vardo, shouting for Kyra to put on her dancing trousers.

When Kyra came down, Lavinia grabbed her with her other hand and tugged both of them to the dancing space. The other dancers had already trampled the grass and were ready with the long dress. There was no need for instructions. Yubi had watched the rehearsals and he knew what Lavinia wanted from him. He knelt as his father had. Kyra took her seat on his hand, Yubi hoisted her high. He was not as stable a platform as his father had been. He dropped Kyra. She fell upon his chest and they both crashed to the ground.

They were fine. Nobody was hurt, so Lavinia demanded another try. They planned a small, introductory performance that afternoon, and she had no patience. Yubi knelt again and offered his hand. Kyra went up again, more securely, but when she tried to shift to her next pose, he lost her again. This time he was prepared for the fall. He caught her around the waist with his left arm and set her gently to her feet.

Again and again they tried, increasing their success gradually. They spent more time piled awkwardly upon each other than her posing like a mystical queen. But, by late morning, they had nearly perfected the stunts. Yubi had nothing else to do. He could not perform his acrobatics

Stefan Scheuermann

without his father. He was, for the time, a dancer, or at least a part of the dancers' performance. He could not have been happier, and he could not remember a more exciting day. He spent the morning with Kyra in his arms, focusing upon her and she upon him.

It was usually Stoyan who rode into town to declare their presence and advertise their bazaar. Nobody else knew quite how to do it. Kyra chose Vadim to ride into Požega. When he returned in mid-afternoon, he came with only two families. But once they were there, they were treated to the charismatic barking of Stoyan. The injured acrobat could not ride, but he could stand upon a wagon and command attention as well as ever.

Five adults and a total of eleven children, that was their intimate audience that day. And they were treated like royalty. They sampled Romani foods, listened to Romani music, and watched the most innovative hybrid of Romani dancing and acrobatics ever seen on a European field.

The lift went up perfectly. Kyra blossomed out of the other dancers exactly as Lavinia had envisioned it. The guests cheered for Kyra like she was the most important person in the world. When Yubi put her down, he did not stay to watch her dance. He went behind a vardo and waited until he was needed for the ending. Kyra noticed his absence. She noticed more than that. Yubi seemed suddenly angry. He seemed bitter, and she had no idea why. He did not rejoin the dancers at the end and lift Kyra into her final pose the way they had rehearsed.

Kyra's new choreography was a blend of her own unique movements and ancient Romani steps taught to her by Lavinia. The small audience loved it. They shouted and cheered. They were no less enamored than the Swabians who called her "Wilde Jungfrauwe", but their love for her was calmer. After the performance, they wanted to be near her, to get a close look into those eyes that burned with such

293

passionate and painful freedom. They had no chance. Kyra took her bow and left the dancers to find Yubi.

She found him in a calm and casual conversation with one of the herders. Kyra expected to find a very different sort of boy. There was no angst, no brooding. When he turned and saw Kyra, he commented on the success of the lift. He gave no excuse for leaving abruptly, no apology for failing to come back to finish the act. He smiled as if quite pleased with the performance. Kyra was not sure how to confront him.

She began simply, "The ending... the lift at the end."

His smile went sour, and he expressed in forced self-pity, "I am sure it ended well enough without me. I am of little use now that my father is injured."

"You are of use to me... to the act. I am supposed to end high above the crowd, with my long dress wrapped around my waist."

"But they saw that already. It is how you began."

"And it is how Lavinia wants me to end."

His face went from sour to grave. He gazed deeply into her eyes and asked, "What do *you* want, Kyra?"

The question surprised her, and she did not know how to answer.

He prodded, "Does it matter what Lavinia wants, or any of us? What do *you* want, Kyra?"

There was such harsh taunting in his voice and in his words. Kyra's eyes reddened. Her eyebrows furled and she rolled her lips into her mouth, biting on them while she thought frantically for a response. The herder and all the others nearby scooted away from the tension and left the two of them alone.

Kyra's clenched face relaxed, and she matched the sober gravity of his expression, as she answered slowly and lowly, "I want you to finish what you started."

She spoke in a double-meaning. She thought of his commitment to her act. Of course she thought of that. But she thought more keenly of other commitments, of other things he had started, things that started two years earlier, when he sat in the grass, spoke to her in Hungarian, and listened to the horrors of her past. She thought of things begun more recently, in the past year, when budding romance began showing its color through the green casing of childhood.

The brief silence that followed her words was broken by her sudden gasp, as she wondered if he understood both meanings. Sheepishly, she pulled her shoulders in and raised her lower lip, wrinkling her chin, but she kept her grave stare into his eyes. It was clear that she would say no more until he had. At the moment, the key was in his hands.

She judged his insightfulness correctly. He caught her full meaning. He was embarrassed. As she continued to gaze at him, embarrassment turned to mortification.

He spoke suddenly and much more loudly than necessary, "You are right! I should follow through with what I begin. I will be ready early tomorrow for rehearsal."

She expected more. She stared and waited for more. He grabbed her arm, squeezed firmly three times, let go, and walked away to check on his father. She was frustrated, but she understood. He was an acrobat without an act to perform. Stoyan was not young. Although he spoke of a speedy return, it was unlikely. It was possible the shoulder would never heal fully. Yubi knew this. They all knew. The great young acrobat felt like little more than a prop in Lavinia's act. Lavinia's penetrating vision saw it early, and she was already contemplating how to incorporate the range of his talents.

The rest of the day went much as expected. The guests bought very little, but enthusiastically promised to bring their neighbors the following afternoon. They left well before dusk, and the kumpania took the rare opportunity for a long sleep. The camp was dark and silent less than an hour after sundown.

Yubi was true to his word. Lavinia did not have to fetch him. He beat her to the rehearsal ground. He beat them all. When they gathered, he gave a quick apology to the other dancers for failing to finish the act. They were eager to forgive him and move forward. To guarantee Yubi's attendance, Lavinia added some acrobatics. She set her dancers in their circle with Kyra squatting low in the center. Yubi was to flip over the circle and land in the center, crouching behind Kyra before performing the opening lift.

Lavinia set a series of sporadic stunts for Yubi to perform between and around the dancers throughout the act. It was not what she envisioned. She envisioned something similar to what Stoyan dreamed for Kyra, though she had not the skills to teach it, or even clearly imagine it. What she wanted for Yubi and Kyra was something like Stoyan's old act with Yubi's mother.

The rehearsal that morning was light-hearted and successful. In the late morning, as promised, a much larger crowd arrived. They trickled in over the course of two hours, being entertained by food, stories, and music. When the time was right and enough had gathered, the old barker resumed his duties. Stoyan felt much better, well enough to rally the hearts of their guests into a frenzy. The people of Požega were Croatian, but most of them understood Hungarian. Stoyan spoke both perfectly, and he bounced between the two languages, not because he struggled with vocabulary, but simply to impress them. He threw in occasional words in languages they did not know, just to give the moment an exotic air.

Stoyan had them so prepared for wonders that no magic would have surprised them. They did not get magic from their hosts. They got a mournfully soulful lyra, a rich, multi-layered voice, a seductively agile corps of dancers, a powerful young acrobat, and they got Kyra. When she rose like a giant in her long, red dress, their eyes widened and they gasped. Just when they got used to the delights of the dancers, their palates were cleansed by a flying flip from Yubi — sometimes high into the air, sometimes across a wide expanse of ground, and sometimes over dancers.

It was all very exciting, but when Kyra danced alone, when she alone held the breaths of the audience, Yubi turned away. He would not watch her dance. He would not watch the reaction of the crowd. He faced away from it all until it was again his turn. When the act was finished and the crowd gathered tightly around them, shouting for Kyra and praising her strange beauty, Yubi slunk away. Much of the praise was his to bask in, but he left it quickly and quietly. Stoyan would not let her pursue him. He held Kyra with his one good arm and kept her where she needed to be — among her thick and boisterous mob of wealthy patrons.

When she had performed her duties, and the guests were being entertained by other attractions, Kyra found Yubi near his tent. He was trying to erect his father's high bar alone, and he was failing.

Kyra wasted no time confronting him, "You watch me rehearse, but you will not watch me perform. You are fun and happy in rehearsal, but not in performance."

He responded before his inhibitions could censor his honesty, "I love… I love watching you dance… and I hate it."

She stared in confusion with a blank face that he could not read, so he continued, "When you rehearse, I feel like you are dancing for me, like you are trying to tell me something."

At those words, Kyra's heart jolted, not from his feelings for her, but from her feelings for him. Not until that moment did she realize that she did indeed dance for him, whether or not he was watching. Each wave and flick of her body *was* an attempt to speak to him. Even when her dancing spoke of the horrors of her past, it spoke those horrors to Yubi, her only confidant.

He pressed on with difficulty, "But when you dance for the crowds, you speak to them. You dance for them. They shout their love. They make their offers. They want to take you from me... from the kumpania, and cage you for themselves inside of their buildings. Oh yes, they shout of love, but they do not *understand* love. They do not understand *you*."

As he went on, she subconsciously held her hand over her mouth, as if trying to hide whatever response her mouth might give. When he finished, she dropped her hand and said, "You understand me."

"I do, which is why I hate when you dance for them."

"I don't dance for them. I never do. I dance in front of them. I dance *for* the kumpania."

Her response was not entirely true, but it was true enough to satisfy her, and it was close enough to what he hoped to hear to satisfy him.

Stoyan was nearby, near enough to get the gist of their conversation. It was the final justification he needed. His injury, the loss of Yubi's act, the tension between the two of them, it was all he needed to fulfill an old dream and revive the routines he had done with his wife in a new generation of Roma. Once impassioned by an idea, his resolution was unshakeable. He did not know that Lavinia had the same plan and waited only for the right moment to discuss it with him.

The crowds remained later than the day before, but by dusk, the camp was empty of all visitors. The kumpania settled quickly to sleep, all but two of them. Stoyan snuck from his tent to find Lavinia. She startled him with her tall dark figure the moment he stepped out. Neither had to pitch the idea. Somehow, they both knew. They had only to discuss the details, which they did until the wee hours of the morning.

The new day brightened on Kyra's fifteenth birthday. She had no notion of the anniversary, and no notion that a dramatic change in her life had been plotted through the night.

CHAPTER THIRTY-ONE
THE VENETIANS

POŽEGA WAS A SHALLOW WELL into which they could only dip their bucket a few times. One more day there, one more performance, then Stoyan and Lavinia could begin placing their ideas on Kyra and Yubi while they continued to travel to the sea.

The third day was less fruitful than they had hoped. The visitors to their bazaar were the same faces as the day before, the same purses with no more to spend. They were enthusiastic, but the kumpania profited little. This in no way diminished the efforts put in by the performers. They carried plenty of wealth with them already. They performed from their hearts for the sole purpose of altering the lives of those fortunate enough to witness them.

There was something gained that day that none of them realized at the time. Two visitors to their camp were not from Požega. In fact, they had only arrived there three weeks earlier. A young man and woman, brother and sister, fellow travelers and performers, watched with eager interest. They skirted the edges, obscurely watching, learning, and evaluating. They said nothing the entire afternoon, keeping their foreign accents confined within them. They were not Roma. They had never caravanned with the Roma, but the liberty of the Roma lifestyle, the passion with which the Roma performed, and Kyra - most especially Kyra - intrigued them. They left as the others left, having neither done nor said anything of notice.

When the camp was again their own, the entire kumpania shared a collective restlessness. They were tired, but not too tired to travel. The rattling and rolling energized them. Their eyes were forward and they left Požega behind them, but not entirely. Something of Požega followed them as they rolled slowly west — a Venetian brother and sister. The siblings walked at pace, each carrying a large bundle over a shoulder. They kept their distance, waiting for the perfect moment to present themselves.

The moon rose earlier that evening. It was already high in the sky when the sun went away. The caravan stopped as the orange glow of sunset gave way to the bright and silvery cast of the moon. As the kumpania began to set their camp, the Venetians walked boldly forward. They did not want to appear threatening, with a slinking, stalking approach. Appearing quite comfortable and casual, they strolled into the camp.

The herders surrounded them with their long staffs and stern, weathered faces. Stoyan walked up to them with his injured arm wrapped tightly to his side and Kyra behind him, looking over his shoulder. Seeing Kyra, the brother laid down his bundle and began to clap. The sister followed in kind.

They were old enough to have the finished, chiseled features of adulthood, but young enough to sparkle with magical youthfulness under the bright moon. They were handsome, quite beautiful and alluring, enough for several of the kumpania to wonder how they might appear under the full light of the sun.

In broken Croatian, spoken in a thick Venetian accent, the brother introduced himself, "I Luca and this my sister, Chiara. We saw performance outside Požega."

Medieval Venetian was a sister language of Italian, and Stoyan knew that their surprise visitors would understand Italian perfectly. It was a language he knew well.

He told them, "I recognize you from the Požegan crowd. Požega is behind us. We are moving on. What is it we can do for you now?"

Luca smiled in delight to hear Stoyan's Italian, and he answered, "We too are performers. We seek a new company. It seems to us that you could use more... you could use us."

Fewer than five in the kumpania knew Italian. The nature of the conversation was a mystery to them, but Luca's calm and friendly demeanor coupled well with his beauty to settle their apprehensions.

Stoyan called for Yubi and told him in Italian so the siblings would understand, "Son, take their bundles and pitch them a tent for the night."

He turned back to Luca and instructed, "You and your sister have traveled hard. No business tonight. Sleep under our care and we will speak in the morning."

Not another word passed between them that night. Yubi obeyed his father. Luca and Chiara were settled and sleeping within a quarter of an hour. There was much to learn and much to determine in the morning. Stoyan did not know what the young Venetians could do, but he knew that the loss of his high bar act left a large hole, and he was willing to try anything that might help fill it.

It was well after sunrise when Luca and Chiara emerged from the tent. The kumpania were already hours into their day, cooking, sewing, hammering, and fiddling. Stoyan and Yubi were huddled together with Lavinia, debating which of Stoyan's fantastic ideas were actually possible for human bodies to do. They were not at the place in camp where the dancers rehearsed. They were near Stoyan's vardo, where the acrobats rehearsed. Stoyan envisioned an acrobatic act with some dancing, and he needed Lavinia's contribution. Lavinia wanted a dance performance with some acrobatics. Stoyan's words carried more weight. Kyra was to be trained in acrobatics, specifically, an acrobatic duet with Yubi.

Kyra was dressed in her performance trousers. She was warmed and stretched and ready to place herself into Yubi's hands when she left her vardo. As she walked toward the acrobats, Milena caught up with her.

She walked beside her and commented under her breath, "It is too bad you don't sing so well or play an instrument. You could be all of us at once."

Kyra scrunched her nose in confusion and asked, "What do you mean?"

Milena cocked her head to one side, as if to say, "Come now, don't be modest." Kyra was poor at reading physical expressions, so Milena explained clearly, "It is no wonder Lavinia has taken you in. You are Iraja's daughter. I find it astonishing that Stoyan covets you so. He has a peculiar tenderness toward you."

Kyra, feeling insulted by Milena, and not for the first time, asked, "Why is it strange he should want me?"

"You misunderstand me, child. One does not join an acrobatic act. You are born into an acrobatic family or you are not a Roma acrobat. That is how it has always been. Stoyan does not recruit. That is why his son is his only partner. Do you see now how strange it is? By recruiting you into his act, he is inviting you into his family... forever. Iraja is gone, and now it seems that you are Stoyan's daughter. It is an incredible honor. I hope you deserve it."

As Milena walked away from her, Kyra felt an intense blend of insult and praise. She fully sensed the honor of Stoyan's affection, but could not think what else she could do to earn Milena's, nor could she recall a single word, action, or gesture on her part that could explain the continued coldness between them, just as the singer was beginning to warm to her. It was also not in Kyra's character to disregard the bleak in favor of the bright. No matter how thickly wrapped she was in the warmth she received from the kumpania or the crowds that flocked to them, Milena's coldness cut through it and touched Kyra's heart with a chill.

The chill dissipated with her first glance at the acrobats and Lavinia. Stoyan could have told her to turn herself inside out. She would have tried her best to do so. She was ready to obey him like a daughter.

Stoyan and Lavinia decided to begin the act as they had in Požega, with the long dress and one-handed lift. As Stoyan began to describe to Kyra what was next, Luca and Chiara joined them. They did not seem to care what they might be interrupting, nor did they waste time with morning pleasantries. They threw their bundles to the ground and began unpacking the accouterments of their trade. As if their beauty was not intriguing enough, they displayed scorched torches and staffs, and a chain connected to an oil lamp.

Yubi and Kyra struggled to imagine what was to be done with the items in front of them. Stoyan and Lavinia knew well that their new friends were fire artists. The fire arts were rare and thrilling to audiences. Lavinia maintained a healthy skepticism of the newcomers, but Stoyan, always the flamboyant showman, was sold. Without his stunts on display, the fire artists could add a needed flare to the kumpania.

Stoyan gestured to the items on the ground, took one long stride backward, and said, "Well, our young friends, let us see what you do with these tools of yours."

Lavinia's Italian was weaker than Stoyan's, but she understood, and in an attempt to gently tamp down his excitement, she suggested, "It is early, Stoyan. Let us talk with them first and get to know each other."

There was a brief stare-down between them before Luca interrupted, "No, no, we don't mind. We have been waiting all night to show you."

The guests were mysterious, having arrived behind them in the dark of night. Their complexions were radiant olive. The tools on the ground looked exciting. The addition of a language Kyra did not understand gave the final brush of exoticism to the moment. The fine hairs across her arms and neck stood tall in anticipation.

Luca picked up the charred torch and held it out toward his sister. Chiara pulled from the bundle a small, hand-held contraption. She held it against the torch and squeezed. It clicked, it sparked, and it ignited the oil soaked torch. Chiara stepped behind Luca and pulled his shirt off his back. Luca held his hand over the flame, then ran the torch slowly under his arm, across his chest and abdomen, and under his chin. As the flames licked his eyebrows, he did not flinch. In fact, he smiled. He turned his devilishly handsome smile toward Kyra.

Her lungs involuntarily betrayed her feelings with a sudden gasp followed by a choppy sigh. Kyra was not alone in her admiration. Others had gathered, and similar gasps were heard in concert around them. Only one of them seemed to matter to Luca. He kept his face toward Kyra as he withdrew the torch from his face.

There were no burns, no redness, not on his face, not on his chest nor on his arm. Intrigued in the extreme, Kyra stepped to Luca and inspected his skin. She touched his face and found no more warmth than a face should provide. She did the same with the other places the flame had touched. He held his hand out for her inspection. She ran her fingertips down his arm and across his chest.

The inspection was purely academic, but still discomforted Lavinia, who took Kyra by her other hand

and pulled her back, saying in Romani, "Slow down, child. We do not know these people."

Yubi took Kyra by the waist and told her in Romani, "We need to rehearse. Leave the newcomers to the others."

Stoyan corrected his son, telling him in Italian, "Son, it is rude to speak in front of our new friends in a language they do not understand."

Kyra did not understand, but she pulled from Yubi, took two steps toward Luca, and asked him in German, "Do you speak German?"

Luca slowly lifted the same devilish grin before answering in German, "We do."

Kyra turned back to Yubi, and in a voice more like her much younger self, she asked him, "Do you hear that?"

Yubi did not answer.

She pulled on his wrist and demanded, "You *must* teach me more German."

Yubi answered in Romani, "What we must do is prepare our new act. We have little time to get it ready for an audience."

Yubi exaggerated. The next stop was Zagreb, about ninety miles away. At their leisure rate of travel of only a few hours a day, it would take them almost two weeks. It was plenty of time. It was a different sort of urgency Yubi felt, a much more immediate one.

Lavinia read him well and excused them from the Venetians in crude Italian, saying, "We are happy you travel with us. There is time before Zagreb. Now we dance with Kyra and Yubi. Please excuse us."

Chiara timidly bowed and backed away, but Luca asked if he could remain and watch the rehearsal. Before a protest could be lodged by Yubi or Lavinia, Stoyan gave his hearty consent.

Yubi was in no mood to dance, not with Luca sitting and watching. Stoyan's enthusiasm was not matched by the others. He giddily described his ideas. They tried a few stunts. None went well. Lavinia recognized the futility and recommended they try again the next day. When the rehearsal broke, Yubi asked Kyra to join him for a language lesson. There was a sparsely wooded field to their right and a thickening forest to the left. The field looked more welcoming, but the forest was more secluded.

"In the forest?" he asked her.

"Yes please," she replied, "I must learn more German. I have many things to say to them and so many things to ask."

Yubi knew why she wanted to expand her German. It was not to speak to Ernko, whose Romani improved daily. She wanted to speak to Luca and Chiara. They went alone into the forest. It was a sour victory, but one he seized nonetheless. He had a powerful need to serve her and a stronger one to have her to himself. They found a little hidden spot. It would have been quite romantic had romance been the purpose of the outing.

A strange and volatile chemistry brewed inside of Yubi. Many of their happiest moments together were in their private language lessons. He had her to himself behind the cover of trees. But with each new phrase, he prepared her to bond more tightly with the strangers who had joined them in the night. Yubi viewed the Venetians no differently than he viewed the Swabians who shouted for her and called her "Wilde Jungfrauwe". As they sat together in the woods, never had he wanted so badly to hoist her into his arms and run away with her.

When they finished the lesson in the forest and rejoined the camp, Kyra sought Chiara. She wanted to practice her new phrases on her first. Chiara stood alone between two wagons, doing nothing, simply standing. Kyra addressed her in German. Chiara looked at her but did not respond. Kyra prodded further, asking her how she was and what she was doing. Chiara shook her head and replied in Venetian.

Kyra gave her German one more try, asking her, "Do you understand me? Do you know German?"

Chiara stared blank-faced at her. It was clear that the sister did not know all that the brother knew. Frustrated, Kyra ordered the caravan in motion, though it was still early and many in the kumpania were busy. They obeyed her, stopped what they were doing, staged the caravan for travel, and rolled forward toward Zagreb. Kyra spent their traveling hours alone in her vardo, trying to understand the strange agitation in her heart. As the sun set, they stopped and set camp for the night. They had not traveled far. Their path was hilly and densely wooded.

It was a cold autumn night, but Yubi spent it sitting on the ground, leaning his back against a wheel of Kyra's vardo, watching and waiting for who-knows-what. It was far from a restful night, and he awoke at sunrise stiff-backed and weak-legged. His eyes had just opened when Lavinia reached out with her hand and helped him to his feet.

She whispered to him, "If we are to set this act of yours, we must get away to do it, away from the Venetian."

She knocked softly on the side of Kyra's vardo until the door opened slowly. She did not wait for Kyra to show her face.

She demanded, "Come my dear, dress quickly and join me." She turned to Yubi and ordered him, "Get your father, and do it quietly."

Once the four of them were gathered together, Lavinia laid forth her plan, "Stoyan, get two horses. We are going over the hill to the north, just the four of us, and we are not coming back until we have set this new act."

There were no protests. Kyra woke Vadim and told him they would be gone all day. She ordered him not to come for them. Stoyan came to them riding his horse and leading another by the reins. Kyra tried to mount behind him, but Lavinia beat her to it. She pushed Kyra aside to take her place in front of Stoyan, seizing the reins from his one good hand. Kyra took the reins of the other horse, and Yubi mounted behind her.

"Hold tightly to her, son," Stoyan warned, "She rides fiercely."

Stoyan winked at Kyra then spurred his horse into action. Kyra did the same, and the four of them rode north, through forest and over wooded hills.

About an hour later, they came to a clear valley. The sun was high enough to set the lush grass aglow. In her years with the kumpania, she had traveled far and seen many things. Never had she beheld such a magical place. Dark trees surrounded the bright valley. In the center of the sun-filled valley, the air was much warmer than at the camp.

"This place is magical," she said aloud.

"Yes," Lavinia answered, "and we must do magical work while we are here."

The ride pained Stoyan's injury, and he was clearly worn down by it, but his face was bright and eager. They trampled a plot of ground and began. There were no gawking young fire artists, no bustling camp, only the sweet and dulcet sounds of wild nature. They began as they did in Požega, with Kyra seated high on Yubi's outstretched hand. From there the act changed entirely. It delighted Kyra and Yubi both to watch Stoyan and Lavinia working together, blending their crafts into one another.

From the high lift, Yubi lowered Kyra to his shoulder. She draped backward around his neck like a bony scarf. He wrapped an arm around her ribs and flipped her slowly and gently to her feet. They executed the stunt flawlessly. Delighted with the progress, Lavinia and Stoyan put their heads together again.

Lavinia wanted a romantic dance between them, one that captured Roma love. Stoyan wanted acrobatic lifts and stunts that would thrill the most hardened audience. What they produced over the following hours was a seamless blend of both visions. Stoyan did not want to end it as it began, with Kyra seated on Yubi's hand. He wanted something grander, something higher. Yubi lunged deeply. Kyra placed a foot onto his bent leg, then stepped up onto his shoulders. On his shoulders, she was not much higher.

"No... more," Stoyan demanded, "Let her stand on both hands and lift her above your head."

They did as he instructed. She was much higher above the ground than before.

"No, still not enough," he grunted, "Ahh! One hand. Yes, one foot on one hand."

Kyra was terrified. She gingerly pulled her left foot from Yubi's left hand and lifted it in the air beside her.

"Higher!" Stoyan shouted with widening eyes, "Lift your foot above your head."

Kyra slowly raised her leg, but before it reached the height of her waist, fear waved across her, causing her body to tremble and shake. Yubi struggled to keep her in the air.

"Hold still!" he shouted.

She froze, and Yubi regained her balance. He raised his other hand and she stepped her left foot into it. It was not the glorious image Stoyan asked for, not yet, but there she was still, standing tall atop his fully extended hands.

It was a magnificent sight. None of them knew Kyra was terrified until she shouted down in a faltering voice, "How do I get down?"

Her legs began to shake beneath her, wobbling Yubi's arms. Stoyan could not help. His right shoulder was still useless. Lavinia could not have caught her from such a drop. Neither of them were needed. Yubi threw Kyra's feet to the side and she fell. She fell right into his arms with a high-pitched screech. He caught her as gently as if he had scooped her out of her bed from a dead sleep.

She held her breath as he caught her, and held it still as she laid across his arms. It was not until he dropped his forehead to hers and said, "I have you," that she released her held breath and wrapped her arms tightly around him. It was exactly the romantic ending to the act that Lavinia wanted.

"Yes my lovelies," she said, "just like that. Then turn from the crowd and carry her out of sight."

Mimicking a performance, he turned away from Stoyan and Lavinia and carried her slowly in the opposite direction. Her face rested on his shoulder, nestled against his neck. Her hair flowed down his side like a silky brown sash. Her eyes were squeezed shut in an expression of ardent Roma love. Kyra was many things, but she was no actress. Acting of any kind was not among her talents. Lavinia and Stoyan knew this, and they knew the authenticity of her love by the intensely devoted look on her face. Yubi stopped and stood with his back to his father and Lavinia. He continued to hold Kyra, and she continued to squeeze him as the teachers applauded and praised them.

Yubi and Kyra remained like a romantic statue until Stoyan shouted, "Well done. Now, let's do it again while it is still fresh in your minds."

They rehearsed the entire routine two more times. The terror of the final lift did not subside in the slightest. Each attempt to stand on one of his hands and lift her other leg above her head went much like the first. She wobbled and put her lifted foot back in Yubi's hand before she could get it waist-high. Her relief to be safely in his arms at the end did not subside either, nor the tenderness with which they held each other at the end.

When they were done, the two young performers hardly had the strength to mount the horse. They rode back to the camp the same way they rode away — with Kyra commanding the horse and Yubi holding tightly to her from behind. To both Kyra and Yubi, the embrace that held him to her felt differently at the end of the day. To Yubi, it was more possessive, more gluttonously embracing. To

Kyra, the sensation was more mysterious. It was in the realm of her heart, and her mind could not place it. Although her eyes remained ahead of her as she rode, her thoughts were comprehensively on the arms wrapped around her, those arms that had caught her safely out of the air.

CHAPTER THIRTY-TWO
THE MEANING OF A TOUCH

THE FOUR OF THEM ARRIVED BACK to a curious camp and many demands to see what they had accomplished while they were away. Both Kyra and Yubi were physically done for. A performance for the kumpania would have been dangerous. Stoyan ordered them both to bed. The order was given loudly for all to hear, but it was given in Romani. All walked away, knowing they would have to wait — all but Luca and Chiara. They did not understand, and they stood in anticipation.

Stoyan translated for them. He told them that the acrobatic dance would be shown to the kumpania the following morning.

Luca stood tall and spoke with too much comfort for new company, too much familiarity, "I would like to see it now. I have shown you some of what I can do. Now I want to see Kyra."

"*Yubi* and Kyra need to rest. It is a dangerous act that requires their strength. You can see it tomorrow with everyone else."

Luca did not back down. He surprised Stoyan, persisting, "I am sure they could show me part of it."

Chiara interrupted, "Brother, I think he knows best. Afterall, he—"

Her thought was cut short by the harsh glare Luca gave her. There was distinct, domineering cruelty in his eyes. Chiara turned her head and flinched, as if expecting to be struck. Stoyan took one step in her defense, but Luca wrapped his arm around her, kissed her head, and laughed. When he turned back to Stoyan, his manner had softened.

"Of course," he said lightly, "my sister is right. You know best."

Stoyan eyed him up and down suspiciously, trying to determine if he misunderstood what he had just witnessed. The moment was awkward. Luca broke it with a reverent bow and a warm smile. He thanked Stoyan for taking them in, feeding them, and giving them a soft place to lay their heads. Chiara remained timidly in her brother's embrace.

"I am sure," Luca told him, "that you will be pleased with our fire act. I am sorry I came on strong. I was fascinated by what I saw in Požega, and I am excited to see how you have put a Gypsy dancer and acrobat together. I would like to see how I might include her... include them both..."

Stoyan cut him short, "We have a long afternoon of travel ahead of us. I am going to rest."

Luca bowed again. Chiara followed in kind. Stoyan returned a shallow bow and walked away from them.

Yubi escorted Kyra to her vardo. They shared a long embrace, each focusing on the breaths of the other. When they released each other, Yubi congratulated her on the success of the morning. She returned the sentiment, gave him one last squeeze, turned from him and closed herself in her vardo.

Yubi arrived at his tent exactly as Stoyan did. Stoyan crawled in first, but Yubi did not follow him. He needed to be alone with his swirling thoughts. He climbed into their cluttered vardo and shut out the world. Lounged across their possessions, he thought. He thought about Kyra's face nestled against his neck. He evaluated every squeeze, every sigh, every breath, trying to read her, trying to understand her. His pondering bore no fruit, but exhausted his mind to match his body, and he fell asleep.

He was uncertain of Kyra's feelings, but all too aware of his own, and his dreams reflected them cruelly. He dreamed the kumpania was camped at the very point where they first found Kyra. Kyra stood in the grass as she had on that day, filthy and hungry. She was not the twelve year old child, but the Kyra of fifteen. He ran to her, but before he reached her, Iraja appeared like a ghost and wrapped her in an embrace, entirely obscuring her from view. The old woman began to shrivel and reduce. She turned to dust and blew away with the wind. Kyra was gone.

Yubi screamed for her until his attention was drawn to the closing door of Iraja's vardo. There stood Kyra on the porch, blushing radiantly in a bright red skirt and pristinely white blouse. She reached for him. He ran to her and offered his hand for her to sit upon. She sat, and he lifted her above his head and carried her to a trampled circle of grass. They performed many thrilling and many tender stunts together.

When he put her down, holding her hand, he heard the wild applause of a crowd in front of them. They shouted, "Wilde Jungfrauwe!" He looked up to them, but did not see a crowd of Swabians. He saw a crowd of corpses. They were the dead of Szanzar, with plague sores on their necks, ashen gray skin, sunken eyes, and drawn, shriveled cheeks. Their cheers turned to pathetic begging.

"Come back, Kyra," they demanded, "Come back to us. Come back!"

They dove and fell on her, grasping, moaning, and demanding through their grinding teeth, "Come back to us, Kyra. You belong to us."

They pulled her from his grasp and crawled on her, covering her beneath a mound of rotting bodies. Yubi tried to pull them off of her. He tried furiously, but could not lift them.

A voice came from behind him, speaking Romani, but in a strong Venetian accent, "Move boy, I have her now."

Luca ran up from behind him, swinging a whip made of pure flame. He snapped the whip at the pile of corpses, flicking them off of Kyra one at a time, until there, lying alone on the grass, curled into a ball, was Kyra. Luca picked her up with his one free hand and ran several steps away from Yubi. Yubi ran after them, but Luca turned and snapped his fiery whip. It caught Yubi in the eye, sending fire into his skull, burning him from the inside. He was blinded. He screamed a horrid cry as the fire within him spread to his fingertips and toes, finally bursting through his skin until he was nothing but a collapsing pile of burning flesh.

He awoke screaming the same horrid cry. It was only then, as he slowly recovered his wits, that he realized he was screaming her name. He was screaming, "Kyra!" Stoyan burst into the vardo and fell upon his son. He held Yubi's head, kissed him, and gently shushed him until he regained a normal rate of breath. Stoyan continued to hold his son for another quarter of an hour, until they both heard the bustle of the kumpania, striking the camp and preparing the caravan for travel.

Stoyan shot up quickly and told his son, "An idle mind can be poisonous. There is work to be done, and I think it is best if you do it."

When they entered the open air, the kumpania was hard at work. Kyra was helping Vadim hitch his horse to her vardo. To Yubi's surprise, Luca and Chiara were striking a tent. They were rolling it and packing it with obvious skill. Luca was not hanging near Kyra, not making demands, though she was mere steps away. He was in light conversation with his sister, while they both worked for the good of the kumpania. The sight did much to relieve Stoyan. He watched in admiration until he had all but forgotten the tense exchange just a few hours earlier.

Kyra rode on Vadim's horse with an inexplicable need to push forward into the night. Each time someone recommended they stop and camp, she rebuffed. Weary and travel-sore, under the scant light of a quarter moon, they obeyed her. Luca distracted and entertained them with a sample of his fire act. He lit the lamp attached to the chain. Walking beside the caravan, he swung it over his head, making a circle of light. To his right, to his left, in a figure 8 over his head, he swung the lamp. He was tireless, and the dark hours seemed less strenuous and passed quickly.

Luca made a point of lingering beside Kyra. She was not immune to the spectacle, as she stared at the majesty of fire in the hands of an artist. It soothed her as it soothed the others. When it was nearly midnight, she finally gave her blessing to camp. They traveled for another half an hour before finding a plot of land that was suitable, flat enough and with sparse forestation.

As they set camp, Luca helped the others. Once everything else was done, he pitched the tent given to him and Chiara. He did much that night to ingratiate himself to the kumpania. By the time he crawled into his tent, he was very much one of them. Before he did, he escorted Kyra to her vardo.

He helped her onto her porch and said in German, "You need to sleep. I expect to see you dance in the morning."

The comment was strangely presumptuous, but Kyra was too tired to consider it in depth, and she went to bed without giving it another thought. Yubi too was very tired, but he could not easily fall asleep. When he finally did, his poor mind ran him through variations of that same awful dream. He awoke in the morning without the scream, but with every bit of the anguish.

The morning was a race between two young men, a race for Kyra's attention. The sun had not fully breached the horizon when Yubi went to Kyra. Luca was already there, leaning against the side of the vardo, waiting quietly for her to rise. Yubi was angry at first, but then he smiled as he realized that even Luca would not presume to wake her. The fire artist was dynamic, charismatic, talented, and handsome, but he was not of the kumpania. He did not have the familiarity Yubi had.

Yubi grinned at him, climbed the ladder of the porch, gave the door a single knock, and let himself inside, closing the door behind him. Kyra still slept soundly. Yubi sat on the edge of the bed and gently rubbed her shoulder until she calmly woke and turned to wish him a good morning. Kyra dressed quickly and was ready to meet the day. Yubi was reluctant to let her. He knew Luca waited just outside, while he was inside with Kyra. He wanted to rub Luca's nose in it. He sat on the bed and asked her questions about each little trinket in the vardo.

It was at points an awkward hour of forced conversation, the purpose of which Kyra could not imagine, but she humored him. When they finally emerged, Luca was not there. Such a glorious sensation of victory Yubi felt. He drew a deep inhale and let it out slowly as he scanned the newly lit world around him, as if he was master of it all. Kyra cocked an eyebrow atop an inquisitive face. She giggled, punched him in the arm, grabbed his wrist, and yanked him to the ladder. He realized how ridiculous he must have looked. He regained his humility and followed her lead.

Lavinia saw them dismount the porch and ran to them, saying, "Finally! I do not know what you two were plotting in there, but I am ready to see it in action. Move quickly. We have to make up time."

She yelled for Stoyan, who quickly joined them. The call also summoned Luca. The five of them found a flat spot of grassy ground beside the camp. They stomped the grass and prepared a rehearsal space.

Lavinia, Stoyan, and Luca backed to the edge of the space. Kyra and Yubi huddled in the center and whispered to each other, secretly discussing details of their performance. When they were both quite satisfied, Yubi kneeled down and Kyra sat upon his hand.

"Wait! Not yet!" Lavinia shouted, "Today we must add music."

She ran from the circle and fetched Manfri. While the old man tuned his lyra, Yubi stood and wrapped both arms around Kyra from behind. When Manfri was ready to play, he plopped himself on the ground and scratched a long steady note. Yubi went back to one knee and offered his palm to Kyra. She sat. He lifted. And the act began. While Kyra was in his hands, Yubi forgot about fire artists and nightmares. He forgot about amorous crowds. The only thing on his mind was Kyra and the thrilling, dangerous stunts they performed together.

Milena heard the lyra and responded. She began singing before she came into view. She walked up to stand beside Manfri, placed a hand on his shoulder, and wove intricate harmonies with the lyra. It was a portrait of complexly braided disciplines. Dancing blended with acrobatics, an expertly bowed lyra threaded through it, and the voice of all voices wound and wrapped it all together. It was not long before the other musicians and dancers gathered to watch. In several pairs and pockets, they mumbled ideas for their own integration into the revolutionary artistry on display.

Luca also planned and plotted, but he did it alone and in silence. When the act was done, everyone rushed the circle and competed to push their own ideas forward. Amid the conversational chaos, Luca walked to within three inches of Kyra's face. He congratulated her, praising her artistry and her beauty. As he did, he wrapped his fingers around her arm. He squeezed then relaxed his grip, then ran his hand up her arm softly, over her shoulder to the base of her neck.

Kyra felt tinglingly alive. Her heart thrilled, but the nature of the thrill was uncertain. Whether her pulse was raised by some premonition of excited joy yet to come or from the vile touch of a profane hand, she could not tell. In either case, her pounding heart tried to leave her chest with every beat. Her skin became hyper-aware of the slightest breeze. Her eyes darted and circled in search of no particular target. And her lungs frantically drew breaths, as if there were only a few left in the world.

Amid the bustle, only Manfri witnessed it. He tucked his lyra under his arm, walked closely beside Kyra, and whispered as he passed, "Better alone than in bad company."

The comment sobered her immediately from her stupor and provided food for abundant thought. Kyra excused herself and walked away without a backward glance. In his arrogance, Luca assumed she was overwhelmed by his charm and in a romantic fluster. But Kyra was no Chiara. She was not the simple little creature he thought she was. He could not begin to imagine the complexity of her mind, let alone the mysterious workings of her heart.

With a swirling, cluttered mind, Kyra walked to the circle of jewelry makers. She sat beside them and offered to help in the ways they had taught her. It had been a long time since she sat and worked with them. Their delight in her company showed resplendently in their smiles. The slow and redundant motions, the sliding of beads, the loops and the knots, were exactly what Kyra needed. The conversations were not thrilling. The work was not dangerous. Like the rest of the kumpania, the jewelry makers evolved their craft under Kyra's influence. But it was a slow, quiet, subtle evolution.

Her sudden disappearance after the rehearsal was an enigma to Yubi. By the time he discovered she was gone, she was nestled between two jewelry makers, deeply focused on tying a knot. He watched her, chewing his fingernails to the quick. But as he watched her, he saw the comfort. He saw the ease of mind and spirit plainly on her. Her happiness always had a powerful effect on him, and she looked happy. She looked peaceful as she smiled and conversed comfortably with the jewelry makers. He was not like Luca, or like anyone who wanted Kyra's attention. He would not dare interrupt her peace, not even with love. He took her lead and joined the herders in mundane conversations.

Kyra savored the company of the jewelry makers for two hours. She took her meal with them, and ordered the caravan in motion well before planned. She remained among them until she gave the order to roll. She did not travel alone on Vadim's horse. She joined the acrobats. She sat between them, clustered tightly on the narrow bench on the front of Stoyan's vardo. She asked Stoyan for stories of his wife and the life they lived together. Stoyan told one long, uninterrupted story until Kyra slept leaning against his shoulder, and Yubi slept leaning against her.

It was a short nap. She awoke still pressed against Stoyan and blanketed by Yubi. She thought about Luca's touch and compared the sensation with the one she savored then. The difference was extreme. It was not right versus wrong. It was just different, and she sat still with her eyes closed, pondering the comparison deeply, until they rolled upon an ideal site to set camp.

It was the first large field they encountered in Croatia, large enough to raise the large tent with room to spare. Kyra thought about the jewelry makers, and about the herders, cooks, Ernko, and the pottery makers. She thought the kumpania could use some unity, and she ordered the large tent raised. The camp was set. The tent was raised. Kyra had a vivid memory of the dream she had long before, when she held the entire kumpania in the palm of her hand. She felt them in her hand again. She felt uncertain times ahead of them, and she wanted to squeeze them together with her fingers.

In the tent that evening, she asked to see Luca and Chiara's act. Chiara was no more than an obedient servant, but the act she assisted was truly extraordinary. She lit his torch and handed it to him. Luca removed his shirt and ran the flame across his skin without a flinch. Chiara handed him other instruments — a fiery staff, two flaming batons, and of course his lamp at the end of a chain. It was all very dangerous, all very exciting. His sweat made his olive skin glisten and accentuated every muscular contour.

After his demonstration, while the kumpania huddled around him to congratulate him, his eyes were on Kyra. He walked from the others to where she sat on a pillow, between Stoyan and Yubi, at the edge of the tent.

Stoyan congratulated him on his marvelous performance. Kyra echoed the sentiment. Yubi nodded begrudgingly.

Luca squatted directly in front of Kyra, and looking her in the eyes he said brazenly in Italian, "I think your act could use a little fire."

Kyra looked to Yubi for a translation. He answered in Romani, "He thinks we are not good enough without him. He wants you to be his assistant, like his sister."

Stoyan disagreed with the translation but not with Yubi's judgment. He wrapped a hand around Kyra's arm, gave her a few quick squeezes, turned to Luca, and told him

322

in German so Kyra would understand, "Your flames are a welcome addition. I hope you will be happy with your place among us."

Luca was far too full of himself to catch the hint. He continued to gaze at Kyra flirtatiously. Yubi asked Kyra to excuse him. Stoyan stood with his son and declared his need for sleep. He took Kyra's hand, kissed it reverently, and walked from the tent with Yubi. In the brief seconds that followed, Kyra compared Stoyan's encouraging, fatherly touch to the strange sensation of Luca's hand on her skin. It raised in her a sudden urge to follow the acrobats from the tent. Luca stood and watched her from behind. He did not pursue her. He did not feel he needed to.

CHAPTER THIRTY-THREE

LYUBEN

IN THE MORNING, still a few days out of Zagreb, Kyra found Vadim and Ernko near the cooking basin, sharing breakfast with Milena's husband and the other herders.

In much improved Romani, Ernko bade her, "Good morning. You join us just in time. There are plans that need considering."

Before further explanation could be given, Patrin, the tailor, and Manfri joined them, followed shortly by Milena.

After appropriate greetings, Kyra returned her eyes to Ernko and asked, "You were saying something about plans?"

Ernko's mouth was full, so Vadim explained, "Zagreb is a big city. It is no Požega. We cannot simply camp outside of town, bark our presence, and fill our tents. More complex preparations must be made. Ernko and I will ride into Zagreb. With luck, we will return in less than a week with arrangements for a suitable time and place to set ourselves."

After a long moment of silent staring, Kyra asked, "What is it you need from me?"

Quickly, sharply, and with a sarcastic tone, Milena answered, "Your blessing, of course. Nothing can be done without your blessing."

Everyone in the circle, including her own husband, gave Milena a chastising glare before quickly returning to the business at hand. All eyes went back to Kyra.

"You would know much better than I," she told him humbly, turning her eyes timidly to Milena and back again, "What you think is best will always have my support."

They continued to stare at her, waiting for something more.

She added in a low, vocalized whisper, "You have my blessing."

It was all they needed to hear. Ernko and Vadim saddled two horses with supplies for a week, and bid their farewells.

As they mounted, and many gathered to see them off, Luca ran to Vadim and instructed him, "I need you to buy some more lamp oil while you are away. I have used the last of it."

Vadim knew enough Italian to understand the request. He said he would try, and he and Ernko rode toward Zagreb in haste. Kyra watched them ride away, and continued to look in their direction well after they were out of sight.

Yubi startled her from behind, taking her firmly by the shoulder and speaking closely into her ear, "Come with me. I have an idea."

She followed him to a clearing behind a row of low trees. They were alone. Nobody was near and nobody could hear, yet he still pulled her tightly to him and whispered, "You dance with love and you dance with pain. I know your past. I know what churns inside of you."

Kyra was still very grateful to him for having long been her encouraging confidant, and she responded, "I know you do."

He continued, "You need no fire, no high bar. You only need to tell your story."

"What are you suggesting?"

Yubi reminded her that the pain and death of her past was the fire behind her dancing. As romantic as the end of their act was, he suggested an alternative.

"I carry you at the end, as we rehearsed, but just as we hold each other tightly, I drop to my knees. I will gasp and writhe and go limp to the ground, then you fall on me and weep. Weep for Szanzar, for Menowin and Iraja. Then dance. Dance alone. Dance heartbroken."

Kyra puckered her face as she considered it. The idea clearly made her uncomfortable.

Yubi noticed and explained, "We perform for people... people who have lost loved ones, people who grieve. You will show them they are not alone. You will place their own grief in front of them and tell them their own stories in a way they cannot. It will strike them as familiar, and they will unite in the shared experience."

It was a profound insight into the human condition from one so young. More importantly to Kyra, it showed that Yubi could reach beyond the Roma notions of grief. He understood her. He could see her spirit as clearly and colorfully as a brightly painted vardo at noon on a clear day. They set immediately to rehearsing the new ending.

At the end of their routine, Yubi rehearsed it as he described it. Kyra was deeply shaken by the horrible realism of his theatrical seizure and death. It drew grief and pity from her very depths. She danced. With no music but the rhythm of her own heavy breaths, she danced her sorrow. Still lying twisted on the ground, Yubi watched her through one slightly opened eye. It was, in his opinion, the most beautifully expressive thing he had ever witnessed.

She finished her dance by collapsing to her knees beside him, pulling him onto her lap, and weeping profusely over him. When her tears — true, authentic tears

— fell from her cheek and landed on his, he knew his plan was successful. When her heavy sobs slowly settled to shallow breaths, she released him. They kneeled facing each other, neither sure what to say. She looked at him in admiration for his artistic vision.

To him, he had just danced with the world's most amazing creature. His mother had danced. Iraja and Lavinia had danced. His father had done many inhuman stunts. But none of them had done anything like this. The people of Zagreb were in for an experience they could not possibly foresee.

Kyra suddenly sprang to her feet and announced, "Your father and Lavinia! They must see this. Do you think they will approve?"

"No!" he blurted, "I mean to say, yes, they will approve, but no, we should not show them. Let them and the others experience it with the people of Zagreb. Until then, it stays between us."

She agreed, and for the first time in a long time, he savored a secret between them. But he wondered where her heart was while she danced, and while she held him and cried. Was she thinking about her family in Szanzar, about Menowin and Iraja, or was she thinking about the person she was holding? His need to know seared inside of him and singed his very bones, but he would not ask her. They stood together and walked hand-in-hand back to the camp, delighted in their shared surprise, while something deeper simmered beneath the surface.

Kyra spent the afternoon in her vardo. Her mind was too agitated to read or write. She could think of nothing but her experience that morning with Yubi. She did not want to see anybody else, but could not bring herself to go to him. Yubi — well nobody knew where Yubi was, not even Yubi. What began as pacing around the camp mindlessly, became a long, contemplative walk in increasing circles outward.

It was late in the afternoon, while plenty of autumn sun still lit the colorful camp, when he came to a sudden stop. He did not know where Kyra was, and he did not know where Luca was. With an urgency he had never before known, he ran to Kyra's vardo. He burst in without warning, startling her into a loud gasp. His face had the glow of exertion. She anticipated something of profound importance from his lips, but nothing came.

She prompted him tentatively, "Yubi?"

He reached his hand to her. She took it, and he led her from the vardo and several youthful paces away from the camp. He sat on the ground, and she sat looking at him and smiling.

His face turned grave, and it cooled the air around them. He demanded, "I need you to look at Lyuben and tell me now if you love him."

Kyra's high smile dropped. She shook her head berserkly, as if she had been accused of murder.

Yubi released all air from his lungs in one sudden exhale. He drew the next breath slowly, only enough to say, "You don't. You don't."

Kyra looked to her left and right, then back to Yubi, and she asked, "Who is Lyuben?"

He stared at her with an expression of disbelief on his lowered eyebrows. As the truth of the moment dawned on him, he dropped his shoulders, lifted a boyish grin, then broke into hearty laughter.

Through his laugh, he answered, "Me! That is my name. Lyuben... Yubi."

As he spoke, his laughter increased until he was buckled over himself, hardly able to breathe. When he looked up again, he saw a face brightened red with embarrassment.

He tried to stop his laughter on the spot, but it was not to be caged. It continued to burst through with every other exhale.

Kyra tried to excuse herself, "I.., I didn't…, nobody told me."

Her awkwardness was unbearable to him. He tried to relieve her, saying through his loosely leashed laughter, "How could you know? Nobody has called me Lyuben since I was very young, not since my mother died."

The air around them chilled again, as they gazed stone-faced at each other. Another giggle popped through, but not from Yubi. It was Kyra's giggle, and she tried to push it down. Her attempt was hilarious to him, and they erupted together into deep-bellied, seizing laughter. It slowed together, then ended together with a long hummed sigh. She looked at him red-faced and aglow.

His face was suddenly stern again, and he asked, "Well?"

"Well," she answered.

"You have not answered my question."

It took a moment for Kyra to recall the demand that initiated the strange exchange between them, but when she recalled it, she too went solemn, and she answered, "I look around me and I do not see Lyuben. I do not know him."

He let out a curt sigh and bit on the inside of his lips. His hands began to shake.

She continued, "I see Yubi, my Yubi, my dearest friend Yubi, and I love him more than anything."

It may not have been the exact answer he hoped for, but they had just shared a wonderful moment that was so distinctly and uniquely *them*. There was such comfortable, affectionate warmth between them. He took her hands and responded with words she had already chosen, "And I see Kyra, my Kyra, my very dearest Kyra. I love her more than anything."

Kyra smiled as he spoke, but when he finished, his penetrating eyes said more than his words. Her smile flattened. Her eyebrows raised. Her eyes began to well. She drew a sharp inhale and held it in. After a frozen eternity under his intense gaze, her face slowly formed a grimace. She fought back a grand smile that was intent upon its purpose.

When she could hold it back no longer, she let out another giggle, then said in a tone of forced loftiness, "You must introduce me to this Lyuben. He sounds very useful. I think I will have him carry my things and wash my clothes."

He wanted the intensity of the previous moment to continue. He wanted it to intensify further. But she destroyed it. It was adorable to him. Her forced lofty tone through her rolling giggle was quintessentially Kyra. He released her hands, rolled back, and laughed with her.

Kyra bounced to her feet, offered him her hand, and demanded, "Come... *Yubi*! Come eat with me."

By the time they joined the cooks, many others were there, including Luca and Chiara. Luca described in dynamic detail the wonderful things he would perform in Zagreb, and how his talent would profit the kumpania. The same words from any other mouth would have been boorish, even offensive. But Luca had a rare brand of charisma. Even Yubi found himself intrigued.

It grew to quite the cozy, familial gathering. As night fell, they broke off a few at a time. Kyra slipped away unnoticed and went to bed. Again her door flew open without warning. This time it was Stoyan. His intrusion did not come with the gravity of Yubi's. On the contrary, he had a calm and pleasant look about him. Kyra began to sit up in bed, but Stoyan gestured her back down with a subtle lift of his hand.

He sat on the edge of the bed and told her, "I know you have shared many secrets with my son."

She held her breath in anticipation, not sure which of the secrets he referred to.

He continued, "You have told him your past. Now I will tell you the past he does not remember. Yubi was different from other babies. He never cried, not even when he was hungry. His eyes were always wide to the world around him. You should know he came from a perfect love. My wife was a superior woman. Our love was extraordinary. I cannot tell the story of Yubi without beginning there. He was the product of the most beautiful love, and he was the most beautiful child."

"I can believe that," Kyra interrupted.

Stoyan smiled at her and added, "He drew long gazes from every eye to behold him. We were very proud... perhaps too proud. We manufactured opportunities to place him before an audience. He was always on display. As soon as he could walk, we had him performing."

Stoyan tilted his head in a reminiscent trance, giggled, and went on, "His eyes were oversized, so much so that they might have appeared awkward, even unsettling, if not for the light that shone from them. As it was, those huge eyes suited him perfectly. The little Gypsy boy with an angel's face. He loosened purses before he knew what money was."

Kyra's face betrayed her disappointment, and Stoyan quickly excused himself, saying, "It was not about the money, not for us. We were proud parents, and we wanted the world to delight in our beautiful child. Still, it was too much, too early. As he grew, he never delighted in the crowds, never cherished the performance."

"But he is such a passionate performer now."

"He was always passionate, but not about the performance, not about the crowds. When his mother died, he became more internal. Although he tried to hold it in, the light in him still shone out. The more it did, the more he tried to bottle it, ...until now. When he dances with you, I see a fire release from him with blazing freedom, one that neither I nor his mother could ever bring forth."

Kyra had again been holding her breath. When it finally demanded release, it did so dramatically. She gasped as if finally reaching the surface of a lake after having nearly drowned.

Stoyan sighed, shook his head, patted Kyra on the leg, and said, "I don't know why I feel I need to tell you this. I don't imagine anything will change because of it. But my love, you should know. It might tell you as much about yourself as about him."

She nodded to him. He nodded back to her, patted her leg again, and left the vardo.

CHAPTER THIRTY-FOUR
THE KYRA IN THEM ALL

THERE WOULD BE NO TRAVEL until Vadim and Ernko returned, giving them long afternoons they were not used to having. The craftsmen used the time industriously, building a healthy store of wares to sell in Zagreb. Lavinia rehearsed the dancers. Milena worked with Manfri and the musicians. Stoyan removed his injured arm from the sling and painfully tried some menial and mundane tasks.

Lavinia brought the other dancers into Kyra and Yubi's rehearsals. They began as they had in Požega, peeling away from Kyra like a blossom as she rose slowly on Yubi's hand. They incorporated the musicians and finally brought the entire act together. The rehearsal ended as Lavinia and Stoyan had set it, without the dramatic addition. That would be revealed in Zagreb.

Vadim and Ernko returned late one morning with great news. Zagreb was short on skilled blacksmiths. Ernko had set himself up with enough personal commissions to keep his hammer swinging for weeks. Vadim arranged a performance in the prestigious Medvedgrad Castle. It is the first opportunity to place themselves in front of a crowd of such important, wealthy people since the wedding performance two years earlier. The leaders of Zagreb had influence and connections from Venice to the southern end of the Dalmatian coast.

Vadim called for representatives of each occupation in the kumpania, including their new fire artist. He presented them with a sketch of the castle's layout. There was a large courtyard on the far end. To get to it, one must pass through a long, wide corridor. It was all arranged. The fine Roma wares, from the jewelry to the pottery and canisters to the colorful clothing stitched by Patrin would line the corridor. Guests would have to pass the wares on the way to the performance, and pass them again when they left.

Poking the sketch of the courtyard with one fingertip, Vadim declared, "Look at this space. We will all fit in this space, I tell you. We can all watch the performance. It will be perfect, and it will bring more opportunities than we can imagine."

"Why is that?" Kyra asked.

"That is a surprise."

They all begged to know, but he held firm, and only offered one hint, speaking to Kyra, "You will be our jewel, our *crown* jewel."

Vadim delivered his report in Romani, and Luca did not understand. He looked concerned and impatient. Vadim, reading him well, added, "And I have purchased Luca's oil. It awaits him in the castle, more than he could use in a month."

Stoyan translated it into Italian, and Luca gave Vadim a grateful nod.

Less than an hour after the meeting broke, the caravan was moving toward Zagreb. For two days, as long as there was the faintest light in the sky, they traveled. They arrived before noon on the third day, setting camp about a mile from the castle. The event was scheduled for the following evening. All those who attended Vadim's meeting accompanied him to the castle. They were graciously accepted, given a grand tour, fed a luxurious meal, and sent on their way.

During the whole tour and meal, none of their hosts or servants acknowledged Kyra. Their eyes passed over her as if she were nothing more than a bland accessory. It was a sensation she knew well as a child, but one she had nearly forgotten. The remembrance of it haunted her as they returned to the camp. She was offered a seat on Stoyan's horse, but she insisted upon walking.

Walking with her shoulder nearly touching Stoyan's foot, she looked up to him and said, "You all make too much of me. I am as plain as I have ever been. Nobody in the castle saw me."

Luca was walking behind her. He skipped forward to her and asked what they were talking about. Kyra translated it into German.

Luca answered in her defense, "If they did not see you, they are blind."

Stoyan immediately contradicted him, but in Romani, for Kyra's ears only, "They are not blind, Kyra. But you have become very good at obscuring yourself when you do not wish to be noticed."

She searched her heart and admitted, "I was intimidated by the castle, and by the pageantry of it all."

Luca, wanting to remain in the conversation, added, "But they will see you tomorrow!"

Stoyan answered him in Italian, "Yes Luca, they will see her, and when they do, everything *but* her will be obscured."

Luca did not much like the sound of that, but even his confident heart agreed. From that point until he crawled into the tent with Chiara, he thought of ways he could draw Kyra into his fire act.

They rose early and brought the caravan to the castle. It was a thick, stone fortress, perched on a hill, ensconced by a band of thick trees. There was a path through the valley that led to the castle. The vardos, wagons, horses and livestock had no room to cluster. They were strewn in single-file, so that the center of the caravan had no view of either end. They had often traveled so, but rarely camped.

Until the evening, they were strangely placid. Nobody sang or played or danced. The canisters were polished, the clothing folded, and the jewelry bundled for sale. The only movement noticeable from the walls of the castle was the steady pacing of the herders through the trees along the caravan. When the time came, they took their things, walked the path, and entered the castle.

As they passed through the gate, Luca asked Stoyan, "Am I to perform immediately after Kyra?"

"After Kyra?" he asked with surprise, "You perform before her, before the dancers. You have an exciting act. It will warm them well for Kyra and my son."

Lavinia was walking beside them, and Stoyan told her what Luca had asked. Luca began to protest but was silenced by Lavinia's look. She was a soft, nurturing, maternal figure, but when she turned stern, she wore an expression that was not to be challenged. Luca bit his tongue, turned his eyes downward, and entered the corridor in silence.

The castle seemed empty. Only a few servants passed them as they set their wares in the corridor. The performers were escorted to the courtyard then left entirely alone. It was surrounded by walls that stood fourteen feet high. As twilight darkened the walls, a line of servants, each carrying a large torch, paraded along the perimeter of the courtyard, mounting their torches to the walls and lighting the area brilliantly. The triumph of Vadim's efforts were becoming apparent. It truly was perfect. How magical they would all appear under such conditions!

The true triumph came through the corridor after the honored Croatian guests. Trailing behind them all, announced by a blast from a polished horn, was the King of Hungary and Croatia, Louis the Great. The Croatians clapped for their king, but not the Roma. They stood dumbfounded. Vadim smiled victoriously.

Kyra leaned into him and said, "The surprise you spoke of?"

Vadim nodded, took her hand, squeezed it, released it to her side, and joined the Croatians in their applause.

There were no chairs in the courtyard, no pillows, nothing upon which to sit, lean, or recline. The dancers took their place, establishing the performance perimeter. King Louis stepped to the head of the audience, and the rest of them filled in behind him. The musicians were against the wall behind the dancers, except for Manfri and Milena, who had perched themselves upon the courtyard wall. The music started, and the dancers held the perimeter, while Luca and Chiara strolled dramatically to the center.

Chiara lit her brother's torch, then took her obedient place by the fire tools, while he swung his torch over his head. He performed well, removing his shirt and exposing under the orange glow his well-made physique. A torch, then a flaming staff, fiery batons, and finally, his lamp and chain, were all handed to him in their time by Chiara. The audience was enthralled. The king leaned forward, fascinated with the fiery tricks. When Luca finished, the music stopped, and he took his bow to mild applause.

The dancers closed into their circle. Kyra took her place amid them. With no more than two steps in preparation, Yubi flipped over the dancers, and landed amid them behind Kyra. He fastened the long dress around Kyra's waist and disappeared beneath it, and the performance began. It began with echoing sounds coming from the top of the wall. Manfri and Milena wove their rising and cascading notes tightly around each other. The acoustics of the courtyard played games with the minds of the guests. To them, it seemed like the sounds descended upon them from the sky above. The dancers peeled away, Kyra rose. The king and the Croatian nobles were transported and transcended.

The theatrical ending was not all Yubi and Kyra had changed. At one point, he set her down in front of him and vaulted in a flip over her shoulder. The whole act was more dramatic, more theatrical, more passionate. When he threw her, he threw her like a wild animal. When he caught her, he caught her like a lover, which made the tragic ending all the more soul-stirring. When it came time for the final stunt, she stood on his two hands, but she did not lift one foot and try to raise it. In that courtyard, with the torches so far beneath her, she felt twice as high. She was too frightened to lift her foot from Yubi's hand.

She remained standing firmly on his two hands. It was impressive enough for their noble audience. He pushed her feet from under her, caught her in a passionate embrace, and walked with his back to the king. Yubi faked a dramatic death, and Kyra danced a mournful lament. When she held him tightly to her chest at the end, crying a cry that could not be faked, she drew tears from every face in the courtyard — every face, royal and Roma alike.

As she held him on her lap, her cry bellowed from her and echoed from the walls of the otherwise silent courtyard, until the dancers encircled them both and lunged over them, covering them like a burial mound. The whole thing was a poignant metaphor for the tragedies of life and love, and it struck to the deepest chambers of the heart.

Beginning with a slow and steady clap from the king, the audience showed their appreciation. This was no howling mob. It was a manicured gathering of Zagreb's most respected families, in the presence of the king. Their applause was exuberant, but controlled. King Louis shouted his approval. This liberated the other guests to elevate their praise. The performers stood in a line holding hands, facing the king, with Kyra and Yubi in the center.

Such prestigious eyes were on them. The most influential voices hollered for them. It was nothing peculiar to Kyra and Yubi, or to the dancers and musicians who shared the moment. But to Luca, it was like a crazed dream. He was ravenous with ambition.

They all took their bows and they all received their praise. When the elegant guests returned their attention to the king, praise for Kyra and Yubi's new ending came from a more intimate source. The entire kumpania was within the walls of the courtyard, and they shuffled among each other for their turn to question and congratulate them. They had experienced the performance differently than the strangers in attendance, and not only because they knew and loved the performers. Kyra's dancing at the end was a brand and degree of sorrow that had been unknown to the Roma.

When the evening wound down, the Roma craftsmen attended to their wares, and King Louis himself led a procession of wealthy people down the corridor, each wanting to impress the king with the money they could spend on the Gypsy guests. Many items were crafted in preparation for the evening. Nothing returned with them to the camp. Even the blankets laid out to display their items were sold as souvenirs of the great event.

The pockets and purses of the kumpania were brimming with Croatian coins, with jewels and rich trinkets, and with everything the honored guests could pass to them in exchange for a small sample of Gypsy passion. What they did not know was the evening was less traditionally Roma and more Kyra. The tales they told as they returned to their homes redefined the reputation of the Gypsies, and the "Gypsy spirit" has had at its core a strong and bright strain of Kyra ever since.

When the kumpania had settled back into their camp, their hearts were stirred and their eyes were wide. None of them, not even the very youngest, were ready to sleep.

There was no space to raise the large tent, so they clustered as well as they could near the center of the caravan to enjoy a moment of unity. In contrast to their exuberant hearts, their lips were mostly still. Those few murmurs that rose were whispered. They were waiting for Kyra and Yubi to say something, to explain their performance in words the Roma could understand.

Yubi and Kyra were leaning against her vardo, with most eyes fixed on them.

"I think it is time," he told her, "time to tell them your story."

"But your father said that part of me is dead, that I must come to you."

Yubi turned to face her, took both her hands, and explained, "That was before you changed us. The truth is, we have come to Kyra as much as Kyra has come to us. Don't you see it? It shows in everything we do. Your past is inside all of them. They may as well understand it. They should know what it is that has swelled in their hearts and tinted their lives in a new color."

Kyra was not certain, but he gave her no time to consider it. He pulled her up the ladder onto her porch, then hoisted her onto the roof. She looked down to him, waiting for him to join her. He did not. He dismounted the porch and joined the others as they gazed in anticipation.

With no preface, Kyra sat on the roof and told her story to a captivated audience of affectionate friends. Stoyan stood near Luca and translated for him. Kyra started at the beginning, when the first fevers and sores appeared in Szanzar. They had all heard tales of death and loss, but never told like Kyra told it. She did not just list facts as they occurred. She gave them her experiences. She scraped the very edges of her vocabulary to express every thought and every feeling, her fears and her hopes as she toddled away from her childhood home. She spoke honestly of her embarrassment as she stood alone in an endless field and soiled herself. She described the moment when she no longer cared, and when she resigned herself to die alone in the tall grass.

She stood up tall as she recalled and explained the feeling that the Romani song gave her as the caravan rolled by her, and the heart-dropping fear that they would not notice her. She spoke of every pleasure and every frustration during her first weeks with the kumpania. And she spoke of Iraja. She reminded them of when she stood on the porch of that very vardo, newly cleaned and dressed, while the kumpania applauded her transformation. It was her heart alone that chose the words as she described the slow development of trust and love.

She recounted every moment of her time with them. It was their memories too, but placed in terms of Kyra's heart. Stoyan's rescue, Menowin's death, Lavinia's love, Yubi's lessons, and of course, the loss of Iraja. Yubi was right. As Kyra told their shared stories through her richly unique sensibilities, they began to understand themselves. They came to see clearly that piece of Kyra that resided in each of them, and they began to understand how dynamic and saturating it was, and to see then, only then, how altered they had been by the filthy little girl they had plucked from the grass.

To a caravan of Roma nomads, death was a normal part of life. But they did not listen to her story with Roma ears. They listened with that little piece of Kyra that resided in each of them, which she had slowly and unwittingly implanted in them since she was twelve years old. Yubi already knew her past, and he had discussed every pain and triumph with her since. The sensation he felt as he listened to her was not new to him, yet he cried most profusely as she spoke, for his feelings were acutest. His compassion for her was the strongest, and his love for her the dearest.

When she finished, Yubi climbed back onto the porch to help her from the roof and back down to the ground. The moment she turned away from the ladder, Milena stood glaring at her with a cocked eyebrow.

Kyra spoke quickly and apologetically, "I am sorry I went on like that. Yubi told me I should—"

Milena interrupted her, "You misunderstand me, my sister. Mine is not a face of judgment, but one of admiration."

Kyra's surprise was apparent in the way she leaned back with her eyes almost comically wide.

Milena took her by the shoulder and pulled her closer before continuing, "I have only one principle to guide me... Love. Those I love affect me comprehensively. Those I do not love have no power to affect me at all. You should not look for my affection in the things I say to you. Nobody finds it there. Look for my love in your ability to alter me. I am affected by *you*, Kyra. I am changed and improved. That can only mean one thing. I love you. And since you have altered me *profoundly*, I must love you *profoundly*. You are still such a strange little thing. That opinion will never change. But I love you profoundly, *and I have for a long time*."

Of all the monumental moments in Kyra's life, this speech from Milena was near the top. She wanted to climb back on the roof, gather everyone's attention, and add it to her story. She did not. She threw her arms around Milena, kissed her cheek repeatedly, told her she loved her, and skipped away like a carefree child, along the caravan to mingle with the others.

Luca waited for a moment to corner her alone. When he found it, he told her, "Many times, you died, and each time, you rose. You are a phoenix."

"I am no phoenix," she humbly replied.

"Of course you are! Your village turned to ash and you flew out of it with blazing beauty, soaring into the air for all to see."

He spoke quickly and excitedly, too quickly for Kyra to translate. He slowed his speech and reworded the same sentiments to fit within her German vocabulary.

"Is that what you got out of my story?" she asked him with a puzzled look on her face and her head tilted inquisitively to one side, "I never felt like a phoenix…, no, that was not it at all. I *crawled* out of Szanzar. And when the kumpania found me, I was only a little less broken than the bodies I had left behind."

"Do you not see yourself? You are a blazing beauty and an inspiration to all who see you."

"If I am blazing, it is because the kumpania set me on fire, just as any old stick can be lit to flame."

Clearly her words did not penetrate. He grasped her shoulders, then slid his fingers down her arms until he was holding her hands, and he said, "No, no. no, you are a phoenix, and we must present you as one."

It was his own act he was considering. He did not recognize Yubi's abilities. He saw Yubi as an undeserving benefactor of Kyra's talent, and he wanted the same benefit for himself.

Luca released her hands, took three skipping steps backward, and pointed at her while shouting, "You are a phoenix and I am a fire master. This will be unlike anything before."

He turned and ran along the camp, out of Kyra's sight. She gave the encounter no more thought. She mingled with every member of the kumpania in their turn, then went to bed — delighted for the first time by the uncertainty of her future.

CHAPTER THIRTY-FIVE
BLISTERS ON THE PHOENIX

LUCA HARDLY SLEPT THAT NIGHT. Kyra's story had moved him. That is to say, it moved his ambitions. By the time Kyra stepped from her vardo in the early morning, he had already spoken to Patrin. He commissioned the tailor to make a new costume for Kyra, one with flaming red wings of fabric hanging from her sleeves, one that fit his image of the phoenix. He knew he could not remove her from her duet with Yubi. That was not his plan. He wanted to move his own act to the end, and have Kyra rise like a phoenix from the "ashes" of her duet with Yubi.

He told nobody of his plan, but prepared himself and Chiara to light his torches as Kyra and Yubi finished, then pull her into a new fire act, a dangerous and revolutionary act, one that would present Kyra as he saw her. Luca was an artist. His thoughts may have been deceptive, but they were not entirely selfish. He wanted to amaze people, to give them something special that would change them forever. His own skills fell just short of that goal. He needed something. He needed Kyra.

Vadim and Ernko left the camp early that morning. They returned to the castle to finalize deals that were struck the night before. They remained as guests for two meals and only returned to the camp when they were hungry for a third. Many special performances were arranged, each promising to be lucrative. When they described the opportunities to the others, Luca's eyes gleamed. He already had a focused image of how those performances would go, with Kyra, the glorious phoenix, glowing by the light of his torches.

The first performance arranged was in the private home of a noble merchant. The man's name was Bogdan, and he had been the most enthusiastic of the previous evening's audience. Bogdan was hosting a party, a celebration of his business' swelling success in the wake of the plague. Wealthy merchants from across the Adriatic and Mediterranean Seas would be in attendance. His home was deep in the business district of Zagreb. The urban setting would naturally divide the kumpania, with many streets and buildings between the performers and the camp outside of the city. After one more night near the castle, they traveled to the southeastern side of Zagreb and set their camp in a wild field.

By the time they set camp, the weather had turned. Wet snow fell and the temperature dropped sharply. The weather made their appointment in the city all the more seductive. They would be indoors, in a grand hall, warmed with numerous fires, at least that is how it was described to them by Bogdan. It was grand in its splendor, not in its size. With a bulky table down the center of the room, there would be little room for the dancers, no room for the musicians. Everyone else would remain in the camp.

One musician, only one, could come. Everyone assumed it would be Manfri. But while the details were being discussed, Kyra exercised her authority.

"Milena will perform with us," she proclaimed.

"Just one voice, no instruments?" Stoyan questioned.

"Not just a voice," Kyra answered with a wink at Milena, "*her* voice. Her illustrious voice will fill any grand hall."

There was some debate on the matter, all in Romani, so Luca understood none of the words but Milena's name. It was enough with the gestures for him to know what was demanded and what was being discussed.

Whether it was his authentic opinion or he simply wanted to show unity with Kyra, he could not have known himself, but he shouted out in German, "Kyra is right! Oh yes, she knows best. Milena should sing for the performance."

Luca's word carried little weight. Kyra had spoken and that is how it would be. Nevertheless, when all came into agreement, Luca smiled at Kyra and winked at her as if he had done her some favor for which she now owed a debt. He left the gathering with a self-congratulatory strut, went directly to Patrin, and urged him to sew more quickly.

Bogdan's party was still a week away. The kumpania was rich with money and poor with supplies. Vadim and Ernko made trips into the city every other day. Zagreb was not the most exotic port of trade they had seen. There was nothing in their shops and markets to dazzle a well-traveled eye. But there were plenty of raw materials for the craftsmen of the kumpania to work their magic in the long, idle, cold and snowy hours in the camp.

The regular urban excursions had another purpose. They wanted to get to know Zagreb, to place their fingers on the pulse of the people. The birds, the breeze, the very air itself promised a long and cold winter. Their reception from the elite of the city was already warm and inviting. The camp was well-situated, and more importantly, the next four weeks were already booked with private performances. Rumors circulated around Zagreb that King Louis himself sought to hire them, but no direct offer had come from him. It was never an easy feeling being settled for long near a city, but Zagreb looked promising.

Word of the performance in the castle filtered quickly down from the nobles to the common people, and each one of them wanted a share of their exotic visitors southeast of town. During the week before the party, brave adventurers from the city wandered out to the camp to spy on the Gypsies, and maybe, just maybe catch a glimpse of the mythical young dancer whose performance had bewildered a king. Each as they came were welcomed and served. No matter how rich or poor, they were taken in by the kumpania, treated to some fascinating new flavors and well-wishes in an exotic language before being sent on their way.

They met Kyra and found in her, not the mythical figure of her growing reputation, but a girl, a young woman with an understated but undeniable authority over everything and everyone around her. She was never the first to greet the curious voyeurs to their camp, but she was always the most attentive once they were welcomed and settled and nibbling on something warm. Conversations with the visitors, if they existed at all, were rough and sparse. Most who came to them were poor and spoke a crude version of medieval Croatian. That mattered little. They communicated in the timeless and universal language of hospitality.

The day of the party came, and the performers made their way through thick, heavy snow to Bogdan's home in the city center. Only four dancers came, Lavinia and three others. Milena, Luca, Chiara, Yubi, and Kyra were the only other performers. Vadim had arranged the performance and was the voice of the kumpania to the nobles of Zagreb. For that reason, he led the group into Bogdan's house. All others remained in the camp.

It was not a large home, but every plank, furnishing, shelf, and trinket displayed the wealth and influence of the proprietor. Although the house was rich with servants, Bogdan greeted them at the door and led them to the grand hall. Lavinia paced around it, measuring with her steps and counting out loud. She finished her laps and nodded to Bogdan, who clapped his hands together loudly and gave Lavinia a tight embrace.

Lavinia demanded a few adjustments to the room, which were gladly provided. The large table was scooted nearer the wall, and several chairs were removed from the room entirely. This would mean that some members of the coming party would have to stand for the performance. Bogdan did not care. He would stand if he had to. Having a private performance from the Gypsies that entertained the king gave him a rather royal prestige among his peers.

The performers talked through and walked through their acts. As they finished, and the first guests arrived, Luca pulled from his bag a wad of bright fabric. He bowed to Kyra and handed it to her. When she unfurled it, she saw Patrin's creation. It was a red blouse, cut low in the front, with tight sleeves that hugged the wrists. From the arms hung strips of fabric that resembled the feathered wings of a bird. There were two broad strips at the bottom that wrapped around the waist to accentuate her figure.

Kyra had not forgotten the phoenix conversation. She knew what he was doing. But the blouse was stunning, and Patrin's effort and talent were written plainly upon it. She accepted it and changed into it on the spot. Yubi was not certain how to feel about it. Luca's motives for the gift were unclear to him at first, but the flame artist's wide-eyed gaze at her once it was on her spoke plainly enough. Yubi wanted to yank it off of her and throw it in Luca's face, but he could not. The blouse complimented her perfectly. As she presented it to him, spinning with her arms out to the side, and the wings of the sleeves flowing behind her arms like smoke from a burning stick that a child waves overhead, she was stunningly beautiful.

"What do you think?" she asked him.

He had to admit, "It is amazing. It is perfect... You are perfect in it."

The rest of the guests arrived and pressed together along the perimeter until they filled every inch of wall space in the grand hall. Luca marched with regal pageantry to the center of the performance space, with Chiara trailing timidly behind him like a beaten dog. She lit his torch and he began his act. The tight space made Luca's performance all the more thrilling. The audience felt the heat of his flames and heard the swooshing roar with every swing of his hand. By the time he extinguished his lamp, Bogdan and his friends were in a delighted frenzy.

Milena replaced Luca and began with a long-held, pure, mid-ranged note that sustained much longer than a pair of mortal lungs should have been able. After one quick breath of recovery, she rolled up and down mysterious scales that challenged and defied musical theory, but were in no way unpleasant. Like the exotic spices back at the camp, her scales simultaneously stung and seduced the palate. She performed those cascading scales in a single breath.

Bogdan kept no meticulous guest list. There were no guards at the door to scrutinize every person coming through the gate. Milena's voice reached far beyond the edges of the property and drew, in a siren's trance, anybody and everybody who happened to stroll within its reach. The rooms and halls of Bogdan's home filled with strangers from the street, strangers of every sort and flavor.

As Milena drew her next inhale, Kyra and Yubi came to the center. He wrapped her long skirt around her and took his place beneath it. The four dancers closed in and draped themselves over them. Milena belted her next note as the act began. Kyra erupted into the air in her fiery, winged red blouse, like a heavenly bird, to the enamored gasps of the guests.

Kyra and Yubi performed their routine precisely as they had in the castle. Again, she was too frightened to attempt the final lift as Stoyan wanted it. When Yubi held her at the end and walked with her in his arms, the audience exploded with exuberant applause. Yet amid their clamor, Milena's voice still dominated the room. Yubi stood and held Kyra until the applause died down. He seized and thrashed and fell to his theatrical death. Milena's decadent voice continued to fill every nook of the house, like water poured into an oddly shaped jug, completely saturating everything within and flowing over the edges. Yet it became the less prominent feature in the room as it began to push Kyra's body around. Milena was simply an exquisite utensil used to serve Kyra to the audience.

In the previous rehearsals and performance, Kyra had recalled many horrible memories as she wept over Yubi to finish the act. That evening, she had a single image in her mind. It was the same image that was in her eyes — Yubi lying lifeless on the floor, caged by the walls of a house, in the center of a populated city. Each tear that rolled down her cheeks had a richly authentic, pungent aroma that the audience swore they could taste in their mouths.

Milena retired her voice for the night. When Kyra stood, before she could take Yubi's hand and help him to his feet for their bow, Luca walked to them, took Kyra by the hand, and pulled her away from Yubi. With Kyra in one hand and his torch extended out with the other, Chiara lit the torch and backed away. Luca waved the fire in front of Kyra. The light of fire rippled across her blouse incandescently. Her blouse was the less radiant feature. Her sweat-glistened skin picked up the light and appeared to juggle it between every curve and crevice of her face and neck. The room went silent.

Luca whispered to her, "You are the phoenix, bright and beautiful."

The heat from the torch, coupled with the wide, entranced eyes upon her, heated her to her marrow. She looked to the ceiling and raised her arms to her sides. The wings of her blouse flowed downward, and she looked as if she really could sore upward, leaving a trail of smoke in her wake.

Luca danced around her, licking Kyra's skin with fire, lighting her from every angle. She truly glowed. Even Yubi, who had stood dumbfounded by Luca's audacity, had backed away and watched in fascinated curiosity, that is, until Luca brushed the fire too closely to Kyra's face, and she winced in pain. He took a bold step in interference, but was halted when Kyra's angelic smile returned and she lifted her arms higher.

It was not only the fire caressing her skin. Luca ran his fingers across her. He did not light her up and stroke her for his own satisfaction. He did it to seduce the audience, to make Kyra even more desirable to them and set himself as her auctioneer. It worked. When their heavenly bird glowed with flame, every man, woman, and child watching wanted to take her home and keep her for themselves.

Luca was never satisfied. With each circle he danced around her, he brushed her more closely with the flame and stroked larger swaths of her body with his fingertips. He singed her hair and reddened her face, forehead, and neck. On his final pass, he held the fire against her face and scorched her. She grabbed at the torch and pushed it away from her, burning her palm.

Yubi rushed in, but as he got to her, Luca instructed him, "Lift her like a phoenix!"

He did not know why he obeyed, but he placed his hand as if for their opening lift, Kyra sat down, and Yubi hoisted her above Luca, above the torch and the dancers, and high above the stunned guests. Luca extinguished his torch and took a long bow. Yubi set Kyra to her feet. Luca pushed himself between them, took them both by the hand,

and took another bow. Kyra and Yubi bowed with him. The thunderous approval of Bogdan and his friends, and of all the nameless additions who were drawn in by Milena's voice, might have been heard by Stoyan and the others back in the camp, had they known to shush themselves and listen for it.

Many things were shouted at them as Milena and the dancers joined them in their bows. Most were shouted directly to Kyra. Most were respectful declarations of admiration from the mouths of Bogdan's honored friends. But the room had filled with every sort of human creature, clean and filthy, noble and otherwise.

One young man had squirmed his way into the great hall. He was neither poor nor rich, respectably dressed but clearly not in Bogdan's intimate circle. He too shouted at Kyra. The words he chose and the vile sentiments they portrayed shocked and silenced the people around him. In the sudden silence, his voice carried to Kyra. He shouted in Hungarian. Vulgar proposals, carrying the most depraved visuals, blubbered from his thin lips. Luca's fire had burnt her, but this man's words scorched her more deeply, and the expression on her face showed it. The noble crowd surrounding him, booed him, and pushed him from the room.

As he left Kyra's sight, while still within reach of her ears, he promised, "I will have you for my own if I have to chain you to my bed!"

The man had no idea that the crowd of people forcing him from the house served as a shield of protection from the furious Roma who would have torn him to pieces. But he *was* pushed from the house. The ruckus subsided, and a gentile celebration of the evening's triumph ensued.

The vile man was all but forgotten by all but Yubi. Violent, seething, vengeful rage surged within him. Horrid urges pulsed through him as the intruder's depraved threats echoed in his head. It was too much for him, all of it —

Luca's surprise ending to the performance, the burns on Kyra's face and hand, and the man who burst into the room and insulted and threatened Kyra. His own thoughts were almost as offensive to him as the words that had angered him. His mind could not be blamed for the eccentric and deviant workings of his heart. Were his wits fully about him, he would have censured himself harshly for his thoughts.

The house was cleared of all but the invited guests. The evening turned calmly celebratory, and every heart but one treasured the friendships being formed over dinner. Yubi saw little. His mind was occupied with a single image. He saw only those thin lips, spitting forth the vile desires of a depraved young man. He did not settle. As he sat and ate, his legs bounced and jigged beneath the table, with a darting eye open for the man who had insulted Kyra's virtue, ready to run, ready to sprint, in violent pursuit in defense of her — his most lively passion and his deepest love.

CHAPTER THIRTY-SIX
BLOOD IN THE BATHHOUSE

As Bogdan's party wound down and guests trickled out, Yubi's agitation began to calm. He became less vigilantly protective and more his tender self. He wanted to talk to Kyra alone, to discuss Luca's intrusion into the end of their performance. He pulled her from the dark corner where she sat, into a well-lit hallway. It was then and there that he saw the extent of her injuries. Her left eyebrow was nearly burned away. Blisters were forming on her cheek, neck, and forehead. It was her hand that took the worst of it. It was blackened and obviously painful.

Just as Yubi's rage had settled, it rose again, and he questioned her, "Kyra, these burns…, why didn't you say something?"

Kyra's straight face began to grimace as she stared into the fiery fury in his eyes. Her shoulders raised, and she reached both hands to him as she started to cry. He took her very gingerly into his embrace, careful not to touch her burns.

When he could grind his teeth no harder, he said, "That selfish bastard."

He pulled away from her, took her unburned hand, and dragged her aggressively back to the grand hall.

"We have to leave!" he announced in Romani.

The hall was nearly empty of guests, and they would have left soon anyway. Vadim bid Bogdan a very diplomatic farewell. He collected their payment, and they were kindly escorted from the property by their grateful host.

Once in the streets and walking toward the camp, Yubi took Luca by the arm, saying in Italian, "Not you."

Luca turned to face him and scolded, "What is wrong, boy? Are you angry because I took attention from you and gave it to Kyra? She is the brightest among you."

Yubi clenched his fists, bit the inside of his cheek, then calmed himself enough to respond, "She is the best of us all, and have you seen how you injured her?"

Luca gestured to the others, who kept walking from the city center and were nearly out of sight. Yubi was happy for the separation, for the increasing distance between Luca and Kyra. He made no response to the gesture but glared at him, waiting for an answer to his question.

When no answer came, he asked again, "Have you seen her burns? Her face…, you burned her face!"

Luca scoffed and answered, "She is much tougher than you think."

Yubi drew an inhale that flared his nostrils, releasing it all as he shouted, "What do you know? You have been with us for less than a month."

Luca looked around to see who might have taken notice of the shouting. The street was empty. Their fellow performers had turned around one building or another and were well out of sight and sound. It was only them.

Luca rolled his eyes, entirely dismissing Yubi's concerns, and he pretentiously instructed, "When you play with fire, sometimes you get burned."

"No, Luca! *You* played with fire and *Kyra* got burned! She is in pain!"

In a matter-of-fact tone, Luca rebutted, "Beauty is painful. Ask Kyra if it is worth it. I am sure she is with me."

"She is not with you. She is with me. She has always been with me!"

The statement revealed to Luca that there was much more at play than Yubi's concern over the burns. He was jealous, fitfully jealous. Luca was older. He was taller and had a man's muscular development. But Yubi, thin as he was, was stronger by far, and both of them knew it. Luca did not want a fight in the street. He did not want a fight at all, even if he was sure to win. He foresaw a long stay with the kumpania, at least as long as it would take to convince Kyra to leave with him.

He patted Yubi on the shoulder and said in a much more sympathetic tone, "It is all for the art, Yubi. You should understand that."

The words did nothing to dampen the fire in Yubi's eyes, so he went further, saying, "I did not realize I was burning her. We had no chance to rehearse. I will be safer next time, careful to brighten her without burning her. I promise."

His calm charisma unruffled Yubi. His fists unclenched and his shoulders dropped. Luca walked away satisfied. He followed the path the others had taken, southeast from the city center, toward the Roma camp. Yubi stood frozen in place, serene on the outside but wildly agitated on the inside. He did not want Luca's company during his walk back, so he waited where he stood for several minutes, then turned in the same direction and began to walk.

He had just barely cut the first corner when a voice came from behind him asking desperately, "Where has she gone? The phoenix! The Gypsy dancer! Where is she? Can you take me to your camp?"

Yubi turned around to see, mere inches from his face, the same man who had shouted his vulgar desires and sinister threats at the party. Without a moment of thought, he swung his fist at the man's head. The punch was barely dodged, and the man turned in fear and ran for his life. Yubi pursued him up and down streets, left and right and around buildings. He chased him with no notion or care where he was being led.

The heated pursuit left the city center and entered the old Roman ruins. The man ran to the ruins of the Roman bathhouse. Unable to shake his chaser and unable to run farther. He stood in the center of the dried bath bed and turned to face Yubi. No words were exchanged between them. The man timidly raised his fists but showed no real sign of defending himself. Yubi hit him, buckling his knees and sending him quickly to the ancient stones beneath them.

Who knows what deep and dark part of him commandeered his extremities, but Yubi fell on his enemy and hit. He hit and hit, bludgeoning the man's face with his fists, screaming at him, "You want to take her from us, chain her to your bed?"

He repeated back to the bloody face beneath him every horrible thing that same face had shouted at Kyra that night. When he exhausted those words, he began shouting things intended for Luca, bundling his rage against both men into the beating of one.

With fists still landing and flinging blood into the air behind him with each recoil, he shouted, "You come into my family. We take you in and feed you. You force yourself onto Kyra, burn her, burn her face, burn her sweet face."

The events of the night had stirred him to unmeasured wrath. It was not until his fists fell limp to his side that he regained himself and surveyed the damage. He could not tell if the bloody mess beneath him was alive or dead. The face was hardly recognizable as human. He looked to his left and right and saw that the old Roman bath pooled again. It pooled with the blood of the man he had bludgeoned, and despite that man's intentions, despite the terrible things he had said at the party and the threat of kidnapping and who-knows-what intended abuse, Yubi felt pity.

His had always been a mind teeming with tender concern for the feelings of others, and that part of him, that perpetual part of him, evicted the dark fury that had taken him over. He collapsed off of the man, onto his hip, and sat in the pool of blood. He looked at the mangled face, seeing no movement, no signs of breath, and he believed himself a murderer. It was in no way for himself, but for this terrible man that his sorrow swelled. His pitiful cry echoed off the walls of the Roman ruins.

He wanted out of that bathhouse, out of those ruins, away from the city with its walls and buildings. He wanted the open fields of Hungary with only his own kumpania around him. He wanted to be sitting in a field with Kyra, teaching her the vocabulary of some language or another. His desperation for flight was not motivated by fear, but by disgust in himself. But his guilt and pity forbade him to move. He could not leave the bathhouse. He could not leave the man he had chased and beaten. He sat in blood, but he felt like he was swimming, paddling but not moving in a foul, polluted harbor, unable to get to the dock or to the clean sea beyond.

His swirling thoughts were interrupted by a gurgle, then a gasp from the mangled face beside him. Yubi did not waste a moment of thought. He acted. He hoisted his victim over his shoulder and ran toward the city buildings. At the first home he came to, he laid his victim on the doorstep, banged loudly on the door, and ran away from the scene.

He ran with burning legs at a full sprint, to the sound of barking dogs. He ran in no particular direction, changing direction several times suddenly and without intention until he was out of the city and long clear of any buildings or roads. When he reached the welcoming womb of a wild, snowy field, he stopped running. His legs did not slow until he came to a safe and gradual stop. He simply stopped using them, as if they were suddenly severed at the hip. He careened, crashed, and tumbled to a bruised and bloody stop in the snow, like a rag doll thrown to the ground by a child with no love for it.

There, strewn awkwardly across the snow, with no notion of where he was and no thought of what to do next, he cried. He cried for what felt to him like a breathless eternity, entirely unaware that he had been followed out of Zagreb. An approaching figure called to him, not in anger but in concern, and by name. It was Luca.

Any rage he had for Luca had been expelled on the face he had so viciously hammered with his fists. What remained was the relief of hearing a familiar voice. Luca helped him to his feet. Yubi began a blubbering, half-witted account of the chase and assault.

Luca hushed him, "Shushhh, none of that matters. We must get you safely back to the camp, back to your father."

Yubi's legs wobbled beneath him. He could not trudge through the snow on a long hike, not even to such a desired destination. Luca assisted him with the first few steps, but found it too difficult.

He instructed Yubi, "Stay here. Lie low and I will get your father."

Yubi was afraid to be left alone. He was not confident Luca would do as he said. He tried to protest, but before he could utter a syllable, Luca was off, running away from him, holding Yubi's fate in his hands. He was true to his word. It took him three hours of steady hiking to get back to the camp. He arrived at a scene of muted hysterics. When Kyra saw Luca, she ran to him in delight and embraced him, assuming Yubi to be with him.

When she realized he was alone, she asked him, "Where is Yubi? He is with you. He must be with you."

Luca shook his head and Kyra's hysteria found its voice. She screamed half words in multiple languages, none of which could be understood by Luca.

He calmed her, assuring her, "Yubi will be well."

He explained to Kyra all that he knew. He had seen the confrontation in the street, and he followed the pursuit as well as he could. He lost them before they reached the ruins. He only found them again when he heard Yubi banging on the door. He saw the beaten man left on the doorstep, and he knew well enough what had happened. It was for the best that Luca did not hear all of the things Yubi shouted while his fists flew in violent frenzy. He followed Yubi through the city and out into the snowy field where he left him.

Stoyan and Ernko had gone back into Zagreb in search of Yubi and Luca. Vadim insisted that Luca ride with him and lead him back to Yubi. His Italian was weak, but he made his point well enough.

"No no," Luca answered sharply, "I can direct you to Yubi, but I am needed here."

Vadim looked at him like a horn had just sprouted from his forehead. Luca repeated in German. Kyra translated it into Romani.

Vadim continued in Italian, demanding impatiently, "Why? Why would you be needed here?"

"I should stay with Kyra..., and we should move the caravan now. The sun is almost up and people will blame you. They will blame the Gypsies. You know they will."

Vadim did not understand. Again, Luca said it in German, and again Kyra translated into Romani. Vadim lost all patience, and he shouted, "Where is Yubi?"

Luca pointed, and Vadim vaulted onto his horse and rode off in the indicated direction.

Kyra embraced Luca again and thanked him for following Yubi, "If you had not chased them…, if you had not followed him…"

Luca squeezed her back, kissed her head, and pulled from her to examine her burns.

He ran his thumb lightly on her blistered cheek and whispered, "I was right. You are tough." He touched his lips to her burns, pulled away again and added, "Tough and tender."

Her feelings were pulled to two opposite extremes. She was worried to death about Yubi and had no patience for Luca's garish flirtations. At the same time, she held in her heart profound gratitude for the fortunate service he had provided. It is hard to say why Luca was hanging around Yubi after their confrontation on the street. Kyra would not risk offending him by asking. But there was little doubt he was Yubi's savior. If ever he had sought to separate Yubi from Kyra, the events of that night provided the perfect opportunity. Yet he acted rightly, right by Yubi and right by the kumpania.

Kyra's nerves were overwhelming her, and sitting still while Vadim rode to find Yubi, while Stoyan and Ernko were somewhere in the city, would have been the death of her. She decided to ride through Zagreb, find Stoyan and Ernko, and bring them back quickly.

As she saddled a horse, Luca stopped her, asking, "No, no, where are you going?"

"As you said," she answered with a calmness not at all reflective of the turmoil inside, "We need to be on the move as soon as Vadim comes back with Yubi. So Stoyan and Ernko must be back first. Someone has to find them and bring them back."

She was prepared to defend her actions further, but he agreed, adding, "Yes, and Stoyan should be here to receive his son. Yubi will need his father. Come, we must hurry."

She could not believe her ears, and she asked incredulously, "You want to come with me?"

Luca buckled the strap of the saddle, mounted the horse, reached for Kyra's hand, and said, "Come, we will do this together."

She took his hand, and he pulled her up, but she did not swing around behind him. Still wearing her performance trousers, she stepped on his foot and swung her leg in front of him. He scooted back to give her room and wrapped his arms around her as she hollered at the horse in Romani and they rode toward the city.

He had been near her. He had run his fingers across her skin. But he had never wrapped his arms tightly around her. He noticed immediately that she did not bounce clumsily on the back of the horse. She seemed rather an extended muscle of the beast, just as graceful and just as powerful. His flirtations had been playful, but as he held to her on the back of the horse, a true infatuation formed.

He had never spent time in a Roma kumpania, never encountered Roma women. The women he had known were submissive and entirely victimized by his charm and beauty. Kyra was unlike any feminine creature he had ever imagined. She seemed to possess the horse and control each of its muscles with her mind, muscles that were much more powerful than her own. He could not have known that Kyra and this horse had a history, this horse she called Gellen, after her father, was her first friend in the kumpania. She spoke to Gellen when she could speak to no one else, and Gellen listened well to her then.

Luca held more tightly, not because he feared falling, but because he wanted to explore her strength, to feel more closely her unity with the horse, and the rhythmic flex and release of her muscles. The ride into Zagreb was not long. He wished it was longer, and he wished she would ride past the city and on indefinitely beyond.

Another half an hour later and the shops of Zagreb would have come to life. The church bell would have rung. Those who conduct their business by the light of dawn would have taken to the streets. As it was, the streets were still quiet. Kyra took note of this. She stopped the horse and calmed it with a few pats on its shoulder and a few whispered words.

Luca began to question, "Shouldn't we contin—"

"Shush!"

He obeyed, still intoxicated by his new image of her.

She listened for the sounds of horse hooves. She heard them, off in the distance to their left. She had no need to spur the horse or yank the reins. She simply leaned to the horse's ear and whispered, "Za Gellen. Stoyan zeravo."

They were off to the left in pursuit of the sound. Everything Kyra did in the wee hours of that morning, every movement and every word, was another sip of the intoxicating wine of infatuation on Luca's lips. The horse took them directly to Stoyan and Ernko. Kyra gave her report in rushed Romani, and the four of them rode back to the camp.

Stoyan was surprised to see Luca riding with Kyra, but less surprised to see how he held to her, how he nestled his cheek to her back and tried to experience every twitch of her body. He gave it only a fleeting thought as they raced to the kumpania. Luca was a concern for another day. That morning was about Yubi and the actions necessitated by his violence.

CHAPTER THIRTY-SEVEN
WHAT LOVE LOOKS LIKE

STOYAN RETURNED TO A CAMP that was still without Yubi. The next few minutes were wretched. Relief came with the sight of Vadim riding in a triumphant trot toward him. Yubi sat behind Vadim. He looked well, better than expected. He did not slump weakly, but rode behind Vadim in high posture and with alertness in his eyes. Safely and soundly within the camp, and surrounded by a halo of concerned friends, Yubi sprang from the horse to stand between Stoyan and Kyra. Stoyan pulled his son into a protective embrace.

Vadim looked to Kyra and asked, "Are we all here? Is everybody back?"

Kyra nodded, and Vadim suggested, "Perhaps Luca is right. Should we move on from Zagreb?"

Everyone looked to her for an answer. She had no room in her heart for such thoughts. The moment was about Yubi. She ignored the expectations on her, turned to Yubi and inspected him scalp to toe. His clothes, his hair, his face, arms, and hands were all covered in blood. Zagreb and any dangers swelling within it might as well have been on the other side of the world, for all it meant to Kyra.

She turned her eyes to Stoyan and ordered him tyrannically, "Take him! Clean him up and tend to him!"

Stoyan led Yubi away from her, toward his vardo. Kyra took a step in pursuit when a hand took her from behind. It was Luca. His palm burned with hot-blooded passion for her.

"Yubi is in his father's hands now," he told her, "You and I have other work to do."

"You and I?" she questioned him.

He pulled her in, nose to nose with him, and continued, "We have to leave this area immediately. Vadim awaits your answer. Tell him to pack the camp and move."

Nobody else standing around them understood his German. They all looked to Kyra to translate. She scanned their eager faces but bit her tongue.

She turned back to Luca and demanded, "Tell me straight, what is our danger?"

"Yubi bludgeoned a man, possibly killed him, a man of Zagreb. This man will have family and friends, neighbors and colleagues, who will seek revenge on us. The law will come after me."

"Why would the law come after you?"

"Not after me… after him, Yubi. We need to get clear of here immediately. Come with me! You and I should leave now."

"Alone? Without the kumpania? Why?"

He leaned his face closer to hers and parted his lips slightly.

She pulled away and repeated, "Why?"

"You and I can ride ahead of the others, find a safe path. Make our own way for a while."

It was a very good thing for Luca that the others could not understand him. Yubi's would not have been the only bloody hands that morning.

Kyra did not give Luca's suggestion the honor of an answer. She turned to Vadim, who was still mounted on his horse, and she ordered him, "Prepare the caravan for travel, but for now, we remain here."

He nodded and the kumpania responded without further instructions, doing what they had done a thousand times before.

With those efforts in capable hands, Kyra turned her thoughts comprehensively to Yubi. She ran to the acrobats' vardo. They were not inside. She looked into their tent, and found them there. Yubi sat with his bloody shirt piled beside him. With a wet cloth in hand, Stoyan was wiping blood away from his son's arms and shoulders. Kyra focused on Yubi's hands. They were cut and swollen. One of his fingers looked dislocated.

Kyra gasped. It was not a gasp of astonishment, not one of terror, but one of immense compassion and concern.

She took an instinctive step toward him, but Stoyan raised a hand toward her and said calmly, "He will be well, and you can tend to him soon, but for now, can you leave us? Right now I need to be alone with my son."

The timid little newcomer that she once was surged back to the surface. Her shoulders slouched submissively, and she backed from the tent and joined the others in their efforts, making a particular point to avoid Luca.

Stoyan returned to cleaning his son. Not a word had passed between them since they were reunited by Vadim. Yubi waited for the questions. He waited for a lecture that never came. In Yubi's place, Stoyan would not have done what his son had done. He would not have chased the man and beaten him down. But he understood why Yubi did it, and as much as he believed a lesson should come from the incident, he had nothing to teach, nothing to correct. He had heard about the intruder to the party. He knew the vile and vulgar things that were shouted. Without judgment, he just cleaned the blood from his son's body.

The blood on Yubi's face and hair was not his own, but the blood on his hands and arms was. It still trickled from his mutilated hands and blended with the blood of his victim. With nurturing care, Stoyan cleaned Yubi's injured hands. It should have been painful. It must have been, as Stoyan scrubbed over broken skin and broken fingers. Yubi felt nothing. His mind and heart were in a heated tug-of-war, and he was not sure what his father thought, for Stoyan did not say a word.

Yubi could take no more silent care from his father. He began to cry, to blubber like a baby child, and he blurted out, "I love her. I love her, father. I love Kyra."

Stoyan made no immediate reaction. He showed no signs of surprise at the proclamation. He continued to care for Yubi's hands, then placidly replied, "I know you do, son. I see it in you, and I recognize it for what it is… a true love, an intense love, a love very familiar to my heart."

Having his feelings confirmed by his father, Yubi tried to roll onto his knees and stand. Stoyan pushed him back to a seat.

Yubi pulled his hand from his father's care and protested, "I don't care about my wounds. I must go to her now!"

Stoyan gently took his hand back, and continued cleaning it as he warned, "This is not the time to come on strongly. Kyra is not like your mother. You will frighten her. You must let the excitement of the moment settle. And when your love wears a calmer, gentler face, you may profess it to her."

The idea of bottling his passion and shelving it for later use seemed impossible to him. He did not have the strength. How could he hide it? His every breath wanted to scream it. He leaned into his father, as broken as a young man can be, and he wept. Stoyan held him and rubbed him and kissed his head, while Yubi released himself more with each exhale, until he was as an infant in his father's care.

Stoyan had spoken earnestly. His son's pain *was* familiar to him, which only pinched his old heart more ferociously.

By the time the slight brush of color on the eastern horizon had swelled to light the camp, it was struck and in travel formation. Kyra was seated beside Lavinia on the porch of her vardo, discussing everything that had happened in Zagreb, from the performance and Luca's surprise ending to Yubi and his vicious assault.

Luca came to them and interrupted, "We are ready to travel. Give the word, Kyra. We must move on."

He was as easy to read as her father's well-kept ledgers back in Szanzar. Luca was scared, and not for Yubi or the kumpania. His was a personal fear. The only secret was the exact reason for the fear.

Kyra translated his words to Lavinia and asked her, "What do you think? Is it really so urgent? Vadim has arranged other performances in Zagreb, and Ernko has lucrative commissions."

Luca spoke up before Lavinia could answer, "For Yubi's sake, we must go now. Think of his victim, the family and friends. There will be retribution on us all."

Kyra translated again, but for an extra pair of ears. Milena had been standing near the side of the vardo, just out of sight. She heard the entire exchange. She stepped behind Luca and gave him her opinion, "Friends? A man like that is sure to make more enemies than friends. Yubi did Zagreb a favor. I doubt last night was the first time another man's fist was brought to his face."

Kyra continued in increasing discomfort translating between them.

Luca argued, "You were not there, Milena. You did not see Yubi's rage, his violence."

Milena walked between Luca and the porch, stared him in the eyes, and answered, "That man threatened Kyra. He wanted to take her. If I had been there instead of Yubi,

I would have done worse. I would do worse to *anyone* who tries to take Kyra."

As Kyra put Milena's words into German, they were delicious in her mouth, but she regretted them as soon as they hit Luca's ear.

In typical Milena form, the threat was not well-veiled. She leaned an elbow against the porch and added in a more casual tone, "If you need to go, Luca, then go. We are staying here until Kyra orders us to leave."

Kyra began the translation, but stopped. Her heart was stuck between them. Milena had become like a beloved sister, and her defensive threat was an honor. But Luca rescued Yubi. After craving Milena's affection for so long, she finally had it and did not want to risk losing it. But Luca was exciting and brought thrilling new flavor to their performances and their lives.

Kyra's mind went where it habitually went — to Yubi. She declared in Romani, more to herself than to those near her, "Yubi is at the heart of this. His opinion should be weighed most heavily."

Milena and Lavinia nodded. Luca heard Yubi's name, and his jealousy swelled. He could not understand how Yubi held Kyra's heart so tightly. The more he thought about Yubi, the more obsessively he desired Kyra.

Kyra went to Stoyan's tent and found the father and son in quiet conversation. They spoke in a language Kyra did not recognize.

She gingerly interrupted, "Please, excuse me. There is debate about what to do. There might be some danger in staying here, but we have commissions in Zagreb. The kumpania is looking to me for a directive. I don't know what to do."

Stoyan turned his eyes from Kyra to Yubi. Yubi answered simply, "I want to leave."

Stoyan added, "It is true. We have commissions here. But the sea coast waits for us, and we have already made more money than we need. I think we should leave, but not for the reason you say. Let our steps be toward something we desire, not away from something we fear. Kyra, if you decide that we should go, let us go slowly and comfortably."

Kyra needed no higher authority. Yubi wanted to leave, and Stoyan presented a good argument in defense of his son's wishes. She was more than a little excited to tell Luca. She wanted to please him, partially from gratitude, but also from something deeper. She had strange feelings for him that had quickly rooted in her. It was an inexplicable feeling. She could not tell if she was drawn to him or repulsed by him. The truth is, she felt both. Maybe she was repulsed by the draw, or perhaps drawn to the repulsion. In either case, it kept Luca very often on her mind.

She left the acrobats' tent and found Luca standing near. He did not wait for her report. He took her by the hand and pulled her away from the tent, not far enough away. Stoyan and Yubi could hear all that he said.

"You need to give Yubi more space," he instructed, "You are holding him back."

Kyra shook her head to demonstrate her confusion, so he clarified, "He is an acrobat like his father. He should be swinging from his father's high bar or walking on his tight rope. He does neither. Lavinia has him only dancing with you. Let him be an acrobat."

Kyra dropped her head and considered his point closely. Her face began to wince and her eyes began to water. Luca was good at what he did, good at handling fire and good at handling hearts. He waited, letting her think and letting her emotions crest.

Just as her eyes held all the water they could hold, before the first tear fell, he added, "And he is holding you back. You were born to be a fire artist. Your life awaited only me to bring your destiny to you. Have you ever thought that everything that has happened to you was to bring you to me?"

Kyra lifted her fingertips to the blisters on her cheek. Luca grabbed her wrist, pulled her hand from her face, and placed it on his heart, saying with widening, fiery eyes, "There is no fire we cannot handle, no flame hotter than our hearts. Surely you must see it. We are the same and meant to be together…, with or without these people."

Stoyan and Yubi were dismayed at what they had overheard, dismayed but not astonished. It was enough for Stoyan to leave his son in the tent and place two eyes on Kyra and Luca. He watched them from the shadows of his own vardo.

With his hand still pressing Kyra's hand against his chest, Luca leaned into her and gave her a soft kiss on her lips. She did not know whether to commit to the kiss or hit him and run away. She had strong inclinations to both. She did neither. She simply waited for him to withdraw his mouth from hers, then she pulled her hand from him with force, turned, and walked away. The kiss made her think much more than it made her feel. It felt like nothing at all to her.

Stoyan returned to Yubi and reported what he saw. He was relieved by Kyra's hasty withdrawal. Yubi was not.

Stoyan assured him, "Kyra is in little danger from Luca. I know his kind. He seeks the path of greatest pleasure and least resistance. He will find Kyra too difficult, too smart and far too complicated."

"And he is not smart enough to know she is worth the effort."

"Oh, I believe he is smart enough, but he does not crave what she has to offer."

Yubi ground his teeth and contradicted, "He seems to crave her."

"Only the very outer layer of her. He has no interest in the Kyra we know."

Yubi answered wistfully, "... we know and love."

Stoyan nodded and added with unhidden disdain in his voice, "He is nothing to us, just a simple-minded fool who is incapable of admiring her as we do. His admiration takes the only path it understands, the only path at its disposal. Let him remain as he is, beneath us."

The speech had no soothing effects on Yubi.

Stoyan smiled through the pinching pain he felt for his son. He kissed Yubi's head, walked from the tent, stuck his head back in, and added, "Kyra is above him. She will not succumb. He will grow tired of the chase and move on... from Kyra and from all of us. Ours is not a life he wants."

The day proceeded as Stoyan suggested. It had been an exciting evening, followed by a long, fearful, and strenuous night. They were all tired. The afternoon came without danger, without disruption of any kind. They ate together as a kumpania, then began a slow march southwest, toward their destination, the Croatian coastal city of Split.

They were no more than nine miles out of Zagreb when they stopped to camp for the night. In front of others, Luca continued to urge Kyra to travel with greater urgency. In the few moments he managed to get her alone, he timidly suggested they leave the kumpania together and make their way alone.

When the camp was settled, Stoyan found Luca alone. He took him by the wrist and pulled him several forceful strides away from the others. There was a focused sternness in Stoyan's look, one that demanded privacy. All the others walked away. Even the herders led their animals to the other side of the camp. Stoyan had Luca alone, and he had a mind full of words and a heart full of feelings to express.

Stoyan was a full seven inches shorter than Luca, but Luca felt like a child under the strong, paternal gaze. Stoyan got directly to the point, "Handle Kyra with care, young man. She may appear fragile to you, like a thin sheet of glass. But you cannot place her under fire, heat her, and bend her and shape her to your will. You will find her edges are sharp and you will be cut."

Stoyan chose his metaphor carefully. Venice was the glass making center of Europe, and he knew the image would have power to a Venetian.

Luca took the metaphor into his own hands, arguing, "Yes, she is sharp, but it is only over fire that she can be shaped into something lovely. You know her story. See how she has been shaped by fire so far."

"No! Kyra's struggles have not shaped her. They have revealed her. The fires of her life have burned away what her parents and neighbors thought she was, and they have left only Kyra, bright and beautiful, but sharp and dangerous. Watch yourself. She is more than you think. Try to bend her to your will and you will be damaged."

"Damaged by her or by you?"

"Act wisely and that won't matter."

"Are you threatening me?"

Stoyan pushed his lips to one side, shook his head, and responded, "I am not threatening you. You do that well enough to yourself. I am warning you. A woman's heart is of the *strangest* substance in the world. There is nothing stronger. It can cut through solid stone, and yet, it is affected by a whisper. Do not trifle with it. You cannot damage Kyra. You can hurt her, but not damage her. It is you who will be shattered."

Luca retorted with condescending overconfidence, "That might be true of a woman, but Kyra is a girl. She does not yet have a woman's heart. I am safe."

Stoyan stepped closer and looked upward at the taller young man. The short, old acrobat might as well have been standing on a cloud for the power his stern gaze had in humbling Luca, as he spoke in a much deeper voice, "Kyra spent no time between girlhood and womanhood. She has lived and lost enough for a full lifetime in the last few years. She was a woman at twelve years old, and you are still a boy. Tread carefully, for your sake."

Luca sat down on the ground with his head lowered in thought, then he looked up to Stoyan, stood again with a defiant posture, and declared, "I think I am in love with her."

Stoyan scoffed and shook his head, and he responded, "I don't imagine you have ever been in *love*. I have watched you, and you are not what love looks like."

He thought of his son, of his only child crying like a baby, with swollen knuckles and another man's blood spattered across his face, confessing his love for Kyra to his father, and he repeated to Luca, "YOU are not what love looks like."

Luca lost all remaining timidity, as he asked smugly, "How would you know? You are alone."

"I will always love my wife. It was she who taught me what love looks like."

"Well, that is the difference between us. *I* taught my wife how to love."

Stoyan's face went blank. He took one step backward and asked, "Your wife?"

Luca thoughtlessly continued, "Yes, I am a man. I taught my wife how to—"

He realized too late how freely his tongue had flown, and he stumbled to recover, "My wife…, no, not… I meant to say…"

"And who is your wife? Where is she now?"

In the brief silence that followed, Stoyan's vision cleared. It was Chiara. Chiara was Luca's wife, not his sister.

"Chiara is your wife. Why have you lied to us?"

Chiara! Stoyan could not remember seeing her since they left Bogdan's house. He demanded, "Where is Chiara? Where is your wife?"

Luca stared blankly at him, confirming everything by denying nothing. Stoyan thought hard, trying to recall everything he could remember since they left the party. It led him to a horrid notion.

"Why were you so eager to leave Zagreb, to leave your wife behind? Luca… what have you done?"

"I did nothing to her. She saw that I love Kyra, and she let me go."

"She let you go and remained alone in a strange city? You are deceitful. There is no truth to get from your lips."

Stoyan was determined to find poor Chiara and see to the welfare her deceptive husband disregarded. He found Vadim and Ernko gathered with the musicians. He explained what he knew, and he, Vadim, and Ernko rode with haste back to Zagreb.

Before he left, he instructed Yubi, "Take Kyra into her vardo. Lock yourselves in. Do not let her out and let nobody in until I return."

Yubi did not know what was happening. He asked his father, "What? Why? Is she in danger?"

"No, son, not while she is with you. She will never be in danger with you. You are what love looks like."

CHAPTER THIRTY-EIGHT
THE BANDAGING OF WOUNDS

YUBI COULD NOT IMAGINE THE REASONS for his father's rushed directive. He obeyed and locked himself away with Kyra. Stoyan's intent was to keep Luca from her. He had no trust in Luca's decency, and saw no limit to what he might do. He had abandoned his wife to pursue Kyra, a plan he probably formed back in Požega. It was the only reason Stoyan could imagine they would pretend to be brother and sister.

The air between Kyra and Yubi was awkward at first. Neither knew what was going on. Both had a thousand questions for the other and a million sentiments that wanted to spring forth. So many thoughts and feelings log-jammed in their throats, and neither said a word for the first hour together. That is not to say there was no communication. Kyra took immediately to evaluating and tending his wounds.

She forcefully took his hands from his lap as they sat together on her bed. Kyra unwrapped the bandages placed by Stoyan and gasped at the horror underneath. The violence of the previous night was told descriptively by the damage to Yubi's hands. The torn skin had not clotted. Blood oozed from his knuckles. On the middle knuckle of his left hand, his bone could be seen. The little finger of his left hand was broken, and two fingers of his right hand were badly dislocated.

Stoyan knew little of tending such wounds. Kyra had learned much from Iraja. She set the fingers and bound them to each other, then pulled spices from a box, mixed them with crushed nettle leaves, spat into the mixture to make a paste, and caked it onto his broken skin. The spices stung, and he tried to withdraw his hand from her. Her grasp on his wrist was committed to the effort. Strong as he was, he could not pull from her care.

She gazed at his wounds as they brought conflicting feelings into her heart. It was a gruesome sight, obviously painful, though he showed no signs of suffering. Kyra could not help but visualize the violence that caused it, or the face that received the violence. Those feelings were twisted into a new shape as she considered that it was all done for her. Yubi's mind was not capable of such violence. Only his heart was. His love for her was on bloody display on her lap. For the first time, she understood his heart. He loved her far more than he loved himself. He risked everything in her defense. Although the exact nature of that love was still obscure, the depth of it was unfathomable.

She suddenly remembered something else Iraja taught her. She took a spice called lovage and sprinkled over the medicinal paste. As she wrapped his hands, she sang,

Opré rook, adré vesh

(Over the tree, into the woods)

Si chiriklo ta chirikli

Kyra

(Are male and female birds)

Telé rook, adré vesh

(Under the tree, into the woods)

Si piramno ta piramni

(Are male and female sweethearts)

The lovage and the verse were an old Roma spell, detailed in one of the rugged books at the bottom of Kyra's trunk. It was a love spell, not one intended to attract a lover, but one designed to reveal love. Yubi was not familiar with it. To him, the lovage was just another healing spice, and the verse was a song to soothe. Still, the mention of male and female sweethearts made him blush throughout. Hairs raised across his arms as the words melodically left her lips. It affected him so deeply, he imagined even his bones turned blushfully pink.

Once his hands were bound and bandaged, they sat in awkward silence, each with thoughts and feelings fruitlessly scrambling around their brains in search of appropriate words. The strange tension was broken by Kyra when she pulled one of Iraja's books from her trunk and showed him the recipe she used to make the stinging paste. The love spell was in a different book, one she kept out of sight. They spoke of spices and remedies, and the light conversation settled their hearts enough to lie down and sleep.

Kyra awoke to the mumbling of voices outside of her vardo. There was something in the tone that concerned her. She stepped onto her porch and overheard Milena discussing Luca and Chiara with her husband. Kyra heard it all. She found out Chiara was Luca's wife, not his sister. She learned that Chiara had been left to an unknown fate in Zagreb. Her spirit did not consult her mind, but acted by its own precepts. Wearing no more than a skirt and light blouse, she took a horse and rode toward the city alone.

As Stoyan, Vadim, and Ernko reached the southern outskirts of Zagreb in the dark of the early night, the temperature dropped cruelly. It was unusually cold for the region, and snow fell heavily, in large flakes blown by a bitter wind. The streets were empty and silent. They rode side by side, as slowly and as quietly as possible, winding their way from the outskirts toward the city center.

They had no idea what they were looking for, whether to scour the streets or to knock on doors. Stoyan regretted leaving the camp so hastily and impetuously, and not pressing Luca for more information. They made a clockwise spiral inward, reached the city center, then began to spiral outward again. There was no sign of life on the streets. They were cold. They were tired. And they were frustrated with their failure. They decided to find shelter for the night and resume their search in the morning, when people would be out and about and available for questioning.

They tied their horses to a street post and found a space between two buildings. One had a large overhang and kept the ground beneath it dry. It was not the cold that kept them from sleeping. They were used to the cold. It was the terrible images in their heads, images of timid Chiara alone in a strange city. By the time they settled, there was little time before sunrise. They sat huddled together, each silently and fretfully imagining the many horrible things that could have happened since they last saw her.

When the streets were again lit by the young sun, the three men walked their horses through a foot and a half of snow, street by street, house by house. The weather kept people indoors when they would normally have been about their morning business. Markets were empty. Shops were locked up. High drifts of snow were blown against the fronts of houses, sealing the inhabitants inside. The city was large, and Stoyan, Vadim, and Ernko, independently, but at the same time, began to realize the futility of their efforts.

Without communication on the matter, they all decided to return to the camp, retrieve Luca, and bring him back to Zagreb to find and make amends with his wife. They exited the city to the southwest, and there, behind a barn, was an overturned wagon. The front axle was broken and two wheels were missing. It had obviously been discarded by its owner. Ernko stared at it as they rode by, trying to determine its fitness for repair. But it called to him in a different way, in some inexplicably arcane way.

It is fortunate that it did. His eyes drifted to the left and he saw at some distance a horse, not just a horse but one he recognized, one of their horses. With an awful, sinking feeling, he broke from the others and rushed to the wagon, shouting, "Chiara!" Stoyan and Vadim followed him. There was nothing they could see or sense that indicated Chiara was near, but Ernko seemed convinced. They jumped from their horses and peered together under the wagon, and there, looking pale and lifeless, was Chiara. Draped across her like a blanket was Kyra.

The men were stunned motionless. They were troubled to find Chiara in such a sad state under the wagon, but they were looking for Chiara. Finding Kyra with her was a shock that took a moment of recovery.

Kyra heard the commotion and turned to see their faces staring at her. She crawled out from under the wagon, sobbing violently. Between gasps, she explained what she knew.

"I was riding through the farm… I heard a moan, a miserable moan. Chiara! It's Chiara!"

Kyra was frighteningly cold to the touch. Stoyan held her and rubbed her while Vadim and Ernko pulled Chiara out from under the wagon with little hope that she lived. She was deathly white. What remained of her dress was scant, torn, and soaked in frozen blood. Her face was bruised and bloody, and scrapes and bruises covered most of her arms and legs. Entire sections of her hair appeared to be torn out of her scalp.

Vadim pressed his ear to her nose. She breathed! Ever so faintly, she breathed. Our heroes had no thoughts of justice or retribution, no notions of blame. They thought only of Chiara's life. With a blacksmith's strength, Ernko threw her across the shoulders of his horse and mounted behind her. Stoyan fetched the horse Kyra had taken from the camp, and they all rode back as fast as they could.

The ride was vigorous. By the time they got back to the camp, Kyra was warm with exertion. Yubi, as instructed, was locked in Kyra's vardo, but not with Kyra. She had soothed him into a deep sleep before she left. Everybody else was stirring. The camp was abuzz. The riders went directly to Kyra's vardo. Stoyan mounted the porch and shouted for Yubi. Such a sight he opened the door to see. Vadim and Ernko were lifting the limp and bloody Chiara to the porch. Yubi, with his busted and bandaged hands, helped his father receive her. They stripped her, laid her in Kyra's bed, and covered her in bedding. There were wounds that would need tending, but not until she was warmed. Cold was the immediate peril.

Once Chiara was safely in the hands of Kyra and Yubi, Stoyan stepped out of the vardo and shouted, "Where is Luca? Tell him to come tend to his wife!"

Milena stood nearby and answered him, "Come now, Stoyan. You did not believe he would stay here, did you?"

Stoyan growled, puckered his face, and demanded, "Tell me he has not left. Tell me he has not abandoned his wife in this condition!"

He thought about Luca, about their last exchange, and he responded to his own demand, "Of course he did. He abandoned her to the streets of Zagreb, left her in the hands of nobody-knows-whom, to terrors I cannot imagine. Of course he left before we returned."

Milena informed him, "The scoundrel left last night. He was gone when we awoke. The fool left his trail in the snow. He could not have gone far in this snow, and he will be easy to follow."

"For what reason?" Stoyan shouted, "Are we to kill him in the snow? We cannot bring him here. He has no interest in the welfare of his wife. Either *he* can be here or Chiara, not both, and she is going nowhere. Let Luca go. Chiara is our only concern."

Several times over the next hour, Chiara's breath slowed to a near stop. It seemed there was little chance she would survive. Cooks heated blankets at a fire and ran them in constant procession to Kyra's vardo. Kyra treated the cuts and scrapes on her head. After an hour, her temperature regulated and her breathing strengthened.

They finally removed the blankets to inspect her wounds. The cuts and bruising to her arms and legs were numerous, but not severe. The real damage did not come from whatever violence caused them. The cold was her worst assailant. Her fingers and toes were frozen black. Chiara was still unconscious, showing no signs of pain. The frozen digits needed to be removed immediately.

Vadim volunteered for the duty, but Kyra remained as a nurse at his hip. Vadim cut Chiara's blackened fingers from her hands, and the toes from her feet. The poor young woman groaned and whimpered, but did not awaken. When the amputations were complete, Chiara was left to Kyra's care. It was a horrid thing to witness, and Kyra's compassion was stirred to its extreme, as was her resentment for Luca. She regretted every tender feeling she had felt for him, every moment of admiration, and she was nauseated in remembering the flashing moments of attraction. She ground her teeth in a sickening blend of hate and regret.

Chiara awoke confused the following morning. She was unsure where she was, whom she was with, if she was sleeping through a painful nightmare or suffering some hell after death. There was one thing that calmed her. Kyra sang to her. Nobody else was allowed to see her. One face, one pair of hands, one voice alone was all she could handle. Kyra saw two things in her patient. She saw a sister, another poor orphan taken in by the kumpania. And she saw a warning. Chiara had been taken in by Luca's charm and nearly driven to her death. Kyra, too, had been drawn by Luca's charm, and she shuddered to imagine how differently it could have all played out.

In the first break she allowed herself, she went to the cooks for hot stew. Stoyan, Vadim, and Ernko were gathered around the fire. One question burned hotter than the food — how was it they came to find Kyra beneath that wagon, huddled over Chiara? What mystical guide, what esoteric influence led her to the farm and near enough to the wagon to her Chiara's weak and faint moan? One thing was universally agreed upon. Had Kyra not found her and covered her with her own body, Chiara would surely have died.

Kyra explained, but not in terms they understood, "Sympathy. I felt such pain for her, a familiar pain..., abandonment. Her pain and mine were connected. I only followed the connection and there she was."

That dirty little child they had plucked from the grass, what a magical creature she had grown into! Each week a new talent sprang from her, each more magnificent than the last. They listened to her with confusion, but with an excess of admiration. They wanted to soak in her company, but the visit around the fire was short. Kyra excused herself and returned to Chiara.

The cold lasted for two months. More snow was added on top of the old every couple of days. After two months, it began to warm. The snow melted and left a wet and muddy landscape. With all that had happened, they decided to remain in camp until spring, until the land recovered from the wounds of winter, and until Yubi and Chiara recovered from the wounds of Zagreb.

There were many remaining questions about the night of Bogdan's party. What had happened to Chiara? Had her wounds been caused by her husband or some other? How did she come to lie under that overturned wagon? None would ask. Her past was her past and had no bearing on her future. That was the way of the Roma. It was not Kyra's way. When Chiara regained her strength and her wits, Kyra asked. She began her questioning by retelling parts of her own story. She spoke of Iraja and of Yubi. When Chiara was ready, Kyra asked her what happened that night. The story was as bad as the wounds suggested.

Luca ordered her to remain in Zagreb while he ran away with Kyra. She begged him not to leave her, and followed him like a puppy through the streets, crying for him to love her. He ordered her to leave him alone and forget about him. When he realized she would not obey him, he took her by the hair and dragged her down the street. The commotion drew the attention of a seedy band of men. Luca gave her to them. Whether he received some payment for her, she did not know. The men took her behind buildings, beat her and violated her. In which ways, she would not say, but Kyra imagined the worst, and still, her imagination fell far short of the vile truth.

When they were done with her, they dragged her to a farm on the edge of town and left her for dead. Chiara crawled under the capsized wagon. She had no memory beyond that until she regained her wits under Kyra's tender care.

The guilt! Kyra's sense of guilt was extreme. Had she refused Luca's attention sooner, and more harshly, had Luca not been set on stealing away with her, Chiara might not have suffered as she did. She would never again be whole, not of body and not of spirit. Kyra felt responsible. She was determined to be the glue that held the shattered remains of Chiara together, and she silently swore her life to Chiara's welfare.

Over the warming months that followed, Kyra was a nurse. Nurse became mother, mother became sister. By the time Chiara's face glowed with hope in her future, sister became friend. Chiara blamed Luca, not Kyra, and they bonded in their similarities. The timid and subservient wife of Luca was slowly replaced by a woman just getting to know herself. For that purpose, she could not have been in better hands.

At first, Kyra was an enigma to Chiara. Kyra had such command over the affections and obedience of the kumpania, over the lives of women *and* men, yet she was not loud. Kyra's boldness was more spiritual than physical. Her strength existed beyond her body, beyond the things she said or did. In the months under her constant care, Chiara came to understand that strength, and very slowly, sneakily, and secretively, it infiltrated her and began to grow.

Yubi healed well, but the mending of his hands did nothing for his heart. He was relieved to be rid of Luca, but an itchy agitation lingered in the fire artist's wake. Yubi had thought of Luca while beating the man in the Roman bathhouse. He regretted not directing his violence to the appropriate recipient.

Kyra was occupied with Chiara. Her heart and her time was there. That is not to say Yubi was gone from her mind. She feared him and loved him in extremes she struggled to reconcile. One afternoon, she peeled away from Chiara long enough to corner Stoyan alone. She confessed her polar feelings and begged Stoyan for some insight.

Knowing his son better than any, and knowing Yubi's love for Kyra, he told her, "Yubi is a perpetual surprise, even to those who know him best. Usually the surprise is delightful. Sometimes it is awful, even terrifying. But he is pure and dear, and he is mine. I will defend him always."

He rubbed Kyra's cheek with his thumb, gazed at her like a doting father to his daughter, and added, "He is ours... still and always, our Yubi. Kyra, he is yours. He belongs more to you than to anybody. Yubi is very much yours."

With those words, Kyra saw more of the sweet boy who taught her Romani in the grass, and less of the wild violence that flew uncontrollably from him that terrible night in Zagreb. The violence was still there, but it wore a less frightening face. It wore the face of devotion, commitment, and possession.

During those months of recovery, Yubi's passion churned quietly within him. He could not dance. He could not flip. He could not hold Kyra in his hand, drop her into his arms, and squeeze her against his chest. His wrapped hands could not make a fist. They could not take another person by the arm and give an affectionate squeeze. He was impatient to move the caravan again, as if it could roll toward healing — toward the coast, toward new performances, and toward the future he dreamed of, as Kyra's performance partner, as her friend and confidant, as her lover, and as her husband.

CHAPTER THIRTY-NINE
TORNIK'S WEALTHY WIDOW

THE CITY OF SPLIT, THE ADRIATIC COAST, glorious new wares from across the seas, new performances in front of new people, none of these things were their top priority. It was Chiara they considered most deeply. What was to become of her? Where was her husband, and would he return for her? There were as many opinions on these matters as there were languages spoken in the kumpania.

Chiara was not Roma. She was not a Gypsy, nor was she likely to become one, as Kyra had. Kyra's contagious strength continued to grow inside of her, but it changed in Chiara into something less suited for a nomadic life. Unlike Kyra, Chiara still had a family. She had a mother and father, a living home in which she was raised. In other words, she had a life that she could return to. None of the others thought of her that way. How could they? They were nomads, always looking forward. Only Kyra considered Chiara's return to her childhood home.

Kyra was seated on her porch beside Chiara, holding that troubled head against her neck and singing songs. She did not sing in Romani. She knew Chiara would not learn

Romani, embrace the kumpania, and amputate her old identity the way her fingers and toes had been. Kyra sang no words, only melodies, melodies of the kumpania.

Stoyan came to them to represent those who shared his opinions. Just as he had told Kyra years earlier, Stoyan said to Chiara in Italian, "Your old life is dead. Your marriage is dead. Your new life with us begins now."

Kyra was never taught Italian, but her knack for languages was uncanny. She had picked up enough in the things she overheard since Chiara and Luca came to them to understand what he meant.

She surprised Stoyan and Chiara by stopping him, saying, "Not so fast, Stoyan. Has nobody asked her what she wants? Her parents... her family... she might want... need..."

Her Italian failed her, and she transitioned to Romani, "My life before was truly dead when I came to you. Chiara might be different. Has anybody thought of that? She might want to return."

"Return to what?" he asked, "Her scoundrel husband has abandoned her, and it is for the best that he did. Only now can she embrace her future."

"There is more to a woman than her husband," she scolded.

"Oh Kyra, I know there is. If anyone knows, I do."

She had heard enough of his marriage to believe him, but she instructed him just the same, "You have always been a Gypsy. You cannot understand her as I do."

"Are you saying you would return to Szanzar if you discovered your parents still lived?"

"Not now! Of course, not now. I am a daughter of the kumpania. But in those first months, yes. Yes, I would have gone back to my home... had it survived."

It was a point never considered by either of them, and a long thoughtful silence ensued between them, until Stoyan asked her, "You say 'not now'. At what point did it change? Do you remember when it was that you would have stayed with us, even if your parents lived?"

"Have you forgotten Paks? We never discussed it, but I had a choice in Paks. A home was offered to me there... a family similar in many ways to the one I lost. When did I know I was Roma? It was when you were surrounded. I teetered on the edge of two different lives. I had the choice to run to the shelter of a village home or jump on your horse, pull you from that mob, and ride back to the kumpania. You know which one I chose."

The memory of Kyra's heroics in Paks remained always near his heart. She had no need to remind him. But to hear it in her words, from her lips, was a great comfort to him.

He relished a blissful moment, until she added, "But my case is very different from Chiara's. Ask her what she wants. If it is our duty to save her, let us save her in the way that is best for her."

Well, regardless of whatever opinion Stoyan had as he walked up to them, there was no disputing such a clearly made argument.

He asked Chiara in Italian, "Chiara, we are here for you, to do what is best for you. You have a family here with us, but if you have a family elsewhere, one you would like to return to, let me know and we will take you there."

"I have a family," she answered in a mouse's whisper, "I have a mother and father, and I have two brothers who love me."

"Would you like us to take you to them?"

"Why? I cannot return to my life."

Kyra understood Chiara's last statement, and she asked, "Why can you not?"

"If Luca had died, I could return without shame. But my husband lives and I am without him. In my home, I am as scandalous as I am mutilated. I would bring shame on my family. My father would not take me back."

"Your husband is dead," Stoyan challenged, "or he might as well be."

Kyra understood, and she argued, "There is no way for us to know that. The Venetians think very differently. As an abandoned wife, she would live in shame. She could find no income, nobody to take her in."

He looked at the ground in front of him, sighed, looked up to Chiara, drew another inhale, as if he was about to speak, but no words followed. He was at a loss.

Kyra suddenly sat, straight as an arrow, and announced, "Since there is shame in being poor and abandoned, then she will be a wealthy widow. There is no shame in that."

Stoyan looked to Chiara and translated what she had said.

Chiara shook her head and answered, "No, there is no shame in being a wealthy widow. A wealthy widow is always respectable. But I am not a widow, and I am not wealthy."

Kyra suggested, "She is not a wealthy widow in Venice, but she could be one in Split, or in Tornik, or any other place she may wish us to take her."

It was clear what Kyra was offering. Tremendous wealth had come into the kumpania, and she was willing to part with it to set this little stranger up with a new life.

Chiara held up her hands and asked, "And what of my mutilation? How can I account for it?"

Stoyan answered without a moment of consideration, "Say that it happened in the same accident that took your husband. Nobody of decency will push you on the subject."

Chiara lowered her head and said, "Another lie."

"Is it?" Stoyan came back quickly, "I don't believe it is. Was it not the same night, the same incident?"

Chiara pondered for a moment and saw the truth of it. It relieved her enough to accept the proposal.

Wealth came into the kumpania in waves, followed often by long periods of drought. It is true. They had acquired great wealth since crossing the Drava into Croatia. But setting Chiara up with a new identity as a wealthy widow would be expensive and leave them with little. Kyra was aware of this. She understood exactly what she was offering and what it would cost, but she saw no moral alternative.

Matters of such weight were generally debated under the large tent with all leaders of the kumpania. There was no need for that here. They had accepted Chiara into the kumpania, and in doing so, took responsibility for her welfare. Compassion for Chiara's situation was universal. There was a moral imperative, no matter the cost.

Stoyan translated Kyra's proposal to Chiara, and she began to cry.

"In a new town, alone? I cannot survive."

"Of course you can," he assured her, "With money and a good reputation, you will do well."

"I am little. I am nothing. I have no reputation, and I cannot take your money."

"You can take our money. You helped us earn it. We should have seen what your husband was about. We could have spared you from your pain. As to your reputation, that is easier to earn than you might think."

Chiara was still very timid, and Stoyan and Kyra were pleased with the plan. Chiara went along with it. After discussing it with the kumpania, they decided to take Chiara to the town of Tornik, near modern day Sarajevo. The time spent to get there would be used teaching Chiara how to raise her chin and carry herself like a woman of consequence. Kyra was raised by a settled family of consequence, and she assigned herself as Chiara's personal tutor.

Spring weather had warmed and dried the region. They traveled quickly and comfortably, acquiring no new commissions, no new performances. They stopped only briefly to replenish themselves at markets they passed on their way to Tornik.

One evening, while camped and gathered in the large tent, Chiara thought of her husband, and she asked, "What do I do if Luca comes back to me? He is still my husband, if he still lives. They would see I am no widow. They will know that I lied. What would I do then?"

Stoyan shook his head and said, "There will be no discussion of Luca. We will discard all memory of him to oblivion."

Kyra stood and contradicted, "We will not. He brought terror and pain to us. That is true. But pain burns with a different sort of flame, creating a different sort of light than joy or freedom. There are some dark places that only that flame will brighten. Chiara will find herself in those places, as will we all, and we will be grateful for that light."

It was a notion that would have flown clearly over their heads three years earlier, but Kyra had changed them. They saw the truth of it. They saw it in a very Kyra-like way. They spent the rest of the evening exploring that "different sort of flame". With Yubi's translation, they listened to Chiara speak of Luca, of the love she thought they shared, of the gradual revelation of his true character, of her piercing jealousy, and of how she silently begged for him as she was beaten, and worse, on the streets of Zagreb and dragged to the farm to be left for dead. She still loved him. She still wanted him. She always would. Such was her steadfast heart. She felt conflicted guilt, both for loving Luca still and for choosing to move beyond him.

Yubi interrupted her account to tell her, "It is not wrong that you still love him. It speaks to the strength of your heart. It is so much stronger than Luca's. His heart wavered at a whim, while yours remained committed through unspeakable pain. But there are some things we want, things we love and should not have."

Such dark and penetrating wisdom from so young a man moved Chiara deeply. It was at that moment that she became truly committed to the kumpania's plan for her and fully aware of their capacity for love. It was then that she saw the influence Kyra had on them all, particularly Yubi. That part of Kyra that had been growing inside of Chiara had long burst into its full prime inside of Yubi. From that point on, it was plain for Chiara to see. Kyra was their queen for a reason, and not because she was the daughter of Iraja. She commanded them all, not with orders or mandates. She commanded their spirits toward her signature morality. They were saturated with it, and Chiara had the vision to recognize it.

They were in the early days of summer when they arrived outside of Tornik. The sad nubs that extended from Chiara's hands had healed nicely. So had Yubi's hands. They set camp and prepared for guests from Tornik. Word of them had spread from Zagreb, not of a violent assault in the old Roman ruins, not of an abandoned wife, but of the phoenix, of the beautiful woman who flew into the air with her fiery wings hanging from her sleeve. Kyra's reputation was not all that arrived in Tornik before them. They also spoke of the powerfully passionate young man who had thrust her up with one hand, who caught her and held her in a dramatic, loving embrace. For months, word had echoed off the walls of Tornik about the Roma spirit of love and romance that the young dancers shared with the nobles of Zagreb, and they all craved a portion for themselves.

The performers planned to rehearse that first morning, bark their presence that afternoon, and perform that evening, but they had no need of Stoyan's barking. The people of Tornik knew they were there and they came in force that first morning. The kumpania's performance and bazaar, and their plot to place Chiara in the community as a wealthy widow, had to embark immediately.

The musicians set in place. The grass was trampled flat for the dancers, and Yubi and Kyra took their place in the center. They had not rehearsed since Yubi's injuries. Kyra was afraid, afraid of it all, but especially to stand on his one hand and raise her foot to the sky above. The performance began exactly as it had before. She found herself again standing on his one hand, but this time she was not scared. It was a different emotion she felt. She was surprised — surprised by her ease and comfort. She did not wobble. She did not shake as she lifted her leg beside her ear.

As a child, Kyra was afraid to stand upright on a short stool for fear of falling. Yet, there she was, high on Yubi's hand without fear. She never felt so safely situated than in that hand, that hand that had bludgeoned another in her defense. Some of the kindliest embraces she had ever savored were from that hand, and she could still picture it cut and swollen, with his blood and the blood of another on it. Extreme tenderness and extreme violence — the duality of Yubi was represented in that hand that held her over his head. It brought forth emotions in an equal extreme in Kyra.

That is what churned beneath her surface as she stood statuesque above the mesmerized people of Tornik. It was magical to them. The phoenix and her Gypsy lover had come to Tornik and sprinkled them all with their mystically passionate Gypsy dust. The dynamic between Kyra and Yubi while they performed their act that day was different than before. It was more loving, more passionately aflame. It left its mark on those who witnessed it, leaving them with different expectations of life and love, expectations that would last their lifetimes. Such was the powerful presence of Kyra and Yubi when they were united.

The difference was not only in how they appeared to the audience, but also in how they felt about each other. It is always an awkward transition from childhood friends to adult lovers. Kyra and Yubi were waist-deep in that transition, no more certain of their own feelings than the feelings of the other. Luca had complicated that process, but he also quickened it. Tornik was not treated to a "theatrical representation" of Gypsy love.

Yubi caught Kyra out of the air and into an embrace of true devotion, and when he lay still in imagined death, her mournful dance was an authentic effusion of a love she did not yet fully understand. She vividly recalled her fear as Vadim rode toward the ruins to find him. She thought she might have lost him, as he thought he had lost her to Luca. Their dance in Tornik was an expression of their fears and a celebration of their love, expressed to the people around them, but still not to each other. Inwardly, they still wallowed in uncertainty. They may not have spoken to the heart of the other, but they spoke plainly enough to their audience, who were whipped into a romantic frenzy by the performance.

The kumpania had acquired little since leaving Zagreb. After the performance, they did not have much to sell. What they had, if passed to the buyer by the hands of Yubi or his phoenix, sold at a ridiculous price. The plan was in place and executed perfectly. Chiara, drifting among the guests with a fist full of coins given to her by Vadim, bought much of what was available to buy. When it was gone, and many disappointed people held no souvenir of the day, Chiara began giving the trinkets away.

"I am just a lonely widow," she told them, "with nobody to share such things with. Here, take this to your homes and remember the wonderful people who performed for you today."

Her new identity was established and solidified. After the bazaar, the kumpania gave back all the money Chiara had paid them, plus much more. Contrary to the timid bride she had been, she walked alone into Tornik, put her new wealth forward in the purchase of a home and land. She hired workers for her fields. One result of the plague was that estates went empty or under-worked. Land was cheap. Chiara set herself up with a substantial estate.

The kumpania stayed for another two months. Each day, Chiara visited them, and each day, they saw in her a stronger and more independent woman. She hosted them at her home, pouring her gratitude in every way it would flow. But it could not go on in this way. Chiara could either be a wealthy widow or a perpetual part of the kumpania. She could not be both. Her reputation could not survive an endless flow of Gypsies in and out of her fine estate.

As the dog days ended, she saw them off, professing her love and demanding their return. She spent a full hour alone with Kyra. There were no words to express what Kyra had done for her, what Kyra meant to her. They sat mostly in silence together, enjoying a friendship that needed no words to survive. After the kumpania left, Chiara continued to do much to stoke the searing reputation of her Gypsy friends. Her estate prospered in the wake of the plague. She spent the rest of her days as Chiara, the wealthy widow and Tornik's most benevolent benefactor.

CHAPTER FORTY

INTERTWINING OAKS

IT HAD TAKEN MOST OF THE KUMPANIA'S WEALTH to give Chiara the new life she deserved. They gave the money to Chiara to buy their items from them, then gave the money back to Chiara after the sale. They lost their items and their money. The purses of the kumpania were emptied to purchase the estate. Had they the raw materials to produce their wares, their immediate prospects would have been comfortable. But they had little money left and almost nothing to sell. Discharged of their obligations to Chiara, they proceeded toward Split, not certain what was to be gained under their circumstances. One thing must be made perfectly clear. Nobody blamed Kyra for their sudden poverty, quite the contrary. Her act of wise benevolence raised their young queen even higher in their esteem. But that esteem did not change the fact that their situation was rather bleak.

The kumpania never made money from performing. The music, the dancing, the acrobatics served only to make more enticing and more expensive the Roma items they sold. They rolled away from Tornik with little in store and food was turning scarce. They traveled about forty miles away from Tornik and camped in deliberation for weeks, while their scant supplies dwindled further.

They decided on two possible courses before them. The most direct route to Split was nearly 150 miles of travel. It was flatter land, easily traveled, with a series of villages to pass near. None of those villages promised opportunity, and they wanted to arrive in Split with money and items to trade. The more lucrative route was twice as long and swung them southwest to the town of Mostar, on the River Neretva. The path was mountainous, heavily wooded in areas, and sparsely populated. Travel would be difficult and they would not likely encounter another human being along the way.

They needed to sell things they never had to sell before. Two horses, two of their open wagons, and most of their livestock were set to be sacrificed at the first market they encountered. Those things would gather a greater price in Mostar than in the villages along the shorter route. Mostar it was. They readied themselves to tighten their belts and slow their pace.

They traveled for three weeks toward Mostar, moving slowly and eating no more than a single, small meal each day. They stopped for long hours of hunting. With spears fashioned on the spot by Ernko, made of local wood with forged tips, they kept themselves alive on the plentiful wildlife of the forest. They were not living as they always had, fashioning jewelry for sale at one market or another, mixing spices to be sold at a village bazaar, and rehearsing performances to make it all the more enticing. They lived as hunter nomads. It was rustic in the extreme, but after all they had been through that year, it was a simple but perfect spiritual remedy, and their drive toward Mostar and eventually Split became less pressing.

One evening in early autumn, in a scattered camp along a densely wooded valley, Yubi and Stoyan sat alone in their cluttered vardo, sifting through old equipment, tools, and trinkets that could be sold in Mostar. Storied relics took their turns being evaluated, weighing the potential value at market against potential usefulness. Yubi fell so deeply into thought that he dropped the crusty old oil lamp he held.

At a glance, Stoyan saw the weight on his mind and asked, "What is it, son?"

Yubi surfaced slowly from his thoughts, raising his eyes to his father at the same rate. When he looked squarely at his father, he asked, "Isn't this the perfect time?"

"For what?"

"We have done right by Chiara. Last winter is well behind us. My love wears a calmer, gentler face."

"You wish to profess your love to Kyra?"

"Father, it is burning inside of me. Even if it changes nothing, I have to tell her. Do you think she is ready?"

"She is ready. She has long been ready. You must look into yourself and ask if you are ready. My son, not until one enters sympathetically into another's passions is there love. That has long been the case with both of you. You loved her the moment you introduced yourself to her. We all saw that. And she has loved you for a long time. But this is not a question of love. You are speaking of courtship, of marriage, are you not?"

Yubi's breaths struggled as he fought back a cry. Through it he confessed, "I want to be her husband."

"Why? Why do you want to be her husband?"

"I want the ability to make her happy, to be for her everything she needs me to be."

"Well, Yubi, you have answered well. When a man wants a woman less and wants *for* her more, he is ready to commit to courtship. I believe you are there."

Stoyan shifted from his position to sit beside his son. He threw his good arm over Yubi's shoulder like an old friend, and he replied, "We have never lived like this before, slowly rolling through secluded forests, living off the land. Why is this our fate now? I think there is a reason for it. I believe your instincts. The kumpania has never been calmer, never slower. Your love is calm, gentle, and polished like brass. My boy, my dear young man, let me know what you need from me."

It was soundly resolved between them. Come what may, Yubi would tell Kyra how he felt. From that point, the gadgets and ornamental curios that cluttered their vardo were mere trifles. Kyra had long felt like a lover to Yubi and like a daughter to Stoyan. As they speechlessly continued their efforts, the only possessions they had that shined with radiant gleam were each other and Kyra.

The next morning, Kyra emerged from her vardo with a growling stomach. She overheard someone make mention of the date. It struck her memory strangely, then she realized — it was her birthday. It was the first time she took notice of her birthday, or any birthday, since she was twelve. She sank into a string of memories from her childhood, memories of things that were once intimately familiar but whose fine details had faded and blurred at their edges. They faded because they were not worth keeping. Not one of the birthdays she tried to recall had been pinned securely to her memory by a profound moment.

The world around her muted as she sank more deeply into her distant memories, like noises above the surface of a pool. Yubi yanked her rather forcefully back to alertness. He invited her to a small open patch of grass, asking her to work on their act. It was not enough space to rehearse their dance, but it was wide enough to perform the stationary lifts and experiment with some new ones. They talked of Chiara. The conversation spread naturally to Luca.

"I envy him," Yubi announced unexpectedly, "In one way, I envy him."

Kyra scoffed and assured him, "There is nothing that man has that is worth your envy."

"Isn't there? Chiara still loves him. Isn't that true?"

Kyra nodded.

Yubi continued, "Despite everything he has done, Luca still has the love of an excellent woman. Is that not to be envied?"

"Only by those who are without love."

He responded only by repeating, "I envy him."

After a few minutes of tense silence, they began to discuss their ideas for new stunts. One required her to throw herself sideways at him. He would catch her by the hips, spin her over his head and around his neck like a human baton, and set her on her feet beside him. They theorized the mechanics of the stunt, then decided to try it. Kyra threw herself at him. He caught her and spun her, but she slipped from his hands and flew behind him. She braced herself for a painful landing, but there was no landing, at least not on the ground. Yubi dove backward and fell on his back to catch her on his chest.

The mishap knocked the wind out of him. She panicked as he struggled to draw his next breath. When he finally recovered, he laughed. He laughed heartily, which drew her into similar laughter. She was still strewn across him as they winded their laugh down together. When it ended, what was left was a straight-faced gaze into each other's eyes.

They opened their mouths simultaneously and each pushed out a single syllable that crashed awkwardly against the other's.

"You go," she told him.

He bit his lips, afraid that the feelings that had so long demanded release would burst crudely and unintelligibly from him like a wild drunk. Still locked eye to eye, he released his lips from his teeth, drew a long, slow inhale through his nose and puffed it quickly back out through his mouth. Beads of sweat appeared on his forehead. His nervousness was obvious to Kyra. She had been awaiting a profession of his love. She was starving for it, and she hoped with all her heart that this was it. She lifted a slow, encouraging smile that welcomed his words.

That smile was more valuable to him than Croatian coins, Roma jewelry, polished canisters, livestock, high bars and vardos, or any noble castle in all of Europe. He had traveled far and seen many beautiful sights in his short years. As he looked up at her while she still lounged across his chest, with her long hair cascading down one side of her head and flowing across his arm, shining upon him a smile that not only welcomed his thoughts but begged for them, he knew he never had, and never would, see anything more beautiful. He savored what his senses took in — her shine, her smell, the warmth of her pressed against him.

He began to sit up. She lifted herself off of him and sat on the ground facing him with her legs crossed in front of her.

He mirrored her position, pressed closely, so their knees were almost touching, took both of her hands, and he spoke, "Every now and then, you smile at me like you used to, like a little girl first delighting in her new surroundings. That smile is a potent tonic. It cures me of all pain. It intoxicates me and pulls me out of time. When you look at me... directly into me, the world around me melts away, and all that exists is us. I see nothing now but your face. I feel nothing but your hands. You are everything in the world, and I desire nothing else. I want to be nothing but yours. I love you, Kyra. I love you."

Her blush was intense, and her face seemed to put off its own light. She had cried many leaden tears of sorrow in her life. The single tear that rolled down her reddening cheek as Yubi said "I love you" was spritely. It bounded from her eye to her chin like a child frolicking in a sunny field. It was happy to be there, and it leaped from her chin to her lap with the freedom and joy of a Roma dancer.

Her face spoke all that he needed to hear, and he added, "I will always be yours, and when the time is right, I will be your husband."

She did not realize she had been holding her breath, and when she opened her mouth to respond, she was surprised by her body's desperate gasp for air.

When she recovered, in a musical blend of giggling and crying, she told him, "I have always been yours, and that will never change. I will be your wife. I *want* to be your wife."

Led by neither, they leaned into each other and exchanged a short but tender kiss. It lasted no more than two seconds, but in that time, their lips embraced like old oak trees whose trunks had grown together centuries earlier and wound around each other until they were as a single tree.

They did not withdraw so quickly from the kiss because they wanted it to end, but because they wanted to look at each other, remaining as they were, holding hands and gazing into each other's eyes with nothing but their united breaths accompanying the natural sounds of the forest. They carried in their hearts new identities for themselves and for each other. Yubi was Kyra's Yubi, and Kyra was Yubi's Kyra. That was all they were as they sat and gazed, and that was all they cared to be.

They sat for nearly an hour like that until, as if their brains controlled the nerves in the other's body, they stood together and walked back to the camp. Within a few steps they began to talk as they always had, about minute and mundane parts of their daily lives.

She squeezed his hand and stopped, turned to face him, and said, "Thank you for the birthday gift. Nobody has ever received better."

"Birthday gift?" he questioned.

"Yes. Today is my birthday. I am sixteen years old. I imagine many young women turn sixteen today, and none of them have received what you have given me. None of them! In all the world, only I have been given you."

They had spent many hours, over the previous few years, holding hands and walking around the camp. The sight of them returning to the camp in that way should have been nothing new in the eyes of the kumpania. But it was new. It was fresh and powerful. They were one in their shared love, and in their unity they towered forcefully over everything around them. The courtship of Kyra and Yubi had finally begun. How exactly it would go, nobody could know, but it had already created a powerful wave in their wake, as they walked hand-in-hand through the sprawled out camp. It swept over everyone they passed and promised never to subside, but to grow and drench the world around them in a rare and magnificent love.

There was hardly a moment that day when they were not touching one another. Somewhere deep down in them both they feared that a separation, no matter how slight and for how short a time, would erase what had passed between them that morning. Her touch was like a soothing ointment that made everything that once stung in his life feel warm, soft, and tingly. To her, his touch was like a platform she stood upon, which lifted her from the reach of all things sinister and gave her vision to see things once obscured by her immediate surroundings.

Despite these feelings, when the sun fell, they separated, she to her vardo and he to his father's tent, and they were glad for it. In their solitude they were finally able to process the events of the day and only then convince themselves it was real.

CHAPTER FORTY-ONE
THE LABORERS OF SPLIT

THE NEXT MORNING, THE SUN APPEARED to rise faster. It seemed brighter and unashamed of its brightness, almost indecently so, as if it rose from bed scandalously underdressed and it did not care who saw it. The courtship would be long, probably two full years. Yubi wanted to be married to Kyra that very morning. Something inside of him believed that if they sped the caravan, time would speed with it. He wanted to rush to Mostar, to Split, and to wherever they would go from there. The engagement affected the whole kumpania similarly. There was crisp alacrity in every movement. Even the horses and livestock moved with impatience.

When they arrived at Mostar, they camped several miles outside of town. Vadim and Stoyan went together into the town with the horses and wagons to be sold. A member of the town council was sent to greet them. He had no need of a horse or wagon, but he knew who did. Mostar was a friendly town. Connections came quickly, as did fair prices. They sold their horses and wagons, bought food, tools, and other supplies, stayed the night in a small guesthouse of the mayor's, and returned to the camp in the morning.

They remained camped for one more night, struck early, and rolled toward the renowned Mostar Bridge, across the River Neretva. Tolls on crossing the bridge were Mostar's primary revenue, but when Vadim tried to pay, the guard refused it. He was instructed by the mayor to do so. Instead, he gave them an invitation. In an elegant letter, the mayor asked them to stay for the annual Bridge Festival.

"We cannot pay you to perform for us," the letter read, "but if you will honor us at our festival, you may help yourselves to our feast and our gratitude."

There were no notions of refusing. They camped near the bridge and met shortly after with the mayor and the organizers of the festival. Kyra's reputation had traveled the river and found a home in the dinner table conversations of the tradesmen and laborers of Mostar. They called her the Phoenix of Zagreb. They had no idea of her life prior to that eventful night, when the Phoenix was born under the orange light of Luca's flames.

The festival began early in the day with games and challenges, from stone-hauling to races across the bridge. Food was plentiful, at a price, for the people of Mostar and their visitors, but not for the kumpania. They did not pay for a morsel. They ate, but no vendor would take their money. They were the guests of honor.

Lavinia instructed Kyra to dress as plainly as possible during the day, to be as obscurely plain as she could be until dusk, when the torches on the bridge would be lit and the renowned Phoenix of Zagreb would appear, with her powerful lover, from her mystical realm.

The sun fell below the trees, and under the shades of twilight, the mayor stood on the bridge and announced, "My friends, today we celebrated our bridge, but tonight, it is not only a bridge across the river, it is a bridge between worlds, between our world and the realm of a woman you have all been talking about. Tonight..."

He threw his arms into the air to signal the torch-bearers, who ceremoniously marched across the bridge lighting the torches that lined both sides.

When the bridge was fully lit, the mayor continued, "...we welcome the Phoenix of Zagreb!"

The townsfolk gasped, while Lavinia led a line of dancers onto the bridge from the opposite side, shoulder to shoulder to hide Kyra and Yubi behind them. They formed their circle. The musicians remained on the far side of the bridge. When they strummed and fluted, their music seemed to come from the trees. Milena and Manfri appeared on the bridge and each mounted a wall on either side of the dancers.

Manfri began with a long note, then he rolled it up and down the scales, while the dancers held their positions over Kyra and Yubi. Milena's voice sprang suddenly, loudly, and hauntingly full, precisely when Yubi thrust Kyra into the air.

The surface of the bridge was neither flat nor consistent. It was not a flawless performance. It lacked the polish the performers wanted, but under the torchlight, it did not matter. The festival-goers were enamored. When the show was over, everybody wanted to meet Kyra. But to mingle among them would reveal her mortal nature. Stoyan had another plan.

He brought her to the Mostar side of the bridge, near enough the crowd to reveal her face and figure but far enough away to maintain the mystique. Kyra spoke to them. She spoke in Romani, which none of them understood. She told the story of Yubi's profession of love. She might as well have described the smell of the livestock, for all the words meant to the crowd. But in telling the story she told, her blush shined. The hairs on her arm rose, and chills ran across her skin in waves.

In mysterious words, she spoke to them. Some imagined it to be the passing of some ancient knowledge they would somehow absorb without understanding. Some closed their eyes as if receiving a spiritual blessing. In any case, it served its purpose. An otherworldly figure spoke to them in an otherworldly language, peaking the mystique of the Phoenix of Zagreb — that heavenly creature who had performed for the King of Hungary and Croatia.

After her speech and before mingling with the others, Kyra disappeared on the other side of the bridge and changed back into the same plain dress she had worn all day. A few times throughout the night, some man, woman, or child would stare at her, swearing she looked familiar, one or two even suggesting she might be the Phoenix. But Kyra was very good at being plain when she sought to be, and those notions were quickly disregarded. As far as Mostar knew, the Phoenix had crossed their bridge and returned to her unearthly realm. In the morning, the sun evaporated the Gypsy caravan like a fog. They were across the bridge and on their way to Split.

They rolled down the hills east of the coast, to flat, warm, comfortable land, and camped south of the village of Kučine. The village poked out from the eastern outskirts of Split like a button from a shirt. Their rations were reduced. They needed to sell more to buy more, and buy more to be able to sell. They sold the fire equipment Luca left behind during his hurried departure. Each family in the kumpania emptied their trunks and chests of any valuable trinket or heirloom that could fetch a price. Stoyan's cluttered vardo was cluttered no more. He sold all but the essentials. He even sold the rope from Yubi's rope act. He kept his high bar, believing it a necessary part of their performing future, were he ever to heal enough to swing from it.

When the knick-knacks of the caravan fell short, they sold their livestock. Every animal that could not serve as a beast of burden was sold. They all went to a single farm east of the city. The price was fair and their purses were ready for the dockside markets of the Adriatic Sea. Representatives of each of the kumpania's professions went to the market and purchased the materials of their trade. The jewelry makers came back with exotic gems and beads from three continents. Patrin bought lavish fabrics. Spices, oils, and perfumes from the far corners of the map were unloaded from ships at the docks of Split. It was everything they hoped it would be and when the materials made it back to the camp, the craftsmen went to work preparing for the next bazaar and performance.

In two weeks they were ready to lay out their blankets and cover them in Roma-crafted wares. Stoyan rode into Split and barked their presence. He had lost none of the charisma that had served them so well over the years, but the people of Split were hard to entice.

The first day, only two families came, only one of which was from Split. The other was a poor farming family from Kučine. Nevertheless, the performers performed for their intimate audience. Afterward, only a single vial of African perfume was sold. Not a single necklace, not a stitch of Patrin's handiwork, nothing else sold. They went to sleep that night counting on the spreading word of their few visitors.

The following day, nobody came. Stoyan rode into Split again, dressed in wild Gypsy colors. This time, he took Kyra with him. Still, the people of Split were not stirred to curiosity. Split was an exciting city, which boasted fantastic scenery and exotics from across the world. There was little that could entice them to step outside of the city for entertainment and souvenirs.

Had the people of Split given them a chance, had they come to the camp and sampled the bazaar, had they heard Manfri play and Milena sing, had they witnessed the rise of the Phoenix on the hand of her lover, Kyra's renown would have departed Split aboard every ship to leave its docks and spread to the far edges of the map, and the remaining pages of this book would have read very differently, but that is not what happened. No wealth came in and no reputation went out, and the kumpania was beginning to starve.

Vadim hatched an idea — to take their items to the dockside markets and sell them there. Ernko undertook the commission of securing a space at the large, weekly, market. Being a German-speaking ethnic Swabian, he succeeded. Two days later, he returned to the docks with enough hands to help him. But when he arrived with Gypsies at his side, carrying sacks of Gypsy goods, his license was revoked, and his booth was given away. They returned to the camp exactly as they had left.

The circumstances were grave and deteriorating. They gathered under the large tent to discuss their options. There were few to discuss. They would not find their wealth in Split, at least not in the ways they always had. Returning to Hungary was an argument that carried weight, but they did not have the means. They came to the only viable solution. They needed to seek employment and work until they had replenished enough to caravan.

Frustrated, Yubi blurted, "We had prospects in Zagreb, lucrative commissions and money in our purses. Now we have nothing. I wish Luca never would have found us."

Stoyan shook his head, and in a rare stern gaze at his son, he answered, "I am so very glad he did. What would have been Chiara's fate? He would have found another Kyra."

Yubi interrupted, "There is no other Kyra!"

"No, there is not," his father amended, "He would have been drawn to someone else, to another fascination. He would have abandoned Chiara to some other men in some other place. And we would not have been there for her. Under a frozen wagon, in some cold alley, who knows where she would have ended, but ended she would have. Now she is a woman of consequence and means, independent of Luca or any man. How very fortunate Luca found us!"

Yubi regretted his lament, quickly and whole-heartedly agreeing with his father, and they all resigned to a very different state of being for the immediate future.

The herders took jobs as farmhands. They were the first hired. In the wake of the plague, most of the surviving working class went into the cities for work. Food rotted in the fields. The herders were given fair wages. They worked long hours and returned to the camp for a few blinks of rest before heading back to the farms. Yubi took a job scrubbing the streets of the seaside markets. He made little more than he needed to buy his food for the day.

The best employment opportunities were in skilled labor. Ernko began working for a blacksmith, making door hinges and latches, and installing them at the homes of the customers. Were he trying to survive on his wages while maintaining a home in Split, he would have been poor indeed. But he had no home to maintain. He returned to the camp every evening and proudly handed his money to Vadim. They were slowly rebuilding their resources. At their rate of earnings, they could comfortably caravan back to Hungary in late spring, with enough new inventory to entice the provincial towns and villages speckled across the Hungarian plains.

Fortune came suddenly and surprisingly while Ernko was installing a door. He was in the home of a newly formed dynasty. The Horvat family were laborers before the plague, but had risen to fill a void left by the wealthy dead. Being so new to prominence, they needed to establish all of the things a family of that status must have — a stately home in Split, an imposing family crest, and of course, a set of hereditary armor and sword. It was in this last status symbol that Ernko saw opportunity.

While he nailed into place the hinges he had forged with his own hands, the eldest son of the Horvats spoke of the armor, describing every detail he thought it should have.

Under his breath, but wanting to be heard, Ernko commented, "Oh yes, I agree. I could do that."

Enough of the comment was understood by Mister Horvat, and he asked Ernko to repeat himself and speak up. Ernko abandoned the door, turned to his clients, and described the armor as he would make it. The Swabians were notorious for magnificent sets of hereditary armor, and Ernko's description was a glorified version of what the son envisioned. They must have asked him ten times if he was certain he had the skill to construct what he described. He explained that his former master was the foremost maker of decorative and hereditary armor along the entire Drava River, and the commission was finalized.

The Horvats had money, and there was no amount they were not willing to spend to solidify their place within their new social stratum. Ernko suggested a ridiculously high price for the job, and they agreed without negotiations. It would not replace all they had given to Chiara, but it would most certainly pull them well out of their dire situation. After completing the door, Ernko returned to his employer's forge and begged to use the facility for his commission. For a modest fee, it was agreed, and Ernko abandoned all other duties while he worked on the armor.

His employer had something to gain beyond the small fee. He had never forged armor, and it was a skill he wanted, so he set himself as Ernko's apprentice, lending the material for the job until Ernko could pay him back from the profits. The kumpania did not see him for weeks.

He sent a message explaining his absence and describing the commission and what was to be gained by it.

In the weeks of Ernko's labors, the others continued to work. Yubi swept the streets along the shoreline, each day resetting it with polished appeal for the following day's open markets. Kyra could not stand the time away from him, away from all who left the camp for employment. Early one morning, after their daily kiss goodbye, she begged him to take her with him.

"I can push a broom," she insisted, "If we are to be one, we should be one in all things, including this."

Her sentiment was so romantic and so dearly expressed that he could not refuse her. They rode into town together. They swept and scrubbed the dirty seaside streets, sweating together, blistering together, and resigning the broom together at the end of the day. Secured by Ernko's income, they took their paltry wages and bought a small loaf of bread and a few nibbles of cheese.

They took their bread, their cheeses, and each other to a quieter part of the shoreline, north of the docks and market. It was not as picturesque as other parts of the Split coast. The seawall was formed of craggy rocks. The young couple found a place among those rocks where two lovers could squeeze together to enjoy some bread and a sunset without an inch between them. The sea had been at Kyra's side the length of the day, while she labored beside Yubi, but she never took notice of it. It was not until she settled among the rocks that she looked out over the Adriatic, as it reflected the fiery clouds of the sunset. Such an expanse of water! It spawned a thousand mental metaphors as she sat and pondered her future — a future with the young man to whom she had committed her love and her life.

CHAPTER FORTY-TWO
THEIR OWN SILK ROAD

FOR THE REST OF THE WEEK, Yubi and Kyra worked together all day, and each evening they found a new romantic place to watch the Adriatic Sea consume the lowering sun. Their conversations covered every imaginable topic. They both taught. They both learned. They both loved. On the last day of scrubbing streets, the day before the armor was finished, they overheard talk of a merchant ship from China that would be stopping on its way to Venice. It was rumored to be coming with a large hold of royal silks.

There was no bread, cheese, and sunset that evening. They rode back to the camp as fast as they could and told the others what they knew. Silk was a lucrative trade in the exotic ports of the world, but in the inland roads they had traveled, such a commodity would sell at five times the price. In the isolated towns of Hungary, towns they knew, like Siklós or Győr, the profit margin on silk bought in Split would be exorbitant.

Ernko's armor was every bit as glorious as advertised. He collected the payment, repaid what he owed his employer, bade his fare-wells, and returned to the kumpania. The opportunity in silks was too rare to ignore. Stoyan, Vadim, Ernko, Yubi, and Kyra rode together to the market and waited for two days, sleeping in the streets and behind buildings. On the third day, the rumored Chinese ship arrived. Stoyan wasted no time flashing the money to the captain.

He negotiated in an Indian dialect that only Yubi understood. Yubi whispered his translation to the others, and by the time Stoyan was finished, he had secured the purchase of a dozen bolts of silk cloth. He spent almost all of the income from the armor. It was risky. They could not eat silk cloth. But the potential for return was immense.

They returned to the camp with the silks. In the late evening, when the herders returned from the labors on the farms, the kumpania was again whole. They gathered that night in the large tent and plotted the course of their own Silk Road into Hungary. Each proposal ended with the swiveling of heads toward Kyra. She gave no approval without first asking the opinion of Yubi.

His humility tried to decline the honor, but she reminded him several times, "Together in all things."

To the kumpania, her word was everything, but to her, it was nothing without his.

In the morning, they began their slow cut through Croatia, toward the country they had claimed as their homeland. It was not in the nature of the Roma to affiliate themselves so intimately with any particular plot of land. But again, Kyra altered them in unexpected ways. Kyra was Hungarian, so they were Hungarian. Their spirits were anchored to the place they found her and to the places where they grew to love her. That sense of homeland tugged at them deeply when they were in need of healing, nurturing, and revival.

They had very little in their possession, no livestock, few spices and perfumes, and just a dozen bolts of silk. But as they traveled toward Hungary they sang with more unified jubilance than they had for years. Virtually every rotation of the wheels was accompanied by clapped hands and slapped boots, and exuberant hoots and hollers. Those lively rhythms sewed the measures of sung music together.

Whether walking beside the caravan with Yubi's hand in hers, trotting on horseback, or riding alone in her vardo, Kyra sang along. As she did, she thought about her first encounter with the kumpania, and the mysterious song they sang. She felt fully transformed. Music that had once seemed so strange, so unnervingly foreign, felt as comfortable, natural, and as much a part of her as the hair on her head.

When they camped, it was all about the performers. Most of the craftsmen found themselves without employment. The herders had nothing to herd. There was little to be crafted by anyone. Patrin was one of the few in constant effort. Most of the silk was left untouched to be sold in simple rolls. He took some to fashion into extravagant clothing for sale, all with a distinctly Roma flair. But the best of it was not for sale at all. Patrin set aside the very best to make a wedding dress for Kyra, the design of which he would hold in secret until the day would finally come.

The kumpania traveled along the Vrbas River with an eye open for any settlement along the way that might be enticed by their silks. But winter came suddenly and harshly. They had camped out many long winters, but always with stores of food and supplies. They could not wait out a long winter with the paltry supplies in their possession, so they pushed forward through thickening snow and plummeting temperatures. At times, they could not tell if they were traveling along the river or on it.

There were a string of fortresses along the Vrbas. Some were little more than a few shabby walls of lumber, with nothing and nobody to benefit them. Some were massive but foreboding. The caravan cut large circles around them, keeping their distance. They came to a river fortress near the town of Bocac. It looked warm and lively. Multiple strings of smoke rose from its courtyard, from many little fires. From a distance, they could hear the murmur of simultaneous conversations. The Bocac fortress came to them in the nick of time, as they swallowed the last morsels of their stores of food.

Stoyan rode to the gate and introduced himself. He spoke of his experience in the castle at Zagreb, of meeting King Louis and the other nobles. The commander of the fortress knew the region. He knew the nobles and he knew the king. Stoyan gave details of people and places that only a truthful account could give. The commander believed him, and he invited him into the fortress. He was given a stool in front of a fire. The cold meant little to Stoyan, but he accepted the hospitality as if it had saved his life.

Stoyan spoke of their experiences. To an audience of soldiers and their superiors, he told the story of Luca, and the efforts to rectify the harms done to his victim wife. He told stories of romance that brought forth and captivated the tenderest parts of their hearts. Oh, he could tell a story. The soldiers missed their homes. They worked a hard winter behind the walls of a stone fortress. They missed their wives and children. They missed their mothers. They were torn from the romantic flirtations that had seasoned their youths. Stoyan gave it all back to them with his stories.

The commander saw the effect Stoyan had on the morale of his men. The winter was young and vicious, with a long and powerful life ahead of it. Stoyan left a few hours later with an invitation for the kumpania to camp outside of the walls of the fortress. By that nightfall, the camp was wedged between the frozen river and fortress wall.

The Bocac Fortress was not going to be a gem on their Silk Road. It was not the home of lavish royals, but it was heavily garrisoned, and fresh supplies came through the gates every week. The soldiers were from low, labor families. But the snow bound fortress offered them nothing on which to spend their wages, so their pockets rattled with coins. They could not afford Chinese silks, but they could buy jeweled brooches and Gypsy necklaces for the mothers and sweethearts they had left behind. The kumpania had all the things they had fashioned for the bazaars that went unattended and for the dockside market from which they had been turned away.

The kumpania had little interest in coins. They bartered their goods for meals. The winter promised to outlast the trinkets they had to trade. Where their supplies ran short, their talents and charisma took over. In small groups, they spent a few hours here and there within the walls of the fortress, bonding with their lonely hosts. When the musicians visited, they played and sang. The scales of music and the mysteriously foreign words took the soldiers away from the cold and heartless fortress and revived their spirits with a vengeance.

This was not all that impressed the soldiers. They watched the kumpania walk around outside of the walls, wearing little and unaffected by the cold and snow. It was impossible for them to complain of their own discomforts when Gypsy children played in the snow like it was warm grass in the middle of summer. The soldiers admired the nomads. The difference in their behavior was obvious. Embittered complaints were replaced with words of admiration for the toughness of the Gypsies. Soldiers talked of life and love, and not of cold beds and paltry rations. The unity of the kumpania was contagious and spread through the lives of the fortress. The commander had seen many winters in a fortress. He had battled negative morale. Such a blessing to him were the strange people camped against his wall. He made a point of opening the gates more regularly for his nomadic visitors.

By the end of the first month, the kumpania spent as much time in the fortress as camped outside of it.

The frozen months provided many idle hours. Kyra felt herself on the cusp of a new life and craved self-expansion almost as much as she craved Yubi's company. She found them both in the same place. Yubi spent his spare time filling an opulent mind with the fundamentals of every language he knew. The soldiers of the fortress were mostly ethnic Bosnaks speaking various forms of Serbo-Croatian. Kyra was frustrated every time Yubi had to translate for her. Frustration spawned ambition, and ambition turned to joy as she enjoyed not only her advancement but the process.

Kyra gained rudimentary conversational skills in a dozen tongues from India to France. Her mind saw the truths of human language like few ever have. She held the functional simplicity of it easily in her hand. Perhaps it was her natural insights into the human spirit. In any case, she was a prodigy, who consumed what Yubi gave her as fast as he could give it. Permanent, lasting lessons came from every syllable uttered by the soldiers. As the weeks progressed, Kyra found herself as translator between the soldiers and other members of the kumpania.

By March, the soldiers came to see the kumpania as a necessary part of the fortress functions. The Roma received soldiers' rations. They performed laborious details beside the military men, as if they had enlisted together. Such a blessing they were to each other. The encounter with the Bocac Fortress saved the lives of the kumpania and saved the spirits of the soldiers. That is how they passed the hardest winter in decades. And in April, when the weather softened and the ground flowered, they parted from their seasonal friends with the most heartfelt well-wishes.

From Bocac, they traveled the river valley to Banja Luka. Trade in the town's market had been slow during the terrible winter. There was not much wealth there. The performance outside of Banja Luka saw little exchanged. One strong connection was made. A merchant traveling the river visited the camp and saw the performance. He was no more interested in Gypsy trinkets than he was in Gypsy performances. He was very interested in the royal silks. He was Greek and had worked the river systems of the Balkans his whole life. He knew the value of the silks, and he doubted the Gypsies understood the value.

His name was Andie. He was tall and lanky, with a deep olive complexion and a wild head of curly locks. At a glance, he would never have been considered a handsome man. His facial features were oddly chiseled, and pockmarks decorated his cheeks in uneven patterns. Yet he carried himself with poise and spoke with a rich, deep, and oily voice.

Patrin had the silks laid across an open wagon. The Greek merchant with his Greek charm moved in. Andie thought he was dealing with a barbaric band of nomads who had probably scavenged the silks. The notion that he addressed skilled negotiators and tradesmen, who acquired their merchandise in clever, shrewd, and diplomatic negotiations never occurred to him. He barked a crudely phrased offer to Patrin in Serbo-Croatian. Patrin did not understand him, but Stoyan did. He translated the offer into Romani. Patrin commented about Andie's arrogance and the two of them laughed.

Andie misunderstood the laughter. He thought the rustic nomads did not understand the offer. He resubmitted it in Hungarian. From several yards away, Kyra heard her native language and was intrigued. She stepped beside Stoyan and asked about their visitor.

Stoyan told her in Romani, "This Greek thinks lowly of us. He wants to take the silks off our hands for the price of a loaf of bread."

Kyra turned to Andie and asked him boldly in Greek, "Do you think so little of these royal silks, or do you think so little of us?"

Andie could not hide his shock. Kyra may not have sounded like an Athenian aristocrat, but she sounded Greek. She and Stoyan passed a few more comments back and forth, hopping from one Balkan language to another, knowing Andie would understand them. They talked of Split and the market there, of the Chinese ship and its captain. They spoke to each other but for Andie's ears. Andie realized the sort of people he was dealing with. These were not scavengers who had just rolled out of the isolated mountains.

He was impressed by Stoyan's use of the many languages he put on display, but he was astonished by Kyra. This young woman, this girl not yet seventeen years old, displayed an ability to master the regional trade market, at least that is how Andie saw it. He stared open-jawed at her, not at the Phoenix, not at the Wilde Jungfrauwe, but at a girl who possessed the power of communication, someone who could travel the rivers of Europe and speak her way into every circle. He was still interested in the silks, but much more interested in the people who had acquired them.

He suddenly saw them as equals, perhaps even as superiors from whom he could learn. At any rate, he had no interest in cheating them of their precious cargo, or of striking a fair bargain for the silks and departing. He struck a conversation, not of merchandise and money, but of travels, of towns and people, of regional customs and music. He found kinship in his fellow traveling merchants, something he had long been without. By the end of an hour, Andie sat around a fire with Kyra, Yubi, Stoyan, Ernko, and Vadim, while they regaled each other with stories of their travels.

Andie's boat was docked in Banja Luka, and the sun was getting low. Without consulting the others, Kyra offered Andie a tent and a place among them for the night. The memories of Luca were still fresh and stinging. Vadim began to protest in Romani.

Kyra interrupted in Greek, "Look into his eyes. This is not Luca. This one is like us. He might not be Roma, but he is Gypsy. His caravan is the river. His vardo is a boat. But he is Gypsy."

Andie had never considered himself such, and one day earlier, the same sentiment would have insulted him. But his respect for the people who hosted him in front of their fire had swelled to near bursting. They elevated the term "Gypsy" to something quite laudable, even desirable. Andie was honored by the comparison, and he saw himself as one of them. When Kyra drew the gaze of the others toward Andie's eyes, they saw what she saw, the abounding admiration of a man hungry for their approval and acceptance. The others quickly and enthusiastically reinforced the invitation, and Andie delightfully accepted.

In the morning, Andie invited Stoyan to visit his boat at the docks and peruse his merchandise. He had scraps of metal he thought might interest Ernko, and he invited the blacksmith along. They decided to walk together to the river. It would take the better part of an hour, but that was exactly what they all wanted.

When they grabbed their packs and prepared to leave the camp, Andie asked, "Where is Kyra? Is she not coming with us?"

Stoyan returned, "You would like Kyra to come?"

"If I may be honest with you, my friend," Andie spoke bluntly, "you may speak for them, but she is clearly your leader. I see the way you all look to her. I thought it strange at first, so young a woman to hold you all in her hand as she does. But one evening in her company explained it well. She is extraordinary. She is like a small, plain chest, but when you open it, it holds twice what it should and is filled with luxurious riches."

The description impressed Stoyan. Andie saw in Kyra what they all saw. It was not her dancing, not her Phoenix costume, not her blossoming figure or the passion that flowed from it. It was Kyra's mind that impressed him. Andie saw what Luca did not, what the nobles of Zagreb did not, what the Swabians along the Drava could not see beyond their fascination with her dancing.

"She is engaged to marry my son, Yubi," Stoyan felt the need to inform him, "I doubt she will come along without him."

"Then by all means," Andie announced gaily, "Bring the young man along too."

Stoyan called for Kyra and Yubi.

When they joined, Andie placed a hand on Yubi's shoulder and told him, "I assume you know what you have in this one. I congratulate you."

Before Yubi could answer, Kyra spoke, "He knows what I am. He knows because he made me what I am."

She turned to Yubi and he to her. They held hands, and Andie, Stoyan, and Ernko witnessed her profession, as she spoke directly to Yubi, "Everything I am comes from you… everything good. My courage, my loyalty, the very words I speak came to me through you. The best of my heart…"

She let her emotions run away with her. They all witnessed the raw effusion of tears from her eyes while she continued, "I would have died in the grass years ago, cold, dirty, and alone, had I not been seen by your keen and beautiful eyes. You, Yubi. You picked me up out of that grass, held me in your hand, and sculpted me into all that I am today. It was you, much more than anyone else."

Stoyan and Ernko teared and blushed. Andie simply smiled widely and asked, "Is this the wedding? Did I just witness your vows?"

Yubi and Kyra were far too sunken into each other to hear the question.

Ernko answered, "No, no. They are not married. They must court for two years."

"Or less," Stoyan interrupted.

Not until hearing her profession did he truly understand the love between them. A two-year courtship was too long and too cruel.

He continued, "Ernko is right. They are not married, but they may be soon."

At those words, Kyra and Yubi pulled from the depths of each other's eyes and turned to Stoyan for elaboration. He had none to give them. The length of the courtship was his decision, and what he had just witnessed from Kyra changed his opinion on the matter. In any case, it was not a decision for that day. The five of them left the camp together and walked in meandering conversations to Andie's boat, docked on the river in the heart of Banja Luka.

Andie gave his new friends a tour of his river boat. It was long and narrow. The majority of it was a cargo hold for all his merchandise. It had a row of oars on both sides that were never used. They were designed for a crew and rapid movement up rivers. The boat enjoyed a leisurely retirement after coming into Andie's possession. A tall sail protruded from a tiny bump of a cabin that was barely long enough for Andie to spread his long legs. It struck the Roma as familiar. The boat was a floating vardo, and Andie a floating Gypsy.

As Andie proudly tallied the items in his hold, he was struck with an idea. He knew the kumpania had silk to sell. The villages on their path back to Hungary did not present the best possible opportunities for profit.

He suggested, "Let me take the silk off your hands. I know a merchant who will pay top for it."

Ernko, having been rather recently taken in by the kumpania, was apt to trust him. Stoyan and Yubi were doubtful. It was quite a risk, handing over their most valuable product, on which they had banked everything, to a Greek stranger they had just met.

Stoyan began a diplomatic but defensive explanation as to why they would not simply hand him the silks, but Kyra interrupted, "This is excellent. If you can sell it for us, it will save us weeks of travel."

Andie suggested, "I will meet you in Požega when the sale is done. I will pay you then."

Stoyan asked, "What do you have to gain? How much will you claim for yourself?"

"I hadn't thought of taking a commission. I must attend the port and see the merchant anyway. Much of what is in my hold is intended for him. I might as well take your silks with me. It will cost me nothing to make the deal, so I see no reason to charge you a commission."

Stoyan suggested to Kyra that they discuss the matter with Patrin and the others, but Kyra had none of that. She sealed the deal with a grateful embrace of Andie. They all walked back to the camp. Within an hour, Andie was gone with most of their silks.

CHAPTER FORTY-THREE
KINSHIP OF THE KUMPANIA

THE KUMPANIA CERTAINLY FELT LIGHTER without the silks. There was a silently prevailing notion that they had seen the last of Andie and the last of the silks he took from them. It did not break them. They had nothing before. They could survive with nothing again. Their buoyancy had another source. Kyra believed in Andie. She took him at his word and expected to see him in Požega with their money. Her faith was theirs, and by the time they rolled into Požega, they all spoke eagerly of reuniting with Andie.

They had almost nothing to sell, only a few silk outfits that Patrin had finished before they met Andie. Top among them was Kyra's wedding dress. They were all prepared to sell it if the price was good — all but Patrin, who would have starved himself before parting with it.

The memory of their last performance in Požega still lingered in the hearts and tableside tales of its residents. Although they had not seen Kyra's Phoenix costume, or the romantic and dramatic ending of their act, it was the common assumption in the town that the magnificent dancer they had fallen in love with and the Phoenix of

Zagreb who performed for the king were one and the same. They were proven right on the kumpania's first afternoon in Požega.

Before Stoyan could ride into town and bark their presence, small crowds began to arrive at the camp. They walked freely among the Roma, as if already invited to be there. There was no privacy, nor was any wanted. At Lavinia's suggestion, Kyra put on her Phoenix costume and walked among their visitors. They were star-struck by her, following her closely but not daring to address her directly.

They mumbled to each other but for Kyra to hear, "Is that the Phoenix of Zagreb?" and "You see, she is the Phoenix."

A trail of townsfolk followed Kyra around the camp like the Piper's mice. Finally, Yubi met her. She sat on his hand, and he hoisted her into the air right in front of them. They gasped and clapped. Kyra struck a few mythological poses before Yubi set her down. Just as the visitors began begging for more, Stoyan told them that the Phoenix would rise again the following evening as the sun hit the horizon.

Word spread quickly and comprehensively through the town, and the people came in mass the following evening. So dense was the crowd, it was hard to imagine that anyone remained behind. The performance space was cleared. Torches lit the area with cryptic orange light. The visitors felt like they had opened a dark, ancient, mystic-scribed manuscript and fell into the pages. Mythological creatures of any form could have appeared before them and would have seemed quite in their element.

Only one myth appeared that night. Right on cue, the Phoenix rose in her glowing costume with flowing wings. From the height of her opening lift, Kyra saw a welcome face. Andie stood wide-eyed at the front of the crowd. He watched the performance very differently than he had the first time. His economic mind had been opened to view a wider world. It was clear in his face that he experienced the Roma artistry in a spiritual way that had previously been beyond him.

All of the performers saw him and his besotted eyes, which motivated them to perform all the more intensely. He could have sailed away with their silk and never encountered them again. But there he was, as promised, as Kyra promised.

When the performance was over, they greeted Andie like a brother. His embraces were familial, and they quickly learned why. Andie gave Vadim the money from the silks, so much more than they were expecting. He handed Vadim a second purse, filled with as many coins. It was from the sale of his boat.

In the company of Kyra, Yubi, and Vadim, speaking over the noise of the evening, Andie explained, "I have been alone for so long, a caravan of one on the rivers. I have sold my boat and bought a wagon... to join you... if I may. I feel a family among you, so if you will have me..."

"Of course," Kyra shouted more loudly than necessary to be heard. She embraced him and invited him to settle among them.

The decision to admit a stranger into the kumpania had met with mixed results, but Andie alleviated all doubt when he said, "Come, help me set it up."

Nobody knew what he spoke of, but they followed, gathering Stoyan, Milena, and her husband as they went. Andie led them to his wagon, which was filled with unsold merchandise from his boat, plus things he had purchased since the sale. The performance was over and there had been nothing to sell, nothing to keep their visitors lingering and spending. Andie solved that problem. They quickly unloaded his foreign goods onto blankets and opened them for business.

The items were not Roma, but the people of Požega did not know or care. They were still in an emotional frenzy over the dramatic ending of Kyra and Yubi's dance, and they spent more money than they should have. At the end of the evening, between the money from the silks, the sale of Andie's boat, and the things sold on the blankets that night, the kumpania was wealthy again.

There was no awkward transition for Andie. The kinship of the kumpania was instant and saturating. As he worked beside the others to recover the camp, an onlooker could never have distinguished him from the oldest members of the kumpania, not by his ease among them, not by his efforts on their behalf, and not by the warmth of affection that flowed toward him.

They had money in their purses and very little else in their possession. In the morning, they went into town to replenish what they had sacrificed. With only Kyra, Yubi, Vadim, Ernko, and Andie, they bought sheep and dogs, lumber and scrap metal, textiles and decorative stones, and food stores to last.

Kyra stood alone on a dock, staring down the river, imagining the many places the flowing water had carried Andie. She was snapped back to the moment by the yell of Vadim. She turned and saw him confronting a man. Kyra's heart sank when she realized it was Luca. She shouted, "No!" and drew his attention. Luca stormed from the Vadim to stand toe to toe with Kyra.

"Where is my wife?" he demanded.

She calmly answered, "Your wife is a widow. Her husband is dead."

"Where is she?" he demanded again.

The others followed behind and surrounded him. Luca leaned aggressively into Kyra. She stepped back and was dangerously close to the edge of the wooden dock over the water.

Kyra stood her ground and informed him, "Chiara is none of your concern, and you are none of hers."

She spoke to him in Venetian, in clear and eloquent Venetian. It surprised him, and he took one step backward, almost bumping against Vadim. He seemed to relax, and everyone relaxed with him.

Suddenly, he shouted, "You are a liar!"

Before anyone knew what happened, he punched Kyra hard and square in the face. Her head snapped back. Her knees buckled beneath her. And she collapsed to the dock, her hip dangling precariously from the edge. Luca jumped on her and continued punching her, as blood flowed from her nose from the initial strike. Now, Andie had spent his adult life flinging heavy merchandise on and off his boat with ease. So, you can imagine the easy force with which he grabbed Luca from Kyra. He took the scoundrel by the sleeve and belt, and threw him off the dock to the hard, cobblestone path like he was nothing more than a small sack of stones.

Yubi's love had matured. A year earlier, he would have charged at Luca. Now his focus was fully on Kyra. He rushed to her. Luca stood in a fury, focused not on Andie, but on Kyra. He screamed a barbarian's war-cry and charged at her as Yubi helped her wobbly to her feet. Yubi would have been no defense. He forgot Luca existed. His eyes, his heart, and his hands were on Kyra's bloody face.

As Luca ran to attack her again, Andie took an oar that was lying on the dock and he swung it at Luca's legs as he charged. The oar struck Luca's right knee, folding it backward. The pain meant nothing to the enraged man. He would have continued to charge at Kyra had his broken knee been able to hold his weight. But Luca fell to the dock in mid-stride, with his right leg bent unnaturally to his side. Yubi lifted Kyra into his arms and ran her past Luca, off of the dock, and onto the secure cobblestones.

With watery eyes and a bloody face, Kyra stared at Luca defiantly, with fresh memories of the great pain he had caused vividly in her head. Yubi set her on her feet, and the five of them, Kyra, Yubi, Vadim, Ernko, and Andie stood shoulder-to-shoulder as a wall, daring Luca to approach. Luca stood at the end of the short pier, exactly where Kyra had fallen, with his broken leg awkwardly contorted beneath him. He screamed one more time, then fell into the water. They did not know if he fell or jumped. It was a point debated later. In either case, Luca was in the river. They watched, as did the crowd of tradesmen that had been beckoned by the commotion.

They watched for him to surface. He did not. After several minutes of scanning the river on both sides with no sign of Luca, Ernko suggested, "Should we dive in, try to find him?"

Kyra answered slowly, "It has been several minutes. He is either out of the water or already dead. I think he is dead. As I said, Chiara is a widow."

They were not immune to the tragedy of lost life. They stood for some time in morbid contemplation of the incident, all but Yubi, who returned his focus entirely to the welfare of his beloved.

They returned to the camp with livestock and supplies, with one swollen, bloodied nose, with satisfied rage, morbid sadness, and a strong sense of kinship among them. The incident at the dock soured the milk of Požega. They all agreed it was time to move on, to cross the Drava River into their homeland and put the misadventures of the Balkans behind them. They entered Hungary with every bit of wealth they had left with, but with a little extra.

They took the same road that brought them into Croatia, so they encountered the same ferry at the Drava. The ferry had gone into disrepair, and they found the same ferryman laboring away at his only source of income, unable to use it and without sufficient tools, supplies, or skills to repair it. He was happy to see his Gypsy customers again, but he mournfully had to decline them. The ferry could not take a single horse safely across, let alone a heavy vardo.

Andie shouted from atop a horse, "I know this river well, and I know those who work on its banks."

He asked Vadim for a precise sum of money, which Vadim handed over without question or pause. Andie had proven himself trustworthy and much more. He took the purse and raced west down the riverbank.

He returned two hours later with no purse, but with a promise to the ferryman, "I have purchased the repairs to your ferry. The carpenter and laborers will arrive by tomorrow afternoon and begin the work."

It was a gesture of good will that befitted his new company well. The kumpania gained nothing from the exchange, not even a ride across the Drava. They did not wait for the repairs to be complete. They drove the caravan fourteen miles east to the town of Belišće. It was a rising timber town with a new bridge across the river. The toll was steep, but not nearly as much as they paid for the repairs to the ferry.

They crossed into Hungary with a new, crafty, devoted, and defensive member of the kumpania, and with the ripening love of their young betrothed stars. It was the three of them who decided to follow the river west again along the Hungarian bank to check on the repairs to the ferry. When they arrived, they found the carpenter hard at work, and their friend the ferryman shouting orders like an impatient foreman. When his attention was drawn to the Gypsies on the other side, the hard foreman melted away. The gratitude of an old friend shouted and waved at them. They wished him well and turned north.

CHAPTER FORTY-FOUR
SPICES FROM THE HEAVENS

KYRA AND YUBI HAD DONE MUCH TO DISPLAY the depth of their love for each other. Stoyan had already decided that a two-year courtship was not necessary. When he heard of his son's performance at the docks of Požega, where his love for Kyra overwhelmed his hatred for Luca, and his thoughts and actions were entirely on her, he knew Yubi's love was a man's love for a woman, not a boy's love for a girl.

They decided to marry the lovers where they first fell in love, in the fields near Győr. After leaving the ferryman, they performed for the people of Siklós, who were delighted to see them again. They stopped at Pécs, not to perform or sell anything, but to visit the friar Matthais. Matthais came to the camp and spent three days with them in hearty and intimate friendship. From there, the kumpania worked its way slowly into deeper Hungary. There was no urgency. They had supplies. They had wealth. They had freedom and love.

About an hour's travel outside of Győr, they camped. Yubi wanted to marry on the anniversary of their engagement, on Kyra's seventeenth birthday. So, the second half of the summer was spent with little movement. Vadim and Andie rode occasionally into town to replenish what they consumed. Ernko and Andie built upon the wagon Andie bought, transforming it from an open wagon to a Roma vardo. They painted it to match his old boat to suggest to all who saw it that Andie had always been one of them, even when he sailed the rivers as a stranger.

In late September, on a glorious morning of warmth, they prepared for the first wedding the kumpania had hosted in many long years. Patrin had kept the wedding dress from everyone. They all knew about it, but none had seen it. From his glow as he talked about it, the anticipation was for something spectacular. He pulled Kyra to his vardo and revealed the dress to her alone. Patrin had made it in a Chinese style. It was red and orange with floral patterns embroidered across the breasts and down the left side. A deep blue sash wrapped around the waist and hung down from the right hip. It was slender and designed to hug her tightly, accentuating her every contour.

Patrin held it up for Kyra, whose delight and gratitude sprang from her unbridled. She grasped at it, but he withdrew it.

"It is an old Roma tradition," he informed her, "that you shall not wear it until the hour of your wedding. If you put it on sooner, so the legends tell us, your husband will be unfaithful during your marriage."

"He never could and never would," she replied, "Still, since it is a tradition, I had better wait."

"You are right about that," Patrin told her, "I have never seen a man so much in love with a woman."

Kyra drew a deep inhale, trying to wrap her brain around her own life and come to some understanding of the events that had led her from Szanzar into the arms of a loving husband.

At noon, within an hour of the ceremony, Kyra took the dress into her vardo. Patrin and Milena joined her inside to see it on her as it should be. The kumpania gathered in place for the wedding, in a crescent formation facing Kyra's vardo. Yubi and Stoyan waited at the steps of her porch. Patrin stepped out first and walked with beaming pride in the creation that was about to finally be revealed. Milena followed shortly after.

Kyra shook with nerves. She delayed several minutes before stepping out. It was not to raise the anticipation of the kumpania, but that was the result nevertheless. Yubi fidgeted and kicked at the ground beneath him. When the door of Kyra's vardo finally opened, he nearly fainted from the rapid snap of his neck in her direction.

There she stood, like an angelic, glorified version of the child who first stepped cleaned and polished onto Iraja's porch. But this was not Iraja's young child in front of them. This was Kyra, their star, their queen, the very heart of them all. This was Yubi's bride in a dress that would have been the envy of every noble woman from China to Paris. Kyra's blush set her aglow. The silk fabric caressed her from neck to knee, drawing every eye along each cascading slope of her figure.

Many had shouted their admiration for her over the previous years. Many had fallen in love with her. Had they seen her at that moment, she would have been forever on the run from them. In the intimacy of the kumpania, she was only adored. They knew the girl she was. They had seen her grow. They had experienced their own changes because of her. And they stared at her on that porch with all of those memories bouncing off of their hearts like children at play.

Stoyan climbed the ladder, took her by the hand, and escorted her from the porch. He handed her to Yubi, who walked with her, neither led by the other, to the center of the gathered crescent of loved ones. The bride and groom each chose a sponsor of their love. Yubi chose Lavinia, for it was she who first encouraged his love for Kyra. Kyra chose Milena, for her love had been the hardest to earn, and other than Yubi's, the one most cherished.

Lavinia and Milena introduced the couple with eloquent words of what the young lovers meant to each other and to all. For half of an hour, the praises flowed without pause. When they were done, they presented the couple with two shirts.

They were plain, white shirts with long, loose sleeves. Each shirt had straps dangling from one sleeve. The couple was instructed to put on the shirts. They held hands, and the straps on the sleeves were tied together by Lavinia and Milena, while ancient words of binding love were recited.

"You are to remain tied together for the rest of this day," Lavinia announced, "There will be no privacy between you from this point forward. At the end of this day, when the celebrations are over and you enter your vardo as wife and husband, you may remove the shirts and begin your life as one."

The marriage did not officially begin until they were alone in her vardo and the shirts were removed. For the rest of that afternoon, tied together at the hand, they were to determine if a life united with that person was what they really wanted. That was the Roma tradition and they followed it to the letter. Also in keeping with tradition, the couple was mocked and jeered in loving lightheartedness for the rest of the day. They fed each other with their free hand. They danced with each other and others, all while tied together.

When Lavinia and Milena saw fit, the celebration was dismissed and the sponsors escorted the couple to their vardo. Climbing the ladder while tied together was an enjoyable comedy for all, especially the small children, who found the clumsiness of the effort hilarious. Inside of the vardo with the door closed behind them, the white shirts came off and Kyra and Yubi were married. They were undeniably and eternally each other's, and they felt the full weight of that realization in their very full hearts. If marital love shined with a visible light, Kyra and Yubi would have lit the dark half of the world that night from the secluded confines of their tiny vardo.

Yubi rose the next morning before Kyra. He had placed many kisses on her cheek since their friendship blossomed. Marriage changed everything. It aggrandized his existence, compounding every sensation. The little kiss he gave her cheek that morning, as she continued to sleep, was a more profound experience than anything he had felt in his entire life prior to the wedding. He kissed his *wife's* cheek. He held his lips on her with his eyes open, drawing a deep inhale, trying to experience her with all of his senses at once. When he pulled away, he was overwhelmed with feeling. It dizzied him. He kissed her cheek again just to see if it would affect him as much. It did.

He whispered to himself, "This is my life now. *Now,* I am alive."

He stepped onto the porch and greeted his first sunrise as Kyra's husband. The warmth of the infant rays tingled his face. The air he drew into his lungs was sumptuous in the extreme. He felt like a god and the servant of a god, both empowered and humbled, free as the wind and enslaved with responsibility. He was grateful for it all!

Perhaps Kyra was not so deeply asleep when Yubi kissed her cheek that morning. Maybe she had been in that half-dreamy place in between, or maybe the kiss of a husband so deeply in love marks its brand more permanently. She awoke with her fingertips gently rubbing where Yubi's lips had just been. From that spot, warmth spread to every nook of her being. Yubi was not in bed beside her, but she did not wonder. That early morning kiss bound his lips to her cheek. She could feel that chord of connection, and she knew he was on the porch without seeing or hearing him.

She joined him there. With an arm tightly around each other, they looked out over the sleepy camp. The horses shuffled and huffed. The livestock chewed on the grass beneath them. It was quite a normal morning, yet they experienced it together on the porch of their shared vardo with the freshness of newborns. Both had silently wondered how marriage might change them, how differently life would feel. Neither imagined such a transformation, and neither had known how overwhelming happiness could be.

They remained in camp for one more night, giving the newlyweds an entire day with no responsibilities but to love each other. The next morning, they struck the camp. They caravanned, and the things they did as they traveled were not dissimilar to what they had always done. But to Kyra and Yubi, the routines had more flavor, like two people eating what they had eaten every day, but only now, for the first time, adding salt.

They set up on the edge of Győr, much nearer the town than before. There was no need to ride in and announce their presence, no need to advertise a performance and market. They could be easily seen. Marriage gave Kyra and Yubi boldness, and in their new boldness, the others were emboldened. They camped their vardos under the nose of Győr and dared them not to come.

The Győrans came and were greeted immediately with a strangeness they could not identify. The wedding left a residue of tingling liveliness on everything and everyone in the kumpania. It had no name, for nobody had known it. It was as if some divine ingredient had been sprinkled on them in generous portions by a heavenly hand. When this unearthly seasoning touched the Győrans, it opened their pores, widened their eyes, and dilated their pupils. They were primed for a dramatic performance before the first note was struck.

Luca had contributed one priceless thing before departing from their lives. He gave them the notion of the Phoenix. Before Zagreb, performances were usually during the sunlight hours. In Győr, the music began just before dusk, when enough light still hung in the sky to show the colorful intricacies of the costumes. By the time Kyra flew into the air, the scene was brushed with the colors of sunset. She was lit by only torchlight by the time she stood on Yubi's one hand and lifted her leg beside her head. As she fell to his arms, the wings on her sleeves were majestic flickers of light against the dark sky above.

The new intimacy between the two star performers was brilliantly apparent, bringing tears not only to the Győrans, but to the Roma. When Yubi lifted Kyra, he lifted his wife. When he caught her, he caught his wife. When he fell to the ground dramatically, and Kyra danced in mourning for her husband, her soul bled as if severed in half. No matter how many times they had rehearsed and performed, Kyra's cheeks were drenched with tears by the end, tears that caught the light of fire to perfect advantage and made the Phoenix's face shimmer and glow enchantingly.

After the show, there were no proposals, no professions of love. There was something about the way Kyra and Yubi danced together as wife and husband that was untouchably sacred. Kyra was not for sale. She was not even for admiring. It was their love for each other that was on display, with a purity that nobody dared defile with lewd compliments or obscene proposals. The Győrans ended the evening less in love with Kyra than with each other, with their own husbands, wives, children, and neighbors. If pure love could be cooked down and concentrated, then bottled and sold, that is what was served to the people of Győr by Kyra and Yubi's performance, but not only theirs. The passions of the musicians and dancers who accompanied them were also concentrated and poured like thick honey over their audience.

The wedding truly changed everything, seasoning life in the caravan, for Roma and visitors alike, with a holy spice too richly righteous to be devoured barbarically. Kyra was their queen and Yubi their new king, but it was the rare love between them that ruled the kumpania.

CHAPTER FORTY-FIVE
THE BRIDE'S CARESS

BUDAPEST WAS A CITY THE KUMPANIA was eager to visit. Exotic products from east and west collected on its Danube banks, yet it was far enough from the coastal ports for Gypsy performances to be thrilling and new. They were sure to fill the camp and likely to find enchanting foreign things for trade. They left Győr after five days and rolled the caravan east, along the southern bank of the Danube.

As eager as they were, they were in no hurry. The air was too sweet, the sights and sounds too beautiful. Each moment was too delicious to quickly chew and swallow. They traveled for a few hours each day, savored long, leisurely daylight hours in camp, and slept comfortably under the warm autumn night sky. At that rate, it would have taken them nine days of travel, but they did not break camp every day. If the ground was flat and dry, with pleasurable scenery and a body of freshwater nearby, they remained an extra day or two. Two weeks after leaving Győr, they rolled to the outskirts of Budapest.

When they were three miles from the western edge of the city, they stopped to sleep. They slept in caravan formation. As Yubi held Kyra under the folds of their bedding, he realized that the vardo and its bed, the books and trinkets, and the woman in his arms truly felt like his. The excited newness of marriage was being replaced with a comfortable sense of rightness. It was in the calm gratitude of that moment that he understood the eternal reaches of human happiness.

In the morning, they circled to the south in hopes of meeting the river before it reached the heart of the city. The air was crisp. It was noticeably the coolest morning of the season. But the sun was strong. The direct sun and the cool breeze were a magical combination, especially for people whose senses were so recently enlivened by emotion.

As they rolled along, Vadim drove the horse that pulled Kyra's vardo. Kyra rode on a horse beside him. Yubi sat on the porch exchanging flirtatious smiles with his wife. Overwhelmed by a blush and blown kiss, he sprang to his feet and climbed to the roof. On the roof of their vardo, he began clapping his hands above his head. It was not the seductive rhythm that urged the others to clap along. It was the joy that poured down on them from every part of his powerful body, a brand of delirious bliss that shows its face on this planet only once in a thousand years. Those walking along the caravan clustered near him.

He shouted, "Hada!"

And they all echoed him.

Again he shouted, "Hada!"

"Hada!" they returned.

Yubi pressed to a handstand and held it easily through the rocking and shaking of the vardo. The others continued the clapping he had begun, shouting with bright faces, "Hada!"

Yubi came down from his handstand. He stood still, gazing at Kyra. She smiled at him, reflecting his joy. That rare bliss shone from her as well, and she knew that if the happiness of individuals could be stood back-to-back in comparison, hers would tower over all others in the wide world.

Yubi raised his hands in the air and shouted, "Hada, my wife! Hada, my kumpania!"

He threw a high back flip, much higher than ever. He landed loudly, startling the horse that pulled his vardo. The horse stopped sharply, ceasing the vardo on the spot and almost shaking Vadim from its back. Yubi fell from the roof and landed on his side with a thud and a holler. Startled by the noise, the horse jolted forward and the wheel of the vardo rolled across Yubi's neck, killing him on the spot. The horse continued forward and the back wheel rolled across his lower jaw.

Yubi was dead.

It took several seconds to bring the caravan to a complete stop. Kyra stared in disbelief. Her mind would not let her believe what her eyes had just witnessed. When the truth struck her heart, it did so with beastly force. Staring at the mutilated body of her husband, she tried to gasp, but her lungs were immobile. She fell from the horse and landed on her side. She felt no pain from the fall. She crawled to Yubi, screaming as if on fire.

When she reached Yubi, he was hardly recognizable. The back wheel had dislodged his lower jaw from his face. His neck was bent unnaturally sideways. His eyes were wide open, but there was no light within them, no love, no life. Kyra went silent and breathless as she turned her face away and collapsed to lay across him. All stood still with no idea what to do.

Kyra lifted her head from Yubi's chest and stared blankly into the sky beyond the caravan. What began as a low and steady moan grew as her lips slowly parted. Her mouth opened wider and wider as the ghostly cry raised in pitch and volume. She looked down to her lover's contorted face and went silent again. By this time, every member of the kumpania was gathered around gawking in disbelief and pitiful compassion for the grieving bride.

Kyra looked up from Yubi to the faces of her kumpania. There, at the forefront, stood Stoyan. She looked at him with wide, pleading eyes that demanded, "Do something! Fix this!"

Of course, nothing could be done. The gruesome remains of Yubi's mortal self needed to be pulled from his young wife and committed forever to the ground beneath them, but nobody dared. Stoyan was the first to run to them, but not to aid his son. Yubi's death was certain the moment the first wheel went across his neck. He ran to Kyra.

He grabbed her by the waist and tried to pull her from the body. Her painful scream rose in shrill pitch. It frightened him. He had never heard such a sound. He let go of her and she embraced the body more tightly. He looked at his son and his daughter and felt a new brand of grief for the very first time. He stumbled backward, and his mind escaped to images of distant hills and coasts.

Lavinia took Kyra by the shoulder but did not have the strength to dislodge her. Vadim wrapped his arms around her and lifted, as Ernko pulled Yubi by the arms in the opposite direction. When Kyra was separated from her husband, her vicious scream turned to a vocalized wheezing that went on without break, as if it needed no air.

Vadim pulled Kyra away from her vardo and the murderous wheels, to the far side of a supply wagon. He fell to a seat on the ground and squeezed her with all his might. He said nothing, but only alternated between breathing steadily into her ear and kissing the back of her head. He left Yubi to the others. His only concern was Kyra — the girl he cared for, who had become the artist he admired and the queen he obeyed. Now, she was again a child in his arms.

He did not know how long to hold her so. A few of the kumpania assisted Stoyan in wrapping his son's body and placing it on the porch of Kyra's vardo. Beyond that, nobody knew how to proceed. They had had their share of deaths, many sudden and accidental. But this was Kyra's kumpania now, and Yubi was Kyra's husband. They could not do as they always had. They waited to see how she would respond. They waited to see what Kyra needed and what Kyra expected them to do.

One thing was for sure. It did not matter that they were on the edge of Budapest or cutting a circle to the Danube. There was no Budapest, no Danube, no docks or markets. That all might as well have been a million miles away. The kumpania had been transformed by Kyra and by the love of Kyra and Yubi. Their sensations were aggrandized. Their sorrow hit depths they had never known. It bore Kyra's darkness and was made much worse by the height of elation from which they had so suddenly fallen. They were shocked witless by the bludgeoning effect. They did not feel the loss like Roma. They felt it like disciples of Kyra, and the strange, squeezing suffocation threw them into spells of breathless panic.

Andie rode in haste into Budapest and bought some burial linens. He bought nothing else. He sought nothing else. He rushed back to the camp to help prepare Yubi's body. Lavinia and the dancers, bless them, did what nobody wanted to do. They placed Yubi on the back of an open wagon and unwrapped him. They set his jaw and neck as correctly as they could, and wrapped his head with the precious linens. The sun was low and the light was dimming quickly.

Lavinia found Kyra asleep in Vadim's arms, still leaning against a wagon wheel exactly as he had been holding her for hours. She looked peaceful. They had no idea what she dreamed of, but it was probably better than what she would awaken to. It could be no worse.

Vadim whispered, "Please, let her rest."

"We cannot," Lavinia answered, "The body must be oiled and perfumed, and she must be offered the right to do it."

Lavinia rubbed Kyra's head and spoke gently, "My love..., my love..."

Kyra awoke and lifted her head from Vadim's arm. Her dreams were vivid and had taken her far away from the tragedy at hand. It took her a moment to gain herself, to realize where she was, whom she was with, and what had just happened to her. The compassionate sorrow on the faces of her friends reminded her quickly.

When the recollections crashed in on her, she looked at Lavinia, winced her face wretchedly, and slowly raised a pitiful whine, speaking through it, "No, no, no."

Lavinia curled up beside them and wrapped her arms around Kyra and Vadim. She kissed Kyra repeatedly above her ear, and said between the kisses, "Oh, my love. Oh, my love, my love."

Reluctantly, Lavinia pulled away and told Kyra that her husband's body was ready to be perfumed. A sudden and remarkable sternness came over Kyra. She stood from Vadim's lap and took Lavinia's hand. They walked together to Yubi, where the oils and perfumes waited on the wagon beside the body.

Kyra could not see Yubi's face. His head was wrapped. She simultaneously wanted to see him and desperately did not want to. She knew what a gruesome sight hid beneath the wrappings. But the rest of his body was unwrapped and unmolested by the murderous wheels. It was beautiful. It was muscular. Twenty hours earlier, she had been running her hand over those same shoulders and across that same chest, watching and feeling his hairs rise in response. She looked at his body and drew that memory as near to her as she could.

Kyra crawled onto the wagon, and Lavinia mounted beside her. Lavinia dared not touch him. This was Kyra's moment to say goodbye. Lavinia handed her the perfumed oils and Kyra began rubbing them on her husband. Hers were not industrious hands performing a duty. They were the hands of a bride caressing her groom. She focused her eyes on each inch of him as she applied the perfume. Chills ran across her in waves. Her face was stoic, then writhing, then placid, in random and repeating patterns.

Another scratchy whine oozed slowly from her lips, but it turned melodic. It was so low at first that Lavinia did not recognize it as a song, but when it rose, she knew it well. Kyra was humming Yubi's melody, the one he composed to accompany Kyra's poem, the tribute to Iraja.

The song stopped suddenly, and Kyra's tender, perfumed strokes on Yubi's leg turned grasping and squeezing. The reality of her loss cudgeled her again. She turned her head over the side of the wagon and vomited. When she turned back and looked at the body in front of her, she was suddenly repulsed by it, or repulsed by the reality of it.

As if getting away from the body would also get her away from the truth, she crawled over the side of the wagon and fell to the ground, crying, "No, no…, he is not…, no, no. Yubi! Yubi!"

She was lying in a puddle of her own vomit, continuing to protest in that way when Vadim picked her up and carried her toward her vardo. As they got near, Kyra began to shake in his arms. She shook her head from side to side violently. She said nothing, but it was clear she did not want to go to the bed she had shared with Yubi.

Stoyan walked beside them and told Vadim, "Please, give me my daughter."

Vadim passed Kyra into his arms, and Stoyan carried Kyra to his tent. Milena helped strip her of her dirty clothes and wash her face. They dressed her in one of Yubi's shirts and laid her in the tent. Stoyan laid down beside her and held her. His arms were the only ones that could bring her comfort that night. There was something in their shared loss that helped them both.

Lavinia and the dancers wrapped Yubi in the rest of the burial linens. They took turns staying up with the body through the night with no idea how they would proceed in the morning, how or where to bury Yubi, or how to plan for the immediate future of the kumpania.

CHAPTER FORTY-SIX
THE SORROW BENEATH THE SONG

WHEN KYRA AWOKE, she was no longer in Stoyan's embrace. He slept with his back turned to her. It had been a restless night for him. He slept at a strange angle and in a strange position. His shirt was twisted from turning all night. It took no time for the truth of her circumstances to come lucidly to her. She awoke fully aware. When she looked at Stoyan, she wished, for just a moment, that he had died instead of Yubi, and in that moment, she would have exchanged the father's life for the son's. Kyra loved Stoyan and immediately regretted the thought, adding remorse to the already rancid pool of her emotions. She crawled to him, kissed him on the shoulder, and left the tent.

She thought she was running to the wagon that held Yubi. That is, her mind was moving faster than her body. In truth, she walked like she was waist-deep in water, slogging each step forward as if it took a great deal of physical effort.

The dancers had put great care into wrapping the body. A keen and compassionate eye would have seen it at a glance. Kyra was not capable of compassion. Yubi's body was covered, his skin separated from her forever, and a surge of anger at all those who wrapped him flooded her from skin to bone. This was not Menowin or even Iraja. This was Yubi. Kyra, believing they all saw this as just another loss, just another misfortune of the kumpania, resented them all deeply. These feelings subsided and returned in cresting and waning waves that grew in size and intensity with each resurgence.

By the time the whole kumpania was up and alert, Kyra was unable to hide her resentment. She spoke to nobody and hardly made eye contact. She was clearly in no position to guide them, nor would anyone burden Stoyan with decisions. Vadim decided to drive the caravan away from the city, west, into the welcoming womb of the open grasslands. He had a notion to bury Yubi in the same spot where they had wed, but that was a risky idea and Kyra had closed herself off from consultation. So the caravan rolled west to no particular destination, hoping the right thing to do would present itself.

Kyra would not enter her vardo. She would not ride on a horse like she was when Yubi fell. She walked beside the caravan, near enough to Yubi's body to see it, but not too near. The dew was particularly thick that morning, like large teardrops, as if a horde of people had walked side by side, crying profusely as they passed along the countryside. Kyra's vivid imagination, guided by the intense pain in her heart, conjured similar imagery.

The kumpania was not guided by thought, but by feelings. Those free to do so clustered near Kyra or around the wagon that carried Yubi. Not only did they have no idea how to best serve Kyra, they were stricken with confusion over their own feelings. The sensual renaissance they had all undergone since the wedding was still in full force, only the feelings being magnified were now horrible ones. Part of them demanded that they scream a wheezing cry like

Kyra's. The other part wanted to sing a joyful tribute. They tended to both halves of themselves at the same time.

Their song did not begin with the clapping rhythms that usually preceded the voices. The clop of horse hooves and the squeak of wheels provided enough background for the moment. The song began with Milena, with a simple hummed melody as she walked beside the body and thought about the boy who had brought them all so much joy. Others joined in until everyone but Kyra sang. Although they held Kyra's deep sorrow inside of them, stabbing and aching, they had not yet learned how to express it. They sang like Roma.

Had Kyra listened, she would have realized it was a tribute to Yubi, a mournful tribute, in as much as the Roma express mourning. It savored brilliantly of his spirit, of his kindness, his energy, his strength, his intense love, and his ingenuity. Had Kyra's heart been able to hear deeply into the music, she would have understood the sorrow beneath the song and recognized in it a very familiar sort of grief, and she would have been comforted by the sensation. But she was not capable of such awareness. She only heard music and to her, it sounded inappropriately jovial and predictive of a future happiness she could not imagine, she did not want to imagine.

It was the same "La Nanu La Na" and "La Da Na Na Da" that they had always sung while caravanning, but it rang out in Yubi's spirit. Somehow, they captured his very essence and let it fly on their voices through the free, open, Hungarian air. Not one of them sounded like Yubi. Not one had his voice. When singing together, however, with him richly on their minds and decadently in their hearts, their united voices sounded just like him. Kyra would have felt as if Yubi rode right beside her and all around her, singing directly to her, had her heart cooperated with her ears. But her husband was not beside her nor anywhere near her. He was dead, and each note that took to the air and invaded her ears pinched cruelly at her heart and wrenched her in the gut.

The more the kumpania sang their tribute, the less grieving it became. Yubi was a joyful young man and the melodic eulogy took on his spirit and became celebratory of all Yubi had been and still was to them. These were not sorrowful people surrounding Kyra. It was not a sorrowful song. Joy came onto their faces and into their voices — Yubi's joy, a gypsy joy, but not to Kyra. Not to Kyra.

She could not share in their celebratory song. She felt oppressed by it. She was luxurious in her grief. She thought the others were starved in theirs. The truth is, they grieved as deeply as she did. Their grief was not a Roma grief, it was Kyra's grief, only it did not show as Kyra wanted it to show. Hers was deeper, with many layers covering it. Kyra felt as she did when she first came to them, when she could not understand them and thought they did not understand her. For the first time in years, Kyra felt like an outsider among the Roma.

She wanted them to hurt as she hurt. She wanted them to weep, not laugh, to sink inwardly, not sing out loudly. She wanted them to cry because she wanted to cry, and she did not feel that she could, not amidst the joyful singing. She was wrong. Had she only known how wrong she was! She should have mourned openly in her own way. Only then could she have mourned in their way. Instead, she resented them. She wanted to stop the caravan, stop the singing, and scold them all viciously. Even in those first lonely, soiled days with the kumpania, they never seemed so alien to her.

She spoke nothing at all that day, and nobody tried to pry it from her. They served her. They fed her. And they kept their distance, not knowing what she needed. Travel was more burdensome. The free Hungarian air felt oppressive. They were camped by early afternoon and retired to bed before sundown.

Stoyan, torn as he was from the tragedy, tried to be what the others needed him to be. When he walked toward his tent that evening, the old man appeared very much like himself to those who could only see skin deep. He grinned as he always did. He spoke with no difference in his voice. But it was only a façade of himself on display. Kyra knew him better than anyone in the camp. His smile was something put on intentionally, not something that radiated from deep within him, as it had always been. He was a very different man than the one who had lost his wife many years earlier, different than the version of himself who buried Menowin. He hurt more deeply. His pain was sticky and searing, like molten metal poured onto the flesh, clinging and cooking its way to the bone. Kyra saw the pain in him, and it comforted her. She wished desperately that his deep inner pain would come to the surface so they could weep together.

As Stoyan held Kyra that night, and his paternal arms soothed her to sleep, his thoughts were constantly on his son. Yubi was a vibrantly joyful young man, a man in love with Kyra, a man grateful for her. As Stoyan pondered his son, and Kyra's low breaths brushed his forearm, his mind connected Kyra and Yubi. He could not think of him without thinking of his gratitude for her — his love for her. Suddenly, in Kyra's company, he sensed his son's presence. He knew that Yubi had given his heart to Kyra, and his heart still resided inside of her. As he held her, he realized he was embracing them both, and the nature of his mourning changed.

When they awoke in the morning, the grateful grin was not just a façade. Kyra sensed it but did not sense the love that caused the change, and she resented him for his inner peace. She felt like she had lost her one fellow-mourner, and she felt as alone as she had when she wandered away from Szanzar.

A weighty pall rested somberly over the entire camp, nowhere more heavily than on Kyra's aching head. The pall was lifted by Stoyan. He walked jauntily from his tent, smiling broadly and brightly. It was not a fake smile, not one put on before going out, like some fashion accessory. In honor of Yubi and his extraordinary bride, the man clung tenaciously to joy and refused to hand it over to any event or circumstance, no matter how it lacerated him. He carried his abundant spirit *and* his son's, and it spilled forth from his every gesture.

Kyra had wandered in a daze to Yubi's body. She climbed onto the wagon and began applying perfumes. Stoyan walked directly to her, kissed her and began to speak. He personified the spirit of the Roma. As Kyra looked at that face and listened to that still-vivacious voice, she felt immensely out of place. She could not join her spirit to his. His floated upward like warm air. Hers remained chained to cold and jagged rocks.

She was no longer that soiled child in a field. Life with the kumpania had pulled her fully from her childhood identity, but not fully into theirs. What Kyra did not recognize was that strain of herself that ran through the grateful man in front of her. It was not only Yubi's joy that lifted him. There was no Yubi's joy without Kyra's love and Kyra's strength. Kyra, as much as Yubi, was the fire that warmed him. She was the fire that had warmed them all. That signature fire shone from Stoyan with a quintessentially Kyra hue. It was a part of herself Kyra never really understood — very different than the deep, somber light that flickered dimly inside of her then. There, standing beside Stoyan, listening to him talk of joyous days behind and ahead, she held those contrasting lights in comparison beside each other, and she felt as alone as when she toddled aimlessly from Szanzar so many years earlier. For the first time in years, she felt more akin to her father and mother than to Iraja.

Stoyan sensed her turmoil. He placed one hand on Kyra and the other on Yubi. He squeezed them both simultaneously, and he told her, "Your husband died free, and he died happy, happier than any man I have ever known."

The words had no apparent effect on Kyra. She continued to perfume the body in a trance. She was deep in terrible thoughts, imagining all of the things she might have done or said that might have steered their fate down a different path, one that placed Yubi warm and alive in their shared bed at night.

Stoyan continued, "Yubi died in a way many of us cannot even hope for. His last moments were joyful, with his beautiful wife smiling at him adoringly. It is more than I can hope for. My wife is long dead. She will not be smiling at me during my last moments. I miss Yubi terribly. But I am happy. I am happy for him and grateful for his happiness."

While this understanding uplifted Stoyan, it weighed oppressively on Kyra. To her, it made Yubi's death more of a tragedy, more calamitous, and it made her loss more profound. Even with his tender explanation, she could not see it as he did. She still wanted him to hurt, to fall to his knees and sob hysterically, lamenting his inability to interfere in Yubi's demise, just as Kyra did.

Disappointed by the futility of his efforts, but not hopeless, Stoyan left her to her duties. He gathered the other leaders to discuss what to do next. They determined to bury Yubi where he first spied Kyra, where he married her, and where his years-long dream to be her husband came true. With more determination than they had moved with since the accident, they struck the camp and headed for the fields between Győr and Szanzar. In the four days it took to get there, Kyra distanced herself more and more from the kumpania.

She would not sleep in the tent with Stoyan. She found no kinship in his happiness. She could not sleep in her own bed, not while Yubi's body laid across a wagon nearby. She slept on the cold ground beside the wagon, near to Yubi but not with him. Each evening she fell asleep on the ground, and each morning she awoke covered by blankets that had been laid across her by various loving hands.

They arrived at the place of the wedding, and Vadim began to dig the grave. The air had gone cold and the sky promised snow. Kyra sat beside Yubi and watched Vadim. As the hole got deeper, the permanence of death struck her. What was left of the villager inside of her shouted out. She could not bury him in a field, unmarked and unvisited, soon to be covered over with snow.

In the first words she had voiced in days, she shouted to Vadim, "No! Stop!"

Vadim held still, and Milena walked to her and said, "My love, he cannot ride with us any longer. We must bury him."

"Not here, not now, not like this," Kyra whined.

Milena stroked Kyra's neck and offered, "Tell us where. Tell us when and how, and we will obey you."

Kyra's eyes suddenly widened, and she sat erect on the wagon, proclaiming, "We will take my husband to Szanzar and bury him beside the other members of my family."

It was a disturbing announcement. It was the first time in years Kyra had referred to the people of Szanzar as her family. Also, nobody thought the idea of bringing Kyra back to her dead childhood village was very promising. But Kyra had spoken, and Milena promised to obey her. Stoyan did not believe it good for Kyra to spend much time in Szanzar. None were sure what the village would look like after the years that had passed. He ordered Ernko and Andie to ride to Szanzar and prepare a grave and a grave marker. He intended Kyra's return to be brief.

Ernko and Andie left immediately. When they arrived in Szanzar, they did not find a dead, rotting village, but an active community very much alive. Andie spoke Hungarian. He inquired of the condition of the village, saying nothing of Kyra and nothing of the body they wished to bury there. They gathered what information they could and they rode back to the caravan.

Stoyan greeted them and asked, "Is it ready?"

"Things are complicated," Andie answered, "Szanzar is alive. We saw no sign that death had ever come to them."

He explained that the tithing barn was in full function and being run by a man named Vajk. The faces around him went blank. They had heard that name when Kyra stood before them as they camped outside of Zagreb and told her story. Vajk, Kyra's brother Vajk, lived and ran the business Gellen taught him to run. Stoyan and the others who were there when Kyra told her history fell into deep thought. None of them could foresee what the news meant for Kyra and for her life with the kumpania.

They braced themselves for any of a hundred different reactions from Kyra. They wanted the moment to be as warm as possible, and the setting to remind her of better moments with the kumpania. They raised the large tent, warmed it with lamps, and called for Kyra. When she walked in, the rigid stances and concerned faces told her that news of some magnitude awaited her.

"She is my daughter," Stoyan said as he stepped forward, "I should tell her."

Not at all defiantly, but in a timid, almost submissive voice, she asked, "What? What should you tell me?"

Stoyan asked her to take a seat. Lavinia hurried with a pillow and set it behind her. Kyra did not notice. She stood tall and waited for Stoyan to answer her.

He jumped right to it, "Your brother Vajk lives. He runs the Church's barn in Szanzar and has a family of his own."

Kyra should have taken the seat offered to her. Her mouth opened. Her eyes rolled backward. She panted an airy sigh as her knees buckled beneath her. Lavinia caught her and lowered her to the pillow.

They all had the same fear — that their beloved Kyra, their queen and their inspiration, would leave them and seek the comforts of blood relations during her grief. The panic was real, and it showed in their every twitch and gesture. They stared at her, desperate to gauge her reaction.

Kyra simply sat, stared at her knees, and said, "Vajk. My brother, Vajk."

They remained as they were for several more minutes, none of them daring to budge.

Finally, Kyra stood and, with sharp, focused eyes and a sober, lucid voice, she said, "We cannot bury Yubi in Szanzar. They would never allow it. The open field was his home. That is where he found peace and that is where he should be buried."

She walked out of the tent, and for the first time since Yubi's death, she entered her vardo. She would not sit or lie upon the bed they shared. She leaned against a trunk, opened it, fiddled with its contents, and thought about Iraja and her earliest days in the kumpania.

Kyra's directive gave them hope that they could bury Yubi and ride with their queen away from Szanzar. Under the silvery light of a half moon, Vadim finished digging the grave. In the morning, Kyra scented the corpse one more time and they lowered Yubi into the ground. Kyra knelt at the edge of the grave and whispered a conversation to her husband in a rushed stampede of airy syllables. Everything she would have wanted to tell him over the many decades of a full life together hurried through her lips, believing this to be her last chance to tell him before the earth separated them forever.

With each shovel full of soil to fall on the body, Kyra's words came more frantically, cracking from a whisper to rusty vocalization. By the time his body was fully covered, she was yelling at him, drifting through the many languages he had taught her. Only Stoyan understood all that she said, and only then did the cosmic expanse of her grief become clear to him. He saw that her capacity for love was of inhuman, Godly proportions, and her capacity for pain matched it. He wanted to weep with her. He wanted it so badly. He felt his face swell and his tears climbing to the ledge of his eyelids, but they did not jump. A brand new dimension of sorrow swelled in him and begged him for release. But he did not. For some reason, he could not.

By the time the last of the dirt was packed into the grave, Kyra was hollering in fits and alternating between yanking on the grass beneath her and tugging forcefully on the hair on her head.

Manfri began to sing. His voice was his instrument. Seldom did anyone hear him sing. But he began a song and the others quickly joined in. Led by Manfri's raspy old voice and a chorus that would not sing over him, the song stayed low, slow, and mournful. After having buried so many over their years together, this one was different to them all. They did not sing of freedom or love, or in any words at all. They hummed mournfully. There was such ripping sorrow beneath the notes. Kyra did not hear it. She felt no unity from it.

They all left Kyra to the graveside, gathering in tense, speechless circles scattered across the camp. Stoyan remained for a few minutes after the others. He had a strong urge to dig up his son's body, and hold it and Kyra in one tight embrace. The violent sob inside of him found slight release in an occasional cough, but he swallowed it back down and stared at his pitiful daughter. After a few minutes, he left her and went alone into his vardo to touch the things that were Yubi's and intentionally stab at his own heart.

Kyra spent the night lying atop the dirt of the grave, continuing to mumble to Yubi. She did not sleep. She did not rest, but kept herself in tense and contorted, writhing positions.

CHAPTER FORTY-SEVEN

THE INTERRUPTED COUNCIL

THE CLOUD-COVERED SUN FOUND KYRA where the moon had left her. She still did not sleep. Her mumbling had slowed and lowered overnight. By morning, her lips moved, but only short, panting breaths came from her mouth. Snow had begun to fall during the night. When Milena saw Kyra in the morning, a dusting of white surrounded the ground around her. Kyra's hair and dress were wet.

"Please, Kyra," she stood behind and begged, "let me change you. Let me hold you and warm you."

Kyra gave no response.

The day passed with no change but the increasing thickness of the snow on the ground. A halo of wet dirt surrounded Kyra, kept from accumulation by her body heat. Many offers were made to her. Offers turned slowly to demands, but they were ignored all the same. When the afternoon came with no hope of improvement, Milena gathered the performers together.

"She is going to die on that grave if we do not do something!" she blurted.

Stoyan answered quietly, "She wants to die on that grave, and sink into the ground with Yubi."

Vadim had heard enough, and he shouted, "No! Not my Kyra!"

He stormed to the grave and found Kyra asleep. The snow had begun to stick to her hair and pile on her dress. With much more regard for her safety than her wishes, he lifted her into his arms and carried her to her vardo.

"The steps!" he shouted.

Milena responded and lowered the steps of the porch. Vadim carried Kyra up the steps and into the vardo. He laid her across her bed and tore her dress from her. She was truly unwell, such violent jostling should have aroused her. She remained as limp as the wet clothes he threw aside. He covered her in blankets and laid himself over her until she regained her warmth — her warmth but not her consciousness.

If anyone had command of the kumpania in Kyra's absence, it was Vadim. He was related to Iraja and would surely have taken her place if Kyra had never come to them. So when he stormed from the vardo and ordered the caravan to roll away from the grave and farther away from Szanzar, they obeyed.

Kyra slept through the day and the following night. She had spent enough nights in bed with Yubi to expect him to be there when she awoke, enough comfortable hours with his skin pressed against hers for it to be a habit she would need to break. When her mind finally came fully out of dream, and she remembered the awful truth, she knew immediately that they were in motion and moving away from Yubi.

Wrapped only in a blanket, she stepped onto her porch and yelled, "Stop!"

The caravan came to a gradual stop. Kyra leaped from the porch and ran, following the tracks the wagons had left behind them, with nothing on her feet and only a blanket over her shoulders. The blanket fell from her as her sprint grew in desperation. Several people ran after her, but only Andie could catch her. He tackled her to the ground then lifted her into his arms and stood. She did not fight him, but kicked her legs as if still running. Ernko caught up with them, carrying the blanket she had dropped. He covered her in the blanket, and they were escorted back to the caravan by everyone who had chased after her.

Vadim ordered them to set a tent. He instructed the dancers to stay in it with Kyra, to hold her, talk to her, feed her, sing to her, whatever would keep her from running naked into the open field. Kyra followed their lead. She dressed. She drank some water and nibbled on some dried meat. Vadim called an emergency meeting of the rest of the kumpania. Kyra was not only his queen, not just Stoyan's and Milena's, Lavinia's and Ernko's. She belonged to them all, even the very young, and all of their voices needed to be heard.

Everyone over the age of twelve gathered in the large tent to discuss Kyra and her future. Once they were all settled, Vadim announced, "This cannot go on. Kyra will die. Something must be done and we must do it now."

Stoyan stood and took the attention of all. His face was red and his eyes wet. He cleared his throat and spoke, "We all know Kyra well, and we know this is no place for her to recover."

Ernko asked, "What place are you speaking of?"

"Us," he quickly responded, "She cannot recover with us. I propose we leave her at a village."

There was a concerted gasp from every seat in the tent, but he continued, "We will leave her in a small village, a slow and peaceful village, where she can recover in her own way and at her own pace."

Milena shouted out, "How will she get by?"

"Come now, Milena," he answered calmly, "we speak of Kyra. She is the strongest of us all and the most capable.

She will get by. When she is ready, we will come back and get her."

Vadim asked, "But how will we know when she is ready?"

Voices erupted from all parts of the tent. One person said they should bring Kyra to Tornik and leave her with Chiara, suggesting that Chiara would bring out Kyra's compassion and her grief might be buried beneath it. This brought on a torrent of discussion over the plan's merits and faults. Another suggested they appeal to Bogdan and the other nobles of Zagreb, perhaps King Louis himself. They were all taken with her and might house her and treat her like a noblewoman. But then, could any of them be trusted? Was their regard for her authentic or just a fleeting fascination? The kumpania agreed. She could not be left in such uncertainty.

Stoyan stepped forward and demanded the floor. Everyone quieted, but he could think of nothing to say. It would not have mattered if he did. Kyra burst into the tent at that very moment, panting heavily from a brisk and thoughtful walk, and she demanded, "Take me back to my village!"

Every other breath in the tent was held. All that could be heard was Kyra's heavy panting, and she demanded more forcefully, "Take me to my brother. Take me back to Szanzar!"

She stormed from the tent as forcefully as she had entered.

Stoyan sat down and said, "This is perfect, better than I had hoped."

"Better?" Vadim asked, demanding an explanation.

"Yes. She can return to her village and see that it is dead."

"But it is not dead," Vadim argued.

"Not in that way," Stoyan defended, "not with corpses. But it is dead. She will see that her life there is dead. Let her compare it to her life with us. Yubi is dead but he is not gone. She will not find him in Szanzar. She will find him here, in our tents, in our vardos, in our songs and dances, in our food and jewelry. She will come back to us."

Some saw the wisdom in his words. Others did not but had no better suggestions. It would not have mattered if they had. Kyra had spoken. She had spoken forcefully and determinedly. They had no choice but to take her to Szanzar.

Kyra left a bit of herself in the tent when she left. There was a bit of her in each of their hearts. At the prospect of parting from their Kyra, they cried. They cried together as Kyra would have cried, mournfully, sorrowfully. There was no gratitude in that tent, no celebration of their years together. That would have been a Roma reaction to the situation. There was only sorrow and an intense sensation of impending loss.

When they left the tent, Kyra was on a horse, trotting impatient circles around the camp. Despite their reluctance, they struck quickly, turned the caravan around, and rolled toward Szanzar. They rode directly toward it, and Kyra knew the way. She did not ride in her vardo or even turn her head toward it, but remained on the horse near the front of the caravan.

Several hours later, they were within ten miles of Szanzar. The sky had cleared, and the sun was brilliantly reflected off the white ground. Kyra halted the caravan, rode her horse to the head of them, dismounted her horse, and began briskly walking forward. Andie took a few steps in pursuit of her, but Stoyan stopped him.

"She will make it from here," he said, "And it is best her brother does not see her with us."

The entire kumpania gathered at the front of the caravan and watched Kyra diminish toward the horizon until she was gone entirely from their view.

"What do we do now?" Milena asked.

Stoyan answered, "We do what we always do until she is ready to come back to us."

Milena argued, "What we always do is with Kyra and cannot be done without her."

Stoyan turned to her, kissed her cheek, and shut himself in his vardo. They camped there for the night with the hope that a clear morning sun might guide them somewhere.

CHAPTER FORTY-EIGHT
SOMETHING ONCE CALLED HOME

KYRA'S DETERMINED PACE could not be maintained for ten miles in the snow. It slowed, and at points came to a stop. But she made her way to Szanzar before the sun came up.

The first thing she saw was a new graveyard. By the pink light of an infant day, she walked among the fresh stones. The victims of the plague were buried there. She found her father and mother. The baby's name was etched on Eneth's stone. Beside Eneth was another stone, laid flat, not upright like the others. On it was Kyra's name. The circular stone was not over a grave, but placed as a memorial for a twelve-year-old girl, long presumed dead.

Kyra did not look at the graves of her parents. She had already shed every tear she had for them. She stared at her own memorial stone and thought of how unfitting her name seemed among the dead of Szanzar. She was suddenly pleased that Yubi rested where he did. She had been wrong. Within a gated cemetery, under a heavy stone, beside villagers he never knew would have been the wrong place for him to rest.

As the sun got higher, Kyra could hear the faint noises of a rising new day from within the village. Her eyes remained on her stone, but her ears reached for all they could hear. She heard footsteps behind her. They were the steps of a man making his daily visit to the graves of his parents and baby sister, to pray for them and for the sister whose fate he did not know.

Kyra was much taller. Her features had polished up nicely over the years. Vajk did not recognize her. That is not what drew his gasp. Kyra wore a bright Gypsy skirt and a Gypsy blouse that opened low on the chest, drastically underdressed for the temperature. Some stranger, some heathen Gypsy woman stood at the graves of his family.

"What are you doing there?" he shouted.

Kyra turned to him, and although he did not identify her immediately, there was something familiar about her that froze his protest.

Kyra knew Vajk at a glance. She pointed to her memorial stone and said, "I am not under there."

Vajk knew her then, and he walked in slow disbelief to her.

When he was a step away from her, she repeated, still pointing down to her stone, "I am not under there. I am not dead."

How clumsily her native words stumbled from her mouth, knocking against her teeth and crawling over themselves to her lips. She was surprised to hear herself sound so differently from the last time she spoke Hungarian. She spoke with a heavy Romani accent, not one she placed to make a point, but in an honest but foreign attempt to sound like her brother's sister.

Despite the cold, Kyra was warm and her skin fresh and aglow from the rays of the sunrise. Vajk took her hand to see if she was real. Her hand was warm but not angelic. Her skin was rough and told of laborious years behind her. This was no mystic vision. It was Kyra, alive and returned from a mysterious past. Her clothing told at least part of the story, and Vajk shuddered to imagine the rest. He embraced her quickly, then took her by the hand without another word between them and led her into his home.

It had been her home, the same home. She walked through the very door she had escaped through years earlier. Everything seemed smaller, not just in proportion to her growth, but in every way something can be small. Everything, every book, ledger, chair, table, and dish from Kyra's childhood was there, and each threw memories at her more quickly than she could process them.

Once in the house, Vajk did not slow. He moved quickly to grab a plain village dress. "Here," he directed, "this is my wife's. It should fit you well enough. Quickly put it on."

Vajk turned away and shielded his eyes. After a few seconds, having heard no rustling behind him, he turned back to Kyra and found her standing in bright Gypsy clothes, holding a plain village dress in her hand.

"For Heaven's sake, Kyra, change into the dress!"

"Vajk!" she scolded. She softened and continued, "My brother, I saw you fall to the floor. I thought you were dead. You thought I was dead. And now that we are reunited in our parents' home, that is what you say to me? 'Change into the dress'?"

"Forgive me, Kyra. You are right."

He embraced her again, took the dress from her, and led her to the table.

"Are you hungry?" he asked.

"I don't think I have eaten in days. I don't really know."

Vajk stumbled through the kitchen to provide her with bread as quickly as he could get it to her. While Kyra ate, he tripped over several half-words, not sure how to begin. There was much to learn between them. Kyra knew that many stories lived between the dead and rotten Szanzar she ran away from and the clean, revived village she returned to. Vajk could not imagine what Kyra's life had been like. All he knew was her Gypsy clothes made him uncomfortable. They represented a lifestyle that offended him before he learned anything about it.

When she finished the bread, he asked pleadingly, "Now, please, will you change into the dress?"

Kyra gratefully accepted the dress and changed. It had been a long time since she had possessed village-girl modesty. She changed in front of him with no embarrassment. He blushed, turned away, and realized Kyra's transition back into her childhood home would be difficult. When she finished changing, he took her skirt and blouse from her and promised to take care of it.

Vajk took the clothes into his bedroom. He returned just as his wife came home, hand-in-hand with her daughter, Vajk's step-daughter. His wife, Judit, was a young mother widowed by the plague. Kyra knew her. That is to say, she remembered her. She better remembered the eight-year-old girl, Arely.

"Arely?" Kyra asked, squatting down to look the girl in the eyes.

Arely nodded, and Kyra told her, "You will not remember me, but I was your friend, and now I am your aunt."

"Vajk??" Judit questioned nervously.

Vajk looked to Arely and confirmed, "She is right. You are her niece. This is my sister, Kyra."

Arely tilted her head to one side, puckered her nose, and asked in confusion, "The one in the stone by grandmother and grandfather?"

Vajk smiled and answered, "Yes, she is that Kyra, but she was never in the stone. She was only lost, and now she is found."

Vajk may have been a duplicate of Gellen, but Judit was no Eneth. Scarred as she was by trauma, she was a doting mother and a warm host. She stepped to Kyra, took her by the arm, patted her a few times in disbelief, then begged her to sit and be fed.

"No thank you, sister," Kyra answered with authentic gratitude, "I have just eaten. But I am hungry for knowledge of you and my niece, and news of my brother these past years."

Judit squinted her eyes and commented, "Your accent is strange to me. Where have you been?"

"I have been far, and I have seen and heard many things."

Vajk did not like the direction of the conversation. He did not want Kyra's gypsy past to infiltrate his home and inject his wife and daughter with wild, nomadic morality. He interrupted, "She has only arrived this morning and must rest. After that, I have a great many things to discuss with my sister."

Vajk led Kyra to Arely's room and offered the child's bed. At the sight of a bed, Kyra's weariness fell on her and her legs went weak. She took the offer, laid on the bed, and slept until evening. Her dreams were vivid and varied, but when she rose from bed, she could not remember them. Only swirling emotions and flashes of imagery remained. If she had remembered her dreams, they would have been pushed from her quickly. Word spread of Kyra's return, and curious well-wishers maintained a constant rotation of visitors to Vajk's door.

Visitors came morning, day, and evening, to gawk at her as much as greet her. For four years, Kyra had been no more than letters on a stone in the graveyard. But there she was, miraculously revived to living flesh and bone, vibrant, and with the fire of experience and understanding burning from within her eyes. Although she tried to hide it for Vajk's sake, Kyra was quite the celebrity, which she was well used to. But her fame within Szanzar faded after one week and disappeared entirely after two. The people of her village went about their lives as if nothing new had been added, and Kyra became, once again, an ignored underthought of her village.

For the first few weeks, she tried to fit into her brother's pressed mold for her. Vajk's office was outfitted into a bedroom for her. Vajk was busy making her, in every way, a woman of Szanzar. Kyra bit her tongue each day, unable to speak freely of herself. Her Roma identity found escape in her dreams at night. Her bedroom was attached to the house, and her screams in foreign languages echoed throughout. She often called for her husband in the night, "Yubi! Yubi! Yubi!"

Kyra's past was a growing monster Vajk could no longer keep under a pile of his ledgers. One night, almost a month after her return, too restless to sleep, Kyra went for a walk. It was a frigid, snowy night. In her bare feet and no more than a nightgown, she strolled around the house and barn. Szanzar was absolutely silent, except for the subtle sound of snowflakes landing upon each other. The cold meant nothing to Kyra. The Roma walked for miles at a time in the snow and slept under thin tents on frozen ground.

It was not Kyra who roused Vajk, but Arely. The child was developing a fascination with her aunt. She watched from the window as Kyra circled, lap after lap, around the Church's property.

"What are you doing?" Vajk asked his stepdaughter.

"Look at Aunt Kyra," Arely answered, "She looks like a spirit."

Vajk looked out the window and was disturbed by how spirit-like Kyra looked, strolling around the frozen grounds with ease and comfort, wearing nothing more than a sheer nightgown, with the look of a distant world in her expression.

"Go to bed!" Vajk commanded the girl.

Stefan Scheuermann

Arely obeyed, and Vajk stood at the window and stared with just as much fascination, but unlike Arely, his fascination was weighed by fear. He did not call for Kyra. He only watched her, growing more anxious by the minute, until she finally came inside, flush, ruddy, and glowing with warmth, as if returning from a midday walk in the summer.

"I'm sorry," she whispered when she noticed him, "I didn't mean to wake you."

"You didn't wake me. Arely woke me."

"Oh, well, I didn't mean to wake Arely."

Vajk was deeply aggravated, and he let it show, "Kyra, do you see any of our neighbors strolling unclothed through the winter night?'

"I am not unclothed, Vajk."

He was in no mood to argue such a point, and he begged, "Please, sister, we are your family. Szanzar is your family. Please try to be one of us again."

"It is interesting to hear you speak like that. Father never did. He always seemed above the petty movements of the village."

"Father didn't have to rebuild this village after the plague. I did, and I was younger than you are now. Kyra, it was terrible. The rotting bodies did not bury themselves. The homes did not clean themselves."

In the shock of finding her brother alive and her childhood village thriving, she never considered what the recovery was like. Kyra looked at Vajk with such respectful compassion that he felt confident to continue.

"Those who fled Szanzar when the plague hit, and lived to return, rebuilt their homes and their lives beside me. We buried our dead side by side. Their tears are on our graves. Their sweat is in our home. Szanzar is my family. It is your family."

Vajk's words were a fine synopsis of a much bigger story, a story he needed to tell, and one Kyra was willing

473

to hear. She asked him to sit with her and, with eager eyes, she invited every detail of their years apart. Vajk began his story from when she ran from the house. It was a story of horrid misfortune, striking a young man and a community in ceaseless waves. It was also a story of courage, of companionship, a story of trust and faithfulness, of energy and effort. It was a story of recovery and one of expansion.

It was good for Kyra to hear. She saw her brother, sister-in-law, and neighbors under a new, heroic light. Her tears demonstrated her compassion, and Vajk saw in them evidence of kinship and mutual commitment.

When he finished his story, and they had cried together and embraced each other, Kyra began to introduce her story. She told of her flight from Szanzar. In wretchedly colorful detail, she expressed every pain she felt before lying down in the grass to die. But at the first mention of the kumpania, he cut her short.

"You are home now, Kyra, safe in my house, in our father's house."

"Yes, and I am grateful to you, but many roads have brought me here, distant roads in foreign lands, and I want to tell you about them."

"There is no place in this house and no place in Szanzar for that life. You did what you needed to do to survive. I blame you for nothing."

"I did much more than survive, brother. I lived."

"Yes, and I am glad you lived to come home. You are of Szanzar, and now you are back *in* Szanzar. Nothing else matters."

She saw the futility in prefacing her story, so she simply began again where she had left off.

"No!" he commanded, "I will not hear of it, and you will not speak of it, not to me or anyone."

It was not the night for such a conversation. Kyra yielded, congratulated her brother on all he had accomplished, kissed him, and went to bed. In the morning, she asked Vajk for the clothes she arrived in.

"They are gone," he answered.

"Gone? Where? What have you done with them?"

"They don't belong here. They don't belong on you."

"They are mine and I want them back."

"Oh, I see. You want something of your own. I understand."

He smiled broadly at her and walked from the house. He returned that evening with several packages. Each contained a new and expensive article of clothing, each for a respectable, presentable, village maiden of Szanzar, perfect for the sister of the keeper of the Church's grain. The gifts were a sacrifice that came from the limited wealth of the family. Vajk gave them with authentic love for his sister. But he definitely gave them as part of his personal agenda for her.

Kyra accepted the gifts graciously. She returned Judit's dresses with sisterly affection. The truth is, she lived with Vajk and his family. She lived in Szanzar with her neighbors, and she determined to give Vajk's vision of her a try. She demanded her Gypsy clothes, promising they would never see the light of day. Reluctantly, and against his better judgment, he returned them to her.

She continued to take pleasure in long solitary walks in the snow and cold, but not in the middle of the night and not in a sheer nightgown. Slowly, her Hungarian took the form of a native of Szanzar. All Romani was gone from her syllables, from her clothing, and from her behavior, at least when others were around.

The less she acted like a Roma, the more she thought of her kumpania. Thoughts of them fully occupied her snowy wanderings. She knew their routines well, too well as it happened. She could easily and accurately imagine where they were, what they were doing at any given part of a day, and what sort of conversations were being had between and around the camped vardos. It would have been much easier for her if she could not, if they would have dropped her off and disappeared into some arcane mist like the Gypsies of her childhood fantasies.

Whether at sunrise or the height of the day, twilight or the depth of the night, she could see in her mind's eye every particular of the kumpania. She could hear their voices and instruments, see their waving hips, smell their oils, perfumes, and the spicy foods that cooked over the open fires. And when she was in her still and stationary bed, she still felt the rocking and rattling of her vardo — of Iraja's vardo, keeping the kumpania constantly on her mind.

Her wandering thoughts of her kumpania were not altogether accurate. She could not have known how stunted they were, how paralyzed without her. She envisioned them as they would have been had she still been among them. Kyra was not dead. They could not deal with her absence from the kumpania in the way they deal with death. Had she the vision to see them as they actually were, she might have shed her villager dress, donned a bright skirt, and run at full speed into the wilderness. She always underestimated her power over them, and she did so then, imagining their lives returned to normalcy without their bright star, without their queen, without their Kyra.

The more she thought of them, the more her stories knocked on the inside of her lips demanding to be let out. She had a thousand fascinating stories to tell and no audience to receive them. When she thought it might burst from her and destroy Vajk's carefully sculpted sister, she sought a safe and secret release — her niece Arely.

Vajk was the foremost citizen of his village, making Judit the first lady of Szanzar. Neither were often at home, leaving Arely, much as Kyra had been, often alone. Late one February morning, when the snow was falling, Vajk was supplying firewood to the poor and Judit was making rounds with bundles of food. Arely and Kyra were home alone.

"I show a very small part of me, my dear niece," Kyra told her, "but I do not want to be a mystery, not to you. There are things you should know about me, things that must stay between us."

Arely promised she could keep a secret. Kyra sat her down, and one improbable adventure at a time, she told Arely the stories of her life with the Gypsies, of rescuing Stoyan from the mob in Paks, of discovering Menowin's body in the grass, of her athletic performances in front of screaming audiences. She told of Croatia and King Louis, of Luca and Chiara, of Adriatic sunsets and a winter holed up in a fortress. The central strand of it all was Yubi. She could not have hid her tragic passion for her husband if she wanted to, and she did not want to.

Arely was enthralled. Her aunt tripled in size that day. The fact that the stories were their special secret endeared Kyra to her even more. Months went on in this way. Kyra was a conservative, respectable sister of Szanzar's best man. She said the right things to the right people and acted like a young woman just waiting for God to present her with a suitable husband. On the first really warm day of the spring, that all crashed down.

Judit, intending the very best, knew of a man who sought a wife. She introduced the man to Vajk. Vajk approved, and over supper that night, he presented the idea to the family.

As Vajk was describing the man, Arely commented, "He doesn't sound much like her husband."

The frigid awkwardness at the table spoke well enough of the truth. Kyra was already married, or had been. Vajk did not wait for supper to finish. He rose from the table, took Kyra by the hand, tugged her to another room like she was a child, and he confronted her.

Kyra blurted preemptively, "He is dead."

Vajk took an awkward, involuntary step backward, as if he had been knocked in the chest, and he said, "You were married."

Kyra nodded.

"To a Gypsy?" he prodded.

"Of course. When my whole family was dead, they took me in and cared for me. I had a mother among them, a wonderful and attentive mother."

It pained Vajk to hear her go on in that way, and it showed in his sour face.

Kyra continued, "I had sisters, brothers, a father-in-law, and yes, very briefly I had a husband."

Vile images based on wicked stereotypes flashed through his head, and he asked, "When did they marry you to the Gypsy? Were you still very young?"

"They did not marry me to anyone. I married Yubi last year, after a long friendship and a yearlong courtship..., and I was very in love with him."

Vajk was Gellen's son throughout. His life was a ledger that required a wife to balance the figures. His own marriage had nothing at all to do with love, though he had developed affections for his wife.

Kyra's mention of love rattled him. But the details of her marriage relieved him of more horrid imagery. He no longer saw his sister as a forced child-bride in the hands of heathen kidnappers. Still, he felt more disgust than pity for her circumstances.

After referencing her past as she did, she felt a desire to speak more of it, but she knew Vajk had no taste for it. He was most particularly bothered by the knowledge that Arely knew of Yubi, and of God-only-knew what else Kyra had told her. Vajk had lost everything to the plague, including his sister Kyra. As a result, he grew into a doting and possessive husband and father, clinging tightly to everything he cared for, reluctant to release anything he loved from his grasp. He was all too aware of how perilous is the ground upon which happiness and security are built. He took nothing for granted, and much better than his father, he portioned no more of his time to work than was necessary. Now that he had Kyra back, he was ready to dote equally upon her, to cling to her as tightly, and to benefit her by his position. But he would benefit her in his way only, with the help he thought she needed.

He forbade her to speak to Arely. When she convinced him how impractical that order was, he forbade her to speak of her time with the Gypsies, to Arely or anyone. There was a hole in Kyra's heart the shape of the kumpania, and she wanted to fill it by talking about them. She needed to defend them with truth, to tell of Iraja's love, of Stoyan's dynamic ingenuity, of Menowin's courage, Vadim's loyalty, and Yubi's passionate devotion. She could not stand how poorly they were represented in Vajk's imagination. But Vajk stood his ground with authority.

Over the next few days, Kyra tried several times to ease the subject into conversation, but Vajk shut it down quickly, even more so in the company of others. He wanted Kyra in his life and home, but not all of her, not most of her. More than ever, he rejected everything of her past that occurred outside of tiny Szanzar. Kyra had performed for a king in the courtyard of a splendid castle. She watched the sun set over the sea while in the arms of a devoted lover. She had lived and loved on a scale Vajk could not fathom, and she had to keep it bottled inside of her.

CHAPTER FORTY-NINE
IN THE SKIN OF A STRANGER

HEADING INTO THE SUMMER, Kyra managed to become all that Vajk wanted her to be, all except at the very core. That core was Yubi, and she refused to be matched with another man. Other than that, she made the charity rounds with Judit, spoke of the mundane workings of the village over supper, and made fewer solitary walks.

The more time she spent mingling with villagers, doing what they did and saying the sort of things they said, the more she saw the contrast between them. During her years with the kumpania, her transformation into a Roma queen was gradual, obscured in a way by the very events that caused it. She never had the chance to compare what she had become to what she might have been, had Szanzar never been strangled by the plague.

Walking the streets beside her were many young women and men who were very much like what she would have become. She was able to stand herself beside them in comparison. Their hands had not done much and their eyes had seen so little. Kyra could not remove from her inner core all that had happened to her, and she began to feel like she wore the skin of a stranger. She judged neither side harshly, but saw the beauty in both. The village life and the Roma life — although they were both beautiful, they were not both "home". They were certainly not both her. How could they be? "So what am I?" she asked herself daily, "Who is Kyra?"

While mingling about the village, Kyra would make occasional comments in another language — never in Romani. She could not bring herself to utter the language of the kumpania. It was too painful. She would drop a quick and quiet comment on the weather in Italian, or on a meal in German. She would greet a neighborhood dog in Bulgarian and think of lessons in the grass with Yubi.

She produced these quips just loudly enough for the people around her to know the words were foreign, to remind them that to her the world was much smaller and life much bigger. In all other ways, she was just as Vajk wanted her to be, an understated daughter of Szanzar. Like her colorful skirt, she kept her foreign words mostly closeted, bringing them out only rarely and briefly.

Kyra's answer to the question, "Who am I?" needed to be answered once and for all. The moment was forced when a neighbor told Vajk about the foreign words overheard from his sister's lips, interpreted by a secluded village as incantations, possibly devilish, in some devilish language.

Vajk knew she was no devil-worshiper. He was worldly enough. He made regular trips to Bratislava and made deals in other languages. But he knew the power of perception, and he had to address the issue with Kyra.

Alone one evening, he spoke to her. He looked at her with wide, boyish, unjudging eyes, and said, "I am grateful to whomever took you in. You looked well when you returned. You looked cared for. But gratitude is where my affection for them ends, and it is where yours should end.

They are not you, and you are not of them. They live in different ways, by different rules, guided by different principles."

He placed his hand on the pages of scripture he had copied himself, which he had placed conspicuously on the table for the purpose of the conversation at hand, and he continued, "The rules of religion will guide you now, as it once did. You cannot be blamed for how you lived. You were only a child, and you did what you needed to do. But now you must amputate that time from your life, purge it from your memory. It does not serve you anymore. I will never know how you lived. That does not matter to me. You are my sister and I love you. But you are home now. In every sense, you are home. You should not speak of your time away. You should not think of it."

Looking him blankly but fixedly in the eyes, Kyra closed the gap between them. She pulled the pages from between his hand and the table, half-heartedly eyed them up and down, placed them back on the table with their due reverence, and she spoke, "I know of nothing in the tenets of religion that would condemn the life I have lived, that would justify hiding it from my family and neighbors, let alone myself, or necessitate a complete transformation of my character. I was faithful to my husband. I am faithful to him still."

Vajk winced as if in physical pain. It was not a calculated expression. He was authentically disturbed to imagine her Gypsy life with her Gypsy husband.

She noticed. How could she not? It looked as if he had been taken by a seizure deep in his belly.

She had pity for his feelings, but not enough to spare him from them.

She continued, "Although religion releases me, my love does not. Religion tells me I can move on, remarry. My own faithful heart will not. It cannot and it ought not. There is nothing in my past that must be hidden from the good people of this village, and nothing I should have to hide from my brother."

Vajk began to cry. His face swelled red and his eyes watered. He cupped her cheeks with his palms and begged, "Please, Kyra. I am not father and I am not mother. I understand what they did not. I love you. I will not ignore you, and I will not lose you again, not to the plague, not to the Devil, not to anything. You need nothing now but me. Please, sister, let me care for you."

Kyra's compassionate heart responded, as of course it would. Her face reddened to match his. His love for her was real. His feelings were intense. His heart was good and pure, though his vision was limited. And he was right. He had grown much wiser than his parents.

She knew there would be no resolution on the matter that night. She embraced him. He squeezed harder than he had squeezed anyone, and they cried in each other's arms.

They may have cried in unison but they were not united. To an onlooker, they would have appeared to be one of heart and mind. But they could not be. Vajk's love was defensive in nature, fearful and protective, self-bound and caged, and always looking inward. Kyra's notion of love was formed over thousands of miles traveled, under such a variety of people, places, and circumstances that were well beyond Vajk's imagination. But included in this vast love of hers was a love for her brother. In that embrace, she determined to try, for his sake, to live in his world as well as she could possibly fit, not just in her actions, but in her thoughts. She could not be Roma in Szanzar, not even one in a village dress. As Vajk put it, she had to be not only in Szanzar, but of Szanzar.

She made that determination without knowing if it was possible. She had no chance to try. She was not twelve steps from the house when she heard the news. Gypsies were coming to Szanzar! The village saw very little pass their way, and old and young alike wanted to see the dancers and acrobats they had heard of, the notorious Gypsy musicians and items from across the world, brought to their doorstep by the travelers.

CHAPTER FIFTY

THE LEGEND OF THE FALLEN STAR

AS INFLUENTIAL AS VAJK WAS and as much as he feared the Gypsy influence on Kyra, there was nothing he could do to check the enthusiasm in his village. Gypsies camped outside of town. One had already ridden into the village and barked their presence. Kyra's old kumpania was not the only one of its kind on the Hungarian countryside. She could not know it was them. Neither could Vajk, and he would not take the chance. He forbade her to go, confining her to the house until the Gypsies were on their way.

That evening, the rest of the villagers strolled out into the neighboring field, to the camp of Gypsies with their tents and their colorful vardos. Vajk remained seated by the door, a sentry at his post, guarding the exit from any deep inner-calling that might take Kyra from her wits and lead her to her heathen past.

Just as he foresaw, she came from her room and walked to the door. Vajk stood firmly as a barricade. Kyra stepped toe-to-toe with him. He took her by the shoulders, shook her, and told her to return to her room.

In a soft, sisterly voice, she told him, "I love you, brother. I always will. And I am grateful for everything you have done for me and for this village."

Then her posture stiffened, and in the authoritative voice of a queen, she demanded, "Now release me and never seize me like that again. I go where I wish to go, and I do what I wish to do. I am free."

Her boldness could not be refuted. He let go of her immediately, but he gained enough courage to demand, "Do not go to them. They will sweep you away and I will never see you again."

"I promise you this. I will return to you tonight. I will sleep in my bed, in your house. You want me to be a part of this village. Well, they are all at the Gypsy camp, and I should be with them."

He would have argued more had her face allowed it. But it did not. She brushed him aside with her eyes and he obeyed.

Kyra made her way to the camp. She was not very near it when she knew it was her kumpania. Her heart pounded more ferociously with every step. The faces of her Roma friends flashed vividly one by one through her mind. As she mingled with the other villagers, the Roma saw her. They recognized their former queen. But they did not outwardly acknowledge her. She decided to be a villager of Szanzar, and they treated her accordingly.

She watched Lavinia dance, heard Milena sing, swayed her head subconsciously to the swooping melodies from Manfri's lyra. But she did nothing to single herself out from the small crowd. She followed the villagers from blanket to blanket, looking at what was for sale. She bought nothing. She had nothing to spend. The very same jewelry makers who had taught her their craft when she was not yet thirteen saw her, but did not stare. They spoke nothing directly to her, but treated her like every other stranger to visit them. They had been instructed to do so.

At the end of the day, the crowd was invited into the large tent. Stoyan's shoulder had healed well. He stacked his stools and climbed and balanced, just as Kyra saw him do years before. When his act was finished, a child no older than Arely shouted out, "Why do you not live in houses?"

Stoyan had aged visibly in their many months apart. The difference struck Kyra deeply. His hair was thinner and whiter. The few dark locks remaining appeared to be drowning within the sea of curly white. But the fire in his eyes had not dimmed in the slightest. Ageless passion flowed from him in invisible but powerful waves. He stood in the center of the tent and raised his arms high.

"We have a question!" he announced.

The audience's attention was thoroughly his, and he asked the child, "Do you have a question?"

All eyes went to the little girl, and she asked, "Why do you not live in a village like ours? Why do you travel?"

Stoyan turned from the child and walked in a small circle, making brief eye contact with everyone in the tent, and he asked them, "Would you like to hear a legend of our people, a story that explains who we are?"

The response was resounding, and everyone settled in for a Gypsy legend.

Stoyan began, "The world was dark, and we were travelers in the darkness, simple nomads with no light in our eyes. One day, a young man among us looked out and saw a star. It stood alone in the sky, rare and beautiful. He shouted out and stopped the caravan. They all stared in wonder at the star. It must have seen they were in darkness, for it fell from the sky and landed among them."

The eyes of the audience grew wider, except Arely's. She squinted in deep thought. The child knew her aunt's story, and was wise enough to think maybe the old acrobat was talking about Kyra.

Stoyan continued, "The star knew it was too bright for the Gypsies to look at, so it took the form of a woman. She dressed as one of them and lived among them. Her disguise worked. When they passed through towns, the people saw her as a simple Gypsy. She stayed with her new friends, helping them, saving them when they were in danger. But the Gypsies were mortal and she could not save them all. She had grown to love them, and she mourned them terribly. Her sorrow made the starlight inside of her burn brighter, and her human form could not contain it. One evening, when the Gypsies were gathered near a village much like this one, her light burst through her womanly form. It lit the caravan. It lit the village. It lit the sky above. She swallowed her light and again appeared as a simple woman, but it was already in their eyes and would be there for the rest of their lives."

Stoyan dropped his shoulders and let out a sigh. He found Kyra in the crowd and stared directly at her.

In the pause that followed, a man shouted out, "Go on! There must be more."

"There is more." Stoyan answered, "The star never belonged to the Gypsies. She belonged to the heavens. But who could release such a prize? The Gypsies saw how her light spread to the eyes of the villagers, and they took her from town to town, showing her to the people and spreading her light. One night, in a land far, far from here, she danced too near a flame. It burned away her human form, and she shot into the air like a phoenix. The Gypsies watched her fly and they knew she was above and beyond them. But she returned, because she had fallen in love with a Gypsy man, the same man who first saw her in the sky."

At the sudden romantic turn in the story, wives grabbed their husbands' hands, and young girls dreamily tilted their heads to the side and quietly hummed. That was not the end of the story. Had it been, the audience would have insisted on more.

The old story-teller went on, "The Gypsies wrapped her in a silken dress, and she married the young man. In marrying the star, he too became a star who could leave the earth and shine down upon them from the sky. The sky had turned too dark, and it needed his brightness. He left his caravan and took up his duty above them all. She remained with her Gypsy friends until one day, when she was suddenly gone."

Stoyan looked directly at the girl who asked the question, then he turned to Kyra and stared at her firmly. He turned back to the little girl and finished, "You ask why we do not live inside of walls. Why do we travel, you ask! I tell you, the star lit our eyes, and we still shine with it, but we shine in the darkness. You cannot live so long with a star and return to a dark world. The Gypsies travel to find their star. She is out there somewhere."

It was such a quaint and romantic story to most. To Arely, it was the story of her aunt. To Kyra, it was a desperate plea directed at her. They were all correct.

Kyra shouted over the dwindling applause, "What happened to her? How does the story end?"

Stoyan grinned slyly and cocked his head to one side. The eyes of all, even of the Gypsies, locked on his lips, awaiting his answer.

When it did not come quickly, Kyra added, "It sounds like she had seen more death than most. She must have suffered tremendously. How does a normal person survive so much death?"

He hopped with purpose from his stool, locking his gaze hard on her and took three strong steps toward her. He answered in a much lower voice, forcing the entire tent to lean forward to hear him, "A normal person does not, cannot, but I tell of an extraordinary woman. It is true, she witnessed much death, but she also witnessed an abundance of life. She brought life. She saved lives and she witnessed life like no other. Even the Gypsies envied her."

Kyra asked, "Can a star fall twice?"

All eyes went to Kyra, then back to Stoyan for his answer, "I think the star of this story can do anything she wishes."

As the crowd began to trickle from the tent, Arely found Kyra. She looked up to her aunt with starstruck eyes. She opened her mouth and began to speak, but Kyra placed a finger over her niece's lips, took her hand and walked her from the tent.

The Roma bid their visitors farewell, then gathered in a tight cluster to see what Kyra would do. She followed the people of Szanzar, several paces behind the last of them. She released Arely's hand and told her to go home. Arely obeyed, and Kyra turned to look at the kumpania. Such sad and begging faces looked back at her.

Her eyes spent a moment on each individual face, lingering longer on those she loved most dearly. She nodded to them, turned around, and followed Arely back to their home in Szanzar.

Vajk did not expect to see Kyra again. When she walked into the house with Arely, he gave her a tight embrace and congratulated her. He did not explain his congratulations, but Kyra understood him well enough.

That night, Arely did not go to bed. She remained at her aunt's hip. Kyra invited her to sleep in her bed that night. After a few silent minutes in bed, Arely asked for another story.

"I promised your father I would not tell you anymore stories," she sadly admitted, "But I believe I can sing you a song."

Kyra held her niece, rubbed her head, and sang Iraja's lullaby until the girl was dreamily asleep. The melody and the Romani felt so good in Kyra's mouth. They released an aroma into her brain that liberated vivid memories that had gone dusty.

In the morning, she could not fix her thoughts or senses on the world around her. Stoyan's story had her trapped in deep contemplation of events from far away and long ago. Vajk and Judit noticed her absentmindedness. The whole village did. The weather was fine, and for the next two weeks, Kyra spent the length of the days like she had as a child, meandering laps around her village, with Gypsies on her mind. Only this time, they were not fantasies conjured in her imagination. They were memories — they were memories that occupied each chamber in her mind. Each one was stitched securely to her emotions, so when she tugged on it to view it more closely, she was torn inwardly.

Vajk feared for her future. How would she ever marry? How would she progress with her life if she spent her days in solitary, thoughtful walks? He came to a decision, one he thought would be best for her and everyone in the house. He rode out to speak with a friend.

That very afternoon, while Kyra was walking laps around the village, she came across a wooden trunk. She recognized it. It was hers. She looked around frantically, but nobody was near. She opened the trunk, and there, folded neatly inside, was her silk wedding dress.

Atop it was a note in Milena's handwriting. It was in Hungarian and it read,

> We thought you should
> have this. It is dear to us all,
> but much dearer to you. He
> is still here with us. I see
> him in everything we do. I
> know he is still with you. I
> hope he does not haunt you
> terribly.
>
> Your Sister,
> Milena

She pulled the dress from the trunk and held it against her. The silk reminded her skin of the many exotic things she experienced over her years with the kumpania. She thought about the oils and perfumes, the spices and foods. When her thoughts returned to the moment at hand, she noticed a piece of paper at the bottom of the trunk. She kneeled beside the box, took the paper, and saw different words, in different languages, written by different hands. It was all familiar to her.

Patrin wrote in Romani, "You honored my stitches when you wore this dress. You were the most magnificent bride I have ever seen."

Beneath that, Ernko wrote in German, "You are the forge of the kumpania. You heat us. You mold us. You fashion us."

Stoyan wrote in Bulgarian, "You are the star of the Roma and the light of my life, my only daughter, and my only living child. I love you."

Others drew little pictures to fill every corner of the page. It is good that Kyra was kneeling. It saved her the trouble of falling. She collapsed over her legs and cried. When her color returned to normal and her face was dry, she stood with the paper still in hand.

She looked out to the empty fields beyond her vision, and asked herself, "How did they know? How did they know I would walk this way? How did they know where to place it?"

Only Yubi knew of her childhood strolls around her village. Only he could have known. But how could he? He was dead.

She thought, "Maybe Milena is right. Maybe he is still within them and among them."

Kyra left the trunk. She could not have carried it. She took the dress and the two papers and returned to the house. She went directly to her room and remained there through the rest of the day and the night.

In the morning, she put on her wedding dress and walked from the room. Vajk awaited her. He walked up to her and scanned his eyes across the dress. She awaited his chastisement, but it did not come. He reached out, ran his hand across the silk from her shoulder to her waist, and he smiled.

"This was my wedding dress," she told him.

"It is beautiful," he answered, "and must have been very expensive. How could they excuse such an expense?"

Vajk's life was one of ledgers and balanced numbers. He could not make sense of it. Kyra thought about the fortune given to Chiara, to a young woman the kumpania hardly knew. The silk was a very small fraction of that cost. Yet the Roma thought nothing of parting with it. To them, wealth and poverty were both fluid conditions that drained into each other in a constant ebb and flow. Vajk could never understand them, and he would never understand Kyra.

Kyra understood Vajk, yet she was shocked when he told her, "I have made arrangements for you. I have secured a position for you in a Dominican convent on the east side of Bratislava."

Kyra's face dropped, then her eyebrows furled sharply upward.

Her disapproval was clear to read, so Vajk amended, "It is not a cloister. I can visit you. Arely can visit you."

Kyra's face suddenly went calm, as if a great realization dawned upon her. She leaned into Vajk, kissed him, and said, "I can see now how you love me. I see how hard you have worked for me. Thank you, but I cannot go to the convent. I am the Silken Bride and I am the Phoenix of Croatia."

Vajk did not visit the Gypsies. He had not heard Stoyan's story. He had no idea what she was talking about. She told him that she loved him, kissed him again, and walked from the house.

She walked to the edge of the village and turned back to see Arely chasing after her.

"Aunt Kyra," the girl shouted as she got closer, "Where are you going?"

When Arely reached her, Kyra took her hand and answered, "I am going home."

Arely pouted, and her voice went low as she asked, "Aunt Kyra, will I ever see you again?"

Kyra looked over her right shoulder, but not enough to see the child beside her, and she answered with a wink, "Keep an eye on the open field."

Kyra began her next step forward, but froze it in place when the girl asked, "*Can* a star fall twice?"

Kyra turned fully to face her, squatted upon her heels, and instructed, "Yes it can, and more importantly, new stars will form and fall on new people, bright young stars that are hiding in little villages like this one."

They smiled at each other, because this child, above anyone else in the village, understood and saw hints of her own future in the celestial metaphor.

Kyra kissed Arely on the bridge of her nose, stood, turned without another word or gesture, and walked from Szanzar as she had done many years earlier. This time, she did not walk away from something. There was no fear, no morbid sorrow, and no uncertainty in her heart. Her steps were motivated by love. They were self-assured. They were strong and forceful. Kyra knew exactly who she was and where she belonged.

With nothing in her possession but the dress she wore, she wandered into the wilderness, out of sight of Szanzar, with nothing but an arcane pull at her heart as navigation. It had been two weeks since the kumpania entertained the people of Szanzar, but the trunk had been recently left. They could not be far.

She stood still and strained her ears. In a brief moment, when the breeze died down and the air was quiet, she heard a rhythm. She aimed her eyes where her ears pointed, and she walked. She moved at pace, but smoothly and quietly. She came upon them before they saw her.

Ernko saw her first and shouted. He ran to her, pointing behind him to Stoyan and yelling in much improved Romani, "He said you would come. He insisted upon it."

Stoyan was a full seventy paces behind, walking steadily toward his daughter and queen.

Kyra raised her hand and ordered him to stop. He obeyed, and she shouted to him, "No! Don't you remember? 'You must come to us if you are to live with us, to *be* of us'. I must come to you if I am to put my dead past behind me."

The Romani words rolled richly off her tongue. As succulent as it was in her mouth, it was all the more so in Stoyan's ears. His brightening smile was clear to her, even at that distance. She picked up her pace in increments with each step, until she was in full sprint toward him. Stoyan stood in place, slowly lifting his arms in front of him.

She flew into his embrace, and after one deep breath, she said, "Now... I am finally home."

He kissed her shoulder and answered, "And for the first time all year, my dear daughter, I am home."

They held each other under the silent gaze of the others for several minutes before Stoyan began to cry. He finally cried for having lost his son. He cried for having regained his daughter. He released his grief as Kyra would have had him do, and only Kyra's arms could usher it from him. She continued to hold him, more like a nurturing mother than like a daughter. Stoyan's sobs grew full and loud. As they did, the kumpania encircling them began to cry, and with each sniffled inhale, they inched closer, until Kyra and Stoyan were at the center of a tightly packed cluster.

When Stoyan had cried his last, he led Kyra from the circle. As he escorted his daughter to the rear of the caravan, where her vardo awaited her, the kumpania returned to their business. They started singing. The singing began as a quiet hum from one of the herders, but spread quickly. It grew into a brand of unity Kyra had missed terribly while she was among the disconnected lives in Szanzar.

What's more, she sensed her own flavor in the song. Her deep sorrow had seeped into the marrow of the kumpania and in her absence had swelled to saturate them entirely. It blended fully with their Roma joy into a decadently rich and shared spirituality. As Kyra walked hand-in-hand with Stoyan, she recognized it. It was the very same substance that filled her. Their joy had also blended with the sorrow in her, raising her in so many ways above her brother and neighbors in Szanzar. Walking along the caravan, she was no longer like a bead of rich oil floating atop a pool of water. She blended soothingly, peacefully, and comprehensively into her kumpania, into her family, and she recognized her own essence in every hummed note surrounding her, in the swing of Ernko's hammer, in every thump and thud as they prepared the caravan for travel.

When they got to Kyra's vardo, there, hanging over the door, was a sign. It was similar to the one she had made for the acrobats years earlier. It was an image of Kyra seated high on Yubi's hand. Etched in the iron beneath the figures, it read, "Kyra - Queen of the Roma".

Kyra pointed to it, and Stoyan told her, "Ernko made it from my old high bar."

He lowered the steps to the porch and Kyra climbed up alone. She went inside and found everything exactly as she had left it. They had been pulling her vardo behind them like a museum to the most sacred part of them.

The same sights and the same smells that had twisted her heart so cruelly had a very different effect on her. Kyra had spent almost fourteen years in Szanzar, between her childhood and her return, but as she sat on the bed she had shared with Iraja and with Yubi, she realized that she had *lived* more in her handful of years with the kumpania. It was not the majority of her years, but it was the vast majority of her living.

She saw Iraja's jewelry, her chest and her trinkets, her books and her perfumes, and she felt grateful. She saw Yubi's clothes. She held them to her face, inhaled deeply, and she felt blessed.

The caravan was ready to roll forward, and suddenly, isolated inside of her vardo seemed the wrong place to be. She stepped onto the porch and looked at Vadim's back as he mounted the horse that would pull her. She looked at the people lined up to walk and ride beside her, and she adored them. She rolled her eyes across the caravan and all its busy people, and she knew that there, with them, wherever they may be, was the only place in the world she could be where the things she possessed outweighed the things she had lost.

She looked at the horizon, then closed her eyes and visualized the massive world beyond it. She smiled broadly, with a deep inhale that tried to draw the wide world in with her nose. She opened her eyes and ordered the caravan forward — to fields and mountains, cities and rivers, and exotic ports on the sea — to a Roma life, led by their Roma queen.

The End

POSTFACE

THERE IS NO RECORD OF KYRA HAVING EVER EXISTED, no mention anywhere else of Gellen or his barn, not even of Szanzar. They are all fictional. Yubi, Stoyan Iraja, Menowin are all made up. Yet, were we able to perform a comprehensive survey of the human past, there they would be. Perhaps not in every particular of form or character, not of the same names, but lives very much like theirs have played out in the buried and obscure folds of centuries past.

Lives like Kyra's and lives very different than hers — billions of beautiful and fascinating people have shared this rock we call home. Billions still do, and each one of their lives is worth writing about, certainly worth looking at and paying attention to. Let us please observe them, study them, benefit them, and benefit from them, while they are still here with us. Let us find the Phoenix in the village dress. Let us sew her some wings and lift her into the air.

www.ingramcontent.com/pod-product-compliance
Lightning Source LLC
Chambersburg PA
CBHW021837010726
47493CB00005B/1439